"Two Rings: A Legacy of Hope is a trip down memory lane. It speaks of women who greatly influenced my life as teachers, coaches and barrier breakers. It rekindles my fond memories of being a female athlete born 'just in time' to be able to participate in the 1973 MSHSL State Track and Field Tournament, the snowy 1975 MSHSL State Volleyball Tournament and the first 1976 MSHSL State Girls Basketball Tournament. This book reinforces the many conversations about equality and opportunity that I have shared over the years with our two student-athlete daughters and our son, who also appreciate and understand how far we've come as women in athletics. This book will tug at your heart, put a smile on your face, and make you feel proud to be a part of this legacy."

Liz Erickson, M.Div. student-athlete at Austin, Minnesota and Concordia College-Moorhead, Minnesota; teacher and coach, Lake City, Minnesota, currently ELCA pastor in Elkton, Minnesota.

"This book is a double treat: history wrapped in a sparkling good story! Readers will gain a new hero of their own in eighteen-year-old Sarah as she uncovers heroes among the women in her family, and beyond, who battled stereotypes and injustice to expand opportunities for women - including Sarah herself. Alternately funny and moving, and always insightful, the novel interweaves Sarah's own story with her search, and while the history of women's basketball is a focal point, it moves beyond in ways that illumine the fight for equality in all areas of life. Most importantly, Sarah comes to see that 'their' story is really 'her' story. The defeats and triumphs, sorrows and joys, of women who went before her are not a dead past but a part of who she is and what she can be."

Dan Conrad, PhD. educator, Hopkins High School, Hopkins, Minnesota, and University of Minnesota; coach and author.

"The two books, *Daughters of the Game* and *Two Rings: A Legacy of Hope,* shed a needed light on the history of girls' sports over the past century and into the present. Decisions to drop girls and women's sports during the 1920s and 1930s left behind barriers, myths and stereotypes that required blood, sweat and tears for us to break down. We changed the face of sports. Now, we must continue our vigilance to ensure that young women will always have the opportunity to make all the difference in the world."

Paula Bruss Bauck, pioneer athlete, teacher, advocate, and coach, Moorhead, Minnesota.

ALSO BY DOROTHY E. MCINTYRE AND MARIAN BEMIS JOHNSON

Daughters of the Game

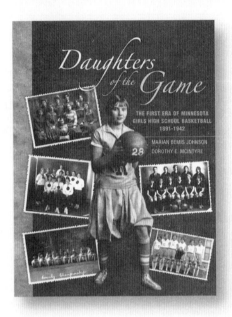

This book compiles the history of girls high school basketball from its arrival in 1892 at Carleton College, Northfield, Minnesota, through 1942 when state and national organizations influenced the ending of competitive teams for girls and women.

You may have a great-grandmother, grandmother, mother, sister, aunt or neighbor who was part of this history. They played for fun, in small towns and larger cities all over the state of Minnesota. They faced all sorts of obstacles, just because they loved basketball.

The book includes first-person stories by the women who played during that era. It is filled with photos of individuals and teams and includes profiles of more than one hundred teams. The purpose of the book is to ensure that this colorful history is preserved for future generations and the athletes who will carry on the legacy of the first daughters of the game.

Two Rings:
a Legacy of
HOPE

*Dream big and make all
the difference in the world!*

Timothy M. Intyre

★ ★

Marian Berris Johnson

Two Rings:

A Legacy of

HOPE

Dorothy E. McIntyre * Marian Bemis Johnson

McJohn Publishing, Mpls.

Published 2012

Printed by Corporate Graphics

by

Dorothy E. McIntyre
Marian Bemis Johnson

The paper used in this publication meets the minimum requirements of the American National Standard for Information Sciences – Permanence of Paper for Printed Library Materials, ANSI Z39.48-1992

For information, contact:
www.daughtersofthegame.com or
McJohn Publishing, LLC,
P.O. Box 390043,
Minneapolis, MN 55439-0043
Printed in the United States of America
ISBN 978-0-9766214-1-6

Cover Design: Blue Tricycle, Inc.
Cover Photo: 1919 Owatonna, Courtesy of Bill Kottke Family
Back Cover Photos (left to right):
Crookston, 1912, Courtesy of Dr. Robert Wright
Owatonna, 1919, Courtesy of Bill Kottke Family
New York Mills, 1979, Courtesy of Janet Karvonen Montgomery
Hill-Murray vs. Mpls. De La Salle, 2011, Courtesy of Minnesota Prep Photo

Type Set in eleven-point ITC Century Std

Publisher's Cataloging-in-Publication
(Provided by Quality Books, Inc.)

McIntyre, Dorothy E.
    Two rings : a legacy of hope / Dorothy E. McIntyre,
Marian Bemis Johnson.
    p. cm.
    Includes bibliographical references and index.
    ISBN 978-0-9766214-1-6

    1. Women basketball players--Fiction. 2. Basketball
for women--Fiction. 3. Basketball for girls--Fiction.
4. School sports--Fiction. 5. Basketball stories.
6. Historical fiction.   I. Johnson, Marian Bemis.
II. Title.

PS3613.C5425T86 2012   813'.6
                    QBI12-600040

Dedication

Our book is dedicated to our heroes, those individuals whose lives inspire and motivate us.

Some of our heroes are known to virtually everyone. Speak the name Amelia Earhart, Sacajawea, Abraham Lincoln, Wilma Rudolph, Rosa Parks, Ann Bancroft, and familiar vibrations begin to stir.

Some of our heroes are close to our hearts, such as our parents, family members, and special friends.

You may have discovered heroes among people whom you have never met, or touched their hand, or stood in their presence.

Maybe you found one of your heroes while reading a book. Their words may have impacted your thinking, and suddenly, you could see a new way to live, to believe, to dream.

Some of our heroes are those whose actions in a time of crisis have left us in awe of their courage and their willingness to sacrifice so much for others.

Heroes leave footprints on our hearts, and on our lives.

The characters in our book also need heroes and they will surface at timely places.

You may wish to acknowledge and preserve some of your heroes, so we provided a section for you, called "My Heroes." Then, one day when you need inspiration or a pause to reflect, your heroes will be waiting for you, to inspire, comfort and encourage you once again.

★ ★ COURAGE ★ ★

Courage is the price that Life exacts for granting peace,

the soul that knows it not, knows no release

from little things;

knows not the livid loneliness of fear,

nor mountain heights where bitter joy can hear

the sound of wings.

How can Life grant us boon of living, compensate

for dull grey ugliness and pregnant hate

unless we dare

the soul's dominion? Each time we make a choice, we pay

with courage to behold the restless day,

and count it fair.

Amelia Earhart, 1927, "Courage"

★ ★ LEGACY ★ ★

Something handed down from an ancestor,

a predecessor from the past.

★ ★ HOPE ★ ★

A confident feeling about what will happen in the future.

TABLE OF CONTENTS

Second Half

Overtime

For the Fans

★ ★

PREFACE

In the preface to our first book, *Daughters of the Game - The First Era of Minnesota Girls High School Basketball, 1891-1942,* the opening sentences read, "It was the look in their eyes when they told their stories. Each woman remembered games, opponents and scores as if it had happened just yesterday. It was, in fact, eighty or more years ago!"

In 2005, Marian and I compiled her years of research about the first era of girls basketball and published our book through our own publishing company, McJohn Publishing, LLC. For the next five years, we enjoyed a wonderful tour of the state and beyond, sharing the history of this first era of girls' sports in Minnesota. We spoke to dozens of civic and community organizations, historical societies, and book clubs; in fact, we went wherever we were invited. Our book programs helped to shine a light onto the lives of young women in Minnesota who had enjoyed sports in the early 1900s, and whose stories were on the brink of being lost.

Daughters of the Game is now being read and enjoyed by interested individuals, families and scholars, as well as being available in libraries across Minnesota and in many other states. It has been sent internationally by families of players featured in the book. The Minnesota Historical Society's magazine featured it and sold copies of the book in its museum store. We enjoy knowing that a copy is in the Schlesinger Library, Harvard University, where preserving women's history, including that of our hero, Amelia Earhart, is their focus and mission.

In 2007, *Daughters of the Game* was the recipient of an *Award of Merit from the American Association for State and Local History* (AASLH). The press release said, "This award is the most prestigious recognition for achievement in the preservation and interpretation of state and local history."

At each opportunity that we have had to tell the women's stories, we wondered how these stories could capture the attention of young people and adults who may not consider history to be compelling reading when they pick up a book late at night.

It was a blustery day last March when I leaned into the wind and drove over to Williams Arena at the University of Minnesota. It was the site of many girls state basketball tournaments that were my responsibility from 1976-2002. It was wonderful to "high five" the guys at the pass gate and see coaches, officials and personnel who had shared so many experiences with me. The memories we recalled were, no doubt, enhanced a little over the real thing.

In the concourse, a book sale was underway and I met the three Foley sisters who had grown up in the community of Le Sueur, Minnesota. The sisters were in high school when the second era of girls' sports of the 1970s was just beginning. They played basketball and other sports before heading off into their diverse careers.

Jeanne coached many years at the university level. One day

she realized that young women needed a novel that delved into the dynamics and challenges of playing a team sport like basketball, i.e., a book that would speak to their experiences as female athletes. So Jeanne wrote it. The result: *Shooting Two, A Story of Basketball and Friendship,* is a book about a 1988 Minnesota girls' basketball team whose season goal was to get to the state tournament and win it. Terri, the youngest sister, had formed her own publishing company, Peppermint Books, and published *Shooting Two.* Patti, the middle sister, and former player on the Le Sueur girls basketball team, would focus on marketing. They have a success story in the making.

As I look at our book, *Daughters of the Game,* it is still amazing how much historical information was gathered by Marian Johnson. As she crisscrossed the state, interviewing women, and mailing dozens of interview forms to others, Marian was gathering and preserving crucial information from a generation who never thought their history would be important to others. They would frequently ask Marian, "Why are you interested in my story of playing basketball? No one has ever been interested before."

A random thought crept into focus. Could we write a historical novel that would incorporate the stories told by these marvelous women? *What if* a high school girl was looking for information for a school report and found the diaries of women in her family tree who had also been athletes during their high school years? What fun that would be!

The fingers on the computer keyboard began to tap out some ideas...where to start...how to tell their stories.

A special "crossroads" friend from Mahnomen, Minnesota, Esther Burnett Horne, Sacajawea's great-great granddaughter, once told me, "Dorothy, preserve your oral history. Keep *telling your stories as our people do. When you write it down to preserve your history, write it yourself* to be sure it is accurate. Someone else may *not* tell your story as it really happened."

In this book, *Two Rings: A Legacy of Hope*, the historical information is accurate to the best of our research and knowledge. The personal experiences shared by the early players can be found in our first book, *Daughters of the Game*. Some stories are adapted to fit within the storyline of this novel. Each pioneer woman, however, is fully credited for her story in the section of the book, "References and Notes."

Sarah is a fictitious young woman, created to tell the story of the two rings. Her mother, Patti, is fictitious, but includes the high school experiences of Patti Foley Good, who did play on the Le Sueur, Minnesota, girls' basketball teams in the 1970s. Patti has granted the author modest license to build her story into the role of Sarah's mother, confidante and mentor. Sarah's family members are fictitious and any resemblance to real people, family or friends is coincidental, mostly. Some of my friends may find themselves in the storyline, but were advised of my intentions and I believe they said, "Go for it."

One disclaimer must be inserted, loud and clear: this is a book of *historical fiction*, based on the real and accurate history of Minnesota high school girls basketball and swimming teams, and the beginning of the second era in the 1960s. The history of the National Amateur Athletic Federation - Women's Division (NAAF-WD) is presented as fairly as this writer is able to do so, since I wasn't a mouse in the corner of their meetings. Also, this book tells our history in Minnesota and does not attempt to include the unique history of other states.

The description of my home state of Iowa and its state girls basketball tournament does reflect real events held at the tournament and its legendary director, E. Wayne Cooley, whom I consider a special friend. As a high school girl, I attended the state tournament with our team in the 1950s and when I revisited the event in 1990, the team cheers were still echoing up in the rafters of the arena.

Please refer to the "References and Notes" section of the book for comments and valuable resources that can tell you the rest of the story. If you want a complete history of women's basketball written by two dozen experts on the subject, read *A Century of Women's Basketball - From Frailty to Final Four*, by Hult and Trekell, editors.

Developing the character of Sarah and her experiences with our history and its wonderful women was great fun. As the story developed each morning at my computer, Sarah begins to realize that she is learning far more than simply how young women played basketball in the early 1900s. She begins to understand life without modern conveniences, such as no electricity or running water. She can feel the bitter cold that would accompany traveling by sleigh or canvas-covered school buses. She can imagine the heat from the stoves in the corner of an opera house turned into a basketball court. Sarah is learning that life on the prairie was challenging, at best.

Sarah also experiences the pain of loss as she empathizes with her great-grandmother's loss of a special ring. And then, she tries to absorb the injustice of losing the opportunity to play a favorite sport, simply because adults "said so."

You may find that Sarah's frustrations mirror your own, as she is confronted with discrimination in its raw, "in-your-face" way. She is angered by the old traditions and "social mores" that limited women in so many ways, such as in what they could wear, how they could travel, and what activities they could enjoy. And most of all, she is angered by the insidious ways that women's voices were stifled, including denying them the right to vote for so long.

As she questions and objects to the discrimination that she encounters, we begin to see her own philosophy under construction. There comes a moment when she realizes that she must stand up like her heroes did. She must get off the bench and "get into the game."

She may be mirroring your own life.

Bringing a story to closure is a challenge. A writer must realize when the story has been told and the torch passes on to the reader. In your hands, the end becomes the beginning.

What will the lives of today's young women be like in another ten, twenty, fifty years? Will they be ready to meet what lies ahead? Have we provided them with some keys to help them open more doors? Have we left a legacy that will serve them well?

We must hope so, for the world sorely needs the talents of today's young women. Then, the sacrifices of so many will have been well invested in building a foundation for today but with an eye for the future. Who will be their heroes? Will you be one of them?

As this story comes to a close, I find a little twinge of sadness, wishing that we all could be there to see what is coming for today's children. It has been said that a teacher is one who builds for a future they will never see.

Well, that may be so. Maybe we can't be there in the future, but we *can* go to our schools and watch young women skillfully competing with confidence and courage. We *will* be seeing a glimpse into their future.

Then we can all smile and say, *"Look at them go!"*

ACKNOWLEDGMENT TO RUTH

"I'm sorry, but my ring is never leaving my hand. It will be buried with me."

Ruth's words were disappointing, but I understood. Our request to borrow Ruth's ring had come about a few years ago when Ruth was unable to attend a MSHSL Leadership Conference to tell her story in person. There was a chance that she might loan her ring for display while we shared her unique story. But when you know Ruth's story, it was understandable that she would not want to part with the ring, even for a day. She didn't, and the ring was buried with her.

As Marian was gathering stories from women who had played during that era, Ruth McCarron Dahlke of Sherburn, Minnesota, had quite a story to tell of her days playing basketball in the 1920s, and the loss of her silver championship ring. Ruth's experiences and anecdotes are told in her own words in our first book, *Daughters of the Game - The First Era of Minnesota Girls High School Basketball, 1892-1942.*

As the storyline of this novel began to take shape, Ruth's story kept returning as a possible focal point: Ruth and her silver ring. What can it teach us?

Let's review her story: Ruth played on the Sherburn, Minnesota, girls' basketball team in 1925, when they won an invitational tournament and players were awarded silver rings with a basketball crowning the top. Ruth treasured her ring and was devastated when, while swimming with friends, her ring slipped off her finger into the deep waters of Fox Lake, never to be seen again.

Some seventy years later, her daughter attended an estate auction and the auctioneer encouraged her to buy a small box with some costume jewelry in it. When she showed the box to Ruth, she said her mother suddenly burst into tears, something she had never seen before. Ruth reached into the box and lifted out a small silver ring with a basketball crowning the top.

You see, the estate sale was that of a *teammate*, a woman who had been Ruth's team captain. The ring had been hers. The family, who may not have recognized the ring's sentimental value, put it in with other miscellaneous jewelry to be sold at the auction. As life would have it, Ruth's daughter purchased the little collection, also not aware of the significance of its contents.

So, the ring of Ruth's teammate was saved, and though Ruth's ring is still resting at the bottom of Fox Lake, it carried the same sentimental value to her. She treasured it and never allowed it to be separated from her ever again.

We enjoyed inviting Ruth, and her ring, to book programs where she could tell her story and show, *on her finger*, her ring. The memories of Ruth's basketball playing days remained vivid and treasured throughout her life. She is one of our heroes and we miss her.

In tribute, how can we preserve the lessons woven throughout Ruth's life, and how can a little silver ring become a symbol of the legacy of that wonderful era?

As sometimes happens in historical fiction, some adaptations and new characters will take center stage. And the fate of the little silver ring in this story? Well, you'll see... I believe Ruth would approve of a truly happy ending.

Please welcome the characters of Ruby McCarroll and her great-granddaughter Sarah, who provide us with a legacy and hope for the future.

Special Acknowledgements

Believe it or not, some of the individuals who helped proof, edit and critique our first book in 2005, came back for more. Even as the number of chapters increased, they continued to read and critique, ask questions and suggest changes that improved the characters and readability of the book.

Chapters went flying back and forth with **Sylvia Logerquist, Jane Christensen, Vel Teichroew, and Liz Erickson. Pat Lamb** and **Ele Hansen** enjoyed the story of their special Carleton College and its unique role in this history. **Allie Cronk** edited and commented, reporting smiles from fond memories. **Joanie Hance** and **Mylla Urban** read, and cheered us on, as they have always done.

Their individual and mutual approval of content and subject matter was crucial to moving to publication. Together, we had lived through the challenges of the 1960s and 1970s and I knew they could verify information simply by checking their own memories, and some scars.

My sister, **Anita Darnell,** read and read, giving her older sister edits, suggestions and feedback. When she said a chapter was "fine, just fine," I relaxed.

Dan Conrad entered the stage when he happened to see a notice back in 2005 about a book program on girls basketball to be held in Minneapolis. He attended, and became interested not only in the history of girls basketball, but also in the life of our mutual hero, Amelia Earhart, and the women of flight around the world. Dan gave me timely advice after reading a draft of a pretty bland first chapter. He said, "You have to have a 'hook' to catch the reader's attention." That did it! Sarah and the lost ring were born. Dan has a great perspective on women and their place in history. Thanks for all the early morning e-mails. Every author needs one editor that is a "night owl."

A big thanks to **Nita Onnen** for telling me that I needed to go to the State Girls Basketball Tournament and meet these three sisters and see their new book. I did, and it has made all the difference. **Patti Foley Good** was a key to personal memories and scrapbooks about Le Sueur, her team and community. **Terri Foley**, Peppermint Books, generously shared her experience and insights into writing and publishing a historical novel. **Jeanne Foley,** author, encouraged me to try my hand at writing a novel. And here we are!

Sue Neuhart, as a native Iowan, edited, and analyzed the family picnics and life on the prairie, pronouncing them authentic.

Karen Luedtke is a marvel and career expert at catching punctuation and incomplete sentences. Her background in researching ancestry provided the expertise in determining "great-greats," etc.

My special thanks to **Grace Hall** who helped to fix computer formats, and answered questions about all of those toolbars. I still can't understand how simply opening a dozen files of different chapters, or hitting one button, *okay, maybe several,* in frustration, can cause so much trouble.

Neighbor **Dale Sattler** was still ready to drop everything and come over "for a minute" to see what gremlin had crept into the system.

Brother **Gary,** sister-in-law **Nancy** and nephew **Ben** recalled many family memories and life on the farm with their creatures, great and small. Ben has give me many lessons on superheroes and flying WWII missions. I learned by watching his flying fingers.

"Up North" was a fun chapter. **Tammy Berkich** verified my descriptions of the Iron Range and her alma mater, the beautiful Hibbing High School. Years ago, **Lawrence Belluzzo,** Chisholm's historian, provided me with the history of Anne Govednik and her wonderful story. Wouldn't we have loved to hear the radio broadcast of her race as a 16-year-old in the 1932 Olympics, and heard that town whistle blow the race results to the folks waiting in Chisholm.

Thanks for the memories from **Gail Nucech,** who truly is a legendary coach at Hibbing, though she would prefer the emphasis be put on the young athletes whom she has mentored over forty years.

As an authentic basketball official, **Deb Weinreis** edited and checked the technical accuracy of many chapters, especially the basketball championship game so we wouldn't commit a "foul" there.

I was fortunate to cross flight paths with **Patti Sandusky** and **Jean Knox,** of the Minnesota Ninety-Nines, when they participated in a play on Amelia Earhart's life that we put on in my living room. *That's another story.* Patti and Jean shared their love of flying up in those blue skies, as well as our mutual fascination with Amelia's life. (In case you didn't know, *either,* the steering wheel in an airplane is called a "yoke.")

Maxine Menely, 93 years young, read each word of each chapter with her magnifying glass, and would call to share her thoughts. When she said a story was just as she remembered it during her young life in Illinois, it stayed as written.

My Irish cousin, **Hazel McIntyre,** who lives next to our ancestral farm in County Donegal, Ireland, is a real author of six novels. I can't insert her Irish brogue but you can imagine how it sounded when she encouraged me to "give it a try." I am her Amazon. Kindle publisher and her books are all "up there" for you to enjoy.

Many friends accepted a draft of the book and offered suggestions, each helping to ensure we stayed within the parameters of the rules of punctuation and history. **Lorry Anderson** helped reduce the volume of commas and suggested her favorite "dashes" in their place. **Lynn Scearcy** didn't expect to edit, but made the telling statement, "I love to proofread."

And, of course, a special heart-felt thanks to my friends, the **"Women of the Federation,"** and my compatriots who shared similar careers on the staffs of state associations for "lo, those many years," including **Susan True,** our hero "on watch" at the National Federation Office. Your individual and collective support was so important and always will be. **Ola Bundy,** Illinois and **Sharon Wilch,** Colorado, were the first two pioneers in our state associations. Each of these women could write their own book on life at the state association, the Federation, and the early days of high school girls' sports. Special thanks for their help with this book to **Sue Hinrichsen,** Illinois and **Karen Kuhn,** Wisconsin. **Ruth Rehn,** South Dakota, **Marie Ishida** and **Donna Zavada,** California and **Brenda Langdon,** Virginia, kept sending their support. To **Sheryl Solberg,** North Dakota - it has also been fun to share our mutual hero, Sacajawea. And to each and every woman who was, or is currently a member of a state association staff serving young women in your respective states...*thank you* from all of us who have 'been there' and still share your road. *Stay the course!*

Our hearts still ache at the loss of our great friend, **Claudia Dodson,** of Virginia, who was my anchor during the trials of publishing *Daughters of the Game.* If Claudia didn't know the answer to one of my frequent questions, she could find it. We had a running commentary about the number of commas in my writing. She would say, "Darrr-ah-theee," I don't know who taught you punctuation, but you put a comma wherever you pause or take a breath." And I assured her *that's what we did* in the Midwest. She said people in the "East" didn't have time to pause that often. We had so many good laughs together. I always wondered how I could be so lucky to *have* a friend like Claudia, though her years were far too few. We wish she could have *paused* with us longer.

I had replied to all inquiries that a second book wasn't on the radar. The reservoir is empty, *I said.* However, memories did fade of the challenges experienced while publishing our *Daughters of the Game* book. And it was enticing to think about a smaller book with the history condensed into a story that would be an appealing 'read' in front of a crackling fire, with a cup of hot chocolate.

I knew there was a good reason why I was keeping those boxes full of the history of my teaching days, life at the League Office, and *all those speeches.* Have you noticed how many piles of "important papers" can emerge from just *one* of those storage tubs?

What is truly amazing is to realize how lucky one person can be to experience a career filled with the opportunity to make a difference, with friends alongside.

CHRONOLOGY

1833   Oberlin College, Ohio, founded, first to admit women after nearly two hundred years of college education open only to men

1848   A convention to discuss the social, civil, and religious condition and rights of women was held at Seneca Falls, New York

1849   Amelia Bloomer began publication of *The Lily*, a monthly paper that became an active voice for women's rights, including changes in the restrictive clothing worn by women. It recommended shorter skirts and the knee-length undergarments that came to be known as "bloomers"

1858   Minnesota became the 32nd state in the Union

1869   The University of Minnesota became the first state university in the country to open its classes to both men and women

Sara Burger Stearns started Minnesota's first suffrage group in Rochester

1886 The first true safety bicycle, the Rover, with rear chain drive and direct steering, established the design of the bicycle very much as it is today. The 1895 Ladies' Schwinn New World bicycle came at the height of the bicycle boom

1887 Married women achieved the same legal existence as single women; they were no longer the property of their husbands

1891 James Naismith, a teacher at the International YMCA Training School in Springfield, Massachusetts, invented a new indoor game that he called "Basket Ball." The game was spelled with two words until the 1920s

1892 Max J. Exner, a friend and roommate of James Naismith, was a student in Naismith's class and played in the first game. Exner moved to Northfield, MN, to serve as director of physical culture at Carleton College. He brought with him the rules for the new game of basket ball. He taught the game to the women of Carleton in the lower-level gymnasium of Gridley Hall

1892 Senda Berenson adapted Naismith's rules for her Smith College students. She wanted a game that would be vigorous and yet "womanly" and acceptable to her college and the parents of her students

1899 The Women's Basketball Rules Committee held its first meeting at Springfield College, Springfield, MA

1900-45 The Golden Age of railroads

1914   World War I began

1917   The United States entered World War I

1917   The National Women's Party staged a non-violent civil-disobedience campaign by picketing on the sidewalk in front of the White House demanding rights to vote for women. Women were arrested and incarcerated in a workhouse where they were force-fed, chained and beaten

1918   President Woodrow Wilson announced that women's suffrage was urgently needed as a "war measure" and strongly urged Congress to pass the legislation

1918   A basket with an open bottom, instead of a closed basket with pull chain, became official in the game of Basket Ball

1918-19   The influenza pandemic was the most devastating epidemic in recorded world history, killing between 20 and 40 million people around the globe. 675,000 Americans died in the worst epidemic the United States has ever known

1919   Treaty of Versailles ended World War I

1920   Nineteenth Amendment to the U.S. Constitution secured suffrage for women

1921   Women win the right to serve on juries

1922   The Amateur Athletic Union (AAU) incorporated women's basketball into its program offerings

1923-24   The National Amateur Athletic Federation - Women's Division (NAAF-WD) was organized. The first meeting was held in Washington, D.C., in 1923; its organizational meeting was held in 1924

1924 The NAAF-WD began disseminating information and recommendations throughout the country that competitive teams for girls and women should be replaced with "competition of the right kind," i.e., competition for enjoyment and without the stress of winning and losing

1924 The Minnesota State High School League sponsored its first state tournament for girls in the sport of swimming and diving. The tournament ended in 1942

1925 Thirty-seven states held state girls basketball tournaments. Minnesota did not sponsor a girls state tournament in basketball until 1976

1926 The Amateur Athletic Union (AAU) held its first national basketball championship for women in Pasadena, CA

1927 Iowa superintendents discuss NAAF-Women's Division recommendation to drop girls basketball in Iowa and decide to create the Iowa Girls High School Athletic Union (IGHSAU) and continue their state girls basketball tournament

1928 The NAAF-Women's Division protested women's entries in Olympic track and field events (and protested participation in all events in 1932 and 1936)

1929 The Wall Street stock market crashed

1930s The Great Depression plagued the United States

1932 The NAAF-Women's Division recommended that no women's events be conducted in the Olympics held in California. The recommendations were not implemented by the Olympic Committee

1932 Anne Govednik, Chisholm, MN, placed sixth in the 200-meter breaststroke. Babe Didrikson won two gold medals in track and field

1936 Olympics held in Berlin, Germany. Naismith observed games and awarded gold medals to the winning U.S. men's basketball team

1936 The All-America Red Heads women's basketball team was organized; using men's rules, and competing against men's teams

1938 Official basketball rules for women changed from a three-court game to a two-court game with six players

1939 Harold Jack, the second Supervisor of Physical Education, Minnesota State Department of Education, reported to schools that "Interscholastic competition for girls of high school age was reported in 92 schools in 1938-1939 and in 38 schools in 1939-1940. This represents a decided change for the better"

1941 The United States entered World War II after the bombing of Pearl Harbor

1942 The first era of Minnesota girls high school sports ends. All girls high school basketball teams had been discontinued and the last state swimming and diving meet was held

1945 World War II ended

1960 Wilma Rudolph won three gold medals in the Rome Olympics for track and field, raising questions as to why other U.S. women were not competing

1960s   Advocates for change in Minnesota became active in promoting and developing competitive opportunities for girls and women in sports

1963   The First National Sport Institute was held in Oklahoma to provide teachers with skills to teach gymnastics and track and field. Four additional institutes were held to emphasize other sports and to promote adding competition into these activities

1966   Unlimited dribble for women's basketball was introduced

1969   The Minnesota State High School League voted to add girls' sports to their sponsored programs of boys' sports, music, drama and speech

1971   The National Federation of State High School Associations published a high school girls basketball rules book

1971-72   The first MSHSL State Girls Track and Field Meet was held at St. Cloud Apollo High School

1972   Title IX of the Education Amendments of 1972 was passed. "No person in the United States shall, on the basis of sex, be excluded from participation in, be denied the benefits of, or be subjected to discrimination under any education program or activity receiving federal financial assistance." Included athletic programs

1974-75   The first MSHSL State Girls Volleyball Tournament held at Anoka High School

1974-75   The first MSHSL State Girls Tennis Tournament held

1975   *Title IX Guidelines* published. These interpretations were issued to schools from the U.S. Department of Health, Education and Welfare (HEW) regarding the intent of Title IX. Schools were instructed to be in compliance by 1978

1974-75 The MSHSL sponsored fall and winter season basketball playoff tournaments for schools playing in separate seasons

1974-75 The first MSHSL State Girls Gymnastics, Tennis, and Volleyball Tournaments held.

1975-76 First MSHSL State Girls Cross Country, Swimming and Diving, and Skiing Meets held.

1975-76 At the end of the first official winter season, the first MSHSL State Girls Basketball Tournament was held at the Met Center, Bloomington. All games were played with the five-player, full-court game

1976 Women's basketball was added as a competitive sport in the Olympics held in Montreal, Canada

1976-77 The First MSHSL State Girls Golf Tournament held

1976-77 The First MSHSL State Girls Softball Tournament held

1980-81 The First MSHSL State Girls Soccer Tournament held

1984 The U.S. Women's Basketball team won its first gold medal in the Los Angeles Olympics and repeats in 1988 in Seoul Olympics

1994-95 The first MSHSL State Girls Hockey Tournament

2011 7,667,955 girls participated on sports teams, compared to 3,960,932 in 1972. Reported by the National Federation of State High School Associations

1

SARAH GETS AN ASSIGNMENT

"Oww!" Sarah winced and rubbed the stinging sensation on the back of her arm. As she glanced back to locate the perpetrator of the rubber band attack, Jordan's mischievous eyes danced and she quietly whispered, "Got'cha!"

The bell rang and the stragglers slumped into their desks. Sarah's chair seemed determined to hit every sore muscle and bruise from last Friday's game.

It was the last period of the day and after a pop quiz in chemistry and a fitness test in physical education, Sarah was "beat." Basketball practice was going to be grueling today with the big game coming up on Friday night.

Her history teacher's voice cut through the fog of her fatigue. "And your assignment is to find a woman in your family whose life left a legacy for you, and perhaps others. She must be at least a generation prior to your parents, i.e., a grandmother, or great-grandmother or great-great-aunt, etc. That goes for you boys too. Our current unit is about women and their struggles for suffrage, legal rights, and the right to participate in sports. We should all be aware of our female ancestors who made a difference in our lives."

Some of the boys' eyes rolled back in their heads and a snicker was heard in the back of the classroom. The teacher strode to the back and found the offender, a young man who had unwisely exhibited disrespect in her classroom. He ended up with an extra assignment for the next day on the subject of "Respect for Others."

Back at the front of the room, with everyone's attention, the teacher continued, "You have the entire semester for this assignment. Your written and oral report will constitute fifty percent of your grade in this class. The final exam will be thirty percent and it will cover the information gathered in all of your reports. And the remaining twenty percent will include your participation in this class."

At the word "participation," the teacher's look seemed to send a laser beam zinging its way toward the young man with the extra assignment.

As the teacher wrapped up the class, the bell rang. It was 2:45 p.m. and time to head for the gym. Coach Johnson did not appreciate any tardiness and an extra lap or two would usually resolve anyone hanging around with friends after school.

Yolanda passed the ball and a question to Sarah during their layup drill, "Who you gonna' find for your paper?"

"I have no idea," Sarah answered as she drove in for the layup. "I want to find someone in sports, and I've never heard of anyone other than my mother who played basketball, or any other sport. I could be in big trouble."

After basketball practice, the activity bus bumped and jolted Sarah into a drowsy nap until the driver yelled, "Hey, Sarah, you getting off tonight or riding back to the bus barn?"

As she walked into the kitchen, her mother, Patti, was chopping vegetables for dinner.

"And how was your day?" she asked.

"I survived. Basketball practice was brutal. Of all of my volleyball, basketball and track coaches, I don't know who likes to torture us the most. Then we had a pop quiz in chemistry. Lucky for me, I knew what was going on there, so it didn't ruin my morning. And in physical education class, I qualified for the Presidential Physical Fitness Award. But the assignment in history could be trouble."

"Why is that, honey?" her mother inquired.

"Well, we have a research paper and oral report that is going to count for half of our grade. We have to find a woman in our family who left a legacy for me, and perhaps others. I've got to look up just exactly what 'legacy' means. I don't think it means money."

Patti grimaced a little, "No, Sarah, in this instance, it doesn't mean money. There would be good information on the Internet for you."

Sarah said, "Yeah, I figured you'd say that. Anyway, it would be fun if I could find someone who participated in my sports, like volleyball, or basketball, maybe even track and field. Do you think I could find a woman from years and years ago who was an athlete? I know you played sports in high school, but you don't count, Mom."

"Well, thanks."

"No, I mean that it has to be someone like a grandmother, great-aunt, or someone from a generation earlier than you - a person even older than you are."

Patti laughed, "Well, good thing you aren't trying to make points with me tonight, but I understand what you are trying to say. Perhaps you could consider your Great-Grandma Ruby who played basketball at Sherburn in the 1920s. 'Seems like she fits the requirements for your paper."

Sarah's eyes lit up, "Really? Great-Grandma Ruby played basketball? I know she loved sports and never missed watching a Twins game, but it's hard to imagine her running around a basketball court."

"Oh, indeed she did. You might be surprised what you could learn about Great-Grandma Ruby. After she played high school basketball, she played at Mankato State and coached a girls' basketball team at East Chain."

"Really?" Sarah exclaimed. "She actually played real basketball and coached a high school team? What a woman!"

Patti laughed, "Yes, and Grandma Ruby played softball and she was on a golf league well into her senior years. After she married Grandpa, she raised her own family and took time to be very active in what was happening in Sherburn, including helping abused women and their children.

"It's too bad we didn't ask her about her life before she died a few years ago," Patti stopped chopping for a moment. "She would have loved to tell you some stories herself. But we do have a trunk upstairs in the attic that came from her estate and no one has looked in it for years. Maybe we could find something that would help you with your research."

Patti opened the refrigerator door and began pulling out the makings for a big salad.

"But, here, help me with dinner and we'll take a look later."

2

THE TRUNK AND THE DIARY

The trunk looked old, dark and rather ominous, sitting in the attic with dust motes floating in a shaft of sunlight from a nearby window.

Sarah's mother patted the lid fondly and said, "You know, Sarah, this trunk traveled from the 'old country' with the first generation of immigrants in my family. Think of the stories it could tell."

Sarah carefully slid the latch until she heard it click. As she lifted the heavy lid, a strong fragrance of mothballs assailed her nose and she turned away. The uncomfortable smell soon dissipated and Sarah turned back to look more closely at the trunk's contents.

She reached in tentatively so she wouldn't carelessly disturb or break something fragile that had been resting there for so many years. On the top was an old, yellowing newspaper. The ads made Sarah smile. Grocery ads listed items with such low prices, some only pennies: fresh eggs, 25 cents a dozen; coffee, 47 cents a lb; flour, 31 cents for five pounds.

"Look, Mom," Sarah said, "this newspaper says milk in 1924 was only 13 cents a quart."

Her mother smiled, "With the gallons we drink around here, that would be a wonderful price to pay."

As she turned to go down the stairs again, Patti reminded Sarah, "I have to drive Lauren and Holly to their piano lessons, so keep an eye out for your brother."

"Okay, will do." As Sarah continued to look though the fragile, yellowing pages, she noticed a page that had articles about sports, mostly about high school sports teams.

With no professional teams taking up most of the space in a big metro newspaper, Sarah noted, a small town newspaper would have space for local teams and high school activities.

One headline caught her attention, "Local Girls Win Basketball Tournament." As she scanned down the paragraphs, she saw her great-grandmother's name: Ruby McCarroll. The article reported that the local businesses in Sherburn had sponsored an invitational girls basketball tournament. Teams were invited from Ceylon, Elmore, Welcome, Triumph, Granada and Jackson. The Sherburn girls' team had won the tournament.

On page two of the sports section, Sarah saw a photograph of the team with the captain and coach holding a large silver trophy. The article stated that each girl on the team also received a silver ring with a half a basketball on the top and the initials "SHS" engraved across it. The local jeweler had offered to engrave each girl's initials inside her ring.

"Well," Sarah thought, "what a fun tournament, and such nice awards for the team."

Sarah heard the family's SUV coming up the driveway. It didn't take Mom long to get things done, Sarah thought, as she ran down the stairs to the kitchen.

"Mom, the article says the players were awarded silver rings. Have you ever seen Great-Grandma Ruby's championship ring?" Her mother slowly shook her head.

"No, that's a sad story," responded her mother. "Here, put the vegetables to steam in the microwave and I'll tell you more of her story. My grandmother used to tell us about her basketball playing days and she was very proud to have worn the uniform of Sherburn High School. She told us that girls basketball in those days was the biggest game in town and everyone came to see their teams play. They had regular officials in charge of the games, so it was serious business and winning that tournament was a highlight for the team."

"How neat those girls were treated so well during those early years. It must have been fun to have so many people coming to their games and cheering for them," Sarah said.

"Oh, yes," her mother agreed. "Years after they graduated, the team members would get together every now and then to reminisce about their basketball playing days. Most of them continued to live around Sherburn. One was in charge of polishing that beautiful silver trophy."

"I wonder where that trophy is today," Patti mused.

Sarah pulled up a kitchen stool and pondered, "So, do you know what happened to Great-Grandma Ruby's ring?"

Her mother paused as she was putting dinner on the table. "She never wanted to talk about it. All she would say was that they had been diving off a raft out in the lake outside of town. She realized when she came up from being pushed off the raft by one of the boys that the ring was gone. The water was too deep and they couldn't find it. It was always a sad finale to her basketball memories."

"Oh, how awful she must have felt!" Sarah felt a pang of empathy for her great-grandmother's loss.

"All right," her mother ended the discussion, "Call everyone for dinner."

Sarah yelled from her resting spot at the counter, "Come and get it while it's hot!" And the look from her mother told her that she'd better get up and go find them.

Later that evening, Sarah and her mother continued investigating the contents of the trunk. They carefully unwrapped many special treasures that had been carefully saved for many decades: hand-kerchiefs with initials stitched in them, doilies with slips of paper attached with a straight pin, listing who had made each one. There were small brooches for a dress or coat.

Then, wrapped carefully in tissue paper, they came upon an evident treasure to be preserved: Great-Grandma Ruby's basketball uniform! The white middy blouse had a black ribbon tied with a bow in front. The black bloomers were made of a woolen material gathered with elastic at the knees and waist. A small pair of leather shoes and long black stockings were in a small box. In a cardboard frame was a black and white photo of the team. A yellowed copy of what appeared to be a tournament program was inside a scrapbook, along with other memorabilia and some news clippings.

"Look at the stitches on the uniform, Mom," Sarah said, looking carefully at the seams. "Someone must have made this uniform. It doesn't have any company label."

"Yes," her mother said, "I would guess either Grandma Ruby, or her mother Clara, would have sewn this uniform. They wouldn't have spent money on something they could make for themselves."

Sarah lifted out a large piece of black paper that appeared to have come from an old scrapbook. It had an article on the front that looked like it was from a city newspaper, probably the *Minneapolis Star*. On the back were torn remnants of other articles. One was about how to purchase a pattern for a striped poplin dress. Also, there was an interesting remnant of a headline, 'Gertrude Ederle Writes Story of How She Set World Record in Channel Vic....'

On the front, the article appeared to span the width of the newspaper page. There were head shots of eleven high school girls and one adult woman, all wearing their basketball uniforms. The headline was, "Are Modern Girl Athletes Risking Their Looks?" The sub-title was, "Judging by These Pictures, the Answer is No - And Sports Are No Longer Considered Unmaidenly."

Sarah pointed at the article, "Look at this headline! Can this be 'for real?'"

Patti reminded her daughter, "Well, in the 1930s, some people still questioned whether girls should play sports like basketball. They didn't seem to mind girls participating in individual sports like golf, tennis and swimming, but they saw basketball as a rough team game."

Sarah scanned down the article, reading aloud, *"Is the modern girl in a sorry plight? Must she make a choice between beauty and brawn? Can she spend hours on the tennis court, in the swimming pool, on the golf links or even on the basketball floor, and yet expect to be so attractive that she will be invited to senior proms and other nice parties? Do the young men like the athletic type of girl or do they prefer the less energetic ones because they are prettier? Apparently the answer is that a girl can be both athletic and pretty, that she can possess feminine fascination and charm, but at the same time have supple muscles and the vigor of an Amazon."*

At that, Sarah smirked, "'...the vigor of an Amazon?' Well, I guess that includes me. Listen, this is interesting."

She continued reading, *"There was a time when it was considered unmaidenly for a girl to participate in any sort of sport, and she was barred from games and contests. Of course, there were always a few who disregarded the dictates of convention, but they were called tomboys and pointed out as bad examples by careful mothers. But no one ever hears of a tomboy these days. Perhaps the new styles in clothes have liberated girls from the situation which denied them the opportunity of exercising; perhaps with the dismissal of the old ground trailing skirts went a host of other traditional inhibitions."*

As she read down the page, Sarah commented to her mother, "Look, they are quoting Dr. Anna Norris from the University of Minnesota. She is the head of the Women's Physical Education Department. It says she is an advocate of sports for girls attending the university and believes that they can take part in athletics and 'yet be very charming.'"

The article identified the photos as basketball players from Litchfield, Brainerd, Princeton, Buffalo and Montevideo. Two players were listed as Dorothy Burshek and Winifred Roth of Buffalo. One adult woman was Marian McInerny of the First National Bank team of Minneapolis.

Sarah was fascinated by the history that was new to her. She said to her mother, "This article was saying that girls couldn't compete with their long dresses and corsets and high-buttoned shoes. Now, in 1930, they had thrown away the dresses, and played with bloomers and even shorts."

Have women's sports always gone through these cycles of being accepted or being discouraged, and then accepted again, Sarah wondered.

Sarah set aside the article for future examination and resumed her search of the trunk.

There was something tucked under some handkerchiefs near the bottom of the trunk. Sarah picked up a small leather book. *It appeared to be a diary.* Inside the cover, it said, "Property of Ruby McCarroll - Hands off!"

"Mom, look at this!" Sarah couldn't contain her excitement. Risking the potential repercussion of her great-grandmother's warning, Sarah carefully turned the pages and began to read her daily entries. Ruby described her days at school and then, midway through the journal, there was a description of the 1925 basketball tournament.

Ruby had written, "It was really fun to win the big tournament. There was a snowstorm and one of the teams couldn't get there, but we called another school and they came later in the day. The girls from the other teams stayed over in our homes and we played the championship the second day. There were lots of people there. My parents came too."

The diary contained several pages filled with comments about her teachers and friends, and Ruby had drawn caricatures of faces. One appeared to be Ruby's little dog.

As Sarah carefully turned the pages, Sarah noted that school ended in mid-May as the children of the farming community needed to be available for spring planting. Ruby had drawn big fireworks of celebration on two pages. They had an all-school picnic and there were games and races, and the best part was a big bonfire.

Everyone roasted wieners and toasted marshmallows. The mothers had brought delicious cakes and Ruby's mother had made gallons of the Watkins cherry drink. It was her favorite.

Ruby had written, "We ate until we were as stuffed as those hot dogs."

Sarah came to a page dated June 24, 1925: "This is the saddest and worst day of my life. My silver ring from the basketball tournament is lost forever. I was wearing it when we were diving off a raft on Fox Lake. I came up one time and the ring was gone. It must have slipped off when I was playing around, splashing one of the boys. We dove and dove but the raft kept swinging around, and it was so deep and murky at the bottom. The ring is gone forever. I shall cry all night."

Oh, no. Sarah could feel the agony of the young woman's loss. It must have been a terrible feeling to lose something so special, knowing that it couldn't be replaced and was gone forever.

As she closed the lid of the trunk, she thought, "I wish Great-Grandma Ruby's ring could be found somewhere, somehow!"

3

A New Game Comes to Town

As Sarah slowly trudged across the kitchen floor, her mother gave her a concerned look. "You look, as we used to say, like something the 'cat dragged in.' What's happened now?"

Sarah began a litany of her problems. Her advanced math teacher had loaded on an extra page of problems to bring in for tomorrow's class and promised a quiz. The choir director had added another rehearsal for the school musical. The basketball coach wanted them at a special practice on Saturday morning.

Sarah complained, "There's just too much to be done!"

"Stop, stop, and stop," her mother interrupted. "Sarah, you have to stop piling up things like you are building a pyramid. Lay them out, decide what must be done first and put the rest in order of deadlines and importance. Take things one at a time. It's called *prioritizing* and it's a good thing to learn now before you hit the real world."

Sarah's dad, Gary, walked in and caught the last phrase. "What's this about the 'real world?' Let me tell you about *my day*."

With a quiet "please excuse me," Sarah left her parents to discuss their days, and dropped into a chair in the living room. Her younger brother, Ben, was playing a video game with superheroes and monsters crashing and smashing the world into pieces.

"Hey, Sarah, wanna' play with me?" he asked with a hopeful look in his eyes.

"Sure, why not?" Sarah grinned, "I'll just make defending the world from aliens my first priority."

Her brother looked sideways at her as he handed her a remote, but decided not to ask any more questions or he might lose his playing opponent.

After a half hour of smashing, screaming sounds and missiles flying all around, the voice of Sarah's dad rolled out of the kitchen, "Ben, turn that thing down!"

Sarah thought to herself, it is fun to work off a little stress with a superhero that can save the world. My history teacher says we could use one right now.

"Well, buddy," Sarah finally sighed, "it's fun, but my superhero needs a break to regroup. I like being on the same team with you and you really are good at this stuff."

Ben smiled at her compliment and continued his bombardment, his fingers flying. "Thanks," he said, "maybe for awhile after dinner?"

"I'll see if I can get my homework done," Sarah responded. "Right now I have to go read a diary."

Ben shook his head...another answer from a sister that didn't make sense to him.

Sarah's desk was piled high with books, so she moved them to a nearby chair and sat down to do her math problems and review her class notes. It was a tough class and the test wouldn't be easy tomorrow, but she liked the challenge. It helped, she thought, to have a teacher who treated girls the same as boys, and didn't act as if they couldn't learn math too.

"Hey, Sarah, got time for a little game of 'horse' with Ben and me?" Her dad was at her door.

"Sure thing," Sarah smiled, "you two coming back for more after last night?" They both laughed.

"But Mom says I have to *prioritize*," Sarah said, "and I have about twenty minutes of homework left."

"That's a deal," her dad teased, "and in the meantime, Ben and I will take a few warm-up shots."

The ball swished through the net and there was a moan from Ben, their dad, and Kevin, a neighbor friend of Sarah's who had joined the action on the court.

"All right, Sarah," Gary said, wiping the perspiration from his forehead. "We've had enough for one night, haven't we, Ben?"

Ben nodded, heading in to start his homework, and happy for the reprieve from watching his sister sink those shots. How could she make it look so easy?

Sarah and Kevin had a final quick game, with the same results, and retired to the kitchen where they caught up on their day at school, reinforced by Patti's freshly baked chocolate chip cookies and a glass of milk. Soon, it was time to get to their homework.

Kevin grabbed another cookie on his way out the door, "See you tomorrow in history class, Sarah. And don't forget our Team Captain's meeting!" Sarah nodded. It was going to be a difficult meeting because there had been a weekend party, reportedly with members of both the girls' team and the boys' team involved. There would be consequences for those who had broken their commitments to their teams to be chemically-free.

Being a captain is not easy when you have to follow through with your responsibilities too, Sarah thought. It's like that song that says, "There is a point when you cannot walk away, when you have to stand up straight and tall and mean the words you say..." Let's hope we can mend the damage to our teams' unity.

Sarah was back on her bed, this time with her research papers spread around her. The break had been good and she felt energized to take on an evening of homework.

Well, she thought, Mom says every journey begins with one step. I have found an ancestor, Great-Grandma Ruby, who played basketball in the 1920s, but now I'd like to find out when basketball came to Minnesota.

Sarah looked at her notes. The Internet had information on some guy named James Naismith who was teaching in a school out in Massachusetts, somewhere in the early 1890s, and he needed an indoor game that would interest his male students during the winter between football and baseball. He made up this game with two teams that would throw a soccer ball around, trying to score a point.

This is such a funny part of the story, Sarah laughed to herself. Naismith needed something to use as goals that could be hung on the end walls of the gymnasium. The challenge for the players would be to toss a ball into the air and get it to land in the opponents' goal. Naismith asked the custodian to find two boxes. Pretty soon, the custodian came back and said he couldn't find any boxes, just two peach baskets. So, without a better idea, Naismith told him to nail them onto the end walls.

I'm going to describe it to the class and ask them to imagine how a peach basket is shaped. It has a round top, with sloping sides and a round narrow bottom. They'll notice how similar it is to the shape of the basketball nets that we use today.

The class will enjoy this part. The peach baskets had bottoms in them, so whenever the ball went in and scored a goal, someone had to climb a ladder and take it out, or lift it out from the balcony. Honestly, wouldn't you think they would figure out how to take the bottom out of the basket?

But, according to what I read, Sarah thought, it took *years* for someone to figure that out. In fact, they even made the basket with metal chain netting, with a chain to pull that would open the bottom of the net so the ball could fall out.

Sarah fell back on her bed and laughed again, thinking, can you imagine the officials in our game tomorrow night pulling a chain to get the ball out of the net?

And then a thought struck her. What do you think would have happened to the game of basketball if the custodian *had found* boxes and hung them on the wall? Imagine shooting a ball into square boxes. Do you think we might have been playing "box ball" instead of "basketball?" Or worse, maybe the players would have thought it wasn't any fun and the game would have been dropped as a bad idea.

She shook her head, considering basketball's narrow escape from obscurity. Can you imagine, she thought, our lives without basketball?

Now, to connect this Naismith and his game of "basket ball" to Minnesota, she thought. I have to remember that it was spelled with two words until the 1920s. At least it wasn't called, "peach basket ball."

Sarah shifted her position until she was comfortable again and opened an envelope that had arrived in the mail for her.

Was I ever lucky, Sarah thought, when I told Mom about my dilemma. She called her mother and got the telephone number of Grandma Mary's sister who researches our family tree. Mom said that if anyone would know, she would. So I called Great-Aunt Karen and could hardly believe it when she said that she had information that one of our ancestors had played basketball at Carleton College in Northfield, Minnesota. She said she would send it to me right away. And she sounded rather mysterious.

This could be the link between Massachusetts and Minnesota. Could I be so lucky? Sarah wondered.

Sarah carefully removed several sheets of handwritten stationery covered with her great-aunt's beautiful handwriting which her mother had identified as the Palmer Method taught years ago when writing by hand was important.

The letter said, "Sarah, I am so happy that you are researching the history of our family for your paper. I think you'll find this information to be very useful. It comes from a diary written by your Great-Great-Grandmother Clara when she was a student at Carleton College in Northfield, Minnesota. Good luck, and let me know when you want to join me discovering our roots."

Enclosed in the mailing package was a small diary.

As she scanned down the letter, Sarah nearly stopped breathing.

Wow, this is awesome. Great-Great-Grandmother Clara played basket ball in the *first game ever played in Minnesota*. And it was in the lower level gymnasium of her own dorm.

Darkness fell outside as Sarah began to read the diary. Clara's first entry as a college student was in 1891, when she enrolled as a freshman in the highly respected, private coeducational college in southeastern Minnesota.

Imagine, Sarah thought, Clara was the first woman in our family, as far as Great-Aunt Karen knows, to attend college.

As Sarah scanned through Clara's diary, she noticed the young woman's sense of responsibility to do well and be a credit to her rural farm family who was sacrificing so much for her education. In those days, many parents didn't see the value in educating their daughters, so Clara realized that she was fortunate indeed.

As Sarah read the next page, her pulse rate increased in anticipation of what she was about to learn.

During her sophomore year, Clara had recorded a new experience and her excitement popped off the pages. A new teacher had arrived on campus and he brought rules for a new game called "basket ball."

Clara wrote, "Dear Diary: November 18, 1892. We had the most fun tonight. Our new director of physical culture put a notice on our Gridley Hall bulletin board: 'Come to the recreation hall downstairs tonight at 7 pm and learn to play a new game, Basket Ball. Wear your tennis slippers. Signed, Max Exner, Director of Physical Culture.'

Clara's diary continued:

"Mr. Exner was a student at the YMCA Training School in Springfield, Massachusetts. Last year, his instructor, James Naismith, invented a new game that he called 'Basket Ball.' Mr. Exner said he played in the first game and the men all liked it. He said that women from nearby Smith College saw them playing and wanted to learn the game too. So, he thought we would benefit from learning the game as well.

"We spent an hour as Mr. Exner showed us how to move around the floor, tossing the ball from one to another. He had hung a fruit basket on each end of the floor. If the ball went in, we scored a point. We asked Mr. Exner if we could practice again tomorrow and he said 'yes.'"

Sarah smiled. I imagine that Clara felt like I did when I first played in a basketball game. There's such an excitement being on the floor with other players, watching the ball being thrown from one to another, and then to be the one to toss it up and see it land in the basket. That's a feeling that would have been the same for Clara as it is for me.

Another entry in the diary appeared two weeks later:

"Dear Diary, December 5, 1892. We are having such fun playing basket ball. A reporter from our college newspaper wrote an article about us. I will send it home to Zumbrota as I know my sister would enjoy this game too.

"This is the article (see clipping attached to this page). I'm not bragging, but I played in this game and scored two points.

'Gymnasium Work for the Year 1892-1893, Spring Issue, ALGOL (Carleton College yearbook)

... A little later Basket Ball was introduced and you should have seen the fun. See the ladies on the floor, attired in loose dresses permitting free action of the body and tennis slippers upon their feet. They are divided into two sides, standing at opposite sides of the gymnasium; their eyes sparkling with excitement, ready to dash at the ball when put into play. The ball is thrown into the field of play and the fun begins. Now they are all in a bunch endeavoring to get the ball, now they scatter and again they rush together, every eye following the ball which is never for an instant in one place, and every energy bent upon obtaining a clear throw for the basket. Watch an individual player. Now she

dashes to obtain the ball, now darts to obstruct an opponent and again to protect the goal; running, dodging, squirming, throwing the ball, again catching it, and all the time exercising her vocal organs to the best of her ability. When in the course of the game a well-directed throw sends the ball into the goal, a cheer arises which shows the complete relaxation of the mind to the enjoyment. Are girls fit for the drawing room only? Can they participate in active games as boys can? Were you permitted to witness one of these games, you would surely conclude that they can.'"

Clara's diary entry concluded, "As you can see, we are so enjoying this new game. I hope other young women will have an opportunity to learn it too."

Sarah thought how wonderful it was that Clara and her friends were encouraged by their instructor and the college. She decided she would leave Carleton College on her list of potential colleges because they have a long tradition of championing the rights of women.

Wouldn't it be fun, she thought, to be a student-athlete at the same college where my ancestor played in the first game of basketball in Minnesota? Sarah's eyes sparkled with the thought.

It was growing late and Sarah's energy was fading. Yet, her detective work was so intriguing that she didn't want to put it away for the night.

Her mother tapped on the door, opening it slowly to check on the light that was visible under her door.

"Sarah, it's time for some sleep. Did you get your biggest priorities finished?"

"Yes, Mom," Sarah replied. "I got the homework for tomorrow done.

But look at these diary pages that came from Great-Aunt Karen. You must read this! Can you believe that we have a relative who played in the first basketball game in Minnesota?"

Her mother's eyebrows went up as though a bit skeptical at that news, but as she scanned down the pages, she became very animated.

"Sarah, this is simply unbelievable! How could our family be part of such an important event in the history of basketball? To think that one of our women played 'basket ball' at Carleton."

Patti sat down in a chair, "And just think what that means - *women learned to play basketball first in Minnesota.* It boggles my mind! Women have never been credited with being the first to play basketball. What an important piece of sports history! I am so proud of you, Sarah, for uncovering this information."

Sarah smiled at the unexpected praise from her mother, especially so early in her research.

As her mother got up and turned at the door, ready to turn off her light, they both smiled at each other. What fun to share this with my mother, Sarah thought. *She gets it!*

Basket Ball Sweeps Across Minnesota

Sarah was anxious to get home and back to her research paper. Even basketball practice seemed a bit tedious and Sarah struggled to keep her concentration so her coach wouldn't notice. She didn't need to spend time doing extra laps today - those diary pages were waiting for her.

Finally, she was sitting at her desk at home. She hadn't been able to finish reading her great-great-grandmother's diary and the correspondence from her Great-Aunt Karen. Sarah noticed a folded sheet that turned out to be a copy of a letter from Clara's sister, Alice, who was in high school in Zumbrota.

"January 8, 1893. Dear Clara, I was so looking forward to spending the weekend with you at Carleton, but never would have guessed that you would show us this new game of basket ball.

It was so exciting that your professor, Mr. Exner, put me into the game for a few minutes. It was such fun to throw the ball around from one girl to another and try to toss it up so it would land inside a basket hanging on the wall and score a point. The game reminded me of one we played in our elementary school, called 'duck on a rock.'

On Monday, I went to see our English teacher and asked if she would supervise us and help us learn how to play this game of 'basket ball.' Mr. Exner had given me a copy of the 13 rules.

Our teacher is young and she doesn't think we girls should just sit and watch boys play football or baseball, so she posted an invitation to the other girls in the school. We found a round ball and went downtown to the community hall. We nailed two fruit baskets to the walls at the ends of the floor and found a ladder to retrieve the ball after a score. Twenty girls showed up for the first practice and more are coming every day. Our teacher said we could invite some of our friends from neighboring schools to come and we could teach them how to play. She said that if the principal approved, we could get together and play our team against other schools. Wouldn't that be fun?

The boys are starting to hang around and watch. They act like it is a game for girls, but I saw a couple of them pick up the ball and try to score a goal.

Mother, Father and the boys send their love, your sister, Alice."

Sarah considered the timeline. Alice and her friends probably played until she graduated in 1895. Maybe the local historical society has some information. So she called them.

How neat, Sarah thought, that the woman at the Zumbrota Historical Society was so willing to help me. She said they had a copy of a booklet that had photos of the Zumbrota team in 1904, 1910 and 1915 and she faxed copies to me. There is one page from the "Zumbrota Centennial Booklet" that says *"The girls and boys played in the same facility where they had to be careful about hitting low ceilings or dodging low-hanging light fixtures. In 1912 they played in the City Hall."*

That means, Sarah thought, girls' teams spread out from Carleton College pretty quickly. Plus, the boys had picked up the game too.

Patti ran up the stairs and rushed into Sarah's bedroom. From the look in her eyes, Sarah hoped there wasn't trouble somewhere.

"Sarah, this is your lucky day." Patti was waving a big, heavy-looking book. "Our women's book club invited two women to speak to our group today. These women have researched the history of girls basketball in the early 1900s, and published a book. It is filled with stories told by the women who had been in high school during those years and played on girls' basketball teams! And you should see the photos of teams. The authors said that the women, just like Grandma Ruby, had kept their team photos, scrapbooks and even uniforms. I bought the book for you. I also got one for the school library, but I'll wait to give it to the librarian until after you make your report."

"That's really cool, Mom…" Sarah began.

Her mother wasn't finished. *"Sarah, you'll never believe this - the authors of this book had the Sherburn trophy with them. It was the one with Grandma Ruby in the team photo, all polished and the silver was beautiful.* The plaque on the trophy said, "Invitational Tournament Champions, Sherburn, 1925."

"Look," her mother pushed her cell phone toward Sarah. "I took a picture of it. Isn't it beautiful?"

"That's really cool," Sarah enthusiastically repeated. "But why did these women have it?"

"It appears," her mother replied, "that when Sherburn and smaller nearby schools were going to be consolidated into Martin County West, the athletic director found the trophy in a storage room. His daughter is a school administrator and coach in the Cities, and she contacted the woman at the Minnesota State High School League who is also co-author of the book. So, they loaned the trophy to the book authors for display at programs when they teach people about the history of Minnesota's 'daughters of the game.'"

Patti dropped down alongside Sarah on her bed, nearly exhausted from the excitement of her day.

They sat together, turning the pages of the book, *Daughters of the Game - The First Era of Minnesota Girls High School Basketball, 1891-1942.*

"Look at this, Mom," Sarah exclaimed, "they had parties after the games and after 'away' games, they stayed in the host team's homes. They sure had a lot of fun."

The stories told by women who played during those years were full of anecdotes and interesting descriptions of their uniforms, how they traveled and where they played. But, thirty years into the history, something must have happened because there were stories of regret and sadness that told of teams being dropped.

The light stayed on in Sarah's bedroom for another hour as the two heads bent over the book, exclaiming over photos of all those young women smiling back at them from so many years ago.

Finally, it was Saturday and Sarah had the entire afternoon to research how basket ball had spread around the entire state of Minnesota. Sarah was back on her bed with her new reference book, *Daughters of the Game.*

She noted that there was a photo of a 1902 St. Paul team and another of a 1902 Brainerd team. It hadn't taken long for basket ball to sweep across Minnesota.

As Sarah turned the pages of the book, she was amazed at the amount of history that had been gathered by the authors, Marian Bemis Johnson and Dorothy E. McIntyre. It would be a great help for her research.

Sarah took a closer look at the team pictures and noticed that their uniforms weren't very "uniform." The Brainerd team had dresses with skirts over the bloomers. The collars were cut differently and had trimming in different places. Some girls had ribbons tied on the top of the dress. The young women, or their mothers, had obviously made the uniforms. Maybe, she thought, they called them "costumes" because they weren't very "uniform."

The dark stockings and slippers, plus the long sleeves confirmed that girls were not supposed to show any "skin" in those days. Sarah laughed, thinking, those wool uniforms must have been pretty hot.

She noted that most of the girls had long hair, some swept up into the "Gibson Girl" style of the decade. They would have loved the way we wear our hair in pony tails now, she mused.

The 1902 St. Paul team photo was a different style. The players wore jersey sweaters, bloomers, and the ball looked very heavy with its leather seams. No wonder they didn't want to bounce the ball very much in those days, Sarah thought.

Sarah bent over the book to read the description of the early game. It appeared that the women teachers at Eastern colleges liked the idea of teaching basket ball to their female students, but wanted a game that wouldn't alienate school administrators or parents who thought women should exhibit only feminine behavior and dress. So, they began to develop rules unique to the women's game. By 1899, a Women's Basketball Rules Committee began to divide the playing floor into two, three or more sections and restrict players to stay in each section.

When Sarah read stories told by Minnesota players, it appeared that schools simply decided which rules they would follow. Some played with three courts and some played with two courts. A few schools played the full-court "boys' rules" until they were told they had to stop because it was against state association rules.

Players told stories of not knowing what rules they might play until they arrived at the school. One player said they decided to play half of the game with three-court rules and half with two-court rules so everyone would be "happy." Imagine, Sarah thought, of not knowing what game you would play.

Sarah mused, it seems like they made it far more complicated than it needed to be. Clearly, every little "dot on the map" of Minnesota had a girls' basketball team by the 1920s. If only the state association had set statewide rules, they could have had state tournaments too, like Iowa and other states did. I wonder why no one stood up for girls basketball and gave them a tournament when the boys in Minnesota had a state tournament in the 1920s?

Sarah had found a team in 1919 who challenged area schools and only one accepted their challenge. When Owatonna defeated New Ulm, 24-18, Owatonna declared themselves "state champs."

Good for Owatonna, Sarah thought. If no one will give them a state tournament, they'll do it themselves!

At least now, she thought, girls and boys play by the same rules, and both have state tournaments. Better late than never, she thought wryly.

As she turned the pages, Sarah saw more stories by women who played in the 1920s and 1930s, stating that their teams were being dropped. She remembered that Great-Grandma Ruby's diary had said that her team was dropped the year after she graduated.

From all accounts, it looked like *by 1942, the girls' teams had all disappeared. The first era of girls basketball in Minnesota lasted only fifty years. What had happened?*

There was something else beginning to irritate Sarah. Why were women constantly being limited in what they wanted to do? When the bicycle was invented in the mid-1850s, there were warnings that riding a bicycle might cause women to leave home without chaperones. Or when women wanted to play more active sports and began throwing away corsets for bloomers, what a furor that caused.

And their legal status was terrible. The *Daughters of the Game* book says that in 1887, married women achieved the same legal existence as single women; they were no longer the *property of their husbands.*

How ridiculous! Imagine being considered someone's "property," Sarah shuddered at the thought.

Her history class had studied the suffrage movement and had been horrified by the treatment of women who simply wanted the right to vote. They were ridiculed, and spit upon, even by other women. They were jailed in terrible conditions. Sarah thought, how awful it must be for any group when they are treated differently and can't enjoy the same freedoms that others have.

Sarah stood up and walked over to her window where she could see the flag waving on the flagpole in front of their home. Her dad was a veteran and he made sure that they faithfully respected the flag in every way.

Don't we pledge, "*... with liberty and justice for all?*" Sarah questioned. We are taught that some things have gotten better, she reflected, and they have in many ways, but there is still injustice in the world that my generation needs to change.

Her fingers closed into a determined fist as Sarah realized that she felt a *new stirring*, a commitment to learn more about the injustice that had been perpetrated against women and to find a way to help bring about change.

"Listen up, World," she announced to her empty room. "When my generation gets involved, there's going to be another new game coming to town - *and we're going to play!*"

5

WHERE DID ALL THE SNOW GO?

"Tonight, Great-Grandma Ruby wrote in her diary, "we are going to play an 'away' game and we have to go by sleigh, bobsled and train to get there. And it is an overnight too. I'd better start getting my warm clothes ready."

As Sarah lay on her bed reading the diary, she could feel the young woman's excitement and thought... how fun it would be... to go with Ruby and her team....

Sarah's eyes were slowly closing.

The snow felt like hard little pellets blowing into her face. Sarah pulled her warm coat around her and wrapped her long woolen scarf tightly around her head. Together with her boots and mittens, she looked like a veritable moving mound of clothes with snow accumulating on the very top.

"Hop in, be quick!" her father said, and Sarah jumped into the sleigh with her overnight bag. The harnesses on the horses had brass bells attached and she always loved to hear them jingling as they glided along the trail. "I'll get you into town and then they'll have a bigger bobsled ready to take you all to the train. We'll stop and pick up Marie along the way and meet Ruby there."

It was dark and the lanterns on the sleigh cast small circles of light. Fortunately, there was a full moon rising and it helped to outline the fences, with the snowdrifts leaving their long shadows. It would be even colder tomorrow after the storm moved on. The big horsehair lap robes and heated soapstones for their feet helped keep toes warm. The wind wasn't blowing as hard now, so the trip was actually fun.

The sleigh bells almost sound like my alarm, Sarah thought, as she snuggled down, pulling her blanket around her shoulders.

Sarah smiled, anticipating the night ahead. They were going to stay overnight in the hotel in New Prague. That was a real treat. In the morning, the teams would take the Minneapolis and St. Louis, the M&St.L, train back home.

In a few minutes, they could see Marie, another snowy figure, standing by her driveway. Marie shook off the snow before she stepped up into the sleigh and sat down by Sarah. Her cheeks were rosy and her face adorned with a big smile. Marie was such a happy person and Sarah enjoyed being her friend.

"Well, was your mother okay with you playing tonight?" Sarah inquired.

"Yes," Marie responded with a rueful shake of her head, "she got over not wanting me to 'play in bloomers in front of the whole town,' and telling me I was 'bringing disgrace to the family and making a spectacle of yourself.' You know how hard it was for me to stand up to my mother and tell her that I wasn't going to quit basketball. She finally agreed, but said she would never come to a game. And she hasn't."

Marie smiled, "But lately, when I get home, she does ask me if we won the game. At least now I don't have to fib and tell her that I'm playing in the orchestra at the game. I didn't like having to hide my flute in the bushes outside the house. Lucky for me, it was always there when I got home. And listen to this, Sarah, yesterday my mother told my younger sister that she *could* play basketball next year. So, my sister is lucky I didn't give in or she wouldn't have been able to play either."

"Did you bring your stuff for our overnight in the hotel?" Marie asked.

"Yes, I have the fudge," Sarah responded. "What did you bring?"

"I have popcorn already popped and more corn if the hotel will let us pop some there. With the boys' team around too, I couldn't bring that much popped corn on the sled, and the train," Marie added.

The sleigh glided quietly down the road, with only the breathing of the horses and the rhythmic sounds of the sleigh bells breaking the silence of the Minnesota prairie evening. As they came into town and approached the school, Sarah could see other sleighs and a group of players standing around, stomping their feet to keep them warm. Ruby was waving at them and she had a bag full of treats too. It was a happy group whenever the girls and boys' teams played double-headers. The chaperones would have their hands full trying to keep the players in their rooms tonight.

Soon the big bobsled was filled. The coach's instructions were clear: boys were to sit in the back and the girls in the front. Sometimes it was hard to check out the seating arrangements with those big horsehair blankets covering everyone up. There was a little stove in the back and the boys were responsible for keeping the fire burning with some corncobs and small pieces of coal. The stove pipe poked up through an opening in the roof of the bobsled but sometimes smoke would escape from the stove, causing some coughing and burning eyes.

Marie tried to brush off the steamed up window coverings but it was difficult to see out, even on a good night. The important thing was that they blocked out the cold wind.

The snow had picked up again and the driver was muttering to himself as he sat inside on the front seat of the sled, trying to see the edges of the road. Ditches weren't very deep but it didn't take much for the sled to tip over. If that happened, everyone would have to get out and the boys would lift it back onto the road again. It was always easier for the driver on the way home because the horses seemed to know the way.

Across the fields, Sarah could occasionally catch a glimpse of lanterns flickering across the snow as sleighs with parents and fans were making their way to the neighboring town. The smaller sleighs frequently just went cross-country as farmers didn't mind neighbors crossing their fields on a cold winter night.

When they reached the outskirts of town, they pulled into the train station and the M&St.L engine was huffing out its big black clouds of smoke.

Everyone climbed out of the bobsled, reminding each other to bring their bags. No one wanted to find that their uniform was on a one-way trip home in the bobsled. Sarah checked to make sure her fudge was still intact. It was only somewhat squashed by someone leaning on the bag.

It was nice and warm in the train and it didn't take long to cover the last seven miles to the next town.

Tonight they were playing in the New Prague Opera House as the school had no gymnasium. It had a nice floor, but there had been a dance there the previous night and the floor was very slippery. Fortunately ,the coach had some resin.

"Here, Sarah," Ruby said, as she shook some on the floor, "step on this resin and walk on your heels until you get back on the playing floor."

Ruby's team was happy to learn that they were going to play the two-court game and would be allowed two dribbles before passing the ball. They could play a fast game with those rules. There were small rooms where the visiting teams could change into their uniforms. The home teams had to put on their uniforms at school and then run two blocks to the Opera House. Brrrrr, Sarah thought. It would be even colder after the games.

After the games, the three young women and their teammates trudged along the street toward the school. Ruby linked arms with Sarah and Marie.

"Wasn't that a great game?" Ruby squeezed their arms. "I can hardly wait to tell my mother about it. She still talks about learning how to play basketball when she was at Carleton College."

Sarah's eyes widened at the connection with her family members. This was sweet, she thought.

Ruby added, "When I saw the high baskets and that balcony on one end with the New Prague boys hanging over it, I thought we were in for a time of it. There were so many people on the stage at the other end, and not many were cheering for us."

Marie laughed, "And those posts in the middle of each court! Did you see how they planned their plays so we would be looking the other way and would have to dodge them at the last minute? Poor Jane hit that one post pretty hard. It made me laugh when she said, 'Good thing I have a hard German head.'"

"And the stoves in the corner," Marie added, "It was lucky for me that one of the New Prague fathers caught me as I was falling toward that hot stove, or I'd have been 'toast.'"

They all laughed.

Ruby said, "Well, it was nice to have those stoves. I remember when we played at Dodge Center in that hall above the hardware store and there was no heat at all."

Sarah squeezed her arm around Marie's shoulders, "Marie, your score at the last second was wonderful. We haven't beaten them for the last two years. And my guard told me there is going to be great food at the school and they have a concertina band, so we can dance too."

Marie's smile was very happy, "Well, you know that the cooks around New Prague are really good. I love the Czech sausages and pork schnitzel, and the apple strudel. *I'd love to have to stay here for an extra day, just for the food.*"

As they approached the school, the sound of the concertinas playing waltzes and polkas came rolling out into the street. It didn't take long before the assembly room was filled with students and, it seemed, the entire community of New Prague too.

All too soon, it was off to the hotel where the girls were assigned to rooms on one floor and boys on another floor. The girls got out some playing cards, the fudge and popcorn and before long, the boys' noses led them to where they were. A tapping on the door and soon the room was filled with games of cards and lots of good laughs, but it didn't take long before there was more knocking on the door and a weary chaperone stood in the doorway, shaking his finger and ordering the boys back to their rooms.

It seemed to Sarah, Marie and Ruby as though they had just gotten to sleep and it was morning. A loud pounding on the door startled the young women. Marie peeked out the door to find one very angry, red-faced coach.

"Girls, get dressed and downstairs, right now!" They hurriedly threw their playing clothes into their bags and rushed down the stairs. On one side of the room stood the boys, some with heads hanging. On the other side were the coaches and the two chaperones. The girls joined the boys and stood silently, waiting for an adult to speak.

"It seems," said the coach, "that someone sneaked into my room last night and *turned off* my alarm. Now we have missed the 6:00 a.m. train. Since it's Saturday, there is no train until 3:30 p.m., so you will all have to sit in their school until we go to the station. The principal will take care of you on Monday. You can expect discipline, including potential dismissal from school, for the 'guilty party.'"

With a sly grin, Marie turned to Ruby and Sarah, and whispered, "Maybe the New Prague mothers will bring us lunch!"

When Monday came, the two teams sat in their seats after the last bell dismissed the rest of the students.

The principal came into their assembly room, and announced, "When the guilty party, or parties, from last Friday night's incident in New Prague comes forward and takes responsibility for turning off your coach's alarm clock, the rest of you may leave."

No one moved.

"All right," the principal said with a deep breath, "you have each chosen to be 'guilty by association.' You can all plan on meeting me here after school every day this week. You will write 100 times every day, 'I will never do that again.'"

And they never did.

"Sarah, wake up! You'll be late for school. Did you sleep all night with your clothes on?" Her sister was standing in the doorway to their bedroom, with a piece of toast in her hand. *"Didn't you hear your alarm?* Hurry up - you have ten minutes before the bus comes."

Sarah opened her eyes, bleary with sleep. Great-Grandma Ruby's diary was next to her on the bed, her hand still holding it. Her mother must have come in last night and covered her with a blanket. She wanted to nestle down and sleep longer; maybe she could get back into that dream again.

No, she remembered, I can't do that today - too many things going on. Sarah carefully replaced the diary in her top dresser drawer, a safe place for now.

Sarah brushed her teeth, pulled on her clothes and ran a brush through her hair. It would have to do for today. She smiled to herself. *That certainly was an interesting dream!* It was fun to be with my Great-Grandma Ruby and her friends when they were all young, like me. It must be what happens, she thought, when I'm reading her diary before I fall asleep.

As she ran out the door to the bus stop, she looked around, laughed, and said to Ben, *"Where did all the snow go?"*

Sisters...Ben shook his head, who can understand them?

★ ★

6

Why Did They Take That Game Away From Us?

The land line rang. With all the cell phones in the family, it was unusual to hear it ring. Ben loved to answer the telephone and prided himself on informing the unnamed caller to put their number on a "do not call" list.

This time, however, Ben's smile was spontaneous, "Hey, Uncle Dan. How ya' been? Are you still coming to my game next Friday?"

Uncle Dan was a favorite in their family. He always had time to support his nieces and nephew, and was a familiar face at plays, concerts, and games. He was interested in all facets of their busy lives, and he seemed to know so much about everything. They knew he must be a good teacher.

Ben handed the phone to Sarah, "He wants to talk to you now."

"Sarah, I've been thinking about your report and I think I have a place that would be interesting for you. Would you take a ride with me to Cokato where your dad and I grew up and went to high school?"

Uncle Dan was one of Sarah's favorite people. He knew so much about women's issues and had recently returned from England where he had made a presentation on Amelia Earhart, one of his favorite heroes.

Sarah had also enjoyed going to the World Champion Minnesota Lynx games with him last summer. He said he believed that Lindsay Whalen from Hutchinson, Minnesota, is one of the wonders of the world. Sarah agreed.

Sarah was happy to ride along with him that late autumn morning. As they rode west along Highway #212, the rolling hills and their trees seemed to be showing off their most brilliant reds and yellows. Many Minnesotans, Uncle Dan said, were either farmers or only a generation or two away from their rural upbringing. He talked about their Swedish heritage and the family history he was researching.

As they came into the town of Howard Lake, he pointed out the building where the upper level had been the site of many exciting early boys and girls basketball games.

On impulse, he swung into the parking lot and said, "Let's see if someone will let us in so we can see it for ourselves." The lower level was now the town's little grocery and gas station. The manager listened to her uncle's explanation of their interest in seeing the second floor.

"Sure enough," he said as he reached for keys hanging behind the counter. "This used to be a busy place with community meetings, but now it has to be fixed up in order to meet codes. You know how that goes - it takes money our community doesn't have, so now it sits empty."

They climbed up the long stairway to the second level and the manager jiggled the key in the door until it finally clicked. When the door swung open, there was the basketball court, still intact with its wooden floor and some boundary lines showing around the edges of the court.

There were no baskets remaining from those early days. A dropped ceiling had been put in to accommodate the community's meetings.

"I suppose," Uncle Dan said, "that leaving the baskets would have been too tempting and they didn't need them for holding meetings or dances up here."

Sarah wished they could find a ladder and lift up a section of the ceiling to see if they could see any remnants of the basketball backboard or nets. Windows lined the wall facing the street below. She tried to imagine how people would have set their chairs around the edges of the court. The ends of the court had an open area and there would have been enough space for quite a number of people to sit or stand.

"I wonder if they had bleachers?" Sarah pondered.

As they walked around the floor, Uncle Dan told of hearing a woman aged 97 years telling stories about playing basketball for Buffalo High School, a school not far from Howard Lake. Vera Ilstrup-Templin had played in the 1920s, and she was one of those unforgettable people, Uncle Dan said, feisty and enthusiastic about life. She had outlived two or three husbands, as he recalled.

Vera told about playing in her bloomers and middy blouse, but had said that the local doctor's wife made uniforms for their team of purple corduroy. "Mrs. Dr. Catlin," as the girls called her, made purple knickers with a white heavy rayon blouse with a purple corduroy collar. Vera had said, "We thought we were pretty foxy."

"Vera was quite the story-teller," Uncle Dan said. "She told us how a bus had replaced cars named Franklins and Hutmobiles, their previous mode of transportation to their games. The bus had a cab with the driver and an assistant. Along both sides of this long bus were wooden bench seats. The boys sat on one side and the girls on the other. Vera had added, 'at least, *most of the time* we sat that way.'"

Sarah decided she would have liked Vera.

Uncle Dan went on, "Vera described how one night on their way to a game, a big winter storm had blown in. Without the benefit of Doppler radar, television or even a radio, the team had no idea they were heading into one of the worst snowstorms of the year. When the snow began to obliterate the sides of the road, the boys took turns walking in front of the bus to guide it down the road and keep it out of the ditch. The team finally arrived in Howard Lake at 9 p.m., two hours late, and found that the bleachers and chairs were full of fans, still waiting for them."

Sarah couldn't imagine her team's fans waiting like that.

"Vera told of how the girls' team won their game against Howard Lake and won the Wright County Championship. Then the boys played their game and they also won. The snow had continued and when they reloaded the bus for home, they repeated the same cold procedure with the boys wrapping the girls' long woolen scarves over their faces, taking turns leading the bus down the road. She said they arrived back in Buffalo in the wee hours of the morning."

Sarah tried to imagine the determination it would have taken for teams to travel through storms in those days. She had read of teams staying overnight in farm homes and one-room schoolhouses along their route. Then they'd finish their trip in the morning when they could get through the roads again.

She said, "My parents would be beside themselves with worry and calling everyone to find out where we were. I suppose in those years, parents just had to wait and worry."

They stood looking over the gymnasium floor, now dusty and empty, but full of memories. Sarah thought if she listened carefully, she could almost hear the crowds cheering, the officials' whistles and the bouncing of the basketballs - echoes of those happy years when basketball was king *and queen* of the court.

Sarah and her uncle started again on their way to Cokato. Their "flight plan" was to visit a woman in Cokato that Dan had met at a meeting of their local historical society.

Uncle Dan drove up to her home in Cokato. Its lawn was neatly mowed and the flowers were putting out their last blooms before a hard frost hit. A woman came to the door with a friendly smile, beckoning for them to come in. A plate of freshly baked cookies and a quart of cold milk with glasses waited on the table.

After talking about the weather, a Minnesota custom, Uncle Dan steered the conversation to Adalyn's basketball years in Cokato, from 1917-1925. She clearly had been looking forward to the opportunity since Dan had called.

Adalyn's eyes sparkled at Sarah as she recalled her high school basketball days that began in the seventh grade.

"You know, Sarah," Adalyn began, "our games were played in the town hall and there was no place to change into our uniforms."

"What did you do?" Sarah asked. It seemed unbelievable that there were no indoor locker rooms for the teams to use.

"Well," Adalyn replied, "there was a coal room downstairs and we usually used that, especially when it was bad weather."

"A coal room?" Sarah's eyebrows shot up. "What was it for?"

"Oh, Sarah," Adalyn shook her head. "I forget how many years have passed. You young people today don't even know about coal furnaces. You do know what coal is, don't you?" She laughed.

"Yes," Sarah smiled too, "but we were studying coal as an environmental problem with the chemicals it produces when it is burned by big factories. I didn't realize that homes and small buildings in your day actually burned it for heat too."

"Oh, yes," Adalyn recalled. "Our father delivered coal around the area. He had lots of horses for the delivery wagons. He and another man would put a chute through a small window that led into the coal room near the furnace. Then they would shovel the coal down the chute. I can tell you, it made an awful oily film and dust, hard to get off your clothes and anything else it landed on."

"So," Sarah wondered, "wasn't it hard to put on your uniform without picking up coal dust?"

"Yes, but there would usually be enough room to stand on the floor and we'd spread some newspapers. When that's the only place girls could have a little privacy, you just did it. And it was better than running outside to the outhouse. You know what an outhouse is, don't you?"

Sarah laughed, "Yes, my Great-Grandma Ruby's farm still has one sitting behind the house, but it is just to show the little kids how it used to be 'in the good old days,' as they call them. They plant flowers in the holes now."

They all laughed and reached for another cookie. Sarah couldn't believe that she was sitting with a woman whose life had been so different from her own.

"So, Adalyn," Sarah began again, "what was it like playing in the town hall? Were there baskets hanging on the ends of the floor?"

"Yes," Adalyn smiled, "they had nailed baskets to the walls. For the first year, there wasn't a backboard behind the basket and you had to try to shoot the ball so it would land in the basket and not hit that rough wall behind it."

Uncle Dan laughed, "So, 'all net' for your shots, right, Adalyn?"

Sarah smiled and Adalyn did too. She understood his humor. After all, she watched lots of basketball games, especially the girls state tournaments and women's games on television.

"What kind of floor was in your town hall?" Sarah asked.

Adalyn laughed, "Oh, it was a wooden floor, but it was terrible. They held every kind of event there. One weekend they had a county chicken show and there were still chicken feathers and straw, and other 'stuff' on the floor." They all laughed at the images of the teams slipping and sliding on the remnants of the chicken show.

"Wasn't it dangerous to play on that floor?" Sarah asked.

Adalyn winced at the memory."Well, it was. One time we were playing a game and I got tripped and ended up with a sliver from the floor in my back. I ran to Dr. Peterson's office up over the drug store. He took it out, gave me a shot, and I went back and played the rest of the game."

Sarah winced too. Who could ever say that those early pioneers weren't capable of withstanding the challenge of playing basketball? It seems so unfair that their style of basketball games has been so unappreciated.

"Did you have rivals with the other schools?" Dan inquired.

"Oh yes, Howard Lake and Dassel were really 'dog-eat-dog' games. Beating them was our big goal."

"Did it ever get rough?"

"You'd better believe it! One night we were playing at Howard Lake upstairs in their town hall and we had no dressing room, so we just laid our clothes on the chairs. When we weren't looking, someone threw our clothes out the window. We had to go downstairs and pick our clothes off the street!"

Adalyn shook her head as if the "score" might not have been settled even yet.

"Sarah," Adalyn's voice carried a note of excitement, "with your young legs, would you run up those stairs into my attic? There is a 'hope chest' up there with my basketball uniform and a scrapbook. I never put sheets and doilies and stuff like that in it like a lot of women did. I put important things in it- *like my basketball uniform.*"

Sarah quickly climbed the stairs and lifted the attic door, using the flashlight Adalyn had given her. There sat the "hope chest."

With the basketball uniform and a scrapbook in her arms, Sarah carefully descended the narrow steps.

Adalyn's uniform was a traditional middy top with its long neck ribbon, and a pair of bloomers. But the middy was red with a black ribbon, and the bloomers were made of black corduroy.

Uncle Dan observed, "The photos of teams of your era are always black and white. So I'm finding out that many teams had colorful uniforms."

Adalyn smiled, "Oh yes, teams frequently wore their school colors. The town photographer had the best camera in his studio, so that's where team photos were taken. They were good quality but all black and white in those days before color film."

"Adalyn," Sarah asked, "I've read that wool was usually used for bloomers. Why are yours made of corduroy?"

Adalyn smiled, "Well, one game was with Buffalo and they had these purple corduroy bloomers. We thought they were pretty neat, so we made ours out of corduroy too. And they were easier to wash. With wool bloomers, some teams didn't wash them from one season to the next."

"Oh, imagine, no dry cleaners," said Sarah. "You had some interesting challenges, Adalyn."

And the two basketball players laughed together.

For the next hour, Adalyn carefully showed Sarah and Uncle Dan each article in her scrapbook, turning the pages slowly to prevent any cracking of the yellowing pages and occasionally pointing out her name as a high scorer for Cokato.

"Did people come to your games, Adalyn?" Sarah asked.

"Oh, yes, the hall would be full of people. We were really the 'big show' in town. People put chairs along the edges of the court, and more than once a player would end up in the lap of someone's parent." They were smiling and chuckling, as they visualized her stories.

Adalyn laughed, "When our fans got really excited, their Swedish heritage came out and they loved to cheer: '*Rockar, stockar, Thor och hans bockar. Kor igenom! Kor igenom!*'"

Uncle Dan spoke up, "I know what that means, '*Rocks, Logs, Thor and his steeds, Drive on through, Drive on through.*'"

They all laughed, imagining the community building vibrating with the familiar language.

"Adalyn," Uncle Dan began, "your information is very helpful to Sarah for her school research paper."

"Yes," Sarah added, "with your permission, I would like to include your stories in my report so my friends will also learn about your playing days."

"Well, that's very nice," and then Adalyn hesitated. "I've been thinking - there is another woman in town who loved basketball too. Her name is Lorraine. She is in the Memory Care Unit of our assisted living home. She is about seven years younger than I am. Lorraine was always so unhappy about what happened to her team. She might remember those days, if you have time to stop there."

"Please, Uncle Dan," Sarah asked, "let's go to say hello. Even if she doesn't remember playing basketball, it would be good for her to have a couple visitors stop by. I'm doing some volunteer work at our assisted living home, and it is so sad to see the people who keep looking at the door, hoping someone will come to visit them, *or take them home.*"

As Uncle Dan and Sarah reluctantly bid their goodbyes and thanked Adalyn for her memories, she pressed the remaining cookies into Sarah's hands. "You need these, young woman; you need to add a little 'meat on your bones' to stay healthy." Sarah smiled at the familiar gesture of that wonderful Minnesota hospitality, always ensuring that no one would leave hungry or without a snack on the way home.

On the edge of town sat the assisted living building which was now home to so many local residents.

As they quietly walked down the hallway, Sarah said, "Think of all of the stories these people could share of their lives. I wonder if their families have written them down."

As they walked into the room, Lorraine's eyes opened when she heard their footsteps.

Uncle Dan pulled two chairs near her bed and they sat down on either side of her bed. "Hello, Lorraine," he said gently, "My name is Dan and I grew up here in Cokato. And there is a young woman with me who would like to meet you."

Sarah began, "My name is Sarah and I play on my high school basketball team. I know you liked to play basketball and I wonder if you could tell me about the years when you played?"

Unexpectedly, a sad look passed over Lorraine's face. As she looked intensely at them, she took one of Sarah's hands in both of hers and asked, "Why did they take that game away from us?" She repeated the question, clearly distressed by the memory. *"Why did they take that game away from us?"*

She said sadly, *"I never got a chance to play."*

Sarah was shocked at the emotion that Lorraine was sharing with them. She had expected her to share the stories of fun times that other women like Adalyn had experienced. But this was different. Lorraine was very upset and Sarah hoped she hadn't done something that would cause her any problems. Decades had passed, but the memory and pain of that thwarted dream was still vivid.

Lorraine tried to raise herself onto her elbows, still grasping Sarah's hand. Uncle Dan placed a pillow behind her for support.

"I was a good player on the B team," she said. "When I was going into the 9th grade, I knew I would be on the A team. I'll never forget the day the school principal came into our classroom and told us that the girls' team had been dropped. *Gone.* We asked, 'Why won't we have a team?' He didn't give us any reasons. He just said that the decision was final and that was that. *He just walked out of the room.* No reasons. No reasons. *He just told.* And in those days, you did what they said."

Lorraine fell back on the bed, exhausted from the exertion and the flood of memories.

Sarah felt tears roll down her face and onto her hand that tried to share its warmth with Lorraine.

As Sarah and her uncle drove home, they were somber, thinking of Lorraine's words.

Sarah said sadly, "Just think, Uncle Dan, this woman is now 91 years of age, and many of her life's memories are slipping away. Yet, she clearly remembers and is still so upset to think that she should have been able to enjoy basketball as I do now. Why didn't her parents go to a school board meeting? Why didn't someone object to this decision? Why wasn't it against some law to give boys a team and not the girls? This was so unfair to Lorraine and her teammates, and girls all over the country."

Sarah felt such a deep sadness for Lorraine.

"You know, Uncle Dan," Sarah said, "I'm beginning to understand that when someone has been wronged, time can't be rewound and history can't be rewritten. But we *can learn* from history so we don't repeat the same mistakes. So, it really requires each of us to make a personal commitment to do something when things aren't right."

Sarah continued, "First, I am going to find out why their school, and so many others, made that decision and then I will tell everyone *why it happened* so it won't happen again."

"And," Sarah added, with conviction, "I will never allow that to happen to *my* daughters."

If things are going to be made right, Sarah thought, it's up to people who care, like Uncle Dan - and me.

UP NORTH

"Wheels up." The Piper Warrior soared off the runway and Sarah relaxed her hands on the yoke. This was no time to have her muscles freeze. Her reading about women aviators had taught her that in the early days, instructors had a small club that they would use to knock a novice student on the head when they froze with their hands on the controls.

"Good job," Jean, her instructor, said, and her compliment helped Sarah relax just a little. Takeoffs were still a new part of her training. Landings would soon be her next challenge.

"Awesome, Sarah," came Tammy's voice from the rear seat. "I never thought I'd be with you when I had my first ride in a small plane. And with you as the pilot. 'Guess trust is part of being friends, right?" And they all smiled.

It was a beautiful day for a trip in the blue skies - heading *"up north."*

Their flight plan was to fly north to the Iron Range towns of northeastern Minnesota and find information for Tammy's research paper.

A few days earlier, Tammy had burst into Sarah's bedroom, "Sarah, you'll never guess what I found out. My ancestor was a *swimmer!* I thought I'd find a basketball player like you did because my dad and his brothers were all high school and college basketball players. But it turns out that my mother's family lived up on the Iron Range and her grandmother was a swimmer and diver. What a surprise!"

"Hey, that's terrific! What do you know so far?" Sarah asked.

"My dad drove me up to the office of the Minnesota State High School League in Brooklyn Center. I asked their staff person who keeps the history records about girls swimming. She brought out the old League handbooks and some of them had results from the *first series* of MSHSL Girls State Swimming and Diving Meets. Can you believe this? *They had a state swimming and diving meet for the schools on the Iron Range every year from 1924-1942.*"

Sarah smiled with a tinge of sadness, "I'm happy for those swimmers and divers. It's just so unfair that there was no state tournament for the hundreds of girls' basketball teams. They must have had a strong person from the Iron Range on the League's board of directors to advocate for them."

"Well, listen now," Tammy wanted her full attention. "It seems that the schools on the Range had swimming pools so they were all in the state meet. The meet results listed: Virginia, Eveleth, Aurora, Biwabik, Ely, Mountain Iron, Chisholm, Hibbing, and Nashwauk. The meets usually had about 130 swimmers and divers participating in them."

"It's interesting," Sarah realized, "that the girls state

swimming and diving meets ended in 1942, which coincides with the disappearance of the girls basketball teams. We'll have to see what we can find out. Seems like an unusual coincidence. Did you find out why the League stopped holding the meet after 1942?"

"That's the funny part," Tammy said. "The League person and I looked through the minutes of the board meetings, and there was nothing mentioned about ending the state meet. After 1942, it just wasn't held. Isn't that strange?"

"Now," Tammy started a free-fall toward the bed alongside Sarah, who quickly pulled papers away from the falling body, "I have to find a way to get some photos and information from my great-grandmother's school. And I did find her name in one of the meets. She was on a relay team. Her name was Frarey."

Sarah grabbed her book, *Daughters of the Game*, "I remember something about swimming in here." She flipped through the index and soon found the section, "Look, here it says that the State Department of Education told the schools that they should drop their *girls' basketball and swimming teams*."

Tammy stopped, her finger almost jabbing at the page, "*Oh, my gosh, Sarah, look at this!* There is a quote here by a woman named Jean Frarey Walters from Virginia. *SHE'S MY GREAT-GRANDMOTHER!* Her voice had reached into the higher octaves.

Sarah and Tammy huddled together, barely able to hold the book steady in their excitement.

Tammy pointed to a paragraph, "Here, it says that in 1942, Jean Frarey won the last championship in the girls' freestyle competition and her medley relay team established a record for that meet. Just like your great-grandmother, Sarah, they were both on the last teams before their schools dropped them. Look, it says Jean's dad was on the school board at Virginia and he fought dropping the girls' swimming teams."

The two "high-fived" that terrific father.

Tammy went on reading, "It looks like a man named Harold Jack sent out letters to the schools several times, recommending that the schools drop their girls swimming as well as their girls basketball teams. Here it says that in the fall of 1939, the superintendents voted to drop the girls swimming teams, but there was so much negative response from their communities and news media that the superintendents 'reconsidered' their decision.'"

"Ha!" Tammy pumped her hand in the air. "Finally, someone stood up for the girls! Those Iron Rangers are all right."

"Then what? Keep reading," Sarah prompted.

"Well, let's see, Tammy continued, "it says the superintendents then voted to allow each school to decide for its own community. Listen, the schools decided to continue swimming for two more years through the 1942 state meet!"

"So," Sarah calculated, "that's why the swimming championship just doesn't show up in the League Handbook. They knew the Range schools were dropping their teams after 1942, so there was no need to make an official decision."

Tammy dropped back on Sarah's bed, throwing her arms up in frustration. "It's hard work being a detective. Look how the history of girls' sports has been hidden away in so many places. If it hadn't been for that woman...." She flipped back to the cover of the *Daughters of the Game* book. "Let's see, her name is Marian Johnson. She's the one who wondered why she couldn't play in the 1940s and her mother could in the 1920s. If it weren't for her, this all might have been lost."

Sarah smiled, "Well, it's a good thing those two women wrote a book instead of letting it sit in some boxes somewhere. Mom says it is important to know our history and that I should journal to record my life like my ancestors did."

Tammy said, "I guess we'll be 'old' someday too, huh, Sarah?"

Sarah laughed, "Well, let's not think about that yet. But, I hope we will be friends for life like some of these women were. I'll have to show you the story about the two friends in Milan who lived their last years together in the same assisted living home."

The two young women smiled at each other, barely able to contemplate their lives as senior citizens.

"It sure would be fun to go to those Iron Range schools where they had girls swimming meets," Tammy sighed.

"Hey," Sarah's eyes brightened, "let's fly up there! We can do it in one day. I'll contact my instructor out at Flying Cloud Airport and see if she could arrange for a plane. I need flying time because I want to have my license by the time I graduate next spring."

"Awesome," Tammy bounced off the bed and nearly landed on Sarah's foot. Fortunately, Sarah pulled it away in time. This was no time to go to practice with a bruised foot.

"When can you find out? We have next Saturday off, no practice and no game."

"I'll check today and text you later."

Both young women were more than ready to go on an adventure that surely would be waiting for them up in those blue skies … "up north."

"Look, Sarah," Tammy exclaimed, "there is the first little glint of the sun coming over the horizon. Isn't that just awesome? And here we are, heading 'up north.'"

Jean, Sarah's instructor, smiled as she watched the thrill of flying being shared by these young women. She knew the feeling. She had first felt the tug of flying as a young girl, looking up into the sky and wanting to be "up there" with the birds. It hadn't been easy to get her license. It meant taking extra jobs to pay for her lessons and trying to find an opening in aviation.

Lucky for me, Jean thought, I had heard about the Ninety-Nines, the organization founded for women pilots by Amelia Earhart in 1929. One of their missions is to encourage young women to fly and my scholarship from them helped pay for my lessons. Being around other women pilots continues to be wonderful too.

The three women gazed out the window, watching the outlines of the terrain, and enjoying the last of the fall colors on some trees. They flew a few degrees west so they could fly over the east edge of Mille Lacs, the huge body of water in central Minnesota that would soon glisten with ice. In summer, it was a haven for fishing boats seeking walleye, the state fish. In a few weeks, a winter phenomenon would begin. Areas of the lake over popular fishing spots would be covered with little communities of ice houses. They were occupied by people who fish with tiny rods and lines dipping down through holes in the ice. The ice house of early days had now taken on the conveniences of home with generators for electricity, television, and cots for overnights. For obvious reasons, refrigerators weren't required.

As the plane hummed along, Sarah pondered aloud, "I wonder what all this looked like a hundred and more years ago? No freeways or speeding cars, no planes disturbing the farm animals. And no lights at night when everyone turned off their lanterns and kerosene or oil lamps. Our ancestors lived such a completely different life that it is hard to imagine now. What was it like without e-mail, cell phones and all of our gadgets?"

"I guess," Jean joined the conversation, "people talked directly to one another, read books printed on paper, and even played checkers, cards, marbles, and other games. Those days had their advantages."

"Maybe," Tammy said, "that's why my parents say we have to plan one night a week where we talk and do that kind of stuff. We aren't allowed to have any television, cell phones, or any of that. It took a while for us to get used to it and we grumbled at first. Now it's kind of fun. We eat dinner together and then each night one of us kids gets to pick what we are going to do. One night we played a funny game called Sardines. It's like a reverse of hide-and-seek. 'It' goes and hides and when someone finds 'It', they hide with them. Eventually several people are packed like sardines under a bed, or in a closet. Imagine trying not to laugh. It's really fun."

As they neared Duluth, the view was spectacular as Lake Superior came into view. The great lake was Minnesota's "ocean." The Ojibwe called it "Gitche Gumee," which means Big Water. In science class they had learned that the lake was so large that it had its own six-inch tide. Sarah remembered how her family could hardly wait to get out of the car and run down to the shore and dip their hands into the always frigid water.

As they flew over the immense body of water, they saw barges filled with taconite slowly making their way out of the harbor. One of the most famous tragedies on the lake was the 1975 sinking of the *S.S. Edmund Fitzgerald* in a fierce November storm.

Sarah's thoughts wandered to some of their family vacations

another 150 miles north of Duluth in the Boundary Waters. It was such fun to drive the Gunflint Trail from Grand Marais to Poplar Lake. When they stepped out of their vehicle, their first breaths were exhilarating. The air was so fresh, so clean and crisp.

Staying at Nor' Wester Lodge with owners Carl and Luana was an experience not to be missed. Luana's wild blueberry pie - Sarah's mouth watered at the thought. She could see Carl hoisting a big canoe complete with paddles and life preservers onto his shoulders. Sarah saw Carl as a real-life Paul Bunyan.

Sarah's mother always said that dipping a paddle into Poplar Lake could heal many cracks in the soul. Sarah remembered the haunting call of the loons that seemed to say, "Stay awhile longer."

A little bumpy patch jolted Sarah back to their flight plan. She was happy that Jean was handling this part of the trip. From Duluth, they were headed northwest another 80 miles to the small cities in the Arrowhead area of Minnesota known as the Iron Range. She knew the huge open-pit mines had been so important to the region and the entire country when they supplied essential iron ore during World War I and World War II.

The towns were tucked among the pine trees and lakes and built near the vast open mines. The first strip mine on the Mesabi Iron Range, the Hull Rust Mahoning Mine outside Hibbing, is roughly three miles long, two miles wide, and more than five hundred feet deep. Sarah could see why they said that the mines "bled iron." There were steep terraces and broad canyons, all dark red. At the bottom, they could see the huge electric power shovel that could gobble up 33 cubic yards and spit the rubble into a 240-ton production truck that was the size of a house. Its wheels were twice the height of a person.

"Little wonder," Jean said, "that the mine has been called the Grand Canyon of the North."

As they circled the city, Jean pointed out the area where the city of Hibbing had first been built. She said, "When the valuable mineral was discovered under the town, the town was actually relocated to have access to the ore." She explained that the nearby taconite processing plants have experienced slowdowns because of soft demand for the iron ore pellets, which is hard on the local economy.

"Imagine moving your whole town," Sarah said, trying to fathom the undertaking.

The runways at the Hibbing Airport were welcoming and Jean landed the plane with nary a bump. Sarah watched and hoped that she could soon work on her landings again. Today, she would learn from her skilled instructor.

Jean had friends in the area and a quick call brought a big SUV and a friendly voice from within, "Hop in, I'm Gail."

Jean introduced Gail as the legendary girls volleyball coach at Hibbing, one of the pioneers who had brought girls' sports into her school as early as 1969. Jean pointed out that Gail continues to coach after 40-plus years, and her teams frequently made trips to the state tournaments.

"Cool," said Tammy, "just think of coaching kids like us for over forty years."

"'Doesn't seem that long," Gail chuckled and glanced back at the young women. "Every year there are new memories. Like in 1976, we headed down to the second state volleyball tournament at St. Cloud State University and ran into a huge snowstorm. They closed the roads and we ended up staying overnight in Mora in a church basement."

"Did you get to the tournament?" Tammy asked.

"Oh, yeah," Gail grinned, "the tournament director kept rescheduling the start of matches because teams from all over the state were late getting there. Whenever two teams arrived that were scheduled to play each other, they would start the match. One team from Sartell was transported to Hallenbeck Hall on snowmobiles. And the team from Windom, down in southwestern Minnesota, followed a snowplow most of the way to St. Cloud. Bet you've never had to do *that*."

The young women shook their heads, thinking of their nice warm buses. Sarah thought, the pioneers of the "second era" of girls' sports had their challenges too, just like our great- grandmothers did.

The first stop was Hibbing High School. It was a huge, multi-story brick building that resembled an old medieval castle. As they walked in, Sarah nearly gasped, "Is that *real marble* covering the floors?"

Gail smiled with pride, "Yes, the schools on the Range received taxes from the iron mines. Our people emigrated from Europe and wanted their children to have a good education. In the heyday of the mines, they built beautiful schools. Hibbing High School was built between 1920 and 1922 for over $3,900,000. It is estimated that it would cost over fifty million to replace today."

Gail pointed out, "Our school has been called 'the school with the gold door knobs' because the brass door knobs and railings have a golden appearance. You can see how the railings decorate the sides of the eighteen foot wide solid marble front entrance steps. Now, take a look at the designs on the main floor hallway. They braided *horse hair* into the hand-molded plaster designs. The pillars are three feet thick and solid marble. They call it the Elizabethan Period style, much like the state capitol."

Sarah looked in awe at the intricate designs. "This beautiful artwork is within reach of kids going to class several times every day. Doesn't it get damaged?"

Gail smiled wryly, "Our school is so beautiful and it is respected by the students. *No one* would risk their family's wrath if they damaged the school their parents, grandparents and neighbors had built and attended."

With a flourish, Gail opened the doors to the 1800-seat auditorium and turned on the lights. The four solid glass chandeliers had been manufactured in Czechoslovakia in 1924. Gail explained that the plant had later been destroyed in World War II, making the crystals literally irreplaceable. Each chandelier weighs nearly six hundred pounds. The orchestra pit in front of the stage looked ready to be occupied for a performance. Gail explained that the organ has over 100,000 working parts and provides amazing sounds, including bird whistles. Two private boxes flanked the stage, just as it would have been in the early days of theatre. Gail noted that the auditorium was modeled after the Capitol Theater in New York City and is the pride of the community.

She smiled and pointed to the auditorium seating. "The velvet -covered seats have been reupholstered only *once* since the school was built. Then she chuckled, "And the custodians tell me they still use the original fabric for dust cloths."

Near the door, Tammy pointed at the fire extinguisher box. "Look," she said, "the box is made with stained glass. This is amazing."

The tour concluded with the "new" five-million-dollar athletic and music complex built in 1991; complete with a new swimming pool.

After a tour of the library with its murals of the mines, they bid a reluctant goodbye to the beautiful and historic building.

Gail said, "Now, we are going to stop at my house for a bite to eat before we go to Chisholm. I know you must have worked up an appetite getting up here." Soon, they were zipping down the roads and into the pine forests. Their noses told them they were truly in the north woods.

Gail's home was nestled among the trees with a large garden protected on all sides from the deer and other creatures. Before they went inside, Gail took them around to the back of the house where her huskies were in their kennels.

"My husband and I race our dogs during the winter. There are some great races up here," Gail said proudly. "You should come up sometime, but dress warm." It sounded like a great idea to the young women. What a story *that* would be to tell their friends!

As they walked into Gail's kitchen, Sarah and Tammy could hardly take it all in. The table was full of food, obviously for their "bite to eat."

As Gail filled their glasses with milk and poured some "curl your hair" coffee for Jean, she explained what she was serving.

"This is called 'porketta.' It's the traditional ethnic meat served at every important function on the Range, from birth to death. It is a pork roast that has been rolled and filled with what you smell, fennel, plus some other spices. You won't find anything like it anywhere else. And, by tradition in my family, it must be served with hard rolls, potato salad, baked beans, and dill pickles. If you are a busy coach, you stop at Fraboni's Market in town. So dig in!"

The invitation came just in time, as Sarah and Tammy could hardly wait to put their taste buds to work.

With sighs of satisfaction that almost sounded like groans, the four women finally slowed down, chewed more slowly, looked at one another and smiled.

"This is the best meal of my *life*," Tammy said. "How could I be eighteen and never have tasted food like this?"

"That is because you haven't been to the Iron Range before," Gail laughed. "I get to the Cities quite often because our teams have qualified for state tournaments many times. We've shown your 'city teams' that we can play well up here too."

Sarah thought, here I am, sitting in this legendary coach's kitchen, eating their legendary food. How great is that!

"Now, even though you don't think you can eat one bite more, try a little piece of potica (pronounced 'po-teet-sa'). It's also a Range specialty. You can see that the dough has been rolled many times and each layer is filled with honey, cinnamon and walnuts."

The pastry melted in their mouths and no one could refuse "just another little piece."

"I'll wrap up a roll of potica and a bag of porketta sandwiches for you to take with you on the plane. You may think you'll never be hungry again, but you may change your mind when you get back up in the air again."

This woman was, indeed, a role model of what an Iron Range woman and coach was all about. She and her husband had worked out a partnership where her coaching, though time-consuming, was supported and encouraged.

Gail added, "I just heard of a new training program called 'WeCoachU,' which works to recruit and support women coaches. 'Sounds like a good idea. You should consider coaching; it's a great opportunity to give back."

Sarah thought how many more women coaches there might be if

they had support and encouragement. She said, "I'll have to tell our coach about this new organization. Tammy, why don't we volunteer to coach the little girls this summer?"

"Good idea. Now let's hit the road for Chisholm."

A few miles down the road, they saw a sign that read, "Chisholm, population 4594." They pulled into the parking lot alongside the junior high building. Doors were open and as they walked the halls and auditorium, they saw similar intricate gold decorations and paintings that reflected this community's pride in its school.

"Let's walk over to the natatorium."

Sarah and Tammy's eyes widened, *"Natatorium?"*

Gail smiled, "That means swimming pool."

As they walked down the hallway, an amazing sight greeted their eyes. Above the doors to the pool was a huge mural of a young woman in her swimming suit climbing out of a pool. The sign said, "Anne Govednik Pool."

Tammy smiled and was ready to share her knowledge about this young woman. "When I was in the League Office trying to find out about Minnesota high school swimmers, the staff person gave me this copy of the *MSHSL Bulletin*, Winter 2000."

She held it up for the other two to see. "See her picture on the cover? It includes an article about 'Anne Govednik's Special Summer.' A man named Lawrence Belluzzo is the historian in Chisholm and he recorded the details of her participation in the 1932 Olympics."

Gail's head nodded at the familiar names.

Tammy checked the notes that she had brought with her, "Anne was one of our Minnesota state champions in the 50-yard and 100-yard breaststroke during the years when the State League sponsored a Girls State Swimming and Diving Championship.

"Here's what is really interesting: outside the season, Anne competed through the Amateur Athletic Union (AAU) and qualified for the Olympics in 1932 and again in 1936. In 1932, she was only sixteen years old! She and her high school coach traveled to Chicago where she qualified for the Olympic trials in New York. There, she qualified as one of three swimmers in the 200-meter breaststroke to represent the United States in the Olympics being held in Los Angeles.

"Can you imagine Anne traveling from New York to Los Angeles on the Olympic team's special train?" Tammy's eyes sparkled at the thought of the fun those athletes must have had.

"So," Tammy returned to business, "the Olympic swimming competition begins. Anne qualifies in the prelims and then swims in the finals of the 200-meter breaststroke. It was a very close finish and she placed *sixth in the world.*"

Sarah responded, "How exciting! How did the people in Chisholm learn the results of her swim?"

"Well," said Tammy, "someone had a short-wave radio, and they spread the word that they would blow the town fire whistle for Anne's place in the finals. In other words, the whistle would blow once for first, twice for second, etc."

"So," Sarah said, "They blew the town fire whistle six times?"

"Yes," Tammy almost shivered, "can you imagine that loud fire whistle blowing six times? They could hear it all over the town and probably 'way out in the country too."

Gail said, "Yes, they tell that story around here even yet."

"Well," Tammy continued, "Mr. Belluzzo wrote that when Anne returned by train from Chicago to Duluth, hundreds of Chisholm people drove down to the station to meet her. They were joined by people from other Range towns plus lots of Duluth people who turned out for the ceremonies. Anne had been worried people were disappointed by her finish, so imagine when she stepped out of the train and saw those thousands of people.

"Listen to this," Tammy said, "By the time the miles-long caravan traveled back to Chisholm, they estimated that there were over 5,000 people packed into every nook and cranny of the community building and outside on the streets. Hundreds more couldn't even get close. They had to put loudspeakers outside so everyone could hear the 'welcome home' ceremonies. Don't you just love it when a woman's success gets celebrated?"

Jean, Sarah and Gail nodded enthusiastically.

Sarah asked, "You said she was in the 1936 Olympics too. Weren't they held in Berlin with Jesse Owens and Babe Didrikson winning medals?"

"Yes," Tammy said, "but it was a sad experience for Anne because she got really sick on the ship going over to Europe and there wasn't enough time for her to recover. She competed, but her times weren't good enough to qualify for the finals. It's so horrible to think that she couldn't be at her best. They didn't have antibiotics then. It must have been awful for Anne. She was 20 years old and this should have been her year. Don't you just wonder why things like that happen to nice people? Her big chance lost, all because of the flu and an earache."

"But, once a hero," Gail added, "always a hero on the Range. Anne became a teacher here, and lived many years in the Chisholm and Duluth area."

As they opened the door to the parking lot, suddenly the town fire whistle blew - *one long blast*, sending shivers running up Sarah's back. The whistle seemed to be proclaiming once again that Anne Govednik would always be *number one* in the hearts of Chisholm and the people of the Iron Range.

As they drove back into Hibbing, Gail handed them their picnic treats for the ride home. She added, "And, if you want to treat your team to porketta sandwiches, should we stop at Fraboni's Market?"

Without hesitation, everyone responded with an enthusiastic, "YES!"

Gail waved as she drove away from the airport and the trio headed toward check-in prior to boarding their plane. Sarah made sure the porketta was safely in its bag. Even so, the fragrance was unmistakable.

As she laid the bag on the desk, the security guard asked, "What's in there?"

Sarah winced, hoping there was no problem. "A porketta," she replied.

With a smile, the guard waved them on, "Go right on through." Clearly, anyone traveling with a porketta in Hibbing was *not* considered a security risk.

My Mother Played ~ Why Couldn't I?

"Why wasn't I allowed to play when I was in high school in the 1940s and my mother played in the 1920s?" ~ *Marian Bemis Johnson, sports historian*

Sarah was getting frustrated. She pounded on the bedspread as if it alone was covering up the answer to her question: why did those girls' sports teams get dropped?

Sarah was determined to find an answer. Why did Lorraine's team in the early 1930s get dropped? Why did the state swimming meet get dropped in 1942? Why did my grandmothers not have any sports when they were in high school in the 1950s? What could cause so many schools to take such a step? It's like some huge wind swept across the country and obliterated almost everything in its path.

After all, she thought, it's not like it happened today and some video went viral and suddenly everyone said, let's drop the girls and women's competitive programs. It had to have taken a lot of talking and correspondence to get that kind of nationwide reaction.

Sarah reached over to the headboard of her bed and picked up her book, *Daughters of the Game.* She looked again at the photos of those early girls' basketball teams. How happy they all looked.

As she scanned through the early history, she came to a chapter called, *The Third Quarter.*

And there it was. She found her answer, a complete narrative of what happened to those girls' and women's teams - just waiting for her to pay attention to it.

Okay, Sarah thought and took a deep breath...here goes.

From the book, *Daughters of the Game,* she read, "In the early 1900s, as girls basketball in Minnesota was rolling happily along, storm clouds began gathering at the national level."

Yes, they were happy, thought Sarah, riding to games in their sleighs and buses, playing hard, and having great fun. So, what happened?

Two hours passed quickly as Sarah took notes, trying to untangle this collection of organizations and people.

She felt her eyelids getting very heavy. . . .

"This meeting will come to order." The room became instantly silent. Dr. Anna Norris, the chair of the National Amateur Athletic Federation - Women's Division (NAAF-WD) platform committee was apparently not someone you wanted to annoy, Sarah thought.

Dr. Norris was director of the physical education department for women at the University of Minnesota. The room was filled with women who also were directors from large universities across the country plus others Sarah couldn't identify, but likely were individuals and representatives from national organizations who were interested in girls and women's sports.

Sarah tucked herself into a corner of the room, trying to be inconspicuous.

"Mrs. Lou Hoover, the chair of our NAAF-Women's Division, is here to participate in the meeting of our Platform Sub-Committee," Dr. Norris began. "Lou, we want to thank you for your time and financial support for our goals. Your work with the Girl Scouts of America and your interest in encouraging fitness for all young women place you in the vanguard of our mission to root out the unacceptable practices and abuses in competitive sports for girls and women."

There was loud applause and Mrs. Hoover politely nodded her acknowledgment.

Sarah decided to sit as quietly as she could. This could be very interesting, she thought.

"We have a long agenda today," Dr. Norris continued. "The first item on the agenda is a review of the platform of the NAAF-WD which we adopted earlier. As you know so well, the foundation of our platform is our recommendation that schools establish a comprehensive girls physical education department taught by women trained in our universities. The platform itself has twelve goals that specify the type of recreational and sports activities that are recommended, and, of course, under the direction of our trained and qualified women administrators, teachers and officials."

Dr. Norris summarized, "We believe that competition should be 'of the right kind,' which means games without the pressure of winning and the trappings of competition such as uniforms, trophies and teams limited to only the elite athletes. This platform should eliminate those competitive programs that clearly exploit our young women. The winning of championships, the setting of records and bringing in of gate receipts should be replaced by competition that is enjoyable and develops good sportsmanship and character in all young women, not just the elite athletes. Our slogan is 'A Team for Every Girl and Every Girl on a Team.'"

The group enthusiastically applauded.

Mabel Lee from the University of Nebraska raised her hand to speak, "But, the men promoters of girls' sports are not giving up without a fight. They are accusing us women of trying to ban all competitive sports for girls. Nothing could be further from the truth. We are fighting to correct abuses and to abolish only the *wrong* kind of sports."

Dr. Norris agreed, "That is where our mailings to schools and organizations must continue to correct this type of misinformation and propaganda. The report of the national medical association expressing support for our concerns carries a great deal of weight with the organizations for school administrators."

Agnes Wayman stood to speak, "As president, I intend to present the following statement to our American Physical Education Association: *'External stimuli such as cheering audiences, bands, lights, etc., cause a great response in girls and are apt to upset the endocrine balance. Under emotional stress, a girl may easily overdo. There is a widespread agreement that a girl should not be exposed to extremes of fatigue or strain, either emotional or physical.'* Are we all in agreement with this statement?"

The group nodded their collective heads in collective agreement.

"Good," Dr. Norris continued, "now we will move to the next item on the agenda, our recommendation that women from the United States should not participate in national and international competition. As you know, we did not support the participation of women in the 1928 Olympic Games in Amsterdam. When women first competed in the modern Olympics in Paris in 1900, there were only three events: ladies singles tennis, golf and coed croquet. They kept adding events and in 1928, there was competition in women's events in track and field and gymnastics. *It is getting out of hand.*"

The group nodded its endorsement of the concerns expressed by Dr. Norris.

Dr. Norris lifted a sheet of paper. "At this meeting in January 1929, in New York City, we propose a resolution regarding the 1932 Olympic Games when the United States will be the host country.

"I will read the first part of our resolution and then we shall discuss and vote. You can read along with me from your copy.

'Whereas competition in the Olympic Games would among other things:

(1) entail the specialized training of the few,

(2) offer opportunity for the exploitation of girls and women, and

(3) offer opportunity for possible over-strain in preparation for and during the Games themselves,

Be It Resolved that the Women's Division of the National Amateur Athletic Federation go on record as disapproving of competition for girls and women in the Olympic Games.'

"As you can see," Dr. Norris continued, "the remaining part of the resolutions offer our willingness to support activities suitable 'to girls as girls' and that we would ask for the opportunity to put on a festival of music, dance, conferences, banquets, etc., in place of the competition."

Sarah's head lifted and her eyes opened wide as she listened to the committee discuss the resolutions. If the Olympic Committee listens to their recommendation, will Anne Govednik of Chisholm be denied her Olympic experience?

Dare I raise my hand, she thought, then *noticed to her dismay, that her tail twitched.* It caught the attention of someone in the audience, and an umbrella came sailing toward her.

"Sarah, Sarah! You almost rolled off the bed and your voice was so high, it almost sounded like squeaking." Her mother's voice crept through her mental haze, "Were you dreaming?"

"Yes, and what a dream! Mom, you wouldn't believe where I was! *I had been wishing that I could have been a mouse in the corner of those meetings when the women of the NAAF-Women's Division were planning how to convince the schools to drop competitive sports. Guess I got my wish."*

Her mother shook her head and decided Sarah must still be half-asleep.

Patti stood, taking in Sarah's bed, covered with sticky notes and sheets of paper.

"I had no idea this research paper would consume you like this. Now you're dreaming about it too?"

"Mom, this is so complicated and I have to be able to explain it so the class will understand why schools dropped teams for girls and women."

"Well, why did they?" Her mother sat down in a nearby recliner. "I'm all ears."

Sarah began to review how it appeared that exploitation of athletes and other abuses may have crept into some of the competitive basketball programs for men and women across the country, and the National Amateur Athletic Federation (NAAF) was formed to take a close look and recommend changes.

"So, Mom," Sarah said, "it boils down to this - the Men's Division *couldn't find any abuses* in their programs and disbanded. But the *Women's Division* of the NAAF believed that the programs they observed required them to take drastic action to correct the abuses in the competitive programs for girls and women. Now remember, this includes *all* competition for high schools, colleges and universities, industrial leagues, groups like the Amateur Athletic Union, national and international competition, the Olympics - the whole thing."

"So," Sarah's mom considered, "the high schools of the country had to be a really large part of this study."

"You got it," Sarah said. "Now this is how they set up their strategy. The NAAF-WD wrote a platform of recommendations and sent them to schools and state departments of education, plus the organizations of superintendents and principals. Thousands of letters were flying across the country."

"So," her mother concluded, "each state would then pass on this information to their schools. The decision was one that only local school boards could make. But when school administrators saw the same messages also coming from their own professional organizations, it must have seemed like 'everyone' was now saying 'girls' teams should go.'"

Sarah nodded, "Sure, just like a bunch of dominoes, teams started disappearing all over the country. And the bigger schools were the first to drop their teams."

"And listen to this, Mom," Sarah held up a letter sent in 1938 from Harold Jack, Supervisor of Physical Education in the Minnesota State Department of Education. "He sent this letter to the school superintendents and girls' physical education instructors. By then, schools had been told to drop teams for over ten years."

Sarah continued, "Harold Jack wrote, '*In the same manner that the interscholastic and intramural athletics provide physical activity of an extracurricular nature for boys, and skilled athletes of the school, so the Girls Athletic Association (GAA) program provides for the girls of the school. If your school does not foster such a program, it is strongly urged and recommended that such a program be adopted."*

Sarah almost flew off the bed in her frustration. "Imagine, this is saying that interscholastic competition is good for boys, but girls only need *GAA and intramurals?* How can GAA be comparable to interscholastic competition? How ridiculous. What about girls like *me?*"

Sarah wasn't finished, "And there is more in this letter: *'In those few remaining schools still sponsoring a program of girls interscholastic athletics, it is recommended that the interscholastic program be dropped and that the Girls Athletic Association program be installed in its place. The GAA program will adequately meet the needs of the girls from a physical and recreational standpoint. Furthermore, it is in harmony with modern educational aims and objectives and contains none of the objectionable features of the girls interscholastic program which women's organizations in physical education and athletics abhor.'"*

"'Adequately? Objectionable features? Abhor? I've tried to be fair about this whole business," Sarah slumped back against her headboard, "but attacking my desire to play competitive sports is just too much!"

Her mother reached over and placed her hand on her agitated daughter. "I can understand your frustration, Sarah," Patti said. "Everyone was being painted with the same brush, so our Minnesota girls' teams were included, even if they didn't have those objectionable features."

"Yeah," Sarah grumbled, "it's like everyone having to stay for detention because one kid rolls a marble down the row and we all have to suffer."

"Now, Mom, get this," Sarah found her frustration rising again, "I found another quote from Harold Jack in the *Daughters of the Game* book. He wrote, 'Interscholastic competition for girls of high school age was reported in 92 schools during 1938-1939, and in 38 schools during 1939-1940. This represents a *decided change for the better.*'"

"Imagine," Sarah sputtered, "fewer teams for girls was 'for the better.' How sad *is that?*"

"So *that's* how it happened." Her mother stood and opened the bedroom window a crack. Sarah's indignation was heating up the room.

"That's why Grandma Ruby said her team came back to school and was told there would be no more basketball for girls. Look, I brought down her 1927 high school yearbook from the trunk.

"Here's what Grandma Ruby wrote in the section for girls' athletics, '*As we go to press, the editor and associate editors have heard the sad news that there will be no interscholastic basketball for girls next year. The girls of S. H. S. have our sincerest sympathy and we hope you don't get so stiff in the joints that it will hinder you from participating in interclass games.*'

"You can hear her sarcasm and frustration because they'd been told basketball competition wasn't good for them and could damage their bodies; even that they might not be able to have babies."

"Those poor teams," Sarah commiserated with the young women who were learning that their teams were gone.

"Mom, I found an interesting statistic," Sarah looked at her mother. "It says that thirty-seven states conducted girls state high school basketball tournaments in 1925. Minnesota wasn't one of them.

I wonder why Minnesota didn't have a state tournament? There certainly were enough teams and the boys had a tournament. I know that Iowa and North and South Dakota had state tournaments for girls. How sad that no one stood up for girls in Minnesota. And then, how sad that most of the states dropped their state tournament based on these NAAF-Women's Division recommendations."

Sarah's mother added, "But not Iowa. As I told you, your great- grandmother begged her parents to move to Iowa so she could play basketball."

"Well, I can see the point of some of the concerns of the NAAF-Women's Division," Sarah conceded. "If I saw things happening that were bad and unhealthy for women's teams, I would want to do something about it. I support their recommendation that all schools should hire a woman physical education teacher. Look at what has happened to physical education, even in my high school. It's not offered every year. And in the elementary schools, recess isn't enough to re-charge those little kids. Too many times, the girls are standing in little groups watching the boys play."

"Obesity in children is coming up at my meetings," her mother agreed. "They are talking about how there should be physical education in the schools again. After all this emphasis on math and science, they are starting to realize that there should be a 'strong mind in a strong body.'"

Sarah threw her hands up, "Seems like adults don't know what they want. Oops, sorry, Mom, I didn't mean you and dad."

Patti laughed, "Well, maybe we are part of the problem. I should raise the question in our next parents' organization meeting and see what we could do. I, for one, would be ready to speak to our school board advocating physical education. It would help our kids become healthy and motivate them to do something other than play their electronic games, like your brother, for example."

Sarah leaned back against the headboard of her bed, looking at her mother. "Good to see you getting into the game, Mom."

They laughed at a little role reversal.

Sarah said, "You know, you were pretty lucky, Mom, to have been in high school when girls competitive sports were coming back again. Just think, you had uniforms, trophies, and people coming to watch you play."

"Yes," her mother said, "good timing for me, and too late for so many others in Minnesota and in most states across the country. I've learned to appreciate it even more now. Whenever I go to games and tournaments, I know there are women sitting in the stands, or watching on television who have tears of frustration for what 'might have been.'"

"Yeah, what might have been," Sarah agreed, as she gathered up her notes and closed the book.

Patti jumped up, "Look at the time! We'd better get downstairs or we may find ourselves with dinner 'that might have been.'"

9

A PAUSE TO REFLECT

Patti poured herself a cup of tea, buttered her toast, and carefully spread a generous amount of her mother's raspberry jam across it. I do enjoy opening a jar of Mom's jam with its covering of wax, she thought. It tastes so fresh.

The hum of her little robot floor sweeper made her smile. It seemed so happy buzzing around into all the corners and under the beds where even her vacuum didn't like to go. Patti laughed. I agree with Roseanne Barr. She said she wasn't going to vacuum until they made one you could ride on.

Patti went out with her "treats" to sit on her back porch, just for a little while. Why do we feel guilty for taking a little time for ourselves, or using those wonderful gadgets that reduce the amount of time spent chasing dust around? When we don't stop to look around, we miss so much. I am going to sit here and enjoy this gorgeous morning. She lowered herself into her favorite patio chair and put her feet on a little three-legged milking stool that had come from the farm.

She sighed, enjoying the good feelings and memories that were all around her.

Fall in Minnesota doesn't get much better than this, Patti observed. It feels like we are living in Garrison Keillor's town of Lake Woebegon, "where all the women are strong, all the men are good-looking, and all the children are above average." He sure got that right, she chuckled to herself.

Patti looked around her gardens where she had spent so many wonderful hours with her flowers and other growing things. She especially enjoyed her Dundee Cairn Garden where rocks gathered over a lifetime stood balancing atop others. Most cairns were three to four rocks high and it was such fun to find the delicate balancing points. Sometimes a cairn could be built with six or more rocks, but they were difficult. Two neighbors coming by on a walk had asked if the cairns were held together by glue. Patti remembered smiling at them and replying, "no, just gravity."

Some mornings, a cairn would require rebuilding. Apparently the creatures of the night enjoy nudging a cairn, or the birds of the early morning who like the higher perch. It doesn't take much to disrupt the balance of a cairn, Patti thought, just like our own lives. The lesson is, just keep rebuilding and working to keep everything in balance.

Patti reflected back on her college years, and thought, getting my degree in horticulture at the University of Minnesota was a good choice for me. Now that I'm deeply into organic gardening, there are so many opportunities to share and teach others how to treat the earth with respect. It's been leading me into learning about holistic care in naturopathy and the use of natural therapeutics. We have so much to learn about the earth and how its gifts can improve our health.

A small yellow leaf, tinged with red, floated down to the ground. She smiled, thinking, I remember a Peanuts cartoon where Snoopy saw a leaf floating down. 'Wish I could remember what he said. Probably something like, "Couldn't you have held on a day longer? I'm not ready!"

Patti looked around her yard that she had raked just yesterday until there wasn't a leaf in sight. So much for that, she thought, as the scattering of leaves seemed to mock her efforts.

Fall came so early this year. There were frost crystals glittering on the lawn last week. Patti grimaced a little at the thought of the snowdrifts not far away. But, she smiled, then we get out our skis, sleds and skates. Every season in Minnesota has its bonus.

She smiled at the big archway of morning glories that was now a solid heavenly blue, hurrying to get their blooms open before the frost nipped their noses.

As she sipped the cooling tea, a hummingbird zipped by, hovering near its feeder. How can something so tiny migrate so far, Patti wondered. Today here she sits, sipping the nectar with my special touch of vanilla, and maybe tomorrow she will be on her way south. There was a program on hummingbirds that said when the little birds get to the Gulf of Mexico, they have to travel eighteen hours to cross that body of water with no stops and no food. And I complain when I hit the three-mile mark on my morning run.

Patti sighed. Nature is so wonderful. We should spend more time learning from it, respecting it, and preserving it for future generations. I hope our children are learning from us how important it is to conserve and protect the beauty around us. This weekend we need to get the whole family into the woods and enjoy the fall colors. Plus, it will give us a chance to listen to what the kids have to share with us about their lives.

A monarch butterfly floated by, just over Patti's head.

"Hel-lo," Patti greeted it warmly, "You must be checking out the milkweed again. I saw one of your tiny young caterpillars munching away on a milkweed leaf earlier this summer. They are planted just for you and your family, you know."

Patti had been taught by her parents to plant milkweed because monarch butterflies use only the leaves of that plant for their eggs and then the little caterpillars eat the leaves. In past summers, she had seen some large caterpillars in their beautiful lime green, black, yellow, and white striping. It was always so satisfying to be a part of a butterfly's life cycle.

Patti thought about the story of the person who had come upon a butterfly struggling to get out of its cocoon. It seemed exhausted and the person feared it might not be able to break free, so she gently broke off the end of the cocoon. And the butterfly easily slipped out. She waited for the wings to enlarge and open, but nothing happened. Sadly, the butterfly was doomed to live with a swollen body and small, shriveled wings. It would never fly. Why? *It's the struggle* to squeeze through that small opening that forces the fluid from the body and into its wings. Then, the butterfly will emerge with wings fully nourished and ready to fly.

Parenting is like that, she thought. We want to help our children and protect them, but they need to experience struggle to grow strong and develop their wings. Then, like the butterfly, they will be ready to fly into a gentle breeze or the strong, buffeting winds they will face during their life.

Her cell phone rang, and it was her young son's voice. He was asking, hopefully, could she please bring his cell phone to school?

Patti's response was encouraging, reminding Ben that he could exist a day without his device, and his schoolwork didn't depend on having it in his pocket. A disappointed, but resigned, response could be heard.

Some parental choices are easier than others, she thought.

Another leaf floated down. She looked up at her favorite maple tree, "Okay, I get the message. See you next spring!"

A quiet little scratch on the screen door caught her attention. It was Gen, who wanted to share the beautiful morning with Patti. Soon, the little dog was curled up in her favorite lap.

I have so many wonderful memories, Patti thought. We are fortunate to have a home in which we can raise our family. I loved growing up in the heartland of Minnesota, near the Minnesota River. It's still a mystery to me that the river runs north to join the Mississippi River in St. Paul. There must be a lesson there.

Patti's thoughts flowed southwest against the current to Le Sueur. What a perfect school for us during those "growing up" years, she thought. Our family roots will always reach deeply into the rich soil and our rich heritage.

Oh, Patti sighed, think of those family reunions. They were really something. Everyone would come back to Grandpa and Grandma's farm to share an afternoon of stories, poring over scrapbooks and exclaiming over how the kids had grown and what they were doing.

I will never forget the tables piled high with each cook's specialty - cinnamon rolls, homemade breads, lefse sprinkled with sugar and lingonberries, kolaches, brats and sauerkraut, fried chicken, Swedish meatballs, and smoked ham. There would always be several Minnesota "hot dishes," known in other areas as "casseroles."

Her thoughts continued to enjoy the reunion's spread of food. There was every kind of salad, including that Minnesota standard, a bowl of orange Jell-O with those tiny orange segments.

The desserts had their own tables. There was a variety of pies, cakes, cookies, bars, and pans with whipped cream topping with many a surprise underneath.

Patti could almost taste her mother's homemade lemonade which she served in her beautiful crystal pitchers and filled with slices of lemons. Then, Patti smiled, there was my uncle who would bring those huge green canvas insulated bags that protected the ice cream, at least until we kids got to it. The taste of "The Dairy's" ice cream made on their premises in West Union couldn't be matched.

Patti could envision the obligatory softball game for the younger generation, plus some foolhardy souls who ignored their sedentary lifestyle and would pay the price for the next week. Out by the barn, there would be horseshoes, which usually resulted in some friendly bickering. Sometimes there would be a volleyball match on the forgiving front lawn.

There was a little pond by the barn. Grandpa always had several cane poles and a pail of worms ready so the grandkids could drop a line and catch-and-release some fish that he'd stocked in there. He showed the little kids how to hold their poles just right, so they might catch the "lunker" that he assured them was in there, waiting.

And there had to be the inevitable group photos - trying to get the little kids to stand still, briefly, and maybe even smile a little. Someone was always blocked out by a taller relative and years after, everyone would wonder who that was.

Remembering those wonderful times, the "good old days," Patti thought, makes me wonder if our families will continue to stay connected. The Internet and all that social networking can only go so far. It doesn't replace the smiles on grandparents' faces when children and grandchildren come running through the door. When our children are grown, will they take time to gather the families and see one another "live-and-in-person?" It is so easy to scatter and not even meet your aunts, uncles and cousins. Some families don't even eat meals together. I read the other day how much it can help a child to have just one meal a week with all the family sitting together.

As her thoughts drifted back to her school days, Patti remembered listening to her Grandmother Ruby talk about her years teaching in a one-room schoolhouse. There was one teacher and at least a dozen students, ranging from kindergarten to eighth grade. Or maybe a better description would be from three feet to six feet tall. How did one teacher cope with it all? She talked of firing up the stove when she got to school, and sending two of the older students for a pail of fresh water from the neighboring farm.

Patti slowly shook her head and thought, but those teachers must have done the most important things right: they taught their students *how* to study and stirred their curiosity about the world "out there." It still holds true today, she thought.

Patti remembered her high school fondly. Today they would describe it as a small rural high school with a limited curriculum, but a school is only as good as its teachers. I think our teachers did the same in our small high school as my grandmother did in her one-room country schoolhouse: they taught us how to study and stirred our curiosity about the world "out there."

One thing Patti knew for sure was the advantage she had to enjoy so many things. Our class size was pretty small so we could be in all kinds of activities: music, speech, plays, the boys had sports. And her thoughts suddenly screeched to a halt.

Yes, she thought, the *boys had sports* and for a long time young women in our family didn't have any teams available to them. Girls could be cheerleaders, and sometimes there would be an after-school activity. It may have been fine for many girls, but it only scratched the surface when you wanted to play on a team and hear people cheering for you.

Patti's concentration was pulled into the present when a young voice near her shoulder nearly made her jump.

"Hey, Mom, do you know where my practice stuff is? Did you wash it yet?" Her youngest daughter Holly's questioning eyes were hoping the answers would be affirmative.

"Well, my dear, as you know, washing your 'practice stuff' is your responsibility. Did you put them in the machine when you got home last night?"

Her daughter spun around, muttering under her breath and Patti could hear "be late...in trouble." Footsteps pounded down the stairs to the laundry room. Soon a happier yell came upstairs, "Mom, I found them. Lauren must have put them in for me." Patti smiled, sometimes sisters were life-savers, after all.

Yes, she thought, *sisters*. Aren't they just one of life's wonderful gifts!

My sisters and I were always ready to play anything, anytime. We grew up playing tackle football and baseball with the neighbor kids. We climbed trees, explored the river *(sorry, Mom, I know you told us not to)*, and built tree houses. It was a wonderful world.

Patti took a sip of her tea. Now, let me think, when did girls' sports come to Le Sueur?

Patti paused to consider the years that were involved. Let's see, Jeanne is the oldest, so she would have been in high school during the years when girls had GAA, the Girls Athletic Association. She used to sputter, saying there wasn't much "athletic" about it, especially when they couldn't play other schools' teams. The gym was usually filled with boys' teams so the only chance for girls to get into the gym was Thursdays when the boys had a big game on Friday. Jeanne was pretty lucky, though, because her physical education teacher found ways to provide her and the other girls with things to do outside the school. They would go bowling, hiking, even do some weekend camping and canoeing in the fall. They had an annual GAA Slumber Party, where a hundred and more girls would be up most of the night in the gym, playing games, eating, eating...and eating, and trying to throw some sleepy friends into the showers.

Their physical education teacher also worked with the advisors of other GAA's in our conference to get together for weekend events they called "playdays." Jeanne said the girls were divided up on different teams so it didn't get "too competitive." In those days, interschool competition was still very much discouraged for girls. Knowing my sister, I doubt it slowed her down from trying to win any game she played.

It's such a shame, Patti thought, because Jeanne is still angry that she never had a chance to put on the Le Sueur uniform and she always reminds me how lucky our youngest sister, Terri, and I were because we did play on the early girls' interscholastic teams. When we go to state tournaments, sometimes I think she looks like she'd like to cry. She always says, "I was born too soon." When she went to St. Olaf College, she did get to play on some early college teams. It may have eased the pain a little and it certainly motivated her to become a coach and make sure her collegiate athletes had the chance to play competitive sports.

Patti got up to stretch a little and pull out her grandmother's roasting pan and spices for the roast that would be going into the oven. It made the house smell so good. It's "my night" to make dinner, Patti thought. Well, when they walk in the door tonight, everyone should be ready to sit down together at the table and enjoy the porketta that I ordered from our meat market. Our butcher is from the Iron Range so this will surprise Sarah.

Back on the deck with her tea cup refreshed and hot again, she thought, you know, looking through Grandma's trunk the other day left me wondering where my high school scrapbooks might be. How lucky that I found them in my closet.

Patti smiled as she patted her scrapbooks. It is such fun to go through these pages and look at the clippings and programs from the year we were in the winter playoff tournament.

It doesn't seem so long ago, she thought.

It's hard to believe, Patti realized, that the first statewide tournament for girls in Minnesota was in 1972 in track and field. I'm guessing the state league was trying to encourage schools to get their girls' athletic program underway and a state tournament would grab everyone's attention. Track and field was a good choice. Most schools like ours would have track facilities for their boys teams, and girls would have a unit on track and field in their physical education classes.

We love to tell the story about our cousin Susan and the first state track and field meet. It was 1972, and Susan was a student at International Falls High School, 'way up north near the

Canadian border. When they learned about the plans for the state meet, Susan tells the story that the only place the girls could practice was the gravel road in front of the school. So they helped their physical education teacher, now their new coach, measure and mark off the distances for the dashes and the runs. The shortest race was 25 yards, and the longest was the 800-yard run. Obviously, in the early 1970s, there were still lots of stereotypes and myths about how far girls could run without "harming" themselves.

Patti grimaced a little, remembering how Susan and her new teammates had practiced every day on that gravel road. Susan had said that their old wooden hurdles were the worst. Skinned knees with imbedded pieces of gravel were enough to discourage anyone from wanting to run those events, but they did. Her teacher/coach organized some meets so they had a little competition during their short season.

Lots of snow to melt first, Patti laughed to herself.

There was a qualifying meet and several of Susan's team qualified for the *first-ever* MSHSL State Girls Track and Field State Meet at St. Cloud Apollo High School and she was one of them. They were so excited.

Imagine, Patti thought, how fun it would be to be in the *first* state tournament in any sport. Every event sets a state record. We were so proud of Susan when she won first place in the discus. Because it was one of the first events in the meet, the awards were given out first. It turned out that *Susan was awarded the first gold medal in a statewide tournament for girls in Minnesota.*

Patti smiled. Susan wears the medal on a chain around her neck to this day.

And the fun didn't end there. Susan's team tied for first place and shared the first MSHSL State Girls Track and Field Team Championship with White Bear Lake, a St. Paul suburban school.

Just think, Patti considered, from practicing on a gravel road to being co-champions in the first statewide championship. Does it get any better than that?

I went to St. Paul to watch Susan's volleyball team compete in the state tournament last fall. She's an excellent coach, and she certainly makes sure that the young women in her school have every chance to enjoy the thrill of standing on top of the awards stand.

She knows the feeling.

Patti thought about those first years when there was such a huge transition from the GAA activities to competitive teams. I imagine, she thought, many people must have questioned whether or not it was a good idea to promote interscholastic sports for girls.

Well, she thought, every era has its pioneers. Think of those early 1900s girls' basketball teams when their uniforms were dresses, and no bare skin was permitted except their hands and face. When the "flappers" of the 1920s came into vogue, basketball teams started throwing away their bloomers in favor of shorts. And *that* certainly must have caused quite a stir in some conservative towns of Minnesota.

Then, the era of the "black hole" for female athletes followed when competitive sports were replaced by recreational, just-for-fun activities. Imagine that for over forty years, young women were generally restricted to the sidelines. The attitude was, "That's just the way it is for girls."

Then, a group of pioneer leaders in Minnesota were willing to break with those ideas and create quite a stir when they began sponsoring interschool competitions. Fortunately for us, the Minnesota State High School League listened to those progressive leaders and adopted girls' sports in 1969, years ahead of the support from Title IX.

Imagine trying to overcome the inertia to get things started. I wonder what it was like starting an athletic program for girls from "scratch," especially when many times, they weren't welcome.

Patti shook her head in empathy. It also must have been difficult to be the school administrators facing the requests for coaches, funding, and more teams to schedule in facilities already designated for the boys. But the good administrators made it work, and it always helped if they had daughters, Patti chuckled to herelf.

It was just as challenging at the college and university levels. My sister Jeanne tells of how their college teams would travel to games in station wagons or vans driven by the players or their coaches. Many times, they would pay for their own meals and sometimes even their overnight lodgings. Scholarships were just a dream.

Patti sighed, thinking, that's what pioneers have always had to do. I read a description of pioneers that said, 'They bravely set out to do what no one else has done, to go where others have not gone before.'

Wasn't I fortunate, she thought, *and aren't my daughters fortunate*, that those early pioneers didn't quit, saying, "This is too hard. We're not welcome in this new world of competition. It's hard to find a place to practice, to get budgets, and the media tends to ignore us, or make fun of how we play."

Patti recalled a friend who had such difficulty getting support in her school that she had a file on Title IX information in her desk drawer named, "Sausage and Baloney." She said that was in case someone looked into her files, they would see a file of "recipes."

Yes, Patti thought, there was a recipe: *a recipe for change.* Even today, the struggle for true equality in sports is not over and there is work to be done. My heroes are the ones who fought the early battles and those who continue to fight for equality today.

I need to remember to be supportive of the schools and the coaches, and thank them for what they do for our daughters, and our sons. As parents, we must be alert to the things that need to be changed or improved. Gender shouldn't be part of the criteria of who gets to play; *we are simply talking about what is fair and right for all of our children.*

Patti realized, timing is everything, isn't it? Some women were born too soon and missed the opportunity to play. How lucky I was to have been born at the right time. I was in high school during the mid-1970s when the world was changing and becoming more accepting of women in sports, though the road ahead was long.

We had heard that the League was on the brink of adding several state tournaments. As high school kids we didn't know there was controversy setting the seasons for volleyball and basketball. We just knew that we were playing basketball in the winter but some of our friends in other schools were playing in the fall. Our school had also started a girls volleyball team and we played in the fall. Other schools played in the winter.

It was a dilemma. What to do?

I've read since that the League made two decisions. First, they set a fall season for girls volleyball with its first state tournament to be held in November, 1974.

Then, during the same year, 1974-75, the League invited schools playing basketball in the fall to participate in a "fall playoff tournament," and then invited schools playing basketball in the winter to participate in a "winter playoff tournament." Each would have its own *season champion.*

During that year, the League would select one season for girls basketball with the first state tournament in 1976.

Let's see, my junior year was 1974-75, the big year for playoffs. Unlike my older sister, I was born at just the right time.

One day at volleyball practice, the coach told us about the League's plans. It sounded good to us. We were happy to know there would be a state tournament for volleyball and a playoff tournament following our winter basketball season.

The next thing I remember was November, 1974. We lost out early in the volleyball district tournament. The coach wanted us to see the first Minnesota State High School League Girls State Volleyball Tournament, so we hopped on our bus and rode up to Anoka High School.

It was great fun, even though the lights went out just before the first match started. It had something to do with corrosion on the electrical wiring. What lousy timing. It only held up the tournament for a half hour until the mercury lights could get bright again. I remember so well that the volleyball standards for the nets were held down with sand bags. Imagine having to improvise for a state tournament. It had to be tough to be a director of those early tournaments when anything could go wrong and apparently, usually did.

After the championship match, we got on the bus and rode from Anoka up to St. Cloud State University to see the MSHSL *Fall Basketball* Season Championships between Glencoe and Wadena. Glencoe won and became the champions of the MSHSL Fall Season Girls Basketball Tournament. What fun it was to see the excitement and the crowds that followed their teams.

When basketball started, our team set a goal to make it to the playoffs at the end of the winter season. In early February, our team had eighteen straight wins and was headed to the District 13 tournament. We won the District 13 championship and, it was "so far, so good." Then we won over a tough Rochester Lourdes team in the semi-finals of the playoffs. We were going to play in the championship game at Bloomington Kennedy High School up in the Cities. Holy Angels of Richfield was our opponent and they were good.

What we didn't expect was the response from our community. I can still see the looks on the faces of the team when they saw fifteen, imagine, FIFTEEN buses of fans coming to the Cities for our championship game, all paid for by the Le Sueur Chamber of Commerce.

I'll never forget that crowd, squeezed together like sardines in the bleachers and standing around the entire court, even the end lines. The two women officials did a great job, especially with such a close game and spectators almost under their feet. We came from behind to tie it, but Holy Angels scored last and won by two points. While it was disappointing, we felt that we had played well and had a great season.

We were part of history.

It brings tears to my eyes just to think of it again, Patti thought, as she opened her second scrapbook. *The Le Sueur News Herald*, KRBI Radio, and other groups covered our games and there were such wonderful articles and editorials in the newspaper.

As Patti began leafing through the scrapbook, she remembered how badly the team had felt because they hadn't brought home the championship trophy.

Then, she thought, we read the letters and stories from people in the town that they sent to the newspaper. And they made us feel so good.

She looked at the yellowing newspaper clipping under its plastic protective cover and read the editorial, *"What a tremendous week this last one has been for Le Sueur. For sheer impact on the spirit of the community, nothing, not even Urban Renewal, has carried the clout of the Le Sueur girls basketball team. Their valiant fight for the state championship, their comeback from a seeming rout in the championship game, and their disappointment in a last minute loss has left us feeling a little sad and mighty proud..."*

The writer knew we were disappointed, and added, "... Well, girls, you may not have given us a state championship, but you gave us something a lot more important: you gave us a sense of unity and loyalty and being a part of the community that I haven't felt since those dimly-remembered days when I was in high school. Thank you for reaching for the top and letting us, through you, reach along too."

And there were touching letters from the public in the newspaper.

Patti turned the page to one by a woman who wrote, *"You awakened this town and made it come alive. I've lived here the greater share of my life and I've never seen the whole community back anything or anyone as they did your team. You made us see just how close knit we all really are in Le Sueur – our little town in the valley. You didn't let us down, you lifted us up."*

As Patti looked through the pages filled with basketball memories, she remembered that the school had a banquet for the team and it was a big deal in town. They invited 'that woman' from the League who was the tournament director as the guest speaker.

Patti thought, I don't always remember what speakers say, but I *do* remember what *she* said. She revised the old poem about girls being made of sugar and spice, everything sweet and everything nice - and her poem was, *"Girls are made of strength and grace, with everything moving at a frantic pace. Girls need coaches, rackets and balls; and parents with camcorders to record it all. Girls are athletes in this world today, and that's exactly how it's going to stay!"*

Patti laughed to herself. We all applauded like crazy. Then she said that a "winner" is someone who makes the best use of her abilities, who is committed to a cause, who accepts responsibility for her actions, and who breaks big problems into little ones and solves them one at a time.

And she said that's what we did. *It made us "Winners."* And we believed her.

'Still works for me today, Patti thought.

Her tea cup was empty, but her heart was full.

As she gathered things together, Patti's thoughts turned to her family. I'll have to share my story with Sarah. She has grasped the challenge of the young women in the early 1900s and what they had to do just to play basketball. And she has felt the emotional loss that followed when hundreds of girls' teams in Minnesota were dropped and young women were denied their place in their schools' athletic programs for far too long.

Now, she needs to understand how difficult it was to start girls' sports programs again in the 1960s and 1970s.

Sarah needs to understand *who* gave of their blood, sweat and tears for her. What are their names? What did they have to do to break down the barriers? Only then can she truly appreciate her legacy.

Patti smiled at the thought that even she, Sarah's "old" mother, helped to build the foundation on which Sarah stands today.

I am proud to be part of her legacy.

Patti took a deep breath of the fresh, crisp fall air. We need to enjoy each day, she thought. Seasons come and go so quickly. Our children will soon be grown and they will face challenges we can only imagine. As it was for us growing up, they too, need role models to teach them to stand up and do the right thing; to face life one day at a time.

We try, Patti sighed, to be good role models as parents and hope we are doing the right things. But that speaker at our parents' group the other night really impacted our thinking and touched our hearts. She said their son and three friends had been killed in an accident after prom and alcohol had been involved. She said that she and her husband desperately wanted to find the person who had provided alcohol to their minor children. Then she looked at us and said, "The next time we were going to have friends over, my husband went to the refrigerator where we keep alchol for our guests. He found a little slip of paper between two bottles. It said, "Hey, Mom and Dad, I know you want us to have a good time tonight, so I borrowed a couple six packs and I'll pay you back tomorrow. Love, Tom." She said, "We found who had provided the alcohol - *it was us, his own parents.*"

As Patti wiped the tears from her cheeks, and stood up, Gen woke up from her nap, and knew there might be a treat for her in the kitchen. As Patti opened the screen door, Gen ran through with a look back, as if to say, let's hurry now, I'm hungry!

Patti paused to take one last look at the beautiful morning. *There it was* - a rainbow that had magically appeared, it seemed, just for her to enjoy.

Patti could almost hear Minnesota's own Judy Garland and her beautiful voice in *The Wizard of Oz*. The words of her favorite song always spoke to Patti, "Somewhere over the rainbow, skies are blue, and the dreams that you dare to dream, really do come true. If happy little bluebirds fly, beyond the rainbow, why, oh why, can't I?"

She thought, I've always had so many dreams and I've worked hard to achieve many of them. Now I'm 42, and I still have more goals. And my children...how do I help them reach for their dreams?

A woman at our book club yesterday said,

"How will our children learn to dream unless they see us dream?

How will they learn to defend their values unless they see us defending ours?

How will they learn to care about others unless they see us caring about each other?"

Maybe, Patti smiled, we don't have to fly to a magic land beyond the rainbow, looking for a wizard to make our dreams come true. Maybe *right here* is where we make good things happen, by dreaming, defending our values and caring about others.

Right here, right now.

So, Patti thought, maybe Dorothy was right and there is *"no place like home"*... where we make our dreams come true.

As the hummingbird took its last sip and began its flight south, Patti waved and called after it, "See you next spring!"

★ ★

10

STANDING ON YOUR SHOULDERS

"Hey, Sarah," the voice of her basketball coach rang down the hallway, "would you be interested in going to the State Capitol next week for a ceremony on girls' sports?"

"Sure, what's the deal?" Sarah asked.

"It's called National Girls and Women in Sports Day. It's been held for many years to support girls and women's sports programs and honor people who have made a difference. States all over the country plan special programs and Minnesota has always held theirs at the State Capitol. I think it would be a good experience for the team."

The next day, Sarah and her coach met with the principal.

"Thank you for meeting with us, Ms. Schlueder," Coach Johnson began. We are here to request your approval to take the girls' basketball team to the state capitol next Wednesday for the annual ceremony to celebrate National Girls and Women in Sports Day. If you approve, the team will have their homework turned in for their classes prior to our departure."

Before the coach could continue with her longer rationale for the trip, the principal smiled and nodded, "Yes, you may go."

Sarah and the coach tried not to look surprised, though they were, as permission to be away from classes was not easy to obtain from this principal.

"I wholeheartedly support your request, Coach Johnson," the principal began. "It is an excellent opportunity for our young women to learn about their sports heritage and to meet some true pioneers who opened doors for today's girls' sports programs."

The principal looked directly at Sarah, "I will meet your team on the bus before you leave next week for St. Paul."

True to her word, as usual, the principal boarded the bus as they prepared for their drive to St. Paul.

"This is a special day," she began, looking over the attentive team members, "a national day of celebration for girls and women in sports. Across the country, state and national leaders, young women and their coaches, parents and communities will celebrate how far girls and women's sports have come since the 1960s and 1970s when sports for females were virtually non-existent.

"Today, *you* can select from a variety of team and individual sports offered by our school. You are provided with qualified coaches, uniforms, budgets and facilities for practice and the opportunity to compete interscholastically against other schools. At the close of your season, a series of tournaments enable you to play other teams until there is one team remaining: the state champion. We are proud of our trophy case and the awards and trophies that represent the achievements of those who came before you.

"But these opportunities did not just 'happen.' There were teachers who were the first coaches and who began to organize teams without any budgets and without significant support in the community. They faced resistance from some members of the boys coaching staff when they learned that they would be sharing practice times in the gymnasium, pool and on the playing fields. The local newspapers did not cover the girls' sports as fully as they did the boys' games. And, sometimes, the early athletes endured heckling when they played. Being the first to play in public without having prior years of training was not easy.

"So, you are going to St. Paul to this special ceremony, representing not only our school but your generation of athletes. Stand tall. Look around. Who is there? You will see women who were the first to say that young women should have competitive sports. There will be state legislators and community leaders who supported equity for girls and women's sports by passing laws, and policies that were strong incentives, and requirements, for schools to 'do the right thing.'

"Listen to what they have to say and learn from them. My favorite quote for you today comes from the president of a women's college who was reminding her students of their heritage. She said, 'You are standing on the shoulders of those who have sacrificed blood, sweat and tears so that you can have the opportunities available to you today.'

"This is a unique opportunity for you. Enjoy and appreciate it."

Soon Sarah and her team were headed down the freeways into St. Paul. As she walked up the huge flight of steps into the entrance of the State Capitol building, Sarah thought, how many women have walked these steps to take a seat as our state representative or state senator? How many women wanted to, but weren't allowed to be a candidate or even to vote for the men who were running for office? And why hasn't a woman been governor of our state? Another area my generation needs to address.

As they walked into the rotunda, their eyes lifted up to the open dome above them and the beautiful artistry of its design. She thought, *this is the place* where laws are made that should ensure that all people have equal rights and are treated with dignity and respect.

Sarah recalled the poster in her American Government classroom. The poster depicted the Roman goddess of justice, *Justitia*. Her left hand holds the scales which measure the strength of a case's support and opposition. Her right hand carries a double-edged sword which symbolizes the power of "Reason and Justice." She is wearing a blindfold which represents objectivity, i.e., blind justice and impartiality.

How important it is, Sarah thought, that justice is administered objectively, without fear or favor, regardless of a person's identity, money, weakness or power.

As other teams came into the rotunda, Sarah and her friends saw players that were their competitors on the floor, but here, they were all sharing in the dream of fairness and equity.

As they walked around looking at the displays and talking to representatives from many different organizations and schools, Tammy turned to Sarah, "I didn't realize how many new careers in sports we can choose from that weren't available a few years ago. We can be coaches and officials at all levels from elementary through the pro's. I know they need more women. You know, my little sister has never had a woman coach."

Sarah nodded, "And there's a whole bunch of careers in medical areas, like athletic trainer, and researcher of female athletic injuries. Plus now, there are lots of openings in the media, like game announcer, reporter, journalist, and radio and television commentators."

At the stroke of twelve noon, the chairs in the rotunda were filled; people were standing around the sides and back, filling in the spaces between the pillars supporting the upper level. Standing around the upper railing that circled the balcony, Sarah could see other students wearing their team letter jackets. She assumed that the men and women in business suits and carrying briefcases and folders were likely legislators and lobbyists stopping by before heading off to their next committee meeting.

Sitting on the right side of the podium were individuals who were going to be recognized for helping to break barriers and open doors for girls and women in sports. Sarah knew that Minnesota was one of the first states to begin developing girls and women's sports teams, ten years before the passage of the famous Title IX, forty-some years ago.

A woman stepped to the podium and looked out over the audience. She smiled and said, "Welcome. Today we come to celebrate and to commit ourselves to continue our journey to fairness and equity for girls and women in sports in Minnesota and across our country."

A shiver traveled up Sarah's back as she listened to the stirring words.

The woman continued, "We have already traveled many miles on our journey, but this is a journey that must go on to ensure that young women will have full and equitable choices in the world of sports.

"We come today to measure our progress since we gathered here last year, to celebrate our victories, to recognize individuals who have made a difference, and to recommit to the next year of our journey."

Sarah spontaneously applauded and was happy that others had joined her.

Wow, Sarah thought, I have never heard someone say these words before, so clear, inviting us to commit ourselves to travel this road together.

The woman's voice became serious, "We remember the challenging days in the 1960s and 1970s when we began our quest to take down the barriers and open doors once again to girls and women."

Sarah realized, I am standing with some of the women who opened the doors that had closed in the face of Great-Grandma Ruby and all those young women who came along in the following decades.

"Awesome," Yolanda whispered.

"But the road is not always a safe one," the woman continued. "Not all of our fellow travelers believe in fairness for women, and they continue to work to weaken state and national laws that define equal treatment in sports. It requires each of us to maintain our vigilance and to take steps to confront those who do not play fair."

The audience again broke into applause that indicated their support for these concerns.

The woman raised her hands to illustrate her story. "We fly like our favorite Canadian geese, in a V-formation, where the leader takes on the force of the wind, making it easier for those who follow. When the leader gets weary from the struggle of leading the flock, she can exchange her position and rest while another goose leads the way."

How smart, Sarah thought, to share the burdens of leadership.

"The next time," the speaker suggested, "that a flock of geese flies over, look up, *and listen.* You'll hear them calling to one another.

Why? They are calling out encouragement, saying, 'Keep going, we'll make it.' That's what we all need to do: to fly together, share the responsibilities of leadership and call out our encouragement to one another. Then we all will reach our destination - full, fair and equal treatment for girls and women in sports, and in all corners of their lives."

Those words, Sarah thought, will always be locked in my memory. There will come a time when they will give me encouragement to continue what may be coming in my life.

A woman with a guitar stepped up to the podium. Her name was Ann Reed, and, from their response, the audience knew of her and her music, and were happy to see her.

Ann said to the audience, "Thank you for inviting me here today. I am one of those young women who wanted to play and doors weren't fully open for me. Just seeing all of you here today, those who opened the doors and all of the young women who walked through them and are now strong, confident athletes - *you make my heart happy.*

So, I wrote this song for you. It is called, "Look at Her Go!"

As she began to strum her guitar and sing, her rich voice filled the rotunda and flowed down the halls, where laws are developed and justice is rendered.

> *"If all things were equal, and the world was*
> *sitting right,*
>
> *your mother might have played the game, you're*
> *going to play tonight.*
>
> *Memories caught in photographs, moments win or*

lose, she'll look at them and think of how she'd pass
this on to you."

Sarah felt her heart swelling with emotion...she's talking about my ancestors, my mother, and me.

"Look at her run, look at her go
eyes on the ball, heart on the goal
one of a team, bright fields of hope
part of a dream, oh, look at her go."

The audience didn't move, listening to each word.

"If someone could tell you, from the day that you
arrived that the world is open to you, all you have to
do is try...if you like to feel the rhythm of your feet
upon the track, the beating of your heart, and, oh, the
wind upon your back."

Sarah thought, she understands.

"One breath says, here I am
do my best, oh yes, I can
I am stronger with every chance I take."

Then the words of the song reminded Sarah of her responsibility.

"What you have before you is not a simple twist of fate,
thank the ones who took it on to push upon the gate."

Sarah nodded, yes, I will.

"Look at her run, look at her go
eyes on the ball, heart on the goal
one of the team, bright fields of hope
part of a dream

Oh, look at her go!"

There was a moment of silence, as the audience absorbed the words and music. Then the heartfelt applause grew and expanded, filling the rotunda and flowing down the halls, *where laws are developed and justice is rendered.*

The emcee for the awards program stepped to the podium. She was a tall, blonde woman with a smile that made others smile too, and a strong, confident voice. Lynnette had been in high school before girls' sports had returned. She loved basketball so when she and her twin, Lynnea, learned of a women's professional team called the All-America Redheads, they tried out and were selected for the team.

Sarah whispered to Tammy, "Imagine 6'1" twins on your team. Wouldn't that be our coach's dream?"

Lynnette had played on Minnesota's first professional women's basketball team, the Fillies, which had led the way to today's WNBA program, and Minnesota's world championship team, the Lynx. She was now the color commentator for broadcasts of the Gopher women's basketball games at the University of Minnesota. She's a real role model, thought Sarah.

Then a proclamation was read that had been signed by the governor, making this day National Girls and Women in Sports Day.

"Cool," said Tammy, in Sarah's ear, "I'm glad I'm here, aren't you?" Sarah nodded.

As the ceremony continued, Sarah was fascinated by the challenges faced by the individuals being honored. Their stories were touching and inspiring.

In the 1960s, one physical education teacher wanted to expand her Girls Athletic Association (GAA) activities into sports days and events with other schools. There was no budget to pay for a bus driver, but the school principal said she could use a school bus if she got a bus driver's license and drove the bus herself. So she learned how to drive and off they went with happy hearts.

Another award recipient told of washing cars, selling greeting cards and holding bake sales to make money for their teams. They finally had enough money for one set of uniforms and they were worn for every sport. Their basketball team wore those uniforms when they participated in the first MSHSL Fall Season Basketball Championships and won it.

One woman was a founding member of the first association for coaches of girls' sports and served as its executive secretary for thirteen years. Organizations must have people with that kind of commitment, Sarah thought.

One woman's experience left Sarah angry. She told of taking her softball team to another school to play. The sprinkling system in the outfield came on. They continued playing but the players were getting cold and wet. The host coach finally went into the school to find someone who could turn the sprinklers off. She explained to the visiting coach, "This happens a lot. The school custodian thinks the girls' sports create more work for him so when we come out to the field, he turns the sprinklers on and goes home."

Sarah thought, so some people just used underhanded ways to discourage and make it hard. Well, it hasn't succeeded, but what a shame that coaches and players had to endure such treatment. I know there were "good guys" who didn't do that to their girls' sports teams. I guess the moral to the story is, "keep on, keeping on." That's what my dad says.

One recipient was a man who worked for the park and recreation department and he developed girls' basketball teams for the new immigrant population. Just like Amelia Earhart did when she was a social worker in Boston, Sara thought.

One award recipient, Pat, could not hold back a couple tears. She said, "I spent many years wondering 'what might have been' and being angry because my dreams could never become reality - only because girls weren't allowed to compete. I could only watch boys play and wish I were playing too. Everyone seemed to believe that it was okay to deny me the chance to play, simply because I was a girl."

Sarah felt as though a cold hand had touched her. How awful that must have felt.

Pat continued, "Here I am today, fifty years later, still wanting to cry over what my life might have been like if I hadn't been 'born too soon.'"

Sarah felt as though the woman was looking directly at her.

"Each of you young women here today," she said, *"play* for the women like me who were denied the opportunity to wear our school's uniform, to play in front of our family and friends. *Play* for the women who were denied access to sports because we were female. *Play for us."*

So, Sarah thought, not only did young women like Great-Grandma Ruby have a door slammed in their face when their teams were dropped, this happened over and over and over again, well into the 1970s and 1980s. I feel so badly for women like Pat. Today she is being recognized for being a pioneer coach who opened doors for the young women in her school. She invested her life to give them the chance to put on a school uniform, to compete and win state championships. Most of all, she gave them the opportunity to "play like a girl" and be proud of it.

Thank goodness the barriers have been coming down, year after year, Sarah thought. If they hadn't, I wonder what I would be doing now.

As the ceremony concluded, there was a buzz across the rotunda as the proud friends and families exchanged hugs and congratulations.

This was awesome, Sarah thought, as their team waited for an opportunity to speak with the women and men who had received recognition for their efforts to bring equity into their programs.

As Sarah stepped up to shake the hand of each award recipient, she said, *"Thank you. I am standing on your shoulders today."*

11

FLYING THE BLUE SKIES OF IOWA

"Sarah, this is Lynn," the voice on the telephone said. "Want to fly down to Des Moines with me for a quick day trip? I'm going down to see the Iowa Girls State Basketball Tournament."

Sarah immediately accepted her aunt's invitation. It was another chance to fly with a pilot who could show her some techniques and maybe give her a chance to get in a little flying time, if the weather cooperated.

And, Sarah thought, this is a great chance to see what "might have been" if Minnesota had supported their girls basketball teams back in the 1920s with a state tournament, like Iowa did. She knew her Great-Grandma Ruby had begged her parents to let her live with relatives in Iowa so she could play basketball there.

Sarah had met her father's sister at a family reunion and knew she had played basketball at a small school in Iowa. From what Sarah could recall, family lore had it that Lynn was a great player, setting lots of records during her high school years.

The day finally arrived along with good weather, especially for a cold winter day in early March. Lynn kept her own plane at the Flying Cloud Airport in Eden Prairie. Soon they were lifting over the Minnesota River with a bright sun coming up in the eastern sky and heading due south.

Lynn had some hot chocolate and sandwiches along "for sustenance," she said. After catching up on family news for awhile, they decided that some "sustenance" was in order. As Sarah sipped her hot chocolate, she looked out of the plane's small windows. The winter landscape was beautiful and created interesting patterns of farm buildings, fence lines and the famous cornfields of Iowa.

"Look, Sarah," Lynn pointed out the window, "See the herd of deer in that field? It's been a hard winter but fortunately they should be able to find some corn left from the fall harvest. And there's #35W heading south. We'll follow it right into Des Moines. I'm glad you could ride along with me to the state tournament. I think you'll find another piece of the puzzle for your research paper when you learn about Iowa's history. And I'll get to see some friends from my high school years."

After approaching the Des Moines airport, Lynn demonstrated a perfect landing. Sarah watched carefully. It looked so easy when a good pilot was at the controls.

Soon the taxi was whisking them downtown to the new auditorium where the Iowa Girls High School Basketball State Tournament was underway. The streets were filled with fans and girls' teams; parking lots were jammed with cars, vans and buses with license plates displaying counties from all over the state. Stores were hung with banners welcoming the fans, and appealing sales posters were enticing people into their stores. The city was buzzing with excitement.

As Sarah and Lynn walked into the auditorium, the sounds hit them like a wave. The concourse was filled with Iowa girls' basketball teams, all wearing their letter jackets. Sarah felt at home, seeing all of these young women who loved basketball too. She was glad that she had worn her jacket.

"Cool," Sarah exclaimed, "look at the walls of photos filled with the Iowa Girls Basketball Hall of Fame. There are pictures back to the 1920s. Imagine having a state tournament all those years. Our Minnesota state tournament started in 1976 but Iowa had state tournaments for over fifty years before that. I wonder why they started so early and why didn't they drop their teams like Minnesota and most other states did?"

"And look, Lynn," Sarah pointed to a plaque. "They have an award that has been presented to five women. It says each was "a daughter of Iowa, a daughter of the game... recognizing girls of the Commonwealth who have carried tradition and training of a sport into varied and important careers... and for singularly illustrious and most memorable accomplishments." Sarah's eyes widened as she pointed to one name, "She's from the state high school league in Minnesota. That must have been fun to 'come home again.'" Sarah almost thought she heard a voice whisper, "*It was.*"

Their seats were in the front row, mid-court, a great place to see the games. Sarah was impressed and wondered how they rated such a prime location.

Bands were adding their special music to the atmosphere of the arena. It was championship day, with one session for a smaller school class and another for the larger schools. Sarah couldn't see any empty seats, also a tradition with this tournament. One of the ushers had said to Sarah as she led them down to their seats, "We have a saying here in Iowa during the girls tournament: 'last one in town, turn out the lights.'"

There were voices echoing across the auditorium and Sarah realized that teams were greeting one another. On one side, a team could be heard yelling another school's name, like "Hello, Maynard." A team in the far corner would respond, "Hello, Hawkeye." Back and forth, teams who had played one another during the season were sending vocal greetings as they gathered together to celebrate their state tournament. Each team, no doubt, was also planning how they could be on the floor next year.

"Hello, North Winn...Hello, North Fayette." Sarah had never before heard teams greeting each other at a state tournament. How fun, she thought, to hear the name of your school echoing across the floor.

Two of the state association's executive staff members were headed their way.

"Welcome, Lynn," the woman gave her a warm hug and turned to Sarah.

"And you must be Sarah! Lynn has told us about you. My name is Karen Brown and I'm in charge of special events here at the tournament."

Sarah was impressed with her warm welcome. The man standing alongside Karen also had a uniquely warm smile. His eyes were like a leprechaun from Sarah's Irish heritage. His contagious enthusiasm confirmed that he must be the executive director of the Iowa Girls High School Athletic Union (IGHSAU). He exuded pride and Iowa hospitality.

"Iowa welcomes you to our state girls basketball tournament," announced E. Wayne Cooley. "Sarah, you are in for a treat today. We like to share what has been happening here in Iowa for decades, and today we believe that you will see the national showcase for girls high school basketball. Lynn, of course, is very familiar with this event. Every year we plan events at this tournament that we broadcast and televise all over our state and far beyond. We hope other states will provide the same support and recognition for their young women as we do here in Iowa."

He tilted his head and said, with a sparkle in his eyes, "We know you folks in Minnesota have really made progress in promoting your girls' sports program. Your League hired a 'daughter of Iowa,' so we know you'll do just fine."

He smiled, "And congratulations, Lynn, I'll see you a bit later."

As this charismatic man walked away, he was greeted by people who stood to shake his hand and he waved back at the crowd. It was obvious that he was the driving force behind the success of Iowa girls basketball.

Karen handed state tournament programs to Sarah and Lynn, saying, "We hope you enjoy the tournament, Sarah. And Lynn, I'll see you a bit later, as we planned. Better get your popcorn now because the first game will soon be starting."

As Sarah looked through the thick state tournament program, she was captivated by all of the articles and pictures. Clearly, the state of Iowa did love its girls basketball. One article reviewed the history of the tournament back to 1920 when it was sponsored by Drake University. Then from 1923 to 1925, the Iowa High School Athletic Association sponsored both girls and boys sports and their state tournaments.

Hmm. . . , Sarah thought, it's interesting that another group started the tournament and then their state high school association, like our State High School League, sponsored the girls tournament for only a couple years. I wonder what changed. She continued reading.

"Look, Lynn," Sarah nearly lifted out of her seat, "Iowa schools also received those letters from the NAAF-Women's Division that they should discontinue their girls' basketball teams - just like Minnesota.

"It says the school superintendents of Iowa met in Des Moines in 1927 to talk over this recommendation from the NAAF-WD to drop girls basketball and discontinue the state tournament. There was support from some superintendents to drop the teams, especially if this national organization felt basketball might do harm to the girls.

"Listen to this!" Sarah's voice almost squeaked, "It says that a superintendent from Mystic, Iowa, John W. Agans, had a different position. He said to the statewide gathering, 'Gentlemen, if you attempt to do away with girls basketball in Iowa, you'll be standing in the center of the track when the train runs over you.'"

"So that is what happened," she quickly read on. "It says that *after his strong position*, the small schools of Iowa established a new organization to sponsor the state girls basketball tournament. Since 1927, the *Iowa Girls High School Athletic Union (IGHSAU)* has conducted the basketball tournament. In later years, they added a variety of team and individual sports, as other states did. Iowa is the only state with a separate organization sponsoring girls athletics."

"So," Lynn said, "the smaller Iowa schools saved their girls basketball teams, but the larger schools followed the recommendations of the NAAF-Women's Division and did drop their teams. Even in Iowa, girls in larger schools lost the chance to play. Only girls in the smaller schools came out ahead in Iowa."

"One person can make a difference," Sarah agreed, "but you have to be willing to stand up and fight for what you believe is right."

As the overhead lights went out, a spotlight opened onto a color guard who solemnly carried the state and national flags onto the floor. The audience rose to its collective feet, removing their hats and caps. A second spotlight focused on a young woman standing in the center circle. Her voice began to sing the stirring words of the national anthem, "Oh, say, can you see. . . ."

Flags were being waved by everyone in the audience. What a sight, Sarah observed. At the close of the anthem, the young woman continued on, "O, beautiful, for spacious skies, for amber waves of grain . . ." The flags and the audience seemed to move as one. "...for purple mountain majesties, above the fruited plain... ." As the last notes faded away, tears glistened in many eyes, including those of Sarah and Lynn.

"Awesome, that was beautiful," Sarah exclaimed as the audience also clapped its approval.

"Showing respect for country, and special pageantry has always been a part of this tournament," said Lynn. "Now, I will have to leave you in the fourth quarter to join a group for a ceremony between games. I didn't tell you before, but I am going to be recognized for my years as a player."

Sarah excitedly wrapped her arms around her aunt's shoulders and hugged her. This was going to be some day!

"Welcome to the Great State of Iowa...and our Girls State Basketball Tournament," the rich, commanding voice of the announcer began the ceremony and introduction of teams. His voice was recognized throughout the great state of Iowa.

Wouldn't it be fun to play in a state tournament like this,

Sarah thought.

At the end of the first game, the awards ceremony was conducted and it looked familiar - one team ecstatic and the other bravely attempting to hold back the tears. They held their heads high, knowing their families and community would not want them to show any signs of poor sportsmanship.

Sarah was amazed at the size of the trophies. They stood almost to the shoulders of some players, and it required at least two players to hold it high to share with their fans. They proudly carried it over to their cheering sections.

After the teams left the floor for their locker rooms, very few people left their seats. They knew a ceremony was coming and they didn't want to miss anything.

Popcorn sales were going to be down during this intermission, Sarah thought.

Suddenly, spotlights of all colors roved around the floor and the music began. The announcer's voice called for the attention of the audience, though they were already quiet and listening.

"Please welcome," the announcer began, "the women in your Iowa Girls Basketball Hall of Fame." Applause rolled in waves around the rafters. He announced that the ceremony would begin with women who had been inducted in earlier years.

From Sarah's right, a woman walked confidently onto the court toward the center circle. She politely declined the arm of a young woman escort, clearly sending a message that she was still mobile and independent. Her name was Dorcas Andersen from Audubon. At 93 years of age, Dorcas had played in the first state tournament in 1920-21. The crowd roared its approval and support.

The next player was Irene Silka, from Maynard, who played in 1926 and scored 100 points in one game. She looked ready to score again if she could only get her hands on a basketball.

One by one, each of the women made her entrance onto the court, as they represented the decades of the 1920s through the 1980s. Each one was, no doubt, flooded with memories of those special years.

The Billerbeck twins from Reinbeck joined the famous lineup. Then came Sandy Fiete from Garnavillo, 1954, known as "Dandy Sandy." Sandy had a unique back-over-her-head shot that had been a real crowd-pleaser. The litany of superstars and their stats made Sarah's head swim. Among them were - Sandy Van Cleve from Montezuma; Norma Schulte, Monona; Lynn Lorenzen, Ventura; and Denise Long from Union-Whitten.

Each introduction was followed by thunderous applause from an audience who clearly knew these players, their names and records. No doubt many had watched them play or listened on their radios or, later watched on television. Iowa's pride in its daughters flowed across the court, enveloping each woman.

Imagine, Sarah realized, that the first players were in tournaments at Drake University and later at Veterans Memorial Auditorium. During those years, Iowa became a national symbol of a successful girls basketball program. And what a tradition! These women represent over eighty years of state tournaments in Iowa. *And no one will ever forget them.*

Now it was time for three new inductees, and the first was Lynn, who had played in the mid-1970s. As Lynn walked onto the floor and the announcer read her statistics, Sarah clapped and her eyes glistened with pride.

"How could it be that I didn't know that Aunt Lynn was such a high school star in Iowa? Well, I'll take lots of pictures so I can share this big night with our family at home and on the Internet."

As their plane headed north once again, Sarah's head was swimming with the day's events.

The exciting championship games and the induction ceremonies were just awesome, Sarah thought. Then there was more.

The Parade of Champions was amazing. Dozens of young women dressed in their uniforms, leotards and warm-ups, wrapped round the court, carrying volleyballs, softball bats and gloves, skis, basketballs, tennis racquets, track batons and more.

It dawned on Sarah, *I am seeing state champions from the previous year.* Each one is a state champion in a team or individual sport. This was a sight that she had never seen before.

Sarah was awed by the sight of young women from all over the state of Iowa, here to be introduced and receive recognition in front of this huge audience and far beyond via television.

Colorful spotlights and music lit up the arena.

As the announcer read her name, each young woman walked to the top of an awards stand placed in the center court circle and stood briefly in the spotlight, smiling for the audience, television and, of course, her proud family and community.

Sarah was mesmerized by the sight of so many young women who had achieved their dreams of becoming a state champion. The tournament was a great opportunity to give the people in the arena and millions more on television an understanding of all of the opportunities available to young women in Iowa. Sarah thought, this state really knows how to honor its female athletes.

The sound of the plane's propeller was comforting as it continued to hum its way north over the Iowa and Minnesota landscapes but Sarah had many questions for Lynn.

"You played basketball in the mid-70s, like my mom did, but your teams had been playing for many years and Minnesota was just starting to play again. Did you feel pressure to do well?"

Lynn smiled, "Some. In those days, we had no access to summer camps and traveling teams. It was really up to an individual player to improve her skills out of season, and that was difficult over the summer months when we didn't have access to the gym or a coach. I had committed to my coach that I would shoot 500 baskets a day and the only place in our little town was an outdoor court, full of cracks and uneven pieces of concrete. Plus, I needed money and had also signed up for de-tasseling corn."

Sarah raised her eyebrows with a questioning look.

"Oh," Lynn laughed, "I forgot, you city kids don't understand farm lingo. When the corn gets about six feet high and tassels have sprouted out of the top of the stalks, kids are hired to walk down the rows and yank out the tassels. It has to do with pollinating the corn. You start around 6:30 a.m. and you may get done around 6:30 p.m. You walk down a row of corn and reach up to yank the tassel out of the top of each cornstalk, first on the right side and then on your left. And you better not miss any. In the morning, the leaves of the corn are wet with dew and the edges are sharp, leaving little cuts on your arms. The pollen from the tassels gets into your eyes and you get so thirsty. If you didn't bring a thermos or the foreman forgot the big community jug at the end of the row, you simply kept going. Some of the fields were a mile long. It was usually during some of the hottest days of the summer too. In our crew, the boys usually rode a machine and pulled the tassels as they went *over* the corn. Pretty easy. And we girls walked. Go figure.

"So when we finished our day in the fields, I had my commitment to the coach to shoot baskets. I was so tired, so I would say to myself, Lynn, you don't have to shoot the baskets, just go to the court and stand there with the ball. Of course, I ended up shooting the baskets. But maybe those long rows of corn and those thousands of shots made the difference when we played some of the teams that had some real shooting stars."

Lynn looked over at Sarah and gave her a penetrating look. "Sarah, you've had a pretty protected life *so far*. Do you realize that?"

"Yes," Sarah agreed, "but I didn't realize it until I started researching the history of women in athletics and I kept running into so many things that girls and women weren't supposed to do or couldn't do. Like, there were laws that women could only do something with their husband's consent. And look at the clothes that women had to wear - corsets and long dresses, big hats and high-buttoned shoes."

"Well," Lynn laughed, "when you can keep women in clothes like that and require them to be chaperoned when they leave their homes, you can pretty much control their lives, and their bodies. Have you read about those who fought to get the vote for women and the abuse they endured? It's an embarrassment for a country like ours to have such a chapter in our history."

Lynn's eyes began to narrow, "And it makes my blood boil just to say the word, 'suffragette.' Suffrage means the right to vote, period. Suffrag... ette... ette," she repeated.

"The dictionary says *'ette'* means 'diminutive, smaller,' like kitchenette. But when it gets added to a noun, like major*ette* or usher*ette*, it usually means something a *woman* does, like suffrag*ette*."

"I refuse to be an 'ette' in anything," Lynn was visibly upset at what she considered sexist language. "Women are not doing something in a way that requires a separate word. When it comes to the right to vote, which is *suffrage*, I am a *suffragist*. And so is anyone, man or woman, who believes in suffrage."

Sarah agreed, "I hadn't thought much about that before. When I was reading about the early girls and women's teams in the 1970s, there were some who took the name of their school mascot, which the boys used, but then added an 'ette' to it. Like Hawks and Hawkettes. Words can really carry their own message implying which one is important, and which one is a separate or smaller form. I'm going to listen for those words now."

Lynn offered, "I read a quote by Eleanor Roosevelt, 'It's better to light one candle than curse the darkness.' We simply have to change the world's vocabulary *one word at a time*."

Sarah looked out the plane window at the twinkling lights of the little communities below. A crescent moon floated in its solitary path. It always made her think of her hero, Amelia Earhart. When Amelia was the first woman to solo the Atlantic, it seemed fitting that she would land her plane in an Irish farmer's field, only a few miles from Sarah's great-grandfather's ancestral home near Culdaff in County Donegal, Ireland.

When Sarah had read about Amelia's life, she found a surprising connection with Minnesota. As a young girl living in Iowa in the early 1900s, Amelia's family had vacationed in Minnesota on a farm on Okabena Lake in Worthington.

Then, Sarah learned that Amelia's family had moved to St Paul in 1914 and Amelia had attended St. Paul Central High School. Sarah and her dad had driven to St. Paul to see the house where the family lived for that one year. They also drove to St. Clement's Church where Amelia, her mother and sister had attended. It had been a special feeling to walk into the church and know that Amelia had also walked there as a young woman.

Sarah and her dad had gone to the Minnesota Historical Society where they located the school's early yearbooks. Sarah had hoped to find information that Amelia played on the St. Paul Central girls basketball team. She knew it had traditionally competed with other schools since the early 1900s. So it was *very disappointing to find a page in the yearbook that said that in 1914*, Central didn't play other area schools. It was the *only year* they didn't play interscholastically... what bad timing!

Well, Sarah consoled herself, at least Amelia played in the inter-class and intramural tournaments and wrote friends about how much fun it was.

Things got worse. Sarah had read that because of family problems, Amelia had to leave Central and spend her senior year in Chicago and *that was the very year the Central team won the city championship.* What a bummer.

Timing is everything, Sarah thought, and we can't rewrite history. Wouldn't that have been fun to see Amelia's smile on the photo of the 1915 St. Paul Central championship team, as a senior like me? Amelia slipped through Minnesota's fingers because of family problems beyond her control. So many young women's lives get changed through no choice of their own. *Even Amelia's.*

But, she consoled herself, later when Amelia was employed in Boston at a settlement house, she taught the immigrant girls to play basketball. Obviously, Amelia appreciated how the game she enjoyed could also help these young girls adjust to their new lives in America.

Amelia had learned the game in *Minnesota*. So, Sarah affirmed to herself, *Amelia Earhart will always be one of Minnesota's "daughters of the game."*

How interesting, Sarah thought, that Amelia once lived in Des Moines where I visited today, and then lived in the Twin Cities, where I live. She was a real crusader for opening doors for women. Maybe Amelia and I are on the same "flight plan." The possibility made Sarah smile.

"When did you get your pilot's license?" Sarah asked Lynn.

"That's another story. I wanted to fly since I was just a little kid on the farm. We had a barn where I could make slides in the haymow by pulling the loose hay into a pretty good run. Even a piece of cardboard could give you a good ride."

Lynn smiled, recalling the memories, "After college, I put together enough money to get some lessons and that did it, for sure. My head wanted to be in the clouds and I wanted to be the one with my hand on the controls. So when I was ready, I applied for jobs flying cargo or for small commercial airlines and got turned down 'flat.' They weren't hiring, so they said. They should have just said, 'We aren't hiring *women*.' Instead, I joined the National Guard and finally wrangled my way into flight school. After that training, I naively thought, I'm ready to apply to the larger commercial airlines. Funny thing, they weren't hiring either. Being a woman and trying to break into flying took a tough skin. But I believed in myself and kept at it and, as you know, now I'm flying for an international commercial airline."

"Lynn, what do you know about Amelia Earhart?" Sarah asked.

"Well, for starters," Lynn began with a smile, "I am a proud member of the Ninety-Nines, the organization of women pilots that Amelia founded in 1929. She was its first president. It made sense to organize the women pilots so they could work together to improve conditions for their cross-country races since they weren't allowed to enter the men's races. The Ninety-Nines worked to make structural changes in the cockpits to accommodate a woman. Not every woman has long legs like mine," Lynn laughed.

"It wasn't easy in the 1920s and 1930s to be a woman who wanted to fly. Even after women flew planes all over the world as WASPS in WWII, they came home to find that airlines wouldn't employ them as pilots either. Same ol', same ol.'"

"However," Lynn continued with some pride in her voice, "today there are over 6,000 Ninety-Nines throughout the world who support one another."

Sarah said, "My flight instructor told me about the scholarships, so I'm thinking of applying for one. I'm seeing more women pilots like you on commercial airlines and flying every kind of aircraft in the military. An article I read the other day talked about a Minnesota astronaut, a woman, who had climbed out of an airlock to install a new addition to the international space station. They said she was one of eight women, so far, to become a spacewalker. And there was a woman who was commander of a recent space shuttle. It sure sounds encouraging."

"Yes," Lynn said, "we can applaud those who have broken barriers, while we continue to work for more change. Soon, it will depend on your generation to get it done."

They both looked out the window as the plane encountered a rough patch and they checked their seat belts.

"Flying is a lot like life," Lynn said. "You look out and see nothing but pretty white clouds and it looks like smooth sailing, but in those clouds are unseen little gremlins that suddenly bounce you around and create little air pockets that can put your stomach in your throat. You have to be alert and ready to respond."

"That's a good thing to remember," Sarah said as she tried to move with the plane as it swayed and bounced. "Sometimes I start out a day and think everything is going to be perfect and then, 'out of the blue,' something happens and I get all discombobulated - that's a favorite word of Mom's."

"Sure, and that's understandable," Lynn responded. "Sometimes it helps to anticipate that all may not be smooth sailing and others may not agree with you, or they do something to knock you off your feet for awhile. It's how you react to it that counts. It's like being in a game and you know that your opponent is going to do everything to distract you from making a shot, or try to take the ball away from you. Every day is just like a game, Sarah, and if you can live your life with that attitude, you'll enjoy it more, and, I'm predicting, you'll make a difference in this world."

It sounded like how Amelia faced life, Sarah thought. She didn't let any attitudes or barrier stand in her way.

"The key seems to be," Sarah said, "that you have to believe in yourself. One of my favorite quotes by Amelia is, 'I chose to fly the Atlantic *because I wanted to* ....'"

When I choose the direction for my life, Sarah thought, I first need to do it because I believe I can and I want to, and, who knows, perhaps I'll be the first woman to do it, like Amelia.

As their wheels touched down at the Flying Cloud Airport in Eden Prairie, Sarah was tired, yet sorry to have her trip coming to an end. She had so much to share and so many questions to ask. She needed to spend more time with Lynn and perhaps they could go together to a meeting of the Minnesota Ninety-Nines.

"Lynn, thank you for inviting me to come with you. I learned so much about how another state conducts its tournaments and honors its athletes. I was so proud to see you on the floor being inducted into the Hall of Fame for your accomplishments as a high school girls basketball player. I'd like to include you in my research paper. Would that be all right with you?"

Lynn smiled, and in that flash, Sarah could see the same face reflected back at her from the photo of a young Iowa woman in a state tournament program from not so many years ago.

12

Returning to Her Roots

"An All-School Reunion - in Le Sueur? Mom, that's *your* home-town, but I have never lived there or gone to school there."

Last summer's protests echoed in Sarah's head. Let's see, Sarah thought back, that reunion was before this whole research paper started. As I look back on it now, there were lots of lessons for me on that trip, but I wasn't ready to see them yet.

She leaned back on her bed and retrieved memories from the day to scrutinize them from her new perspective.

It was last August. Sarah was not enthused at the thought of driving down to Le Sueur and spending an afternoon with hundreds of people that she didn't know. There were lots of things she had to get done before Monday.

"Do I really need to go?" she had a little whine in her voice and she knew that wouldn't set well with her mother.

Patti's brows drew down and her look said it all. Sarah knew that she had better change her attitude or the repercussions could be serious.

"Okay, okay," Sarah relented, "I suppose it is fun for you older people to get together and talk about your younger years. I can always take my iPhone along and play a crossword game."

Sarah's mother couldn't help but smile. "Sarah, they'll have your favorite Le Sueur corn on the cob and mini-doughnuts. Why don't you look on the bright side? Stop complaining and help me get dinner ready."

The subject was closed. Sarah had to admit that her mother might be right. After all, her mother had played on the Le Sueur team in the 1970s. It could be fun to see how "old" her mother's teammates looked.

The day had arrived and Sarah's parents, her younger sisters and 14-year-old brother piled in the SUV and headed south down the highway to Le Sueur.

"C'mon, you guys, play the billboard game with me," her brother Ben pleaded. Pretty soon, they were laughing and the miles flew by.

As they drew near to Le Sueur, Patti began to reminisce a little to update her captive audience. "In the 1970s, girls' sports were just beginning. We used to ride this old bus to games, and at first there weren't many people at our games. We had uniforms but they had to be used for basketball, volleyball and track."

"How could you use one uniform for all those sports?" Sarah asked from the back seat, "Why didn't you have one uniform for each sport?"

"Well," her mother replied, "this was pre-state and federal enforcement of equal treatment, and the girls' sports program didn't have much of a budget, so we had to 'make do' with one uniform for all of the sports. In those days, many of us participated in every season. The year we made the basketball tournaments, the athletic director pulled together enough money to get a new set of uniforms so we would look good up in 'The Cities,' playing in front of all those people."

As they drove down Main Street in Le Sueur, it was obvious that the planning committee had worked hard to make it a fun event. There was a big banner hanging over the street, "Welcome to the Le Sueur All-School Reunion."

All of the stores had signs in the windows, announcing special sales and bargains for the alums and anyone that could be enticed to walk through their doors.

Patti suddenly shouted and pointed, startling everyone, "Look, there's Brenda! She was the top scorer on our team and one of our best players."

Sarah's dad kidded her, "Better than you?"

"Oh, yes," her mother confirmed, "'Sox' and Brenda were our big scorers. During our playoff games, Brenda was featured in the *Minneapolis Star*. The writer really thought she was terrific, and she was. After high school, Brenda played on the women's team at the University of Minnesota. I'm sure she'll be speaking at the program this afternoon."

It smelled like a county fair, with booths selling the anticipated mini-donuts and Le Sueur's trademark corn on the cob, dripping with butter. The fragrance of cotton candy and hot dogs was very appealing as Sarah's empty stomach reminded her that she hadn't gotten up in time to have breakfast.

"Now," Sarah's mother explained, "I want you all back at the car in an hour and we'll go to the school gymnasium for the reunion program. *And don't be late!"*

Sarah peeled off from the family and headed down the street toward the building that housed the historical society. Inside, there were posters and displays throughout the main floor. One of the women glanced at Sarah and said, "You must be Patti's daughter. You are the spitting image of her when she was in high school here. She was a good student and I enjoyed having her in my class. My name is Mildred."

Sarah was surprised and pleased to hear the nice compliment about her mother. She had never thought she resembled her mother, but it obviously was a good thing here.

"It's nice to meet you, Mildred. What do you remember about my mother?" Sarah asked.

"Patti was a good student and whatever she did, she always put a lot of effort into it. She was somewhat of a perfectionist. And she was a good basketball player. In the 1970s, girls were just starting to play sports and young women like your mother sometimes had to endure criticism that their skills weren't as good as the boys - at least in some people's views."

"Why would people criticize Mom and her team? If they had just started playing, they wouldn't have had the chance to play on teams, go to camps, or even see other girls and women play. That doesn't seem fair."

"It wasn't," Mildred agreed. "The girls wanted to play so badly, and when the schools finally started girls' teams, they would work very hard and were so excited to play another school. Then they would go onto the floor and hear boys whistling and making comments about how they looked in shorts. Some girls were embarrassed and left the team, but your mother stuck it out. We had some talks at pep fests, but it took far too long to get the students and community to support girls like they do now. I still feel badly when I think about how hard it was for girls in those early years. Today there would be consequences for bullying and sexual harassment."

"I never thought that my mother faced discrimination just because she wanted to play," Sarah realized. She thanked her mother's former teacher and began to examine the displays.

As she walked down the aisle, Sarah stopped at a poster that had early photos of the 1920 Le Sueur team. As she leaned down to look more closely at the photos, she could see the hint of a smile on the faces of the young women, with names still familiar in the community: Schwartz, Schneider, Hartung, Von Lehe.

A local reporter for the newspaper had researched the early 1920s photos and found a player, Blossom, who was living in Sleepy Eye. The article said that Blossom thought her team *"deserved remembering and the fun we had. Basketball was, for us, the highlight of the winter, practicing in the old city hall, going to other towns for games by car, train or bobsled, sometimes staying overnight and eating at a hotel. This was high adventure for us."*

Blossom went on, *"Our team defeated all the neighboring high school teams that we played and Mankato Teachers College. We finally lost to the girls of Hamline University (St. Paul)."* Blossom's daughter attended Sleepy Eye High School from 1943-47 and said, "I was envious of my mother's stories about traveling to other schools while we were restricted to intramurals."

"So," Sarah thought, "Mom's hometown had a girls' team during the early 1900s, and then their team was dropped too. That means that the Le Sueur girls didn't have a team, likely from the 1930s until the 1970s when they started playing again. How lucky for my mother that she was in high school in 1975 when the first playoffs were held."

Then a poster caught Sarah's attention. It was a headline from the local newspaper from 1975, "Le Sueur Girls Lose by a Basket." The article told of the 1974-75 season when the Minnesota State High School League announced it would sponsor a fall playoff championship for the schools playing girls basketball in the fall, and another playoff in the winter for schools playing in the winter.

Le Sueur had won the lead-up games and played, in their new uniforms, in the winter championship game against Holy Angels of Richfield at Bloomington Kennedy High School.

"That must have been quite exciting for Mom," Sarah thought, "After having to go through ridicule and lack of support, it must have felt really good to hear the cheers. Her team really did "win," even though they were two points short of the championship."

"Wow, where did that hour go? I've got to get back to the car." Sarah ran down the street, arriving just as the rest of the family was getting ready to pull out.

"Just in time," Sarah's dad smiled. "Sports are turning you into a punctual person after all."

As they drove up the hill toward the school, Sarah could tell that this was an exciting moment for her mother. She thought she almost saw a hint of tears in Patti's eyes as she caught sight of her former high school.

"Hey," Ben yelled excitedly, "there's Grandma Mary waiting for us." The day wouldn't be complete without sharing it with a special mom and grandmother.

Inside, the hallway leading to the gymnasium was filled with tables for the graduates to sign in and pick up their name badges in the school colors of royal blue and gold. Voices were bouncing off the walls and occasionally there was a squeal followed by cheers and hugs as classmates met after a long absence.

Adjacent to the registration tables was a table displaying a book written by a Le Sueur alumnus, Jeanne Foley. The cover caught Sarah's eye: a young woman in a basketball uniform was going in for a layup. The title of the book was *Shooting Two, a Story of Basketball and Friendship.*

Sounds interesting, Sarah thought, that's the first book I've seen about a high school girls basketball team and it says it was a Minnesota team in the 1980s with a goal to go to state. Well, our team has the same goal this year. Might as well dream big - I've got to read that book!

The book's author, Jeanne Foley, was happy to learn about Sarah and her interest in basketball. She happily autographed the book, "To Sarah, today's daughter of the game from an early daughter of the game. Good luck getting to State and winning it!"

Sarah thought, it must be fun to see a classmate and a friend or teammate after years have gone by. I wonder how it will feel when I go back for a class reunion.

Chairs were set on the playing floor of the gymnasium and they were soon filled with the graduates who would appreciate the back support. Before long, the bleachers were also filled and they began bringing in more chairs. The school band was playing over in the corner and the space became one big sound of happiness.

The microphone on the podium crackled as the superintendent moved it higher. She was smiling broadly at the audience, clearly pleased with the turnout for the event.

"Welcome to the Le Sueur All-School Reunion. Welcome back

to *your school!*"

The crowd all cheered and some stomped their feet on the bleachers, just as they had enjoyed doing at basketball games. The band started the school song, "Down the Field." The cheerleaders ran onto the floor and led the singing. A tissue or two soon appeared here and there in the audience.

The superintendent thanked the planning committee for their hard work, and all members stood for their moment of recognition, receiving a big round of applause.

The mayor came to the podium and welcomed everyone back to their school and their town with the comment, "When you come from Le Sueur, *you can come home again.* Welcome back!" And more tissues were observed dabbing at eyes of the former students.

As the program continued, Sarah looked over the crowd of faces, young and old, all smiling and enjoying the event. Sarah thought, in a small town, many of my mother's family and friends stayed here to live. I wondered what would have happened if my mother had stayed here instead of moving away? The thought gave her pause.

A big screen was lowered from the ceiling and the lights dimmed. A video had been created by the planning committee to present a history of the community and its school. When pictures of students and teachers flashed on the screen, there was laughter and some muffled moans as younger faces reflected hair styles and clothing of earlier years. When a segment featured photos of those who had died, some in service to their country, a respectful silence filled the gymnasium.

One segment of the video covered the school's athletic history for boys and girls. The opening for girls athletics featured a picture of the 1920s girls basketball team, and then skipped to the return of girls' sports in the 1970s.

The video then focused on the team that had played in the first playoffs for girls basketball. There was a big photo of her mother's team and Sarah picked out her mother's smile. She felt a swelling of pride thinking, *That's my mother. She was an athlete too.*

Sarah stretched. It was getting late and she had been lying in the same position for a long time, reviewing her mother's return to her roots in Le Sueur.

It's funny, Sarah thought, how many important things you can miss, just by not paying attention. When I was at the reunion, I didn't know that within weeks I'd be researching the link between the generations of my family's women. And that link was their love of basketball.

Look at the beginning with Great-Great-Grandma Clara playing in the first game of basketball at Carleton College in 1892. Then in the 1920s, her daughter, Great-Grandma Ruby, had such fun playing, but her team was the last one to play at Sherburn for decades. After that, there were no teams for my Grandma Mary or any of my family's women until my mother played on a team again in the 1970s.

Sarah mumbled her thoughts aloud, "And now, here I am, able to play any sport that I choose. I'm glad I'm the last link in the chain, *for now.*"

Her sister in the next bed pulled her pillow over her head and mumbled, "Sarah, please be quiet and go... to... sleep."

★ ★

13

HEROES, WHAT CAN WE LEARN FROM YOU?

"Heroes appear like a friend, to clear a path or light the flame. As time goes, you find you depend on your heroes to show you the way."   *~ Ann Reed, songwriter*

"**M**om, who is your hero?"

Sarah was sitting on a stool at the kitchen counter, her physics book open in front of her. Her mother was stirring with a wooden spoon in one of her Grandma Ruby's favorite bowls.

"Why do you ask, honey?" she said, continuing with the two-minute stir that the cake batter required. Sarah knew it was her dad's favorite white cake and her mom's seven-minute frosting was "to die for."

"One of these days, before I'm off to college," Sarah said, "I should get a lesson in how to make those frosting peaks stand up like yours do." Her mother's look said it might take more than one lesson.

"Well," Sarah continued, resting her chin in her hands, "we had a speaker in our history class today. His name was Ed and he was a Marine Raider, the first to hit the beach in a WWII invasion in the Pacific. His Raiders landed at Guadalcanal, Guam, and Okinawa.

He said it was the most frightening thing he's ever experienced but he knew it was important that they do their job so the next wave of Marines could get ashore. When our teacher introduced him, she read us a quote, 'Heroes aren't free from fear - they're just so focused on a worthy goal that they feel they can't turn back.'"

Sarah's mother nodded in agreement, "Yes, as we sing before each of your games, we are the *'land of the free'* because we are the *'home of the brave.'*"

"Yeah, that's so true." Sarah continued on, "We learned about women in the Civil War who passed themselves off as men so they could be soldiers and contribute too. At least now women can serve our country with their own identity. Why is it that women have to go through so many struggles to do what men can do?"

Patti shook her head, "I wish I had a simple answer for you. It's a struggle here and worldwide where women are still restricted from living full lives and are treated in ways that are unbelievable today. But the good news is, when people start saying they won't accept it anymore, change happens. The bad news is, it comes too late for so many."

"Well," Sarah said, "the more I learn, the more questions I have. History just keeps getting filled with war after war after war, here and throughout the world."

"Yes, wars are so horrific, and our country has been in far too many. We have to learn from our history so we don't keep repeating the same mistakes. One of the worst kinds of war is a civil war when the conflict is between people in the same country, when it is region against region, state against state, family against family. Look at the Civil War; it confronted the terrible practice of slavery right in our very own country. And yet, over a hundred and fifty years later, people are still treated unfairly because of their race, gender, and religion."

Patti pointed her spoon at Sarah, "We must find a solution. I hope your generation can continue the progress we've made so far and get the job done."

As Sarah contemplated her mother's hope for a better world, Patti added, "We know that there are times when we must defend ourselves when others intend to do harm to us individually or to our country. In your young life, you have experienced the horror of the attack on the World Trade Center in New York on 9/11."

Patti vigorously resumed her stirring, "In times of crisis, people respond in amazing ways. Think of those who responded to the attack on the World Trade Center, the Pentagon and on United Flight #93 headed toward Washington, D.C. There were the firefighters who rushed into burning buildings, the first responders, all ordinary people doing heroic things to help others. We must always honor those who died and help those who suffer health issues from their actions, trying to help others."

She sighed as the emotions of those days came back in waves, and turned to the dishes in the sink. "I am in awe of one of our own Minnesotans, Tom Burnett, on United #93, who, as you know, Sarah, was part of the group that knew they had to prevent their plane from reaching Washington, D.C., because it was likely aimed at the Capitol. And his words, 'Let's roll' should guide us in our own lives. Each of us must be willing to *stand up* for what we believe to be right."

"Yes, or *sit down* as Rosa Parks did," Sarah suggested, "when she refused to give up her seat because a person of another race wanted her to move. Sometimes it means that the first person to do the right thing is standing, or sitting, in our shoes."

"Absolutely, I don't understand how people can say they aren't interested in history. How else can we avoid the mistakes of the past?" Patti's frustration was getting her baking dishes washed in record time.

Sarah added, "And we must honor those who gave so much for our freedom. Ed said, *"There is nothing 'free' about 'freedom.'* He said he was on a recent Honor Flight with ninety-nine other WWII vets to Washington, D.C., and they visited their WWII Memorial and many other war memorials. He said it was a sad, but wonderful experience to see veterans and their families from all over the country gathering at the memorial built to honor those who gave so much for our freedom."

Her mother's face brightened, "You know, traveling to Washington, D.C., would be a good trip for our family. I hope we can all go someday and see the memorials, the Capitol, and the White House. That would be a truly great experience for us to share together."

Sarah agreed.

"So, who is your hero, Mom?" Sarah persisted.

"Well, I have more than one. In fact, I have many. They come from family and friends, and others come from reading about their lives and what they did at an important time in our history."

"I remember," Sarah said, "during one of our family vacations when we were younger, we drove across the West to Yellowstone National Park. I bet that was fun with all of us kids asking 'are we there yet?'"

Her mother laughed, "There were times when your dad and I did suggest that perhaps one or more of you might be ready for a timeout and lose some souvenir-buying privileges."

"What I remember most," Sarah continued, "was when we

were driving across Wyoming and you were reading the map and happened to mention that we were driving alongside the Wind River and Dad said, 'Well, we are on the Wind River Reservation.' And you just jumped and almost yelled, *Wind River Reservation? That's where Sacajawea is buried!'* Tour books and maps went flying and you said, 'She is buried in a cemetery outside Ft. Washakie, Wyoming, and that's only twenty miles from here!' Dad made a left turn on the next road and off we went to find her. I figured she was one of your heroes."

"Oh, yes, yes, she certainly was," her mother sighed. "I enjoy reading stories about women who did amazing things, though earlier history books didn't include much about women. Then I discovered a great book about Sacajawea's historic trip as guide for Lewis and Clark on their Tour of Discovery for President Jefferson. She clearly saved the expedition several times. One time they were met by a large group of Indians coming out to meet them, and she recognized one as her brother whom she hadn't seen since she was kidnapped from her tribe as a child. And now he was the chief. So, because of her, the expedition was able to get needed horses and supplies. Imagine a trip like that through unbelievable terrain, rivers and mountains, and all the while caring for a small baby. That made our trip with you kids a real 'lark!'" Patti looked across the counter and smiled at her daughter.

"I think, Sarah," she continued thoughtfully, "Sacajawea became an important hero to me because she persevered through so much adversity during her entire life. Her name meant, 'one who pushes the boat away from land.'

"After their return, Sacajawea took her child and left her abusive husband. She traveled throughout the west, living among several

Indian tribes. Sacajawea became known as a very wise woman; her people gave her the name '*Porivo*,' which means *chief*, highly unusual for a woman to achieve that title."

Sarah perked up, "Think of how it would feel, Mom, to hear 'Hail to the Chief' and see a woman being sworn in as our president. She would be our Porivo."

"That would be great, Sarah," her mother agreed, "and I hope we both live to experience that day."

"So how did Sacajawea end up at the Wind River Reservation in Wyoming?" Sarah pursued her mother's story.

"She wanted to return to her Shoshone people where she could help them adjust to the huge changes in their lives as a result of living on a reservation. Unfortunately, their previous way of life had disappeared, along with the buffalo. The conflict over losing their land is a tragic chapter in our history, a true trail of tears.

"There are differing accounts of her life; some say she died shortly after returning from the expedition, but others say it was her sister who died and that Sacajawea lived to be somewhere around 100 years of age and is buried on the Wind River Reservation."

"How do you know this history so well, Mom?" Sarah asked.

Her mother smiled warmly at the opportunity to share her memories with her daughter, "Because, Sarah, I was so lucky to meet Sacajawea's great-great-granddaughter, Esther Burnett Horne, who lived in northern Minnesota. Again, I was in the right place at the right time. Years ago, we had a meeting near Mahnomen and Esther was the speaker to our group. She shared the life of her ancestor and I was *mesmerized*. I managed to get a seat next to her for dinner, and you know how it can happen, we just bonded. It was the only time that I was with her in person. Over the years, we wrote back and forth and Esther sent me a family history of Sacajawea's life after the expedition. She signed it to 'her friend' - *me.*

"She described how she and members of her family traced Sacajawea's life by interviewing people who knew her during those years. Esther said that her grandfather, Finn Burnett, was employed as a U.S. Government farmer and he lived on the Wind River Reservation for more than a quarter of a century. So, Mr. Burnett worked with Sacajawea for the last decade of her life and spoke with her many times about her journey with Lewis and Clark to the Pacific Ocean.

"Esther has a copy of the letter written by Reverend John Roberts, Episcopal Clergyman for the Shoshone Indian Mission, Wind River, Wyoming. In his letter, he wrote, 'I firmly believe that the old Shoshone Indian woman whom I buried in the Shoshone Agency Cemetery in Wyoming is the true Sacajawea, guide of the Lewis and Clark Expedition.'

"Oh," Patti continued, "and I have a copy of a book about Esther and Sacajawea's lives that you should read. It's called, *Essie's Story, The Life and Legacy of a Shoshone Teacher.* Her stories and those of her great-great-grandmother are in it."

"So, you only met her in person *once?*" Sarah was intrigued with the thought that a friendship could develop from only one meeting.

"Yes, I regret not driving up to see her again, and that's a lesson, Sarah. Don't wait to see people as you may wait a little too long. Esther died just before the dollar coin honoring Sacajawea was issued in 2000, but she knew her ancestor was being honored by her country. It made her so happy. She told me that the Shoshone do not have a word for 'goodbye.' They say, *'gigawabamin menawah,'* It means, *'I'll see you again, my friend.'*"

Sarah asked, "I remember that we found that cemetery outside Ft. Washakie, and there was this tall bronze statue of Sacajawea on a cement platform with big plaques describing her life. Wasn't she holding a sand dollar in her hand?"

"Yes, wasn't that wonderful? I'm so happy you remember it. The artist used the sand dollar to symbolically connect Sacajawea with her amazing expedition to the Pacific Ocean."

"Well," Sarah said, "the other thing I remember was that you had a Sacajawea dollar coin with you. I watched you put that beautiful gold coin by the left heel of the statue, and then you stacked little rocks on top of it."

Her mother's smile carried a hint of sadness and her eyes were moist, "Yes, I built a little cairn to cover the coin and whispered, 'this is for you, Esther, *gigawabamin menawah.'*

Patti brushed a tear away and quickly added, "And I hope that someday a little girl comes to see her hero, Sacajawea, and discovers that coin and just feels that it was left for her to take home as a symbol that she should live her life, strong and brave, as Sacajawea did."

Now, it was Sarah's turn to have tears in her eyes. She stood and hugged her mother.

Her mother quickly wiped her eyes and let the cake batter settle while she greased a cake pan, then quickly poured the batter into the pan and shoved it into the hot oven.

"Who else is on your hero list?" Sarah asked. They both needed a new direction to recoup their emotions.

"Sometimes, Sarah, you don't need to look far to find a hero. Sometimes they are right within your own family. My parents lived most of their lives on the farm where I grew up." She raised her eyebrows at Sarah, "Do you remember being on the farm when you were small?"

"Oh yes," Sarah smiled at the memories, "it was so much fun to go into the barn and watch Grandpa Earl milk the cows, those beautiful black and white Holsteins. Sometimes he'd squirt milk right from the cow's teat into the mouth of a cat sitting by his foot. And the little piglets. You know that was the first time I ever saw anything being born. It was really something. Grandpa said my eyes got pretty big."

"I hadn't heard that story before," her mom chuckled. "The farm is a good place to get some lessons on life and death. Farm kids experience reality and not the misleading make-believe from a television or video game."

Patti pulled up a stool and poured herself a cup of coffee. Sarah sipped on her milk and waited for her mother to continue her story.

"My parents were what some might call 'unsung heroes,'" she began, "people who give and give, for their children, their church, and their community, as well as for others far outside their usual circles. The whole world is better when people simply step up and do the right thing."

She wiped a strand of hair that had fallen in front of her eyes and looked out over their home. "You know, Sarah, our farm home was very different from what you know. When my grandparents moved there, they had no running water, no indoor bathroom, no electricity. Kerosene and oil lamps or candles lit the rooms at night. Imagine your life under those conditions."

Sarah's thoughts were stuck on the images of running outside to an outhouse or pulling a chamber pot from under the bed in the middle of the night. They were vivid enough to make her shudder.

"But people talk about the 'good old days,' she asked, "how could they have been so good?"

"Well, in many ways they were good times. Neighbors helped each other whenever they were asked, or they just showed up to help, especially if word got around that someone was sick or had been hurt in a farm accident. It also might be loaning a neighbor a farm wagon or gathering everyone to put up a new barn. Grandma Ruby used to say that women would 'just know' when a neighbor needed her to drop by for a cup of coffee and a shoulder to lean on.

"And everyone in the family had their responsibilities, whether it be gathering eggs, or hoeing the garden or picking berries. But sometimes, it was very hard - working in the fields with horses pulling the plow, shocking oat bundles, cleaning out the barn 'by hand.'

"And a farm woman had to do everything inside and outside. My mother had big gardens with flowers and vegetables, she was the Sunday School Superintendent and member of the church 'circles.' And I remember the church suppers where her desserts were always the first pans emptied.

"Mom used to tell about times when she had a baby in a crib and Dad would stick his head in the screen door and yell, 'I need you driving on the hay rope.' Mom said she would put the baby in a basket and run outside to drive either horses or a tractor attached to a big long rope that pulled the hay up and into the haymow. Your Great-Grandpa Moses was up there 'mowing hay.' In those days he was in his eighties but still had his loud Irish voice. He would yell, 'Go, go, go... *whoa!*' If Mom didn't hear the words change from 'go' to 'whoa,' Moses' voice, Irish brogue and all, would come rolling out of the open haymow door, way up to the end of the hay rope.

"Mom always told me how her dog, Skippy, would sit 'on guard' by the baby basket she had placed in the shade of an apple tree.

Can't you just see that picture? That was me in the basket, by the way. My older sister was with Dad, pretending to pull on the hay rope and riding on the tractors. She always loved to be outside with the machines. I believe she was harder to catch to teach her how to bake a cake than you are."

They both laughed.

Her mother sighed, and then had another thought to add, "And many days, Dad would tell Mom that his cousin and brother would be there for dinner. On the farm, dinner was the meal at noon and real food was expected on the table. She said she always had a white cake ready to stir up and throw in the oven. It was Dad's favorite cake."

Sarah shook her head in appreciation, "And to me as a grandchild coming to visit or sometimes stay overnight, the farm was a wondrous place. I'll never forget the smells that would come upstairs in the morning - pancakes, bacon and eggs, nothing could have smelled better." Sarah's mouth was salivating at the memories.

At that moment, Ben came running in the door, "Mom, you haven't forgotten, have you? I have soccer practice in half an hour."

"I'm ready when you are," she nodded at Ben. His schedule was pretty frenetic these days and when added to her other responsibilities, it made for one busy mother and vehicle. The calendar on the refrigerator was full of notes and reminders, one of which was to talk to him about the amount of time he was playing those war games.

"Well, Sarah, I'm glad you have such wonderful memories," her mother continued. "That's what makes family, parents and grandparents like ours so special. They just did what they believed to be the right thing to do. When Mom's egg money had to go for school clothes for us kids, that's what she did. And I always thought Dad must be rich because he always had a couple dollars in his billfold to take us to a Saturday night movie and then a stop at The Dairy for ice cream."

Sarah was thinking about the heroes that her mother had talked about.

"You know, Mom, I'm beginning to understand how heroes can be found everywhere. They may be exceptionally brave people, like those who volunteer to serve our country, or firefighters and first responders who are there in emergencies. They might be a person who pulls someone out of a burning car, or jumps into a lake to rescue someone and then remembers they don't swim well. They are ordinary people doing extraordinary things for someone else."

Her mother stood up and went to the kitchen counter where she had taped a piece of paper. "I found this one day and it helps me. Maybe it will help you too. It says, *'If it is to be, it's up to me.'*"

"I like that," Sarah tucked it into her memory bank. "You always tell us that we have to accept responsibility for what we do. I will remember that."

"I almost forgot," her mother reached over and picked up a CD from the counter. "I was at a meeting and this amazing woman sang songs she had composed. Her name is Ann Reed and she lives in the Twin Cities area. She sang a song called "Heroes" and between her beautiful voice and the words, we were all in tears. Here, this is for you."

Sarah accepted the gift and looked at her mother, "This is so cool, Mom, because she sang at National Girls and Women in Sports Day at the Capitol and I haven't had time to tell you about that. Imagine, *you and I like the same music!*"

They both laughed again. It felt good.

Patti smiled at her daughter as the young woman struggled to absorb the complex issues that will be in her life as an adult. Maybe, Patti thought, it might be one of my children, perhaps this daughter, who will contribute to resolving issues facing the world. We don't know what path our children may choose. We only hope we will be there.

Suddenly, the fragrance of a baking cake reached them and Sarah's mother raced to the oven, pulling out the cake that, fortunately, was a beautiful golden brown.

"Lucky for us that our noses were on alert or your dad wouldn't have his favorite cake tonight."

Sarah agreed and thought, I'm in the presence of my biggest hero - the rock of our family and a breast cancer survivor. She's standing in front of me, with a warm cake pan in her hands.

14

PIONEERS PLAY AGAIN

"You want me to make *what?*" Her aunt wasn't sure that she had heard Sarah correctly. "You want me to make *twelve* middy blouses and bloomers? By *when?*"

Sarah laughed and grabbed her aunt's hands, "Please, please, Aunt Betty, you can sew like a whiz. Look at all the different kinds of aprons you make and the programs you do to help people understand how aprons changed as the lives of women changed throughout history. Well, I want to help people understand how basketball, and basketball uniforms, changed the lives of young women too."

"Here's the deal," Sarah hurried on. "Next week there is a big fund-raiser at school. We think it is a great opportunity to play a game dressed like the pioneer players in middy blouses and bloomers and playing with their rules. So, could you *please* make the uniforms for us?"

Well," Aunt Betty carefully considered her options, "I can make two or three sizes with a little extra in the bloomers, and the middy blouse is a pullover so that should fit anyone on your team. Actually, it sounds like fun. I have some material left from my apron projects and can make one team in blue and gold. How does that sound?"

"That would be fun. And maybe you could make the 'home' team in black and white like Great-Grandma Ruby's team?"

Aunt Betty smiled indulgently at her niece. It was hard to refuse such a charismatic young woman, and she did have some friends who sewed. Anita, Chris and Margo have daughters on the team and they did owe a return favor for her help at their bazaar last year.

"Okay, I'm in." She smiled as she watched Sarah rush out the door. As the door closed behind her, Aunt Betty said to herself, "That young woman will go far with her persuasive 'way with people.'"

For the next few days, after regular basketball practice was over, the team practiced the two-court and three-court rules, which Sarah knew were the most popular rules for girls basketball in the '20s and '30s.

Coach Johnson was very supportive and enthusiastic about Sarah's plan. She had called Sarah over during practice yesterday.

"Sarah, a couple of my friends were All-American Redheads. They would like to support your event."

Sarah grinned, "We met one of the Redheads in St. Paul, remember? That would be great!"

"Well," the coach paused, "I'd better give the team some background and make some plans." She gave her whistle three short blasts, "Gather 'round, women."

The players were very happy to have a break and quickly sat on the floor as the coach began her explanation.

"I want to tell you a bit about teams like the All-American Redheads," Coach Johnson began. "Teams like the Redheads were professional women's basketball teams that were popular from the 1930s to the 1980s. They provided an outlet for women who wanted to play basketball. Usually they played 'men's rules' at fundraisers. They entertained the crowds with their dribbling and shooting skills, and other fun activities."

"Kind of like the Globetrotters, but women players?" one of the players ventured.

"That's exactly right. They had colorful uniforms and warm-ups covered with stars and stripes. The All-American Redhead players all had to put red coloring in their hair. Sometimes the color ran and there would be red streaks running down their faces."

The team grimaced at the thought of hair dye running down their faces.

"Any questions?" Coach Johnson inquired.

"Did people come to see them play?" Yolanda asked.

"They sure did," the coach smiled. "They were good players and set attendance records in arenas all over the country. I know there were at least six Minnesota women who played with the Redheads. And another woman in Minnesota, "Peps" Neuman of Eden Valley, played with the Texas Cowgirls and other teams."

"Okay, now," Coach Johnson was ready to get down to business. "Let's talk about the Pioneer All-Star Game that Sarah is organizing. Three of my friends were All-American Redheads and they have volunteered to help."

"Sarah," the coach suggested, "one former Redhead is Lynette Sjoquist. She is the color commentator for the University of Minnesota women's basketball games, so she would be great to do introductions and a play-by-play for the spectators. She has a great sense of humor and would help the audience understand and appreciate the early rules."

"Wow," Sarah said to Jordan, "she was that great emcee at National Girls and Women in Sports Day. She will really add a lot to our game."

Coach Johnson could see that the team needed to catch the activity bus, so she said to Sarah, "I'll talk with you later about the other Redheads and how they can be involved."

And off they went, flying high with plans soaring in their heads.

"Sarah," her mother called as she came in the door, "you have several messages on the phone from people wanting to help with your Pioneer All-Star Game. It sounds like you are having a great response from everyone."

"Mom," Sarah picked up the telephone, "you wouldn't believe it all. The team has made posters and posted them around the stores. The big home supply store has a couple old-style wood burning stoves that they said we could use, and they even offered to bring them to the school for the game. They'll go in the corners to 'keep the place warm' during the game. And Dad and Yolanda's dad volunteered to stand around them to protect the players in case someone heads toward the 'hot' stove."

Gary walked into the room and caught the last sentence. "I did volunteer, didn't I?" he teased. "One of my cousins collects old cars. Wally said he'd bring up the Model T and Model A and park it in front of the door to the gym. And he's known for driving anywhere, across lawns and yards, just to get a laugh. So better warn somebody that those cars will likely be right in FRONT of the gymnasium door."

Patti came rushing back into the kitchen, "Sarah, I almost

forgot! I took one of the calls today that came for you, and you'll never guess who it was! Her name is Vicki, and she is a great official. Not only that, she reminded me that she was the official at our winter championship game at Bloomington Kennedy back in 1975. It's a small world. She said that she and Deb, another veteran state tournament official, will be happy to volunteer to be officials for your game. And Vicki said she could get one of the old larger balls from their historical society. It has leather laces and everything."

Sarah thought, "Isn't it interesting how our Pioneer All-Star Game is bringing people together to support us, just like they did for those 'daughters of the game' almost a century ago."

"Mom, I need your ideas," Sarah said, noticing that her mother seemed to enjoy being asked for help.

"I thought that I could use the book, *Daughters of the Game*, to find some outstanding players from schools scattered all over the state. That would help people understand that there were girls high school teams in towns all over Minnesota."

Her mother agreed, "I think that would be a great idea."

"Well," Sarah said, "There is information on a number of players who were good and others who had such interesting stories in the book. We could have two teams of six players for each half. That way we can recognize twenty-four great players from around the state. The program could be set up like a team roster with a short bio on each player and their school."

"You are really getting into this report, Sarah," her mother said. "You are learning a great deal and looks like our community will too. Your teacher should be impressed with the time and effort you are putting in."

"Funny," Sarah said, "I've been having so much fun learning about young women that were my age and what it was like to live and play in those days, I've almost forgotten that this is schoolwork."

As Sarah looked through the book, *Daughters of the Game*, she found many interesting players and it was hard to select only twenty-four, especially to represent the fifty years and the areas of the state.

She decided, I will tell people that there are even more stories and interesting players in the *Daughters of the Game* book. I'll put the website for the book, www.daughtersofthegame.com., in the program and also tell them that there will soon be a copy in our public library.

Sarah ran downstairs where her parents were sitting at the kitchen table.

"Would you look these over and tell me what you think? And please look for any typos. I don't want anything wrong in my copy."

Her dad began to read the copy, and his eyebrows shot up. "Wow, some of these players could really score. Some of their town's newspapers really gave them good coverage too. We'll have to show this to our sports reporter. Maybe the paper would do an article on these players."

He looked at his wife, "Remember when you started playing basketball in the early 1970s? Girls' sports didn't receive much coverage. Of course, after your team made it to the big winter season championship game in 1975, that caught a lot of attention. Jim Klobuchar of the *Minneapolis Star* wrote a great article. He was a respected writer so when he wrote a positive article on girls' sports, people listened. And now his daughter is one of our state's U.S. senators. He must be one proud father."

He looked at Sarah, "Like me," he added with a smile.

Two days before the game, Sarah gave a deep sigh, "There, Yolanda, the program is done. Now to get it printed. The newspaper said we could bring it down and they would make copies for free. Everyone is being so nice."

Yolanda added, "And the bakery is bringing cookies and stuff for after the event and one of the grocery stores offered soda pop."

Sarah smiled, "This is just like they used to do in those 'old days' when everyone would stay for a party after the game."

One day before 'game time,' Sarah went down to the newspaper office to pick up her programs for the big night ahead. She looked at the cover that featured two players in middies and bloomers jumping for a ball and the big heading, "Pioneer All-Stars Play Ball Tonight." And below, it said, "Everyone Welcome!"

"Awesome," Sarah said to the printer. "Thank you so much. It is just terrific!" The woman smiled and said, "Well, we are all coming too. 'Wouldn't miss this fun!"

As Sarah opened the program, she noticed that it had taken four pages to get all of the information inside.

As she began to read the information, she thought wistfully, wouldn't it be fun if the women could see their stories and the game we're going to play tomorrow?

"Pioneer All-Stars"

"These players are representative of the thousands of young women in Minnesota who played basketball between 1892 and 1942. They represented their schools and communities, proudly wearing their team uniforms. They traveled by sleigh, bobsleds, train, cars and by bus, in all kinds of Minnesota winter weather. They played in town halls, dance halls, gyms and armories, frequently staying overnight with the host team families. They played with spectators like you cheering for them. They played in tournaments and received school letters and awards. Above all, they taught us how important it is for young women to have the opportunity to play."

Hattie Van Buren, 1901, Minneapolis Central. The *Minneapolis Tribune*, Feb. 3, 1901, featured a photo of the Central High School girls basketball team. The article praised the new game of 'basket ball' and said it is an excellent game for girls, requiring 'agility and wits…an excellent physical developer. It makes the girls straight and strong, gives them an independent bearing, a good color and confidence in themselves that a girl or woman who has not full control of her body cannot feel.' Hattie was described as 'one of the most enthusiastic players in the city and is an ardent advocate of the game as an exercise for school girls.'

Lillian Graupmann, 1909, St. Paul Central. Lillian began playing basketball in 1896 in the attic gymnasium of the school. Competition against other schools began in 1901-02. In 1909, Lillian and Central won the Twin Cities Championship against St. Paul Humboldt.

Annabel Hermes, 1909, Grand Rapids. In 1909, the team was the 'High School Champions of Northern Minnesota.' The yearbook reported that after their second game, there was 'dancing in the hall' with the team tearing themselves away in time to catch the midnight train home from Floodwood, singing, '*Lo, The Conquering Heroines Come.*'

Jeannette Page Wright, 1911, Crookston. Her parents both died young and Jeannette attended high school in Crookston. She later joined the army in WWI as a nurse and nearly died during the flu epidemic of 1918-1919. When her sons enlisted in WWII, so did Jeannette and she served in the Women's Army Corps at a tank training school. Her granddaughter played on the St. Charles basketball team in 1982. They were both captains of their teams.

Ruth DeLaHunt Rawn, 1913, Willmar. After arriving at a game, they learned Howard Lake had played boys rules only and Willmar had played girls rules. So they compromised and played the girls rules in the first half and the boys rules in the second half. Willmar won, 26-13. Ruth said, 'The best, smartest girls played basketball. It was the thing to do.'

Frieda Kottke Coleman, 1919, Owatonna. Frieda's team challenged area teams to a 'winner-take-all' tournament, defeating New Ulm 24-18 in the old Owatonna Armory. The newspaper declared, 'Girls' team best in state in 1919.'

Anna Tok, 1922-1923, Greenway. Her team won the Range Championship against their perennial rival, Proctor. Their game with Cloquet for the Northwest Championship was played before the largest crowd ever assembled in the Greenway gymnasium to witness a basketball game. Games were followed by a rousing party.

Irma Nelson Post, 1920-1925, Deer Creek. Irma played the two-court game for five years. The girls and boys team frequently traveled in a truck filled with straw and a tarp over the top when it was cold. Irma recalled a school with a wooden beam just off center of the hall. The other team set up plays to try to get them to run into that beam. Irma recalls a game cheer, 'Vas ist dis, Vas ist das, Deer Creek, Das ist vas.'

Adalyn Eckstrom Wright, 1917-25, Cokato. Adalyn's teams

played in the town hall where they also held chicken shows. Sometimes the floor was still covered with chicken feathers, straw and other debris. The team changed into their uniforms in the coal room.

Dorothy Iversen Viker, 1925, Hayfield. Dorothy's teams were called 'Hayfield's Pride and Joy.' Their uniforms were gold sateen middy blouses and bloomers with purple trim, knee high wool socks, and beanies which they wore to games. They won 'best-dressed team' at a tournament.

Helen Johnson, 1923-1925, Ellendale. Helen scored 290 of her team's 504 points during her senior year and was featured in the rotogravure (picture) section of the *St. Paul Sunday Pioneer Press*. In one game, Helen made a record score of 32 baskets for a total of 64 points. Her team won an invitational tournament, bringing home a loving cup and individual medals.

Marie Weibeler Keeler, 1922-1926, Belle Plaine. Her teams played the three-court game and traveled frequently by bobsled, and the Minneapolis-St. Louis train, staying overnight in hotels like the Schumacher Hotel in New Prague. Marie played basketball over her mother's objections that she was making a spectacle of herself wearing bloomers in front of the fans. Marie was the mother of 11 children, 25 grandchildren and 35 great-grandchildren. She celebrated her 101st birthday, always saying that her life should contradict the myth that participation in sports would be negative to the health of female athletes.

Ruth McCarron Dahlke, 1924-1927, Sherburn. Ruth's team won the Sherburn Invitational Tournament in 1925, winning a big silver ball trophy and silver rings for each player. Ruth lost her ring while swimming. On the way to one game, their car went into the ditch and broke the windshield. They had to ride to and from the game with the broken windshield. It was ten degrees below zero.

Kay Nolan Wetter, 1928, Brainerd. Kay frequently drove the family car to games through mud and roads full of deep ruts. Their games drew crowds but the local newspaper said that 'girls were to act like ladies, not ruffians chasing basketballs with their bare knees teasing the minds of young men. How uncouth.'

Luella Bandelin Anderson, 1924-28, Arlington. Luella and sister Carolyn's teams played in the community hall with spectators sitting in chairs around the sidelines and fathers positioned to protect them from falling into the hot stoves in the corners. In the late 1990s, they were featured on KARE-11 TV and among the pioneers honored at the 1999 MSHSL State Girls Basketball Tournament.

Ruth Olson Kleven, 1925-1929, Milan. In 1927, the team had new uniforms with shorts replacing the bloomers. There was a big crowd ringing the court. Ruth's mother and another mother sat in the stands with their heads down at the sight of their daughters' bare knees. Ruth had four generations of basketball players in her family, including two great-granddaughters whom she watched playing against each other. Ruth and her best friend Edith shared their last years living in the same assisted living facility and enjoying their stories in the book, *Daughters of the Game*.

Aileen Just Luther, 1923-1930, Rapidan. Aileen was known as the 'Sensational Point-A-Minute Just,' scoring more points than the minutes she played. In one season, the team scored 614 points compared to a total of 224 points by opposing teams. Her team won 40 games out of 43 games in 3 years. Her picture was sent to newspapers in Chicago, Massachusetts and Denver, among others. The captions read, 'Aileen Just, Outstanding Girl Basketball player in the State of Minnesota.' Aileen is the player featured on the cover of the *Daughters of the Game* book.

Mabel Thompson Erickson, 1927-1931, Mabel. Mabel from Mabel played running center for their three-court games. At 5'1", she was quick to get the ball from her jumping center. Boys and girls' teams traveled by bus and played doubleheaders in gymnasiums. In 1929, their team was the first team in the area to change from bloomers to shorts. She said the shorts made her feel so 'free.' Mabel received chenille school letters for playing basketball and kept them her entire life.

Blanche Line Kingsley, 1926-1931, Cromwell. Blanche's team won the 1926 district tournament, the 1927 Carlton County Championship, the sub-district championship, and the District #5 championship, which included over 20 schools. They also won the championship of 14 counties from Proctor to Brainerd and from Hibbing to Minneapolis. When the school announced in 1932 that the team would be dropped, the girls marched into the school administrator's office and demanded that they be allowed to play. And they did, but the team was dropped the following year.

Irma Malone Foley, 1928-1932, Montgomery. Irma was known for her tenacity and enthusiasm. She played a hard driving two-court basketball game, noted for feeding the ball to her teammates under the basket. Irma played on the 1930 team that won the District Girls Basketball Championship, taking home a beautiful conference trophy. The traveling trophy is now in the New Prague trophy case.

Florence Urdahl, 1929-1931, Litchfield. Captain. The team compiled a record of 73 wins over six years of play, ending in 1932. The *Litchfield Independent-Review* reported that the team held the nation's high school girls' team record in consecutive games won.

Marie Tommerson Berg, 1929-1934, Grand Meadow.

Marie's teams played the two-court game for ten years. From 1929-1939, the teams amassed an unsurpassed record of 94 wins and 0 losses. In the fall of 1939, the girls returned to school to be told by their superintendent that there would be no more girls basketball teams. Grand Meadow was among the last of the hundreds of teams dropped between 1925 and 1942, leaving a huge void for girls who wanted to play.

Thea Sletkolen Stay, 1931-1935, Montevideo. Thea scored 15 more points than all of Montevideo's opponents. She was tall and opponents could not come up with a defense to stop her. Thea was called by the local newspaper, 'A one-girl scoring machine.'

Saima Saari Savela, 1933-1937, Toivola. The Toivola team was the St. Louis County Champs in 1937. Saima said her team didn't like the two-court game and played full-court whenever they could. In 1939, the team was notified that their team would be dropped. Saima said that they were told the game was too strenuous for girls, which didn't make sense to the girls who worked hard on their farms.

Let the Game Begin!

It was the day of the game.

Fortunately for Sarah, Coach Johnson had left some time at the end of practice for the past week to go over the rules. It was hard for her teammates to remember that they could only bounce the ball once or twice and they had to stay in one section. But, as they became familiar with the changes, the ball was being whipped from section to section very quickly and the ball frequently dropped into the basket, "all air." There were smiles and "high fives" as they found, to their surprise, *that this game was fun!*

Yolanda said, "*Whooo-wouldda-thought?*" And they all laughed.

They were ready.

Coach Johnson assured Sarah that she would take care of marking the floor for the two types of games. She had some special tape and had already planned to get help from the student managers to get the floor marked right after school. Coaches have a knack for knowing when a player needs their support.

At dinner, Sarah's mother noticed, "Sarah, you aren't eating much tonight? Are you nervous about the game?"

"'Guess so," Sarah said, "a lot could go wrong. People could laugh or embarrass us if they think it is a silly game. I would feel terrible if we didn't play as well as the early players did and show the fans what a good, exciting game it was. You know how it is when something is different. People up in the stands can be pretty tough."

Patti patted her daughter's arm, "You've done all you can to prepare, Sarah, and I think it will go just fine. Just go enjoy yourself."

Sarah hoped her mother was right.

The night arrived and it looked as though everyone in town was there. As the girls put on their middy blouses and bloomers, they pulled their hair back into pony tails and some were swept up into a bun with ribbons, copying the Gibson Girl look they had seen in the early 1900s photos. Two players had taken a curling iron and put in waves like they had seen in some team photos from the 1920s. They had decided not to wear their big padded shoes, and each had found some kind of soft, leather slippers to wear instead. One team had striped knee-high socks in school colors. The other team wore black to match their black-and-white uniforms.

Jane, the assistant principal, stopped in the locker room to give them her usual words of encouragement. The yearbook photographer snapped a couple photos and they were ready.

As they stood outside the locker room, they could hear Lynnette, the announcer, say, "And now, let's welcome the Pioneer All-Star Teams, our very own 'daughters of the game.' The East All-Stars are attired in black bloomers, white middy blouses with black ribbons and black leather shoes and sox. Here they are! And right behind them are the West All-Stars, dressed in our school colors, with gold middies and blue bloomers."

The crowd roared its approval as the girls ran onto the court. The band played a short version of the school song that tonight represented both teams.

Lynnette officially began the ceremony for the night. The school's color guard entered with the flags and the audience respectfully removed all hats and caps and stood with their hands over their hearts. The national anthem was played by Grace, a well-known trumpet soloist, who hit all the high notes, and everyone shared the moments as the beautiful sounds echoed off the rafters.

Lynnette briefly explained the rules, "There will be two halves. The first half will be played with three courts, one of the early adaptations for women's basketball from James Naismith's full court game. In each of the three courts, each team will have two guards, two forwards and two centers. Only forwards can score. The game will start with a jump ball in the center section. No dribbling; only *one bounce* is permitted. Each basket scores one point. After a basket, play will start with a jump ball in the center. Balls that go out of bounds will result in a throw in from the sideline. There will be no running down the hallway for the ball. And a word about fouls:

no shouldering, hacking, tripping, striking, kicking, hair pulling, tackling and any other unnecessary roughness.

"And," Lynnette shook her finger at the spectators, "that applies to all of you too!"

The crowd laughed.

Lynnette took charge again, "First, the introduction of the veteran officials for tonight's game. You've watched them at many state tournament games. First, the official who officiated the first winter playoff championship game in 1975, Vicki, from Hastings; and her partner tonight, Deb, from Hopkins, who also played with her twin sister; they were awesome volleyball and basketball players. Please welcome our officials."

The fans respectfully applauded the officials. It was a good start to the game.

"Now," Lynnette's voice took on that special announcer's timbre, "please direct your attention to the rosters in your special program for tonight. You will find the names of the players, their school, when they played, and some special information about each player."

Sarah could see people opening the program, and excitedly pointing out interesting information to one another.

"As you can see, they are each great players, and tonight," Lynnette's voice rose to its full, enthusiastic delivery, *"our 'Pioneer All-Stars' will play again."*

And the crowd roared its approval.

"Now, the First Half Pioneer All-Stars. As I call your name, please run onto the court, and stand in your designated section. And wave to your fans:

For the East All-Stars:

Hattie Van Buren, 1901, Minneapolis Central

Lillian Graupmann, 1909, St. Paul Central

Annabel Hermes, 1909, Grand Rapids

Jeannette Page Wright, 1911, Crookston

Ruth DeLaHunt Rawn, 1913, Willmar

Frieda Kottke Coleman, 1919, Owatonna"

As Tammy, Yolanda, Jordan and their teammates, dressed in their middies and bloomers, ran onto the court, Sarah felt her throat tighten as the names of the pioneers they represented came rolling over the sound system. There's no going back now, she thought.

Lynnette kept the pace moving, **"and for The West All-Stars:**

Anna Tok, 1923, Greenway

Irma Nelson Post, 1925, Deer Creek

Adalyn Eckstrom Wright, 1925, Cokato

Dorothy Iversen Viker, 1925, Hayfield

Helen Johnson, 1925, Ellendale

Marie Weibeler Keeler, 1926, Belle Plaine"

Lynnette continued, "The coach for tonight's First Half East All-Stars, *Lynnea Sjoquist*, a former All-American Redhead and - *my twin sister."* Lynnea stepped out, dribbling the ball between her legs, to the delight of the crowd.

Lynnette's eyes rolled back and the crowd laughed again.

"And coach for the First Half West All-Stars, from the Minnesota State High School League, *Lisa Lissimore*, an outstanding guard on the St. Paul Central *Championship team* in *1976, the first-ever* MSHSL State Girls Basketball Tournament."

Lisa stepped onto the court, spinning a basketball on the tip of her index finger, and the crowd cheered their approval and appreciation for the historic player and director of the current state girls basketball tournaments.

Lynnette introduced the two student managers for the evening, two women who had also been All-American Redheads, Sherri Mattson and Gretchen Pinz Hyink. They came onto the court loaded with towels, bags of oranges and medical aid boxes that, no doubt, held anything else the teams might need.

At that moment, Sarah held her breath as she realized that the game was about to begin. Here we go, she thought, *let's roll*.

One of the officials tossed the ball up and the game was underway. Sarah was the jumping center and tipped the ball to the other center who threw it to one of their forwards. She lofted a shot and it went into the basket. *Point*. The crowd clapped its approval. The officials took the ball to the center section and the two jumping centers went after the ball again. Two players went diving for the ball and Yolanda's father caught one before she came in contact with the "hot" stove in the corner. The crowd clapped its approval for his quick response.

The ball went back and forth quickly and the fans enjoyed the constant action.

Lynnette was keeping the fans informed of the officials' calls when players would forget to stay in their section, or would foul another player, resulting in a free throw. A couple players used the between-the-legs underhand toss which the audience probably had never seen before. A player could be disqualified for going outside her section five times and the crowd began to keep a tally. The scoreboard on the end of the court kept running up the points as they were scored.

The players discovered one problem: the leather-soled slippers were just that - slippery. A student manager reached into her supply box for some resin. The players crunched the soles of their slippers in the resin shaken onto a towel and then walked on their heels back onto the floor. The crowd enjoyed the sight.

It was a fast game with the limited dribble. Passing was fast and soon the score was 6-4. Time went by quickly and, all too soon, the horn blew signaling the end of the first half. The fans stood and cheered the first-half pioneer players.

"So far, so good," Sarah said.

During the halftime break, the teams caught their breath on the benches. The band played songs from the 1920s and 1930s. When they played, "Thanks for the Memories," the crowd sang along with the song. It all seemed to fit this special night.

Lynnette took the microphone again and explained how the second half would be played.

"Ladies and gentlemen, you should know that sometimes these young women would go to a game not knowing which game they were going to play. It might be the three-court, or two-court, and sometimes even full-court (which girls were *not* supposed to play). Lynnette shook her finger at the audience and they laughed again.

"Now, you know that *women can resolve conflict.* When one team played the three-court game and the other team played the two-court game, they solved the problem by playing half the game with one set of rules and the second half with the other."

The audience loved it and the *women* clapped the longest.

She continued, "Here is how the two-court game works: the court is divided in half, with three forwards and three guards in each court. Only the forwards may shoot for a basket. Two bounces are permitted. Baskets will now score two points. If we have any native

Iowans here, this is your game." And a few people in the audience stood and clapped.

"So now," Lynnette turned to the team benches, "Please welcome our Second Half Pioneer All-Stars. Check their bios in your programs. They are each outstanding players:

For The East All-Stars:
>   Ruth McCarron Dahlke, 1927, Sherburn
>   Kay Nolan Wetter, 1928, Brainerd
>   Luella Bandelin Anderson, 1928, Arlington
>   Ruth Olson Kleven, 1929, Milan
>   Aileen Just Luther, 1930, Rapidan
>   Mabel Thompson Erickson, 1931, Mabel

For The West All-Stars:
>   Blanche Line Kingsley, 1931, Cromwell
>   Florence Urdahl, 1931, Litchfield
>   Irma Malone Foley, 1932, Montgomery
>   Marie Tommerson Berg, 1934, Grand Meadow
>   Thea Sletkolen Stay, 1935, Montevideo
>   Saima Saari Savela, 1937, Toivola"

Lynnette continued, "And now, please welcome the coach of the Second Half East All-Stars: *Janet Karvonen Montgomery.* As we all know, Janet is the *legendary star player* of the championship teams of the late-1970s from New York Mills."

Janet stepped out, spinning *two* basketballs and with her smile drew long and loud, appreciative applause from the crowd who well remembered her shooting skills.

"And now, the coach of the Second Half West All-Stars, your very own *Patti Foley*. Patti played on the Le Sueur team in the *first championship winter playoff game in 1975*, and now serves on your City Council."

Sarah watched as her mother stepped onto the floor, waving to her community. Once again, Patti heard the cheers of basketball fans. Sarah's eyes welled up in pride.

As the second half got underway, the crowd began to appreciate that a player could cover a large area of the court in two dribbles. Sarah was playing guard this time, and missed the chance to be able to score, though she found it fun to be able to get the ball away from the other team's forwards and whip it down the court to her forwards.

Sarah thought, "I can see why the players and fans in Iowa loved this game for so many years."

The score was tied at the end of the game, 25-25. There was no overtime: *both teams won*. It was a fitting ending to a wonderful night.

The crowd stood and gave the teams a long, warm "standing O."

The teams wearily sat down on their benches as the president of the downtown business club called for the attention of the audience.

She began, "Sarah, please join me on the floor. As the key organizer of this evening, we want to thank you and your team for bringing to life an important part of our history. Many of us didn't know our town had a girls basketball team during the early 1900s. We have learned what a great, exciting game they played and *we will remember tonight*. So, the Downtowners Club wants to give each of you a memento to *remember tonight*."

She uncovered a box held by another member of the club and held up a row of gold basketballs hanging on their individual chains. The team members jumped to their feet and ran onto the floor, their fatigue forgotten.

"We hope that each of you will wear this basketball and remember this special event. You should also know that wherever your careers take you, your community will remember you, *our daughters of the game.*

"And," she added, "On Monday, you can take your basketball to the jewelry store and they will engrave your initials on it."

Sarah thought, "Oh, Great-Grandma Ruby, *I hope you are watching this now!*"

15

MYTHS, STEREOTYPES AND OTHER BALONEY

"The search for human freedom can never be complete without freedom for women."
~ First Lady Betty Ford 1975

A snowflake floated down and landed on Sarah's coat as she stood outside the door to the gymnasium. I wonder how each flake can be unique from all the other jillions coming down. Just like me - I'm unique. She smiled at her own analogy.

Just then her "sleigh" arrived with her mom at the helm.

Now all I need are some sleigh bells and I will feel just like Great-Grandma Ruby going home from a game, Sarah laughed to herself, as she waved at Yolanda and Jordan heading off in the opposite direction.

A warm greeting was waiting for Sarah as she opened the door to their vehicle. There waited Gen, the family's beloved dog, her tail wagging her entire body, ready to jump into Sarah's arms. What an addition it was to the family when they found the little cavalier spaniel at the humane society. The moment her brown eyes had locked onto Sarah's, she knew this little dog was going home with them. Right now!

Sarah tried to fend off Gen's tongue licking her nose and face as if she hadn't seen her for weeks. Maybe for a little dog, a whole day seems like a lifetime. Gen seemed determined to repay the family's kindness by being the cutest and friendliest dog ever. When Sarah took Gen with her to visit their friend Maxine and the other residents at their assisted living home, there were smiles from everyone. Gen just seemed to understand that each person needed to pat her on the head. She seemed to know that she was reminding them of another special pet from years past, so she patiently waited, and then she smiled back.

Sarah hugged the compact little body, "You look beautiful, Gen, with the little ribbon on your collar. You must have been good at the groomer today." Gen smiled. She loved to go to her favorite store and see Libby, her favorite trainer, and have her coat trimmed. It seemed that everyone loved Gen.

"Hey, Mom," said Sarah, as she got Gen safely into her crate, "thanks for coming out in the storm. Was this predicted today?"

Her mother smiled, "Well, this morning, they said a 'little' snow might be coming. You know what they say about Minnesota: 'wait five minutes and we'll change the forecast for you.' And how was your day?"

Sarah locked her seat belt, and took a deep breath.

"Well, I feel really good about one thing that happened today. Yolanda and I went to the counselor with one of our team members. We had noticed in the locker room yesterday that she had bruises on her arm that looked like finger marks. And she had a scrape on her cheek. She finally told us that her boyfriend got mad again and had grabbed her arm and shaken her. So we talked and she agreed to go with us to see the counselor today. No one should have to put up with that kind of treatment."

"Good for you, Sarah," Patti smiled. "All too often people look the other way. Some people think it's just young people having a 'spat' and they rationalize that it's not serious. You did the right thing by going with her for support. I've been encouraging the other city council members to approve a shelter and counseling service for abused women and children. It's a lonely world out there when women don't know where to go for help. So they stay and sometimes it gets worse."

"Mom, why is it that women's lives are so difficult? I've been doing so much reading lately about women's lives and it feels like this kind of thing has been going on forever?"

"Yes," her mother replied, "it continues to be a worldwide problem. Governments at all levels need to address it, and we intend to start right here in our town. I am a firm believer that everything needs to start at home. For one thing, we need to talk to each other with respect. As you know, words and labels can hurt too."

Just then, another driver pulled out of a four-way stop without waiting for his turn. With a quick jerk of the wheel, Sarah's mom pulled safely out of its path.

"Now, there's an example, Sarah," she said. "When that happens to some people, they get angry and even end up with 'road rage.' I've seen people follow another driver and gesture to them how stupid they were, and even tailgate them. Sometimes it can turn violent."

"Yeah, or call them a 'stupid woman-driver,'" Sarah grimaced. "Words can be awful. I don't like it when someone calls me 'little lady' or 'girlie,' either."

Patti agreed, "We'll have to talk about this at dinner tonight. We should review our family's expectations on how to treat other people. My mother always said to sweep your own doorstep first."

After dinner, Sarah was upstairs with papers spread across her bed. It seemed to be a nightly ritual since she started researching her roots in sports.

She was sitting with her legs crossed and her chin in her hands. As her mother passed her doorway with a load of towels, the small book that Sarah had been holding came sliding into the hallway.

"Whoa, what's going on here?" Patti's voice carried a hint of a warning for her daughter's impulsive action.

Patti entered the room and set the towels in the recliner. As she sat down on the bed alongside Sarah, Patti folded her legs under her. Sarah always marveled at how flexible her mother was, *for her age.* Better not say that out loud, Sarah thought.

"So, what's going on that has you throwing perfectly good books around?" her mother asked. "Is it your research paper again?"

Sarah began to try to defend her actions, though she knew excuses wouldn't fly with her mother.

"I'm sorry, Mom, guess I'd better not say I had 'book rage.'" And from the look on her mother's face, she was right.

Sarah began, "Here's the thing. I started out just wanting to find an athlete among our female ancestors, and I did. Great-Grandma Ruby is my main subject, plus I've found that her mother, Great-Great-Grandma Clara was in the perfect place when she was the first to learn how to play basketball at Carleton College in 1892. Their diaries have been terrific because, through their own words, I can begin to get a feel for the life of a young woman out on the prairie.

"But I've started to notice that sometimes other people said and did things to women that wouldn't be accepted today. Like those people who said girls couldn't have a basketball team because 'it was for their own good.' What does that mean? Sounded like an excuse to me."

"Well, when you starting digging into women's history, you are going to find things that will make your blood boil." Patti added, "but next time save the cover on a good book."

Sarah was contrite, but wanted to share more information with her mother.

"Did you know, Mom, that at the same time that basketball was becoming popular in the 1890s, Charles Darwin had published his theory of evolution, based on biology? According to *him*," and Sarah fairly sputtered, "there was a 'scientific explanation' of the differences between men and women. According to Darwin, *women were lower on the evolutionary scale and therefore biologically inferior to men.*"

They both groaned.

Sarah went on, "Then I read that another man said that 'women's lack of ability was because of their lack of *opportunity.*' Now that makes sense. That can apply to any group of people or race who aren't qualified for jobs *because* they were denied education and even restricted to where they could live. So how can that be fair?"

Sarah rifled through her papers and picked up one sheet. "And here's another example from the mid-1800s when the bicycle was invented. It took another forty years to develop a two-wheeled bicycle that women could ride. Remember the pictures of men sitting on top of this bicycle with a huge wheel in front and a small one in back? Obviously women couldn't climb up onto that seat with those long dresses. So when the smaller two-wheeled bicycle was finally developed, the women were ready, and they either tucked in their skirts or wore these new 'bloomers.' And people didn't like that either."

"Remember, Sarah, in those days women were not supposed to go out of their home without a chaperone, but fortunately," her mother added, "many women didn't listen to the critics and went riding off anyway."

Sarah pushed papers around that were scattered on her bed until she found what she was looking for.

"Listen to this quote. In 1896, Nellie Bly interviewed Susan B. Anthony. Ms. Anthony said, 'Let me tell you what I think about the bicycling. I think it has done more to emancipate women than anything else in the world. I stand and rejoice every time I see a woman ride by on a *wheel*. It gives a woman a sense of freedom and self-reliance. It makes her feel as if she were independent. The moment she takes her seat, she knows she can't get into harm unless she gets off her bicycle, and off she goes, the picture of free, untrammeled womanhood.'"

Sarah cheered, '*Free, untrammeled womanhood!*' What an awesome description. I never knew that the bicycle had such an effect on women being able to break away and feel free. I am going to remember that next time I go for a ride on my 'wheel.' I'll just say, 'Here comes 'free untrammeled womanhood' - move aside!"

Sarah and her mother gave each other a "high five" for that victory.

"And," Sarah went on, "did you know, Mom, that in 1887, married women finally had the same legal status as single women: they were no longer the 'property' of their husbands! Doesn't it just drive you crazy?"

"That kind of thing is even closer in time than you may realize, Sarah," Patti said. "When I married your dad, I had to get his permission and signature to take out a loan for a car, even though I had saved enough from my job to pay for it. In those days a woman going in to look at a car by herself raised many an eyebrow. It was as if it was a waste of a salesman's time to talk to a woman about engines and torque without a man there who could 'understand' such technical terms. I was the first girl to take auto mechanics class at Le Sueur. The salesman's jaw dropped when I started talking car engines."

Patti continued, "I remember one of my high school teachers telling us that when she received her first check as a young, single teacher in the 1960s, she learned that the married men in her high school were receiving an extra fifty dollars for being 'head of a household.' She went to the superintendent to let him know that they had forgotten to include it in her salary and she was told that because she wasn't married, she wasn't 'head of a household! And married women couldn't get it either because their husband worked.'

"And," her mother's momentum rolled on, "one of the ongoing battles is to equalize the salary that a woman receives for doing the same work as a man. I read on *Forbes.com* that women's salaries are stalled at about 80% of men's salaries. They said that women are making up half of the workforce and are more likely than ever to be primary or co-bread winners in their families. So, women are seeking out jobs that will pay them the most. *ForbesWoman* posted a list of the top ten states and Minnesota was #8. That's the good news. But it listed Minnesota women's median salaries in 2009 as $37,284, and that was 81.1% of a man's salary. That means that a woman's salary could annually be almost $20,000 less than a man's salary."

Sarah shook her head in bewilderment. Is this the world she's stepping into?

Patti continued, "Another friend of mine had worked for a company for years, receiving commendations for her work. She did receive slight advancements in position and salary through the years, but she noted that a less experienced male co-worker was moving much farther ahead. When she approached her manager about *her* future with the company and *when she* could expect the same pay level, she was told that she couldn't *ever* expect to see similar advancement because the man had children to support, and she didn't. And, to add insult to injury, he said that her salary was *just a secondary income* to her husband's income."

"Isn't that illegal, Mom?" Sarah was becoming increasingly outraged. These examples of such negative treatment of women felt even more personal when it happened to her mother and her friends.

"Fortunately, Sarah," her mother said, "some of these practices or discriminatory statements are not acceptable today, but we know they haven't been eliminated. Some companies and administrators try to fly below the radar, hoping no one will complain, especially when no one wants to lose their jobs today. We have to keep developing better practices to protect those who can't do it alone. You will have to keep your guard up when you are on your own."

Her mother had more to share. "You see, Sarah, sometimes that kind of thing is hard to change by yourself, but it's like a little stone in your shoe. It just keeps rubbing and reminding you that it needs attention. A fair life for women is in the details. So, that's why women have always had to organize to work together against unfair practices.

"Getting the vote is one example. Remember when Grandma Ruby wrote in her diary about the first time her mother walked into a voting booth in 1920 and voted? Her mother had said it was hard to describe the feelings when she marked an 'X' on the ballot for *her choice* of the candidates. It was a pretty exciting day for the women in Sherburn, Minnesota, and across the country."

Patti laughed, "And it didn't matter how her husband would vote. She said she knew she canceled out his vote many times."

"Every woman should always vote." Sarah pounded the bedspread, "I was talking to Lynn on the way back from Iowa last week about suffrage and women getting the vote. Did you know that *'suffragist'* means a *person* who supports the right to vote? If you use that word, you don't have to call women 'suffrag*ettes.*' You should see the sparks fly when Lynn talks about how things that women do get labeled with an 'ette.' She said it feels like fingernails scratching across a blackboard when women's activities are separated as if they're *not the real thing.*

"Oh, and I almost forgot to tell you this. I watched this news program last night," Sarah said. "A famous woman actor was being interviewed about the many different types of roles she had played. The guy asked her, "Have you ever wanted to play a 'Bond girl?'" *You should have seen her eyes snap.* She looked at him calmly and said, *"No, I want to play Bond."* I just cheered! Imagine that in this century, women still get asked questions that imply that being the 'sidekick' to the main actor is the woman's place in films."

Sarah shook her head in frustration. "Mom, it's just another thing that we have to change!"

Patti leaned back on her elbows, "I read an article written by the woman at the State High School League when girls' sports were struggling to be born again. She used the idea of *looking through a mirror*, and she reversed everything in the story, like a mirror would do. In her story set in the 1970s, it was the *girls* who had always had the sports teams and the *boys* were coming to the school administration wanting teams."

Patti continued, "As the story developed, in this school the boys were not welcomed, and were told there wasn't enough money for boys' teams and uniforms, buses and all. It had already been allocated for the girls' teams. There were lots of reasons adding boys' teams couldn't work, they said. The gymnasiums were already scheduled with girls' teams. If the boys wanted to play football on the girls' soccer field, the objection was that it would tear up that beautiful grass developed for girls' soccer games. And on it went. So the point of the story was: if you reversed everything, how would it look?"

Patti's eyebrows lifted as she looked at Sarah. "Think of it in today's schools: if you divided the budget and told one group, boys or girls, to pick the half they wanted, would it be fair to the other group? Or if you set up a practice schedule, and girls got to choose the practice times first, would it be fair to the boys? Anyway, you get the idea. It is important to look through the eyes of the other group or person."

Patti took a deep breath and sighed, "I've always said it's what mothers understand: when there's only one piece of pie and two children want to eat it, give one child the knife to cut it in half, and let the other child have first choice. That's fair. I've watched you and your brother measure it right down to counting the number of cherries in each piece of pie."

"I'd like to read that article; do you have it?" Sarah asked.

"I'll check my file, *'Sausage and Baloney.'* One of my friends has a file with that title. And there's not a recipe in it!"

Sarah flopped back on her bed and laughed. She had never heard this side of her mother before. She really is "with it."

Patti went over to the bookstand and brought out a book.

"Remember when I used to read this before bed? *Alice's Adventures in Wonderland* was one of your favorites."

"Oh yes," Sarah said, "Please read me the part again when Alice met those three at the tea party."

Patti opened the book and began to read, *"There was a table set out under a tree in front of the house, and the March Hare and the Hatter were having tea at it. A dormouse was sitting between them, fast asleep, and the other two were using it as a cushion, resting their elbows on it, and talking over its head. 'Very uncomfortable for the dormouse,' thought Alice, 'only, as it's asleep, I suppose it doesn't mind.'"*

Sarah sat up, "So, is that what they mean by not being a dormouse- it means not letting others take advantage of you?"

Patti laughed, "You might mean 'doormat,' but it's all the same." They both laughed.

She continued, *"The table was a large one, but the three were all crouched together at one corner of it: 'No room,' they cried out when they saw Alice coming. 'There's PLENTY of room!' said Alice indignantly, and sat down in a large armchair at one end of the table. 'Have some wine,' the March Hare said in an encouraging tone. Alice looked all around the table, but there was nothing on it but tea. 'I don't see any wine,' she remarked. 'There isn't any,' said the March Hare. 'Then it wasn't very civil of you to offer it,' said Alice angrily. 'It wasn't very civil of you to sit down without being invited,' said the March Hare."*

Patti paused for the finale, *"'I didn't know it was YOUR table,' said Alice, 'it's laid for a great many more than three.'"*

Sarah leaned back on her bed, "I never could understand why they didn't want Alice to sit with them when there was plenty of room.

But now, I'm beginning to understand - *they didn't want to share,* even though they had more than they needed. *It's kinda like the way women are treated when they want their share of the sports program, or equal pay for equal work, or have a choice in who should be the leaders in every level of government.*"

Patti sighed, "Exactly. It is such a shame that some people can be so devoid of empathy for others, or be so driven to gather wealth or power that they will deny others a fair and reasonable share."

Sarah had been thinking of all the situations and problems she might encounter soon. "You know, Mom, it could be really scary to go out in the world if you think of all the things that could happen and expect that people might treat you badly. But I don't want to live my life in a cave and be afraid of every noise outside. I think I should just remember that the table is set for a great many more than three, and I am going to sit down alongside Alice and take my place at the table."

Patti smiled, "I can just see you and Alice sitting together - *and inviting many others to join you.*"

Patti looked at her watch. "It's your dad's night to make dinner and I think he's ordering pizza."

"Great, I'm hungry," Sarah agreed, "but stay another couple minutes, please, Mom. I want to tell you about this woman that I found on the Internet when I was looking up information on suffrage. Her name is Alice Paul.

"Listen to what this one woman did," Sarah began. "Alice was born in 1885 and her Quaker family believed in gender equality, education for women and helping others. She even went with her mother to women's suffrage meetings. Alice was a top-notch student and went to England where the women were taking suffrage to the streets in London. Later, she returned with this experience to the United States."

"Imagine this, Mom, in 1913, on the eve of President Woodrow Wilson's inauguration, Alice organized the largest parade ever seen in the nation's capitol. About 8,000 women dressed in *white suffragist* dresses marched down Pennsylvania Avenue from the Capitol to the White House. It said that troops were called to restore order when the women received verbal and physical harassment."

Patti shook her head, "So many times the violence comes from those standing by, watching. As you know, that was also the experience during the later civil rights marches."

Sarah continued, "Okay, so then they have meetings directly with President Wilson, but he said the time 'wasn't right' for women's suffrage. It's an awesome story, but you just have to picture all of the demonstrations and lobbying that went on. Then in 1917, the National Women's Party (NWP) began the first U.S. nonviolent civil disobedience campaign by standing by the gates to the White House, carrying purple, white and gold banners saying, 'Mr. President, how long must women wait for liberty?' and 'Votes for Women.'"

Patti interjected with a smile, "Well, if you are going to demonstrate, the White House is as good a place as any."

"But, Mom," Sarah continued, "For over 18 months, a thousand women took turns standing on that sidewalk in the heat and cold, being insulted and spit upon by men, and worse, by *other women.* You would think the president of the United States would support the idea of suffrage for women. But, no, President Wilson wouldn't come out of the White House and sent the police out to clear the women off the sidewalk."

Patti winced, visualizing the abuse that these women had endured on behalf of all women.

"So, guess what charges were used to arrest these women?" Sarah's face was flushed. "They were arrested for 'obstructing traffic!' How ridiculous is *that?*"

"Well," her mother said sadly, "sometimes laws get twisted, when a little common sense would have defused the situation."

"That's the worst part, Mom," Sarah said. "They arrested hundreds of women and convicted 33 who were thrown into a workhouse, including Alice. And it wasn't the kind of place where some of our celebrities spend their jail sentences. They were force-fed, given worm-infested food and put in awful cells. Alice Paul went on a hunger strike and, to try to break her spirit, they put her in a *psychiatric ward.* This is so horrible: *they force-fed her raw eggs through a tube they shoved through her nose into her stomach.*"

They both shuddered.

"I remember reading that horrendous history on the website for Alice Paul and the *National Women's History Museum,*" her mother replied. "It was a terrible price to pay for her and the other women, to get the media involved so the public would finally pay attention. It eventually became a 'hot button' political issue for President Wilson."

"Yes," Sarah said, with a touch of sarcasm. "Finally, *people got angry* and the women were released. In 1918, the president finally announced that women's suffrage was - *get this, Mom* - 'urgently needed as a *war measure'* and strongly urged Congress to pass the legislation. It took more demonstrations, arrests and hard work before the Nineteenth Amendment to the Constitution was passed in 1920, by a one-vote margin. *Women finally got the vote!* Imagine being the last state to cast the deciding vote."

Her mother shook her head sadly, "Yes, those brave women endured so much on behalf of all of us. It is wrong that it takes political pressure to motivate some of our leaders to do the right thing.

"Sarah, I would recommend you continue your study. Read about Abigail Adams who wrote a letter to her husband, John, to *'remember the ladies'* when the Continental Congress was writing a new code of laws. She told him that he and the other men should be more 'generous and favourable to them (the women) than your ancestors.' And she said, *'Do not* put such unlimited power into the hands of the Husbands.'"

"Did they listen to her advice?" Sarah asked. And the look on her mother's face gave her the answer.

Patti added, "You should also read about the earlier 1848 Seneca Falls Convention in New York that passed a Declaration of Sentiments. It argued much earlier that women had a right to equality in all areas including the right to vote. There are great biographies of Elizabeth Cady Stanton, Lucretia Mott and Susan B. Anthony that you should read to become informed on the issues of those times and the women who changed the course of history. By the way, Sarah, a statue of those three women is in the Capitol Rotunda in the nation's capitol after being in a 'broom closet,' (called the Capitol Crypt), for decades. It would be great to go see it."

Sarah said, almost sadly, "There are so many women whose lives should be talked about and appreciated."

Patti brightened, "That reminds me, I wanted to tell you to look at the website for the new National Women's History Museum building that they hope to build near the National Mall in Washington, D.C. The mission of the NWHS is to reclaim the missing half of history - women's history. It's *www.nwhm.org.* Easy to remember."

Sarah nodded in agreement, "It's hard to find women's history so that museum would be a great resource by preserving the lives of so many women who did so much for our country."

"Did you know that in 1923," Patti added, "your new hero Alice Paul was the original author of the Equal Rights Amendment (ERA) to the Constitution? It simply said, 'Men and women shall have equal rights throughout the United States and every place subject to its jurisdiction.' That's quite another long story. After years of struggle, Congress passed the ERA in 1970, but sadly, it still hasn't been passed into national law and leaves states to adopt the ERA for their own state constitutions."

Sarah's head popped up, "Has Minnesota adopted it?"

Her mother smiled, "'Sounds like its back to the Internet for you, my dear. There are lessons to be learned from the struggle. One thing is clear: there is still work to do and your generation has to pick up the torch, or the hammer and nails. I donate to the NWH museum fund and that's one way to be involved. We will celebrate when that new building goes up. Another step forward."

Sarah looked up at her mother, "Why do you think there has never been a woman president in our country? Many countries around the world have women as presidents and prime ministers, why not the United States?"

Patti paused, "I wish there was an easy answer to your question, Sarah. There have been women throughout our country's history who were qualified for the office of President, and so many other leadership positions. The political process is complicated, some say it can be too easily manipulated, and too many people are selfishly invested in protecting their own interests and getting reelected. We seem to have separated into groups and factions that have lost the ability to work for the 'greater good' of our country.

"However," her mother added, "after listening to our current state senators in Congress, I do think that we have good people working for us. As you know, Minnesota currently has one woman and one man as our senators."

Sarah's mother got up from the bed, "That's why your dad and I are active in our local elections and why I am on the City Council. We have to do our part as individual citizens or we stand to lose our democratic process. Democracy is not guaranteed; it has to be protected."

Sarah had not really asked her mother about her opinions before and she realized that she could learn so much from her, and other women, past and present. She simply had to start asking questions, reading and listening.

The two gave each other a "high five" and went arm in arm down the stairs: *two generations, one heart.*

Sarah's voice came rolling throughout the house, "Hey, Everyone, what kind of pizza do you want? *We're taking a vote!*"

16

It's My Happy Heart You Hear

"Stick your landing," the coach whispered in Allison's ear. She stood waiting for the judge's nod to begin her routine.

The uneven parallel bars were her friends. Allison loved the feeling as she grasped and regrasped, swinging and circling the bars. She felt as if she were flying.

Chalk flew as she swung from the low bar to the high bar. Her body was tight and straight as she balanced vertically on the high bar, swinging into her trademark giant swings that always brought a gasp from the audience. Soon, her Arabian double front dismount was ahead. Here it comes, she thought, the mat was coming up fast. Her feet landed. Both hands went up in the air. She had done it. She stuck her landing, without even a small hop for balance.

Allison's smile said it all; this was the performance she knew she could do. And she did.

Sarah sat motionless in her seat among the spectators. After Allison's dismount, she could finally cheer.

"I haven't taken a breath since Allison started her routine," Sarah said to Yolanda. "It's harder to sit here watching than being out on the floor, isn't it?"

Yolanda sighed with relief too, and nodded her head.

The judges were ready with their scores. As the scores in the high 9's were flashed, the crowd approved. Allison had moved into first place in the individual and all-around competition. There were smiles "all around."

It was "typical" high school state tournament weather: blowing snow and a wind chill of minus thirty degrees.

Earlier that day, Sarah and Yolanda had quickly walked from the parking lot to get out of the biting wind. Sarah knew that she'd better thank her mother for telling her to wear boots and a hat, especially after she grumbled her way out the door, with an "Oh, Moth-errrr!"

Today was the final day of competition when the "best of the best" competed for individual and all-around championships.

The gymnastics coach from their school had invited the young women to meet her after the first session in the coaches and judges area adjacent to the competition floor. She said they would have an opportunity to meet some of the pioneers who had started girls gymnastics in Minnesota.

As they walked in, the judges and meet personnel were enjoying a quick buffet lunch. In the nearby coaches room, they were holding their annual meeting.

"Come over here, Sarah and Yolanda," Elaine, the head of the judges, beckoned them into their room. "I'd like you to meet some people."

She gestured to two chairs near her and the young

women sat down.

Elaine said, "The judges here today are selected for the state meet because they are among our best judges. They are responsible for judging routines based on a set of very complicated rules, and there is no instant replay."

She looked around the groups of judges, both women and men. "Who has been judging between thirty and forty years?"

Several hands were raised. Sarah and Yolanda could hardly believe their eyes or ears. The number of years was twice their age.

Vel, one of the judges said, "Yes, I was a judge at the first state meet at Robbinsdale Armstrong High School in 1975. We didn't get done until midnight."

Connie added, "And, wouldn't you know, there was a tie for the team title and we had no tie-breaking procedure at that time. There were two happy co-champions. The announcer, Allie Cronk, has been the announcer of this meet every year since then."

Oh, Sarah thought, that's why the announcer's voice had sounded so familiar during the first session. She is the legendary "voice of girls' sports" in Minnesota. She also announces at the state volleyball tournament and everyone loves it when she says, *"Let's play volley-ball-l-l-l."*

Another judge, Sue, jumped into the conversation, "Remember the State Meet at St. Cloud State University when the truck coming with the equipment loaned from the gymnastics company in Iowa couldn't get through the snow and we had to borrow the apparatus from one of the high schools?"

There were some heads shaking at that memory.

Jill, another judge, began to laugh before she could begin to share her memory, "Then, remember the years when we were in the

Minneapolis Auditorium and the Shriners Circus was in the big arena? Everything smelled like elephants. Ugh!"

The group clearly loved the opportunity to share stories with these young women.

Sylvia jumped into the story, "And then the time when Ardis parked in the lower level of the Auditorium where they kept the animal cages, and she didn't know they were there. When she walked by one of the covered cages, a lion let out a huge roar. I don't think she needed the elevator to get up to the arena. "

And the group dissolved into laughter.

Sarah was calculating the years. Many in this group have been together since the 1960s.They are like that flock of geese flying together, sharing the challenges and shouting out encouragement to each other. Coming to the state meet is like a "homecoming" for them.

A woman walked into the room and the judges all waved with warm greetings. She was clearly the matriarch of this sport.

Elaine brought her over to the young women. "I'd like you to meet Pat Lamb from Carleton College."

Sarah stood and smiled, extending her hand. It was another "plus" for one of her favorite colleges.

Elaine continued, "Pat was selected to attend the First Sports Institute in 1963 at the University of Oklahoma, along with others from across the country. There was a growing interest in bringing competition for girls and women into the high schools and colleges, but first, teachers and coaches had to be trained. So, they invited Pat and representatives from other states to come to the Institute to receive information on how to conduct clinics in their states. When Pat returned home, she formed the first Girls Gymnastics Committee and they began to conduct clinics and invitational meets all around the state."

I see, Sarah thought, that's the connection between the dropping of girls and women's sports in the 1920s and 1930s and opening the doors again in the 1960s. Someone had to take the first steps and break the stereotypes and myths about girls and women in sports. *It was gymnastics*, and *here they are*. I am sitting in the presence of the women who were the pioneers and who created a new world, all for kids like me. And I get to meet them in person. *How cool is that!*

Pat smiled and Sarah could see how her warm, inviting look would encourage people to follow her as their leader.

"I'm very happy to meet you, Sarah and Yolanda," Pat said. "The story of our Minnesota gymnastics program is fascinating. We were all competent teachers in our physical education classes, but most of us didn't have experience or training in how to *coach* competitive sports. We were ready and willing to learn. And we learned that the more steps we took, the better we were at planning events and teaching the skills of gymnastics."

Sarah asked, "But if you hadn't been a gymnast in school, how could you teach or coach it?"

Pat smiled gently, "You'll find you can teach skills that you may not be able to demonstrate. You have to be able to analyze the skill and describe it to your students. A teacher helps them to conceptualize what they should think about and then gives them the confidence to try. They know you'll be there to 'spot' and keep them safe. That works in life outside gymnastics too."

A second woman had joined them and was introduced as Ele Hansen. She had been head of the Women's Physical Education Department at Carleton College. She smiled at Sarah and Yolanda.

Pat smiled and reached over to touch Ele's arm.

"Remember how our physical education department at Carleton hosted so many events? We watched films over and over, and read any book we could find on gymnastics. There were instructors in private gymnastics clubs and organizations from outside Minnesota who helped us too. And the summers when we conducted girls gymnastic workshops for teachers and gymnasts at Carleton College? It was a memorable time, wasn't it, Ele?"

Ele nodded and said, "It certainly was. No one could forget those ground-breaking events and especially the wonderful people involved."

"And you did this all on your own time?" Sarah asked.

Several heads nodded throughout the group, as if to say, of course, that was the only way to get it done.

Sarah nodded her head with them. Yes, she thought, another example of "if it is to be, it's up to me."

"How did you encourage people to come to your clinics and camps?" Yolanda asked.

Pat smiled, "It was amazing. We sent out letters and it was like igniting tinder with a match. Wherever we went for a clinic, there would be an overflow gymnasium full of teachers and 'wannabe' gymnasts. One of our first clinics was up north in Aurora, Minnesota. It was one of the coldest temperatures on record. It was close to eighty below zero with wind chill. We drove up the night before the clinic and by morning, everything was frozen solid, including our cars. We didn't think anyone would come, but we walked over to the school anyway. And, right on schedule, yellow school buses came rolling up in front of the school and unloaded girls by the dozens and dozens, from all over the Range. Wow, did we work hard."

Sarah smiled to herself. Of course those Iron Rangers wouldn't let a little cold stop them from coming to something exciting like that – a chance to learn something as fun as gymnastics.

"The first year," Pat added, "we conducted seven workshops that included 1,200 girls from 200 schools. And all of us were full-time teachers too. "

"Did you have meets between schools?" Yolanda asked.

"Yes," Pat smiled, "in April of 1966, we had our first invitational meet at Eden Prairie High School. In additiion to coaching skills to our gymnasts, we had also been learning how to judge routines. There were about forty of us who were willing to actually judge at a meet. And we found that we were pretty good at it."

Pat smiled as three women came into the room. Mylla was a former coach and judge and had also been athletic director at Carleton College. Joanie was one of the first students at her high school in Wayzata in the 1960s to volunteer to put herself in the hands of these new coaches so she could try those uneven parallel bars. Joanie went on to coach and judge several sports at Clearbook and St. Francis High Schools.

The third woman was Liz. She was a student athlete on the Austin girls basketball team and played in the very first MSHSL State Girls Basketball Tournament at the Met Center in 1976. Liz grinned at the young women, "And I hold the record of being the first player to foul out of the MSHSL State Girls Basketball Tournament. I had only four fouls, but no one noticed that a foul from another player had been recorded in my column by mistake. So I sat out the rest of the game with only four fouls." Sarah and Yolanda gasped at the very thought of her experience.

"These women," Sylvia said to Sarah and Yolanda, "are prime examples of women who stepped up whenever someone was needed. All of us helped seed entries into tournaments, worked at the finish line of the state track and field meets, were supervisors of bands at volleyball and basketball, organized banquets - literally anywhere we could help to make the event a great experience for the teams and young women participating in them. You are looking at the kind of people who are the 'heart' of a state tournament."

Another woman came into the room. She seemed to have only one speed: *fast*. As she approached, she was already talking to them, "Well, Sarah and Yolanda, where are your gold medals from your relay at state track last spring?"

Their faces reflected their surprise that she had remembered their names. Liz said, "Oh, Nita, you are 'something else' when it comes to remembering names."

Nita gave a hearty laugh, "Well, it's easy to remember state champions who break both the state and national records."

She shook the young women's hands again, congratulating them one more time on their great performance last spring. It was a memory that they wouldn't forget either, standing atop the awards stand, looking out over the bleachers and seeing the smiling faces of parents and friends.

"Look, Sarah," Yolanda whispered. They recognized a woman who was coming into the room as the president of the MSHSL Board of Directors who had hung the blue ribbon with its gold medal around their necks.

"Hello again," she said, "my name is Sharon and we met at the awards stand last spring at state track. Will we see your basketball team at the upcoming state tournament? I'm the Tournament Manager so I hope to see you there. And Nita is Team Manager so you would undoubtedly see her again too."

Sarah smiled. It would be fun to see these interesting women again. They all seem to be able to step into so many different positions.

Yolanda nudged Sarah's arm. "These women are so interesting. I'm going to pay more attention to the people who are working at the tournaments. Maybe we could work there someday."

Elaine approached the young women again and led them over to where the judges were sitting. "We have a few minutes before the next session begins. Let me tell you a bit more about our program in Minnesota."

With a sweeping wave toward the arena, she said, "Minnesota has one of the largest high school girls gymnastics programs in the country. And it all started with many of the people here. I was one of their high school gymnasts during the early days and I've been judging since college. I'm fortunate to have been appointed as the League's head gymnastics' rules interpreter. I attend the national meeting every year to learn the latest rule changes, and then I pass them on to the coaches and judges across the state. I help provide interpretations during the season and help select and supervise the judging at the state meet."

Sylvia added, "And, Sarah and Yolanda, because of the success of the girls gymnastics program, people began to change their attitudes and schools started teams in other girls' sports. In 1969, when the Minnesota State High School League voted to adopt the girls' sports program, it meant that state tournaments were now on the horizon for your favorite sports of basketball and track and field."

So, Sarah thought, I owe these women "big-time." They opened doors for me too. And my mother.

Across the room, a small woman who seemed to have boundless energy, came running toward them. She had the look of a gymnast. Today, Peggy was a coach at the state meet and also judged during the season. She warmly grasped Pat's hand, "Ms. McIntyre said you were here!"

Pat asked, "You still call her 'Ms. McIntyre' after all these years?"

Peggy laughed, "Well, because she started gymnastics when I was in high school, I was able to compete at the university. Now I've been a coach and judge for years. Because of her, gymnastics changed my life. So, she will always be Ms. McIntyre to me."

Peggy turned to explain her history to Sarah and Yolanda, "You see, I was in high school at Eden Prairie in the 1960s, when Pat asked Ms. McIntyre to be on her committee. We had been learning rhythmic gymnastics - you know, with balls and hoops?" The young women shook their heads.

Peggy smiled, "Too bad. You'd love it. We used to perform tumbling and rhythmic ball routines wherever Ms. McIntyre would take us on the bus – she drove it too, you know - and she would talk to people about why girls should be able to compete in sports. She used to say, 'Look at these young women from my school. See their smiles and how happy and healthy they are? That's what sports can do for *your* young women too.'"

Peggy was getting warmed up. "You've seen the equipment out there on the floor today? Those beautiful unevens, beams, the vaulting horse and its vaulting table, and that wonderful spring floor?"

This time, the young women nodded.

"Well," Peggy continued, "Our first uneven bars were metal pipes and when someone was practicing on them, the rest of us would stand on the base to keep them from lifting off the floor. And we put sponges over our hip bones when we practiced on the unevens. 'Didn't do much good though."

The young women's eyes blinked at the thought of contacting that metal bar, over and over again.

"And," Peggy grinned at the memory, "our first practice beams were 'two by four' pieces of wood, and our first real Nissen beam had no padding over the wood. We did our floor exercise routines on the bare gymnasium floor. Sometimes someone would slide a small mat in front of us for a tumbling move. Oh, it was such fun-n-n-n if you love pain!"

And they all laughed.

Sarah thought, so when girls' sports were being started again, there were pioneer-athletes then too. Look at Peggy, who was willing to put herself in the hands of a new coach who was trying just as hard as she was to learn a new sport. She really had to trust her teacher.

"But," Peggy looked intensely at the young women, waving her hand at them for emphasis, "it was one of the most exciting times of my life. Ms. McIntyre got her bus driver's license so she could take us wherever we needed to go to perform rhythmic gymnastics routines or help with a clinic or go to a meet. We traveled all over the state. One night we performed a rhythmic ball routine during the halftime of a men's basketball game at Williams Arena at the University of Minnesota. There were over 16,000 people there and they gave us a standing ovation. I'd never been a part of anything like that before. And I loved the sound of the applause. And still do."

Peggy paused and there was some moisture glistening in her eyes, "In the 60s, there was a popular song by Andy Williams that we used to sing on our bus rides, "It's My Happy Heart You Hear." So we called ourselves the "Happy Hearts," because *ours were. And mine still is.*"

"And the All-Around Champion is . . . . "Allie's rich voice rolled across the arena. Allison stood up among the gathering of the gymnasts on the floor. The gymnasts liked Allison and they cheered sincerely for their new champion. As the gold medal on its blue ribbon was hung around her neck, Allison stood tall on the awards stand and smiled, *inside and out.*

As Sarah and Yolanda leaned into the blowing snow, they too were smiling, *inside and out,* from their afternoon with the gymnastics pioneers and their legacy, the young women of Minnesota.

17

How Full is the Glass Today?

The newspaper was tossed onto the kitchen table as if it was carrying a virus. Patti was startled and her head jerked up, looking for some reason for her daughter's actions.

"Now, was that really necessary?" Patti had been concentrating on the minutes of her council meeting and suddenly, her oldest daughter was standing with her arms tightly folded, clearly in a state of high indignation.

"I'm sorry, but Mom, tell me this. Why do women get treated differently by some of the news media? We don't get the same amount of coverage, or same respect, and even worse, the pictures and the way they describe many women in sports are from the 'dark ages.' Last summer, you would hardly know the Minnesota Lynx were heading into the big playoffs for the first time. And last week, the newspaper had a picture of our team winning a big game and it wasn't even an action shot - it was our team members *on the bench*, cheering for Jordan's great steal and layup. And it looks like it has been going on for a long time. I found this high school newspaper clipping from 1973. It says, "Boys' track finishes fourth, girls *end first*. Most of the article is about the boys and the last line says, *'And the girls also ran.'* THEY WON THE MEET! It drives me crazy."

"Well, sit down and tell me all about it." Patti knew that she may as well stop what she was doing as Sarah needed to share something important to her. They both pulled out a kitchen stool.

Sarah took a deep breath. "A speaker in our class today was from the Tucker Center at the University of Minnesota. They do research on girls and women's sports, and one of their studies is the media's portrayal of women's sports. She had a power point presentation of photos and stories from 'way back into the 1970s and when you see them all collected together, it is unbelievable.

"There were photos of women's college teams in poses that made them look like 'pole dancers' and some of them were dressed in outfits that were embarrassing. One women's college team in 1992 was wearing bunny ears and tails, and the headline was, 'These girls can play, boy.' And these photos were in their *athletic department media handbooks*. So the athletic departments were part of the problem. Why did they allow that kind of photo?

"And listen to this: at a national conference in the 1980s when women's teams were really getting a foothold, our speaker said she was at a national meeting and one session was a panel of *women* who were editors of big women's magazines. One of these editors said, 'If you want your women athletes to get coverage in *our magazines*, tell them to get out their little black dresses.' The speaker from the Tucker Center said that women shouldn't have to be sexualized or trivialized to be covered by the news media. And we all cheered."

As Sarah paused for a breath, Patti took a sip of her tea and waited. Clearly, there was more to come.

"And," Sarah sputtered, "it wasn't all from years ago. She had photos of the men and women who were featured in a recent issue of one of the biggest sports magazines. These athletes were exceptional in their sports and highly respected. One was of a woman tennis player who everyone knows, and this sports magazine had named her as their *Sportswoman* of the Year. She was standing on a tennis court, posing in *a little black dress* with high heels, holding a racquet. Now, the *Sportsman* of the Year was in his uniform, playing in his sport. The men look like athletes. The women look like models and have to hold a piece of equipment like a tennis racquet or golf club to link them to their sport."

Sarah felt the tears of frustration waiting to follow her anger, but she wasn't going to let them embarrass her by crying.

She took a deep breath and looked at her mother. And waited.

Patti saw that her daughter's distress needed a response and she wished that she could easily answer her questions. She reached over and laid her hand on Sarah's arm, still trembling with her rage at the unfairness of it all.

"I understand," Patti said. "A few years ago, one of the professional golfers that I used to follow was quoted in an article as saying that a reporter told her that she was *'lucky'* that his paper was covering their golf event and that she better give him something to write about. So, even the highest levels of female athletes faced that attitude."

Then Patti brightened, "Wait a minute while I go grab my scrapbook." She was back in a few seconds and opened her favorite book, full of articles and photos from her Le Sueur basketball days.

"Let's see now… here it is." Patti stopped at a newspaper clipping and smiled. "There was a great reporter for the *Minneapolis Star* named Jim Klobuchar. When we were playing our semi-final game in the winter playoffs, he wrote a column that had our town talking. Listen to what he wrote, *'The women's revolution is real and irreversible. The loudest sound in town last night was the thud of old barricades crumbling in a gym built as a jock emporium."*

Patti and Sarah chuckled, enjoying his insight and heart-warming words.

Patti continued reading the article, *"'If you are a lady, the sound must have been symphonic. Even if you aren't, you had to appreciate the lyrical justice in it. It wasn't more than a few years ago when the notion of high school girls seriously competing in a Minnesota state basketball tournament was resonantly honked and derided as a corset-burner's daydream. But they played the semi-finals of the winter playoffs in the Osseo Junior High building last night and it was a night filled with remarkable sights and deeds.*

"'There was a guard from Le Sueur with pigtails and green eyes and a face that could launch a hundred proms...'"

Patti laughed, "Oh, how we kidded Brenda about her 'green eyes,' and also because he said her black tennis shoes should be banned!"

Back to the article, Patti read on, *"'And she did reverse layups with the basketball, dribbled with either hand and broke a full-court press. She was feminine, indomitable, nervy and she had a lovely jump shot. Her name was Brenda Savage and she undoubtedly will be canonized with the first wave when they build a Hall of Fame of girls basketball in Minnesota...'"*

They smiled at his understanding and special way with words.

Patti's eyes glistened, "Just think, Sarah, *he was writing about our team, one of our players...it was wonderful."*

Sarah sat quietly watching, absorbing the emotions her mother was sharing with her. She realized that she had never thought of her mother as an athlete, as a young woman committed to her team.

How wrong I've been to have overlooked, and not appreciated *my own mother*, Sarah thought.

Patti wiped her eyes, closed her scrapbook, and smiled at her daughter. "Those were special days, Sarah, enjoy each one of yours."

They both stood to stretch their legs and then resumed their positions on the kitchen stools. Patti clearly had more to share with her daughter.

"Let me tell you about the first official MSHSL State Girls Basketball Tournament the next year in 1976. Our team went to the Met Center to watch the games. Imagine playing in the *first* state tournament, being the first to score, the first to foul out, etc. It was so exciting and fun.

"The next morning when my mother opened the *Minneapolis Star Tribune*, there was a column by another well-known staff writer, Robert T. Smith. Mother handed the paper to me and her eyes were narrowed...not a good sign."

"And what was the matter?" Sarah asked.

"Well, this columnist had written that he had gone to the girls state tournament and the girls couldn't play well. He said something like watching *skunk wrestling with loaded skunks would have been more interesting. He said it should be the first and last tournament.*"

Patti could hardly get the words out.

Sarah jumped up from the stool and her arms flew up in the air. "See! The girls finally get a chance to play after all those years of having nothing - *nothing* - and someone *dares* to criticize them?

How did anyone think they could get to be 'good' unless they had a chance to play?"

The temperature in the kitchen was rising and the oven wasn't even turned on.

"It was awful," Patti agreed, "and there was even more in the article describing the low game scores and his opinion about how unskilled the girls were. It made me wonder if we had been at the same game. I wrote to the newspaper and told them how proud I was to be a basketball player and how hard we worked as a team. I told them how hurtful this writer's words were."

"Maybe other people wrote in too," Sarah noted hopefully.

"Now, here is the *'rest of the story,'*" Patti could finally manage a smile again. "Of course, the Minnesota State High School League didn't listen to his negative opinions and kept sponsoring the tournament, year after year. *Six years later, in 1982,* March 21, the day after the girls state tournament, in the same newspaper, the *same writer* wrote another article."

"Oh, no," Sarah looked intensely at her mother. *"Now* what did he say?"

Patti's smile widened as she pointed to an article carefully preserved in its plastic folder. "In his own words, he 'ate crow.' That's the same as saying he was wrong. The first paragraph in his article said, *'Pardon me a second here while I put a little salt and pepper on my crow... You see, I attended the first Minnesota high school girls' basketball tournament in 1976. I wrote and said then that it was certainly the last girls' tournament, or should be. I wasn't very kind. I said the girls couldn't dribble, pass, shoot or play defense. Watching skunk wrestling with loaded skunks would be more interesting, I allowed. Let's see, maybe a little ketchup on that crow would make it go down easier...'*

Patti continued, "Then he talked about how Janet Karvonen and her New York Mills teams and other great players came onto the scene. His final statements were, *'Well, things have changed, my friends. The girls have gotten good. The tournament has lasted, and well it should have...'*

"Then, at the end," Patti concluded, "he said, *'I know there are those, including many macho males, who preferred 'Dallas' to the girls' basketball tournament on television. I say they missed a better show. Excuse me, I've got to go baste my crow....'"*

Sarah and her mother gave Robert T. Smith a "high-five."

"Sometimes," Patti said, "You have to be patient. Keep people informed and be supportive so they have room to turn around and change their direction."

"Yes," Sarah added, "And don't listen to every criticism someone may throw at you. What if the League had listened? We might not be heading into playoffs soon."

"There is another footnote," Patti smiled. "Twenty years later, Jim Klobuchar wrote another positive column about girls basketball, though he was frustrated with the 'bedlam' and 'merchandised hysterics' of collegiate and professional sports. Then he talked about finding a high school girls state basketball game to watch on television, and how he enjoyed their skills and games that, he said, were competitive, intense and fun. In the last paragraph, he wrote, *'Which meant, finally, that I watched a substantial amount of ball over the weekend. Some of it was memorable. But the only game that gave me a lift, and reasonable joy, was a game played by young women whose names I'll never remember.'"*

"It's important, Sarah," Patti replied, "not to paint all media with the same negative brush. There are those who choose not to acknowledge that women have a place in sports and only see women as an intrusion into 'their' arenas. But look for the men and women who are doing a great job covering girls and women's sports and who understand the issues.

"Our local sports editor said he and his staff are always trying to achieve a balance in the way they display stories of male and female athletes. He said they try to consider the number of photos of girls and boys, as well as covering our community sports. It's not an easy job. There's a Latin phrase, 'via media,' that means 'the middle road.' That would be a fair way to treat everyone."

"I like that," Sarah sat down again. "It means we have to do more than complain. We need to encourage the ones who understand, like Christine Brennan. She has been writing over twenty years and you should see all that she does. She writes a column, and also is an author and a commentator on national television and radio. I saw her on a television program just the other day.

"Think about this, Mom. I saw an article she wrote back in 1992, where she said women's sports had made tremendous strides in media coverage since the 1970s. Christine wrote, '… *so is the glass half-full or half-empty? Look at where women in sports were 20 years ago. Women have made tremendous strides.*' I guess she wanted people to look on the positive side and yet still keep moving ahead."

"So," Sarah sighed, "another twenty years have passed since she wrote that. I wonder what she would say to my question today, '*how full is the glass now?*'"

Sarah had worked through her frustration and now had a

plan for how she and her team could approach the media and be positive. As she set milk glasses on the table, she smiled and filled them *half-full*. It would be a great topic at dinner tonight.

Sarah smiled at her mother, "Mom, you are really something, you know. You stop everything you are doing and listen to what I have to say. I really appreciate it."

Now it was Patti's turn to have moisture in her eyes. The praise from her daughter was heartfelt and would be tucked in among her favorite memories.

Patti stood up, "I'd better get back to the goulash that we're having for dinner. I got the recipe from my friend, Pam."

"Can I help?" Sarah asked.

"Sure," Patti smiled, "take that spatula and stir that sausage and baloney."

Laughter echoed out of the kitchen, as Sarah and her mother stood shoulder to shoulder at the kitchen counter, and in life.

TWO RINGS: A LEGACY OF HOPE

18

COMING HOME

The telephone rang and Ben yelled, "I'll get it." It appeared that going into junior high had opened some new doors for Ben and sometimes a young girl's voice was heard on the other end.

"It's for you, Mom," Ben's voice was clearly disappointed. "Some man asking for you."

"Hello, this is Patti," his mother said.

"Patti, my name is Ray and you don't know me, but I have something that I think you will be very interested in."

Patti's eyes rolled, waiting for a sales pitch about something, though his voice didn't sound like the typical sales person.

"And what might that be, Ray?" she asked politely.

"Well, I am from Sherburn and live on Fox Lake outside of town," he paused and Patti's eyes widened at the mention of the town and lake that were so special to her Grandmother Ruby.

He went on, "I have lived on the lake for years and years. Ruby and I were in school together and we used to gather at the lake, swim and have parties."

Patti wondered where his conversation was leading but she thought it wise to let him move along at his pace.

"You know, Patti," Ray went on, "we used to have such fun out at the lake, but I remember one day when we were out on the raft, not far from shore, your grandmother lost the ring the players were given after winning a big tournament. Ruby figured she lost it after she dove into the lake and it had slipped off her finger."

"Yes," Patti was now listening to each word, "that was probably one of the worst days of my grandmother's life. That ring was such a symbol of her playing days on the girls basketball team, and winning that big tournament in 1925. She always said that she never took the ring off after the tournament until the day it was lost in the bottom of the lake."

"Well, I have some good news for you," Ray's words seemed to drag on so slowly. "Our family has used that raft for years. My son, who has taken over the farm now, had towed it into shore last fall to store it for the winter. The other day, he noticed that one of the boards needed replacing. Our daughter Erin was here and she pulled up the board with a crowbar and let out a yell, 'Look, there's something stuck in between the boards. And it's shiny, *like silver.*'"

Ray paused, and Patti could almost hear the smile on his face, "Erin reached in and lifted this little thing out of the crack where it had been wedged real good. It turned out to be a *silver ring. And it had a little basketball on the top...*"

At this point, Patti couldn't stand it anymore, and she almost yelled into the phone, "Did it have initials inside the ring band?"

"Well, yes, and that's why I am calling you," Ray continued on in his steady, deliberate pace. "There were these initials, 'R.Mc, 1925,' and only one person on the team had a set of initials like that - your grandmother, Ruby McCarroll."

Patti felt her knees shaking and she quickly sat down at the kitchen table. Ben had a worried look on his face, and her husband had rushed into the kitchen at the sound of her excited voice. It could be good news or bad news. He raised his hands as if to say, "Tell me what's happening."

"Oh, Ray," Patti was now in tears, "That's Grandma Ruby's ring and we all thought it was lost forever."

"Well," Ray laughed, with a touch of pride in his voice, "I thought I might just 'make your day,' so my daughter Erin found your telephone number up there in the Cities. We thought you might like to take a drive down to pick up your grandmother's ring."

"Oh, yes," Patti smiled. "We'll come this weekend, if that's okay with you."

As the telephone was being hung once again on the wall, Sarah came walking into the kitchen, picking up on the unusual vibes surrounding her mother.

"Sarah, you aren't going to believe this," Patti was still shaking.

"Try me, and calm down, Mom, this is hard on your heart."

"This is the best news, Sarah! A man in Sherburn *found your Great-Grandma Ruby's ring!* We can drive down to pick it up this weekend."

"What? How could that be?" Sarah's thoughts swirled and tumbled in her head.

It seemed too surreal, as though such as thing could not really be happening. Great-Grandma Ruby's ring has been missing for years, and someone found it *in a crack in the boards of the raft?*

I'll believe it when I see it, Sarah thought skeptically.

It was Saturday and the family was on its way to Sherburn. Even the speed limit seemed to work against them. Her father punched in the cruise control so his foot wouldn't get too heavy. A speeding ticket wouldn't add to their day.

The towns rolled by, Lake Crystal, Madelia, St. James, Trimont. Oh, the stories they could tell, Sarah smiled.

As they drove through the little community of St. James, Sarah recalled the history of this area. I know that one of the earliest games was when St. James played a game with Northfield in 1904. How would those two girls high school teams have connected? The towns are over one hundred miles apart. And I read in my *Daughters* book that in 2004, Northfield invited St. James for a 100-year Celebration. The game was called, "The Game of the Century." The teams and captains were presented with commemorative basketballs at the traditional party held after the games. What a special night that must have been, Sarah thought.

Finally, the sign on the highway said, Sherburn, population 1060. Ray had provided them with directions to the farm and they wound their way through the countryside. The winter had been full of snowstorms, and the state basketball tournaments hadn't been played yet. But it soon would be April and May, and the fields would receive the onslaught of tractors and implements, turning over that rich, black soil and planting the crops of the heartland.

As they pulled into the farm driveway, an old collie came out, wagging her tail. She clearly considered herself a welcome dog rather than a watch dog.

The farm reflected the pride of its long heritage. Farm implements were being oiled, polished and prepared for their busy season ahead. The cows were chewing their cuds in a warm barn, waiting for milking time, and the other creatures, great and small, were quietly nestled in their stalls and nests. Patti knew Ben would enjoy seeing the baby pigs and lambs. Maybe they could go out there later.

As Sarah stretched her muscles after the long ride from the Cities, she patted the collie who wanted some acknowledgement of her role as the welcoming committee. The door to the house swung open and Ray came out, leaning on his walking stick, with a big smile on his face. Farming was a hard life, and he had accumulated enough years to feel some arthritis developing in his knees and back. His wife, daughter, son, and grandson were right behind him. Clearly, no one wanted to miss this occasion.

"Hey, Patti," Ray greeted Sarah's mother, "it didn't take long for you to get here. You must have started early this morning."

"Yes," Patti smiled, "we were anxious to get here. Your telephone call was *so exciting.*"

"And this must be Sarah. She has the look of her great-grandmother, and that's a good thing. I was a bit 'sweet' on her for awhile." He turned quickly to his wife, "That was before I met you, my dear." She smiled indulgently and let him continue enjoying his moments in the sun.

Ray smiled , "Come on inside and we'll meet the rest of your troupe. Mother has made her famous sweet rolls and some good egg coffee. I'll wager it's better than what you can get in your fancy coffee shops in the Cities. And we have lots of fresh milk," he grinned at Ben. "I bet you can drink a quart all by yourself. Let's go in and see what we can find."

Everything smelled wonderful and the table was full. There was a fruit platter filled with grapes, sliced oranges, pears, bananas, and pineapple. A bowl of apples and whole walnuts sat nearby. The wonderful fragrance told them that a basket of cinnamon rolls covered with a creamy frosting must have come out of the oven shortly before they arrived.

"Would you like to have some scrambled eggs and ham? It's all ready," Ray's wife offered.

"Well, that sounds wonderful," Patti smiled at the generous breakfast prepared for them. "You've gone to a lot of trouble for us, but we would love to enjoy your hospitality."

"Yep, that's the way we do things out here in the country," Ray laughed. "You city folks probably do the same thing, but every family around here wants to have a good reputation when it comes to putting out a 'good spread' for neighbors and visitors."

Minnesota hospitality, Sarah remembered, was always evident in the welcome given to the early girls basketball teams when they visited other communities. There were banquets held before the games, and parties and dances after the games. I remember the story of one girl who said she had never had a breakfast at home like the one she had when she stayed overnight at the farm home of a host team player. It was sad to read when the young girl said her family was poor and couldn't serve so much food at only one meal.

Soon, the plates were empty of even second helpings, and the coffee cups, and milk glasses, were refilled again.

It was time.

"Well, Ray," Patti ventured slowly, "whenever you are ready, we would like to see Grandma Ruby's ring, please."

Ray gestured to Erin who went to a cupboard full of special dishes, and brought out a small box. Ray stretched out his arm to give the box carefully to Patti. She looked at it, imagining what was inside, and handed it to Sarah.

"Here, Sarah, you should be the one to open it."

Sarah grasped the top and carefully lifted it. Her breath caught as she had her first look at her Great-Grandma Ruby's silver ring. *There it was, sitting in its special new home. On the top was half of* a basketball, with the letters "SHS" etched into the silver. As Sarah slowly turned the ring, she looked inside, and sure enough, there were the initials, "RMc, 1925."

Tears welled in Sarah's eyes. As she looked at her mother, she felt better to see a tear making its way down her mother's cheek. And she was quite sure that Ray's eyes were moist, though he had quickly wiped his sleeve across his face.

"Now, the ring is back where it belongs." Ray looked pleased with his role in solving the disappearance of the ring. "I remember the day when Ruby lost her ring. I thought she would never stop crying. And we kept diving and diving to try to find her ring. But the raft would swing around and the bottom was murky, especially after we stirred it up trying to see something silver shining down there. I was pretty good at holding my breath, but even then I couldn't find it. Later on, I went back on my own several times, hoping that I could find it. It would have made me quite a hero."

The ring and its box were being carefully examined by Sarah's family, while their hosts looked pleased with their role in reuniting them with the lost ring.

"You know, Sarah," Ray said, "I watch our teams play here and I know you enjoy playing basketball these days too. We had lots of fun back then in the 1920s. The girls and boys teams played on the same nights. If we had an 'away' game, the school gave each of us 15 cents for something to eat when we got back to town.

"We usually went to games in cars driven by families and other people in town. Players were assigned to a car, and one night, I was riding with Ruby and we went into the ditch on the way to Winnebago. The windshield was broken and, oh boy, by the time we got the car back on the road, we were late getting to the game. It was ten below zero. They brought Ruby and me some hot chocolate to drink. Ruby had to go right into the game. At least I could thaw out while the girls played their game. And the worst part was, after the game, we had to ride home in that same car without a windshield. Someone loaned us a big old horsehair blanket, but I still thought I'd freeze to death."

Ray was "warming up" again as memories came rolling back. "You know the girls' teams in those days wore big black bloomers. But in 1926, the school bought uniforms that had shorts instead of bloomers. No other team in Martin County wore shorts. Believe me, there was a lot of talk when rumors flew around town that the girls were wearing shorts out on the basketball floor. When they played their first game in shorts, there was a huge crowd."

Ray's eyes softened as he recalled those high school years that seemed not so long ago.

"I guess that's enough of those old memories," he said quietly, "I just hope you kids today have as much fun as we did."

Sarah could see that there was still something Ray wanted to share.

He paused and added, "You know, we guys always felt bad when the school dropped the girls basketball team. Ruby really stormed around the school about it, especially when someone told her it was because basketball wasn't good for the girls' health. Some of the girls became the cheerleaders for our team, but we knew their hearts weren't in it. It didn't seem fair that they added a boys 'B' team because there was more time open in the gym, and the girls had nothing. It was like rubbing salt in the wound for them."

Sarah knew right then that she liked this man. Sometimes it was easy to think that the men were against teams for girls, but she knew that many of the men coaching girls' teams weren't happy to have the teams dropped and fathers as well as school administrators had fought to keep teams for their daughters. She knew that adding physical education was a good thing, but only the girls competitive teams were dropped. The boys kept their teams and had physical education classes too.

Where were the laws to prevent such things? Sarah knew the answer to that question. State laws and federal laws like Title IX wouldn't show up for decades.

Another refill of coffee and milk and "just a sliver" of those delicious cinnamon rolls and sighs of happiness and satisfaction could be heard around the table. Sarah knew she'd never forget sitting around this table and enjoying the hospitality of these wonderful people of Sherburn, Minnesota.

The hugs were genuine as Sarah's family parted from their new friends. And the silver ring, secure in its box, was carefully zipped into her mother's purse, the safest place on earth.

Great-Grandma Ruby's ring was *coming home*, where it belonged.

★ ★

19

I Believed My Mother

"The doctor said I would never walk again. My mother said I would. I believed my mother."

~ Wilma Rudolph

"All right, class, today we are continuing your reports on women in your family who have left a legacy for you." The teacher movd to her usual chair in the back of the classroom, signaling the next student that it was her turn.

Yolanda walked to the front of the room, looked at her classmates, and began her report.

"In 1940, Wilma Rudolph was born into a large family to very poor, honest, hardworking parents. Her father was a railroad porter and handyman. Her mother did cooking, laundry and housecleaning for wealthy white families."

"She was the 'help,'" Yolanda added grimly, and continued. "Wilma experienced one illness after another: measles, mumps, scarlet fever, chicken pox and double pneumonia. When her left leg and foot became weak and deformed, she was taken to the only black doctor in Clarksville, Tennessee. The local hospital was open to whites only. The diagnosis was infantile paralysis, i.e., polio, a crippling disease that had no cure. Her mother discovered that Wilma could be treated at a black medical college fifty miles away and she drove Wilma there twice a week for two years. Wilma's mother was taught how to provide her with physical therapy exercises at home. By the age of 12, with the support of her mother and family, and her own determination, Wilma could walk normally without braces or crutches. She told the *Chicago Tribune* that 'I was challenging every boy in our neighborhood at running, jumping, everything.' She decided to become an athlete.

"Wilma became a basketball star in high school, setting scoring records and helping her team win the high school championship. Fortunately, she had been spotted by Ed Temple, coach of the women's track team at Tennessee State University (TSU). On full scholarship at TSU, Wilma began competing internationally. She earned a position on the U.S. Olympic track and field team and came home from the Melbourne Games with the Olympic bronze medal in the 400 meter relay.

"Wilma set her sights on winning a gold medal.

"On Sept. 7, 1960, in Rome, Wilma competed as the temperatures climbed toward 110 degrees. Over eighty thousand spectators jammed the Olympic stadium.

"It was her day.

"Wilma became the first American woman to win **three** gold medals in the Olympics. She won the 100 meter dash and the 200 meter dash. Then, running anchor, she brought her team from behind to win the 400 meter relay.

"When Wilma was asked by a reporter how she could accomplish this feat, she said, 'My doctor said I would never walk again. My mother said that I would. *I believed my mother.*'

"It was the first time that Olympic competition had international television coverage. As a result, Wilma became an instant hero and role model for young women starved for the opportunity to compete. She was given ticker tape parades and received an official invitation to the White House by President John F. Kennedy. Wilma's achievement led her to become one of the most celebrated athletes of all time."

Yolanda paused, and her voice was strained with emotion, "When Wilma returned to her hometown after the Olympics, she insisted that the homecoming parade in Clarksville, Tennessee, be open to everyone and not segregated, as was the usual practice. Her parade was the *first racially integrated event ever held in her hometown.*"

The class applauded.

Affirmed by their response, Yolanda continued, "Wilma's gold medals raised an important question: *where are all the other female athletes who should also be representing the United States?* The answer was that schools were not providing competitive teams for girls and women, so there was *no opportunity* for young women to receive training and emerge as potential Olympians."

Of course, thought Sarah, there would be no opportunity when sports for girls and women had been dropped some forty years earlier.

"The flame hit the tinder," Yolanda continued, "It was time to take action. In the 1960s, a series of training institutes were held that would forever change the face of sports. The representatives of these institutes came from states across the country and were charged with the responsibility to return home and begin training potential coaches for their high schools, colleges and universities.

"As teams were organized and doors cracked open, state and federal laws were passed that required equal treatment in sports for girls and women. Change was resisted by some and welcomed by so many.

"The forces of change could not be stopped.

"For young women, like me, sports now offer so many opportunities. I owe so much to Wilma Rudolph."

The young woman again paused and looked over the class.

"And, I am so proud to share with you," Yolanda's voice swelled with pride, "Wilma Rudolph is my great-aunt on my mother's side of the family, and I am named for her sister."

The class jumped to their feet and clapped and whistled.

It was her day!

Yolanda heard the roar of the crowd as she crossed the finish line, and smiled.

20

STEERING THE SHIP OF CHANGE

"Never doubt that a small group of thoughtful, committed citizens can change the world; indeed, it is the only thing that ever has."   *~ Margaret Mead*

T he young man, James, wove his way to the front of the classroom, laid his papers on the podium and took a deep breath.

"I want to tell you about a special woman who helped the schools
in Minnesota do the right thing for girls and women in sports. She
is my grandmother, Paula Bruss Bauck.

"One day a few years ago, my two brothers and I were visiting my
Grandma and Grandpa Bauck. Grandpa was a quiet man and helped
us build forts and fun stuff like that.

"But that day, Grandma Bauck decided it was a good time for
us to learn how to run. She said she had been watching us and we
wouldn't win any races the way we were running, waving our arms
and throwing our heads back. So we listened to her instructions
carefully because she was the track and field coach at the high school
in Moorhead, and she was not a person that you wanted to mess
with. We would get down in the starting position like she told us,
with our fingers pinched and arched just behind the line, lift up our

hips, hold, and when she clapped, we'd take off down the driveway. The winner would be the first to *touch the mailbox.*

"I made a nearly fatal error. On the way back up the driveway, I said to one brother, '*You run like a girl.*'

"I still think that it was real smoke that came rolling out of my grandma's ears when she heard me say that and I was immediately told to sit down on the front steps to the house, alongside my brothers.

"'*James,*' (she always called me by my full name when I was in trouble) 'what did you mean when you said your brother *ran like a girl?* Were you telling him he was running really well?'

"'No,' I replied honestly, another risky move. 'I meant he looked like he didn't know how to run and he was so slow.'

"'So, you meant it as a criticism, *an insult*, perhaps?' my grandma asked.

"Now, I *knew* there was no wiggle room left, so I just nodded my head.

"Suddenly, my grandmother's finger was right in front of my nose. 'Young man, first of all, *you are never to say those words to your brother again*, is that understood?'

"'Yes, Grandma,' I said clearly and sincerely.

"'Now, boys,' Grandma Paula sat down beside us, 'let's talk about why that is not an acceptable phrase to say to another boy, and how you could say it to a girl so she would know that it was a compliment.'

"So, we settled in for a talk with Grandma. She explained how words can hurt, *or* they can make people feel good about themselves. We learned that, under no circumstances, were we to use any word or comment that implied that girls or women weren't just as capable as a boy or man. She told us how girls had stood on the sidelines for many years because there were no sports for them. We found that hard to believe, but we listened carefully because there could be a quiz at the end of this discussion.

"I learned from Grandma Paula that she had been a good athlete at Roseau High School back in the 1930s and she had been called a 'tom-boy.' Those words were in the same category as my first mistake. She said girls who were skilled, as she was, were discouraged from playing and that girls' teams were dropped in the 1920s and 1930s because it was said that sports were unhealthy for girls. My brother and I could tell by the look in her eyes that this was a painful story for her to share with us. Grandma Paula told us how her parents and other adults would constantly tell girls like her to 'act like a lady,' or 'walk like a lady,' or 'sit like a lady.' She said, to our surprise, that she and other girls would say, 'If only we were boys, we wouldn't be told those things.'

"After our lessons in how to run *and* how to show respect for girls and women, I do remember that she had chocolate chip cookies and milk for us. So I guess that means she thought *there was hope for us.*

"When I see my Grandma Paula, I see a strong, determined woman who raised her family while she was teaching at the big high school out on the western edge of Minnesota. During my research for this report, I learned that she had built a strong girls physical education department and was highly respected by teachers and administrators all around the state. At the time, I just knew she had high expectations for her grandsons and made the best cookies.

"My dad, who is a school superintendent near here, told us about his mother because he wanted us to understand why he was so proud of what she had done. We learned that she was an important reason why girls in Minnesota have sports teams. Imagine, *our grandma* helped to open doors so girls could play again.

"The doors weren't easy to open.

"People had said for years that girls shouldn't participate in competitive sports because it might not be good for their health or they might not be able to have babies. My dad said his superintendent friends listened carefully, like her grandsons did, when his mother said, *'What makes anyone think that females aren't physically capable and ready for competition? How ridiculous is that!'*"

James gestured to include Yolanda, "Yolanda's report shared with us the exceptional performance of her great-aunt, Wilma Rudolph, when she won her three Olympic gold medals in 1960. It electrified the world. Then, people started asking, *'Where are all the other women athletes who should be competing for the United States?'*

"The answer was very obvious: since the shutdown of girls and women's sports in the 1920s and 1930s, there were few women being trained in any competitive sport. So, the big question was, 'How do we change that on a national level?'

"Now, follow me on this," James urged the class. "It is important to understand how to go about getting things moving from Ground Zero when nothing is happening. Here's what they did:

"In 1961-1962, the U.S. Olympic Committee and the national physical education association met together and decided to organize *national clinics* where they would invite individuals from every state to attend. At the national clinic, these people would learn how to conduct training clinics *in their states* so that teachers would learn how to train their students.

"Did you follow that? *It was like a bucket brigade* - one expert passes the information to another person who passes the information to the next...like passing a bucket of information from one to the next.

"Do you see how it would work? Start with a national training clinic, then in each state, training clinics would be held. The final bucket would be given to the young woman who wanted to learn how to compete. In her bucket would be information and a qualified teacher who could help her learn new skills.

"So, the master plan was to provide training to thousands of young women across the country. They would become the *first competitors* on high school and college teams. From that group, the elite athletes would emerge and represent the United States in international competition.

"It was an awesome plan, if it would work.

"The first two sports selected were gymnastics and track and field.

"Two individuals were appointed to attend the *first institute in 1963* at the University of Oklahoma: Patricia (Pat) Lamb, Carleton College in gymnastics, and Eleanor (Ellie) Rynda, University of Minnesota-Duluth in track and field. When they returned from the Institute, they started the 'bucket brigade' in Minnesota, organizing committees and conducting clinics all over the state. Thousands of teachers and young women came to learn, *and wanted more.*

"The plan was working. The National Institutes continued, and expanded into other sports.

"When they held a second national institute for track and field in 1965, Grandma Paula was selected as Minnesota's representative. She was a great choice. When she traveled to Michigan State University, I think they learned a lot from her because she was a master teacher in track and field. Teachers came to Moorhead just to watch her coach her athletes. So, it was no surprise when her girls track and field teams later won three state high school championships.

"So, the bucket brigades continued and, pretty soon...*kind of like* *spring in Minnesota...*you could 'smell' that *change was in the air.*

"Now, it was time for strong leaders to step up and say *why* girls' sports should be brought back into the schools of Minnesota.

Grandma Paula was there at the right time and in the right place. Can't you see her telling the school administrators to sit down on their 'front steps' and giving them a lesson on why *change was needed and coming?*

"Her favorite quote was, 'He drew a circle that shut me out - (called me a) heretic, rebel, a thing to flout. But love and I had the wit to win: we drew a circle and took him in.'

"So, Grandma Paula and others who shared her convictions, like Mary Dickmeyer Todnem, Mankato, drew a circle around the Minnesota State Department of Education (MSDE), the Minnesota Association for Health, Physical Education, and Recreation (MAHPER) and the Minnesota State High School League (MSHSL). She especially liked Dr. Carl Knutson, MSDE Supervisor of Physical Education, who worked right alongside them. She said he really listened and didn't just tell them what they should do.

"Another 'bucket brigade' began. Listen to how it worked...*again.*

"In 1967, the state physical education association, MAHPER, wrote a recommendation and presented it to the Minnesota State High School League. The first bucket was, 'You, the League, are the organization of all the high schools in Minnesota. You should be the organization that will administer a new girls athletic program, just as you do for boys athletics.'

"And the Board of Directors of the League agreed. Their leader, Mr. Beverly H. Hill, Executive Director, believed that girls should have a sports program under League supervision.

"Then the bucket was passed to a committee appointed by the

League to write the proposed *Athletic Bylaws for Girls' Sports.*
They did their work and passed the bucket to the Delegate Assembly
of the League.

"This is a really important time. Why? Because this group is
like the state legislature. They will vote on the proposal. If they say
'yes,' girls' sports is *'in.'* But if they say *'no,'* girls stay on the sidelines.

"So, in the fall of 1968, Grandma Paula and her committee stood
in front of the Delegate Assembly. After the meeting, the League
sent the proposed bylaws to all the member schools of the League
to discuss and instruct their delegates how to vote.

"Are you with me?" James asked the class. They nodded.

"At this point, the buckets have passed to the schools. Now,
remember, this is 1968, and for decades, people have believed that
girls should not participate on high school teams. Some people still
believed that girls were made of 'sugar and spice, and everything
nice,' and shouldn't be out on the floor, sweating and falling down,
shaking things out of place."

The young women in the class shook their heads.

James continued, "So you can imagine that the meetings of schools
from December to April were sometimes loud and full of differing
opinions. Some were in favor of adding girls' sports and others were
opposed. It was hard to gauge how the votes might come in.

"Now, 'fast forward' ahead to April 1969. Imagine walking in my
Grandma Paula's shoes into the meeting of the League's Delegate
Assembly and facing these thirty-two men who would decide the
fate of girls' sports in Minnesota. She couldn't tell by the looks on
their faces how they were going to vote.

"A man standing at the door of the room where the vote would
take place said to her, *'Bet'cha a quarter, it doesn't pass!'* Can you

imagine hearing that, after all of her hard work and years of being told that girls shouldn't play and to 'act like a lady?' *He was lucky that my grandma had a lot of self-control.* She walked past him to the podium and spoke to the delegates. Then she and her committee sat down to wait.

"They voted.

"Later, whenever she told me this story, she would hold up a quarter, smile and say, *'He lost. The girls won!'*

"It was unanimous! Each of the thirty-two members of the Delegate Assembly voted in favor of the proposed bylaws for girls athletics.

"Girls Athletics would now be sponsored by the League, right alongside boys athletics, music and speech activities."

James emphasized the importance of the event, *"Imagine the feeling that my Grandma Paula and her friends must have felt! There was a new world ahead."*

James continued to draw his picture for the class. "The League wanted to have a woman on their executive staff who would help schools develop their new interscholastic girls' sports programs. During the next year, the League interviewed candidates and in July 1970, added a friend of my grandma's, Dorothy E. McIntyre, who had been a teacher at Eden Prairie and a member of the same committees. They worked together for the next twenty years, sharing the same commitment to level the playing field and bring equity to sports."

James paused and looked at the class, "You might think that from this point, it was smooth sailing. *It wasn't.* Think of what it feels like when you shove your boat away from land and out into the river where the rapids would love to tip you over. *You'd better put on your life preservers. The challenges were just beginning."*

James continued, "There were questions from every corner, such as: Where do you think we're going to have girls' teams practice?

The gymnasiums, pools and fields are full!

Where do you think we'll get officials for girls' games?

Their schedules are full!

Where do you think we'll get funds for these new teams?

Our budgets are allocated!

Many voices were saying, '*No room...no room!*'"

Sarah thought, I've heard that before!

James asked the class, "Why was it so controversial? Remember, *Minnesota schools had adopted girls' sports in 1969, prior to the passage of the federal law, Title IX in 1972, that would later require equity in sports. There were no trails or roads mapped out. Minnesota had to find its own way.*

"Fortunately, Minnesota had local and state leaders who stepped up, and developed policies and laws that would guide the schools as they struggled and blazed their way through this new territory, just as their ancestors had done.

"In other words, Minnesota explored the new territory, built its own roads, and paved the way for today's girls' sports programs."

James looked at Sarah and Yolanda and the three athletes smiled.

James continued, "Having the right leaders in the right places was very important in those early days. The State Commissioner of

Education, Howard Casmey, stepped up and voiced his support for girls to have their fair share of sports facilities and finances. *His voice was heard across the state.*

"In the schools, the superintendents and their local school boards were the key to making things happen. My Grandma Paula had raised her sons well. My dad, the superintendent, would say, quietly and firmly, '*Our school will find* the gymnasium space; we *will find* the officials and the budgets for our girls program because it is *the right thing to do,* and *our girls* deserve their own teams as much as the boys do. His school board agreed, and soon, an armada of boats and ships had pushed away from shore, carrying the young women in Minnesota safely to a new world.

"My dad believes in the fair treatment of all the students in their school district. He did the right thing, just like his mother had taught him *and her grandsons.* 'Playing like a girl' is a good thing in his school. I am very proud to be his son, *and* Grandma Paula's grandson."

James straightened to stand as tall as he could. "My grandmother was like those pioneer women who left their homeland and immigrated to a new country. She left the old way of thinking behind and stood with her hand at the helm, *steering the ship of change,* helping young women immigrate to a new world of competitive sports."

James paused as he prepared to '*touch the mailbox.*'

"At her retirement, Grandma Paula said, '*Who could have anticipated during those challenging years between 1970 and 1974, that one million high school girls would participate on school teams? This four-year growth period has never been equaled. And today, over seven million girls call themselves athletes. I am happy that I was a part of those years when we changed the face of sports.'"*

James smiled, "Everyone stood and gave my Grandma Paula a 'standing O'!"

He took a deep breath, "Grandma Paula used to quote Margaret Mead who said, 'Never doubt that a small group of thoughtful, committed citizens can change the world; indeed, it is the only thing that ever has.' And my grandma was one of those thoughtful, committed citizens."

James looked out over the class, "I have learned so much from watching the women in my family and in our school compete in sports and in their careers. They are confident, have a respect for their opponents and know how to win and lose.

"They have taught me that our *school* is a better place when all students are treated fairly.

"I believe the world will be a better place when women are in equal positions to share, contribute, and steer the ships of change.

"I know that *I* am a better person because of them, *and my Grandma Paula."*

As James finished and gathered his papers, he smiled as his classmates gave *him* a standing 'O.' Then his eyes widened as he scanned the back of the room. He hadn't noticed when his dad, the superintendent, had slipped into the room.

There was a warm bear hug waiting for him from his proud dad, and included in it, was a special hug sent from his Grandma Paula, *and a box of chocolate chip cookies.*

★ ★

21

WHEN THAT HAPPENS, EVERYONE WINS

"We will be measured in the future by the role women in our society play in this new century, the women who are our mothers, sisters, grandmothers and friends." Sarah's voice was clear and strong as she brought her report in for a landing.

"Are they strong, confident, living without restraint, free to explore, to jump crevasses, fly to other planets or galaxies, raise families, choose their careers, find the cures for today's dreaded diseases, and govern at the highest levels of elected office?"

Sarah paused, *"When that happens, everyone wins!"*

Sarah looked across her classroom. The teacher was sitting in the back of the room and appeared to have a tissue at her eyes and the students were sitting quietly, highly unusual for them.

Oh boy, did I totally bomb? Sarah felt her throat beginning to constrict and a shiver ran down her back. Then the class began clapping and it got louder as her classmates began to stand and even a couple of loud whistles rang across the room.

It was almost too much. The positive vibes in the room couldn't stop Sarah's knees that were now shaking from the adrenaline rushing through her veins. She sat down at her desk and put her hands over her face, partly because she felt like crying and laughing at the same time. Tammy sat in the seat behind her and Sarah felt her hand on her shoulder, patting her gently, saying, "Sarah, that was *awesome!*"

As Sarah lifted her head, she saw that her teacher had returned to the front of the room. To her relief, Sarah saw that the teacher had a smile on her face.

"Class, I am so proud of each of you. You have brought the lives of women in your families into focus. It is my hope that our discussions about the myths and stereotypes that affected your family members will help you to be more alert to discrimination and that you will step up to bring about change. Our country is still a young republic when set against others throughout the centuries. We have survived so far because individuals were willing to make sacrifices, to do honorable things that would improve the condition of others.

"Some say that your generation is only focused on your social networking and playing games. I, however, do not agree. I believe that each of you is on the brink of being an important part of our future. And I believe you understand how important it is that you are willing to stand up and be counted, to make change one day at a time."

As the teacher paused, Sarah found her mind and body beginning to coordinate again. She could hear her teacher explain what was ahead.

"I have asked a committee of teachers and community leaders to review your reports and recommend how we may best share them with the school and our community. Our district media department will also be developing your reports into a presentation that can be shown on the school's website and also be available to members of the public.

"Sarah," she said, "You have been invited to present the class project to our downtown community organization.

"And," the teacher added, "members of the news media will be contacting you for an interview."

Yolanda tapped her on the shoulder, "I'll help you wherever you want. My mom is the president of the Downtowners Club."

Sarah smiled to herself. I feel like a candidate for a political office.

22

One Step at a Time

"The true journey of any expedition is the journey of the mind. Navigating that terrain depends not on physical skill or muscle, but on character." ~ Ann Bancroft, Explorer

The whistle blew three short blasts. That meant the team was to come over to the coach, sit down and be quiet, and don't waste any time.

"Whew," Sarah whispered to Jordan, "I needed a break, how about you?"

Jordan's head nodded and the sweat rolled down her face. At the end of the season, the team expected to have tough practices and the coach had been true to form.

"All right, listen up," Coach Johnson began, "you know we have our first playoff game tomorrow. This is what they call the 'second season'; every game decides who goes forward and whose season ends. *Do you want our season to end tomorrow night?"*

"NOOOOOO," the team all responded in their loudest voices, as they knew exactly what the coach expected and it better sound good or they'd have to do it again until she was satisfied with the depth of their commitment.

The coach went through the plans for the next day; they should wear their warm-up jackets to school. There would be a pep assembly, and the co-captains would be talking to the students.

"Prepare your comments tonight," the coach waved her hand at Sarah and Yolanda. "And don't say 'you know' every other sentence. Sound confident and ready to play and ask the student body and faculty for their support. Got it?"

Sarah and Yolanda nodded emphatically and knew they'd be meeting tonight to plan what they would say so one wouldn't repeat the other.

The coach's voice dropped a little in volume and the team knew when that happened, they'd better listen carefully because this would be a serious "pep talk."

"I've coached you for several years now and I believe that you have the ability to get to the state tournament - and win it!"

The team's collective intake of air, almost a team gasp, hung in the air.

"I know," the coach continued, "some people believe it's dangerous to set a goal like that. We might not reach it. But I'm telling you that we are going to win each game that it takes to get to the state tournament, and then we are going to win the games that will take us to the championship game.

"And then," she paused for effect, "we are going to play the way we all know we can, and we are going to win the state championship." And that was that.

It was very quiet in the gym. The team wasn't sure whether to sit quietly or stand up and cheer. They collectively seemed to choose to sit quietly and think about the goal that had been set by the coach.

Sarah knew that their team was good. It was such fun to play when each player knew her assignment and was willing to do what was needed for the good of the team. Sometimes it meant sitting on the bench when you wanted to be on the floor. And sometimes it meant going in when it might be up to you to help win the game with a big play. Several of her teammates were also seniors and this was their big chance and their big finale. High school would soon be over and no matter what road each player would take, they would not be the same team again, representing their school, and wearing their high school uniforms.

The coach folded her arms, and quietly looked at her team, "I'd like to share a friend with you. Her name is Ann Bancroft. She is an arctic explorer, as many of you know, and we are all proud that she is a Minnesotan and a strong, pioneering woman. Let me tell you a little about Ann. She dreamed of being the first woman to cross Antarctica. When she went to corporations and organizations for support, they looked at her stature and frame, and said, 'but you are so small.' The problem was, they didn't see *her heart!*

"So on a dime, support of friends and family, and a belief that she had to help break stereotypes and myths about what women could or could not do, *she went anyway.* Ann believed in her cause. She believed that when she succeeded, other women would follow, and, collectively, they would change the world order. Once launched on one of her several expeditions on the lands of ice and cold, she traveled for months and covered hundreds of miles on skis, dragging a sled, even using a parasail. She struggled up and down glaciers and occasionally had the frightening experience of falling up to her shoulders into a deep glacial crevasse. She faced blinding ground blizzards, frostbite and unbelievably cold temperatures. When asked how she did it, she said, *'I just took it one step at a time.'*"

The coach continued, "Tomorrow, we face a challenge. For our team to succeed, each of you must make a commitment, as Ann did.

"First, *make the best use of your abilities.* It isn't your physical size, it's the size of your heart. Whatever you know you do well, do it for the team;

"Second, *commit yourself unconditionally to our goal.* That means there is no room for doubt anywhere, anytime. This means you can't be tired or question our goal. You must be totally committed to our cause;

"Third, think of Ann. *Take it one step at a time.* Concentrate on every point, every play, every assignment. One step at a time will get us to our goal. Ann succeeded; she proved the 'doubters' had underestimated her.

"So will we!"

Now, the team needed no prompting; they jumped to their feet as a unit, pumping their arms, clapping and cheering, filling the rafters with the sound of their confidence and commitment.

If it is to be, Sarah thought, it is up to each of us. Together we'll be unstoppable.

One step at a time.

23

GET READY, WORLD! HERE I COME

"Tears will be shed at the Met Center this weekend. Some of them will be mine. It has become a ritual of mine, since moving to Minnesota six years ago, to watch the state high school girls basketball tournament and, briefly, to cry... because I was born female, and I was born too soon."
~ Jacqui Banaszynski, Staff Writer, St. Paul Pioneer Press, March 19, 1987. Pulitzer Prize winner, 1988

"And now, welcome OUR VERY OWN GIRLS BASKETBALL TEAM: THE STATE CHAMP--EEE---OONNNNNS!!"

The school gymnasium rocked with applause as the team walked onto their own floor with the co-captains carrying their championship trophy and gold medals proudly displayed around each neck. As the team looked around, it seemed that everyone was there.

This is some "welcome home," Sarah thought, and smiled to herself. It's as big as when the football team won their championship. Maybe bigger!

Yolanda pointed, "Look, there is the mayor and the school superintendent. Cool."

It had been a long week and some late nights, but today, any lingering fatigue was forgotten as they shared their happiness with their friends, family and community.

Sarah felt that the applause sounded as loud as it was at the end of the championship game last night in the Target Center,

Minneapolis. Their team had taken the tournament "one step at a time," and had reached the championship game.

The game had been a battle from the beginning. For the audience who loved basketball, it was a battle of titans and great fun. For family and friends of team members, it was *pure torture*.

It had been a fun game to play. The officials had been great. The coaches had stayed in their coaching boxes and no technical fouls had been administered. The sportsmanship had been admirable in the stands as well. It was like a championship game should be; two evenly matched teams battling it down to the wire.

Now it was getting seriously tight and close to the end of the game. The score is home-77, visitors-76. Jordan had just made a fantastic driving layup, one of her signature moves, and now they were only one point behind. Twelve seconds left in the game.

As the opposing player came dribbling down the floor, Yolanda was able to deflect the ball from the dribbler to send the ball flying. Sarah grabbed it and went dribbling down the court, pulled up in her favorite spot, and as she shot, she was fouled.

Although she had missed the shot, it still meant two free throws. And Sarah would be shooting the free throws.

The sound in the arena was deafening, but Sarah hardly heard it. One point behind, the championship is on the line. This was what every athlete dreams of - the chance to make the points that win the game and *the state championship*.

Negative thoughts started creeping into her mind, but Sarah pushed them away. She reminded herself that for years during practice and at home on the driveway, she had put herself in this exact situation over and over again, setting the stage: we are one point behind, and I'm at the line. All I have to do is put this ball in the basket, *twice.*

I've been waiting my whole life for this moment. It's up to me and I can do it. I've practiced these free throws thousands of times before. *No problem.*

She got herself set, looked at the front rim of the basket, bounced the ball two times, spun it in her hands, set, and shot. The ball went up in a slow arc and dropped into the bottom of the net.

Point!

A touch of her teammates' hands and Sarah was set once again. Carefully placing her foot behind the free throw line, she eyed the basket. Bounce, spin, set, and the ball headed once more toward the basket. This time, it rolled maddeningly around the rim as Sarah and their fans urged it to go in. Finally, the ball spiraled down into the basket.

Point!!

Sarah's team had a one point lead. Jordan and Yolanda were waiting with arms high as the opposing player quickly brought the ball to mid-court. Just before time ran out, she lofted a long, high ball toward the basket. As the ball dropped down toward the basket, it fell *just short* of the rim.

It is over. We win!

Now the sounds are deafening. Players waving their arms in one big circle together, and jumping, jumping, jumping. It was all a happy blur.

It doesn't get any better than this, Sarah thought. She looked out in the stands and saw her mother and dad, her brother and sisters, all smiling and clapping. It almost looked as if she could see other familiar faces - *was that Great-Grandma Ruby? Clara? Marie?*

Sarah smiled.

As Sarah glanced over at the opposing team's bench, she saw a player with her head in her hands. Heather was an opponent tonight, but Sarah had played on the same team with her at summer camp. They had traveled to tournaments together, even stayed at each other's homes. Sarah walked over and sat on the bench beside her, putting her arm around her friend's shoulders.

"Heather," Sarah began, "you played a terrific game and I am so proud of you. Either of our teams could have won this game." Heather lifted her eyes to look at Sarah.

Sarah continued, "I know it's hard, but right now is the time to hold your head high because you and your team are great. Your fans respect you for how you played and represented your school. So heads up, my friend. Show the world what you are made of!"

Heather managed a little smile, and joined her teammates on the court for the second place awards ceremony. They hoisted the trophy to take to their fans who would always think of them as their winners.

As Sarah's team waited on their free throw line, a reporter touched Sarah's arm.

"Sarah, what does it feel like to win a state championship?" she asked.

Sarah smiled, "I have always wanted to experience the feeling I'm feeling right now...*it's awesome!*"

"One more quick question," the reporter said, "How could you hit two free throws with the pressure of a state championship on the line?"

Sarah thought for a moment and said, "I just did what the coach told us to do - I took it one step at a time, one free throw at a time.

"And," Sarah grinned, "it worked, didn't it?"

As she was leaving the gymnasium and the welcome home celebration, her track coach had leaned over and said, "See you at practice on Monday." There would be no break in her schedule.

Sarah wearily climbed the stairs to her room, dropping her heavy gym bag in the corner. After they had all returned from the welcome home celebration, the family had gathered around the kitchen table for some traditional ice cream.

Her dad had surprised her with a plaque that he had made. They had all come up to her room and Ben ceremoniously pounded a nail in the wall and hung the plaque. They had taken Great-Grandma Ruby's silver ring out of the box and carefully hung it on the chain that was hanging on the plaque. Then Sarah took off her championship ring and slipped it onto the chain, gently guiding it down to rest next to her great-grandmother's ring.

The plaque said, simply, "Two Rings: A Legacy of Hope."

Oh, yes, Sarah smiled, you belong together: my grandmother's legacy and my hope for the future.

It was late. Sarah flopped down on the bed with a huge sigh and thought of the basketball season just ended. I wonder if I'll remember, like the pioneer women could, all the details - the practices, the trips, and the fun we had. Sarah looked at her bulletin board with its newspaper clippings, photos and certificates, the shelves of trophies lining the room, and the research paper that had changed her outlook on life.

Sarah got up and walked over to the plaque on the wall and the two rings resting next to one another.

Now, I think I can understand better, Sarah thought, how

Great-Grandma Ruby felt when she received her ring. It's what the ring *stands for:* trying to do our best, giving up things other kids could do, all because we have a dream and nothing is going to stand in our way. And I've learned that life isn't always easy, but we have to move past the pain of loss and keep looking ahead.

Sarah's eyes brightened as she realized, *so that is what "hope" is: a confident feeling about what will happen in the future.*

I have hope!

Sarah thought, to all of you women, those of my family, my country, those who dared to break down the stereotypes and myths that closed doors to women for so long, thank you. I've learned from you, and now, I'm ready to stand on my own, to do my part.

Sarah straightened her shoulders, stood a little taller, looked at the two rings and announced in a clear, strong voice,

"Get ready, World! Here I come."

24

ATHENA, THE BRINGER OF VICTORY

"Welcome to the 40th Annual Minneapolis Athena Awards," the woman at the podium of the Minneapolis Convention Center announced with a warm smile as she looked out over the enthusiastic audience of six hundred and more.

Suddenly, from the back of the room came a trumpet fanfare that caused a ripple through the audience. It signaled the entrance of the young women from metro area high schools, each of whom had been selected as the recipient of their school's Athena Award.

The band began to play, and the first young woman stepped confidently into the ballroom, followed by the second, and third. Their numbers grew into the twenties, then thirties, and forties, until they numbered *fifty-five*. As they walked down the aisle, many glanced quickly toward the area where their family was sitting. Fifty-five young women, each representing the "best of the best" in their school, with accomplishments that would soon awe the audience when the awards were presented.

"Sarah, would you step in to my office for a moment?" It was the principal's voice. As Sarah followed the principal into her office, Sarah thought the office staff looked as though they knew a secret.

"Sarah, please have a chair," the principal beckoned her inside. And she smiled.

"I have good news for you, Sarah," the principal began, "You have been selected by our Athena Selection Committee to be our school's Athena Awards Recipient for this year."

Sarah's breath caught in her throat. She knew of this event and had always been in awe of the senior women who had been selected in previous years. She knew that only one was selected each year, so it was an honor, that's for sure.

The principal continued, "As you may know, Sarah, our school has participated in this event since its inception nearly forty years ago. You will become part of a long tradition of young women selected to represent our high school in athletic and scholastic achievements, as well as community service. Congratulations, Sarah, from all of us.

"Now, here's what we need from you," the principal said, though Sarah's mind was flying away in anticipation of the experience ahead for her.

Patti sat down in her kitchen chair, looking in amazement at Sarah who had just shared her news about the Athena Award.

"Sarah, I am so proud of you, and your dad is going to bust his buttons," Patti brushed a tear of happiness from her cheek.

At dinner that night, Ben came down and stood behind Sarah, placing his homemade "olive wreath" on her head. They all applauded, both for Sarah and for Ben's desire to share his pride in his oldest sister.

It was the day of the event and everyone was a bit nervous. Patti and Gary's choice of attire had met with Sarah's approval. The parents smiled knowingly at each other, enjoying the small role reversal.

As they drove near the downtown skyline of Minneapolis, Sarah was proud that their Twin Cities were such neat and clean-looking places. Sarah's dad always commented on how the classic Foshay Tower used to be the landmark before being overshadowed by the IDS Tower. Nicollet Mall was a favorite of both "locals" and tourists, especially during the holidays when the Holidazzle Parades featured volunteers who dressed in big, heavy, and warm costumes with hundreds of lighted, colorful bulbs.

Then there was the summer celebration, The Aquatennial. Yes, Sarah thought, it truly was a City of Lakes - Calhoun, Harriet, Nokomis (that means 'grandmother' in Ojibwe, Sarah had learned on her trip 'up north'), and Lake of the Isles. Each had its own character and in summer hosted everything from sailboat races to lakeshore concerts, and always the daily crowd of runners, skateboarders, bikers, and walkers.

Here I am, Sarah contemplated, heading for an event that is a once-in-a-lifetime opportunity for me to be with young women who have also been selected by their schools as their Athena Award recipients. I love the awards that young women can reach for today, like Ms. Basketball, Ms. Hockey and being an Athenian.

The group photos were now finished and Allie, the "voice of girls' sports," had checked with each young woman to verify the pronunciation of her name. This woman just exuded warmth and friendliness.

It was line-up time. Members of the sponsoring committee checked their order and gave them last minute instructions. Their tables were at the very front of the auditorium, directly in front of the stage where the head table would be filled with dignitaries.

Sarah was going to be sitting next to Heather. Looking back at the state tournament where their teams had met in the championship game, Sarah was happy that she had gone to the bench to tell Heather that she had played a great game. It's a lesson to remember, Sarah thought. You might be the winner today but how you treat your opponent is important because you might be meeting again and sharing another experience, like sitting next to one another at the Athena Awards Luncheon.

The chairperson of the committee welcomed the young women and the audience to the 40th anniversary of the Minneapolis Athena Awards Program.

Imagine, Sarah thought, they held the first program when my mother was a freshman in high school. That's awesome...just think that this dedicated committee has recognized over 2,000 young women like me over those four decades. And one of my friends will be part of the St. Paul Athena Awards.

The speaker reminded everyone that Athena was a Goddess of Greek Mythology and the committee had chosen her as the symbol to represent outstanding young women athletes because she had possessed wisdom, courage, strength, and athletic skills.

After lunch had been completed, a distinguished-looking man was introduced. His name was Ray Christensen. The response of the audience confirmed that he was well liked in the community. Ray had been the emcee of the early Athena programs, and when he said "a few words," Sarah could understand why his voice alone had added a special quality to the ceremony.

Two women at the head table were introduced. They were the first mother and daughter to *each* be selected as the Athena Award recipient from the *same* high school. It must be awesome, Sarah thought, to share that experience with your mother.

The next introduction was of an Athena award recipient from the very first awards program in 1973. She may now be years older, Sarah calculated, but from the sparkle in her eyes, and her confident gaze, this woman has successfully incorporated the qualities of Athena into her life. She reminded the young Athena women that over 80% of successful women business executives played organized sports. She said, "The road from your locker room may well lead to the boardroom, the courtroom and any other room you choose to enter."

Then she smiled and added, "They used to tell the young women of my generation that our 'place' was in the *house.* So, I thought, perhaps it is. Today I proudly serve Minnesota in the *House of Representatives* in Washington, D.C."

The Athenians and their constituents all applauded. She had their support with a couple supportive whistles for emphasis.

It was now time for the awards presentation. Each young woman was instructed to walk from her table to the steps leading up to the stage. She would receive her recognition standing in front of the head table, in front of the world.

As Sarah listened to the introduction for each Athena winner, she wished that the pioneer women could see their legacy: the young women who were exemplary in sports, academics and in service to their communities.

Amazing, Sara thought, as she listened to the career paths they had chosen: medicine, law, music, architecture, military, movie producer, engineering, business, explorer, pastor, dietitian, therapist, researcher, pilot, teacher, chemist, zoologist, oceanographer, astronomer, flight controller, astronaut - clearly, these young women envisioned no doors closed to them.

Sarah had listed a potential career choice, but she knew her options were still wide open. Be patient, she thought, you will know when the time comes.

Sarah heard her name and school, stood, walked up the steps and across the long stage in front of the head table. As she reached the awards presenters, she was awarded her plaque and they stood together for the traditional photographs.

As she sat down again at her table, Sarah finally exhaled. She hadn't slipped, or tripped or done any of those things that can happen when your head and feet don't seem to be connected. She thought, I hope my parents are breathing again too.

As the family drove home, Patti was reading from the description of Athena from the program. "This Greek mythology is interesting. Athena created and gave the olive tree to her favorite city, Athens. And following Greek tradition, an olive wreath is awarded to Olympic champions. Ben, you were 'right on' with your award last night."

Ben smiled.

"Athena presided over the Parthenon, was brave and the essence of all that is noble," Patti read. "Legend has it that she possessed the gifts of dignity, power and youth, making her invincible. Today she is considered the *bringer of victory*."

Patti turned, "That's a tall order, Sarah."

"The bringer of victory," Sarah said, *"that's what I want to be.* I want to use my abilities in a way that will encourage people to make good decisions, to be brave and do the right things. I want to be a leader who will help others to work together."

The occupants of the front seat looked at one another and smiled. Those in the back seat gave their big sister a "high-fifteen"!

Home again. The day was over. Sarah pulled back her comforter and crawled wearily into her bed. She turned off the light and tried to close her eyes, but they popped open again. Sarah wanted to hold on to such a memorable day.

One of her congratulatory cards was from the two women who had written *Daughters of the Game*. It said, "Sarah, the daughters of the game have passed their *legacy* to you. Now, you are their *hope* for the future."

The future, Sarah thought, and sleepily remembered the quote from a Dr. Seuss book that her dad used to read to her, "You have brains in your head. You have feet in your shoes. You can steer yourself any direction you choose."

As she began to relax, Sarah kept hearing the words, "the bringer of victory."

That could be me, just like Athena, she thought, as she drifted off to sleep, her olive wreath resting alongside her pillow.

25

All the Difference in the World

As their graduation caps flew high into the air, Sarah's happiness was tinged with the emotions that this was her last moment as a high school student, and her first as a high school graduate.

And the memory of one individual flashed into her mind.

Sarah was thirteen when she met *the Star Thrower*.

As she stooped over to look more closely at a shell, a wave came rolling in, covering her bare feet with the cool water of the Gulf of Mexico.

Sarah smiled to herself. The waves coming in were quite gentle this morning, and shells were rolling in for her scrutiny. They were her morning's "gift from the sea." Sometimes, a wave known as "#7" came rolling in, a stronger wave carrying shells and seawater higher onto the beach, catching many a sheller by surprise.

As she looked down the beach, a figure was stooping down near the water's edge, but was tossing something back into the waves. What is that woman doing, Sarah wondered. Most of us are picking things *up*.

It was still dark, though the glow in the east confirmed that an orange sliver of the sun would soon touch the rim of the horizon. Sarah thought, this is the best time of the day.

The birds were returning from their overnight in the refuge located on the other side of the island. She watched five pelicans as they approached, flying low across the water, their wingtips barely skimming the waves. A snowy egret stalked by, so focused on its search for little morsels of food that it paid no attention to a nearby human being. Sarah's favorites were the tiny sanderlings, the little shorebirds that darted into the waves to poke into the sand for food, and quickly back out, their little legs a blur as they raced ahead of the next wave.

Sarah's little bag of shells this morning was a nice variety of her favorites: olives, whelks, murex, even part of an angel wing. An empty tulip shell also was a temporary home for a hermit crab, so Sarah carefully set it back into the water.

"No need to spoil your day," Sarah commented quietly. "It's hard to find a good home."

One shell was a nutmeg, a pebbly-surfaced, round little univalve shell, with streaks of brownish-gold and white. It is not easy to find a nutmeg; maybe that was why she enjoyed the shell. It is the search, isn't it, Sarah thought, that is the most fun in life.

At home, I like to pour a handful of shells into my hand and catch the fragrance of the sea and hear the sounds again as they click against one another. Sarah knew that her days on Sanibel Island would always be a part of her special memories.

The woman was closer this time as Sarah glanced up, and again, she saw her stoop down to pick up something from the sand and toss it gently back into the waves.

Sarah walked toward the woman and stopped, waiting for an acknowledgement of her presence. The woman straightened up and smiled at the young woman, no doubt remembering her younger days exploring the beach at sunrise.

"I've been watching you," Sarah began, "and I notice that you have been picking up something from the sand and putting it back into the waves again. May I ask what you are doing?"

The woman smiled, kindly, "Of course, I'm happy you asked. You have probably noticed that this morning, there are starfish on the beach that were washed up overnight by the high tide. This morning, the sun will soon be up and the heat will cause them to dry up and die out here on the sand."

Sarah paused and looked around, noticing for the first time that there was another starfish lying near their feet.

"Yes," Sarah said, "I see what you mean, but what are you doing?"

The woman reached down and gently picked up the little starfish, "I am picking up the ones that I see and putting them back in the water where they belong." And with that, she gently tossed it back into the waves where the starfish floated safely down into its environment again.

"But," Sarah's eyebrows lifted skeptically, "there are miles of this beach ahead of you, and there must be lots of starfish in trouble out here on the sand. Even if you put back the ones you see, you can't reach them all, and tonight, the tide will likely bring many of them back in again. *So, what difference will it make if you throw some of them back in the water?*"

As the woman glanced at Sarah, she saw a starfish nearby. She picked it up and held it out toward Sarah.

As she swept her other arm across the vast expanse of beach and water, she said, "I don't know how much difference I can make in this whole scheme of things."

As she gently tossed the little starfish back into the waves, she looked at Sarah and said, *"But I do know one thing – to that one, it makes all the difference in the world!"*

The sun was setting through Sarah's bedroom window. What a day, Sarah thought. I have been a high school graduate for twenty-four hours and whenever I think about what is ahead for me, I still think about that woman on the beach, "the star thrower."

She taught me such an important lesson - to do what I can, where I can, when I can, because to someone else, my actions might make all the difference in the world.

Researching my family's roots in sports opened many unexpected doors for me. When I walked in the footsteps of those pioneer women, like Great-Grandma Ruby, Marie, Adalyn and Anne, I discovered that they were once young women with hopes and dreams, *just like me.* And I met my heroes, some among my family and friends, and others who inspired me by their integrity and courage.

My heroes, Sarah thought, *what did I learn from you?*
She leaned back and began,

> *I learned that we must use our abilities, whatever they may be, for the good of others.*

> *I learned that we must accept responsibilities for our actions.*

I learned that we must commit ourselves to a cause,
even when it involves risk to personal health and safety.

I learned that we can solve a big problem by breaking
it apart and solving the pieces one by one.

Sarah sat back in her chair and closed her book, *Daughters of the Game.* She glanced up at her research paper in a frame, marked "A+," hanging alongside the plaque with its two rings.

"To each of you," Sarah said, "who 'pushed upon the gate' so that I can step into my future - *thank you.*"

As she gazed outside at the blue skies, Sarah said, "I may not know just when or how, but I do know one thing, *I am going to do something that will make all the difference in the world.*"

And her mother, who had stopped quietly outside her door, smiled.

Epilogue

"My dream is of a place and a time when America will once again be seen as the last best hope of earth."
                                                                    ~Abraham Lincoln

S arah sat in the bright January sunlight. She looked out over the huge crowd, the band, choir and dignitaries gathered in the stands around her and rows of people in front, filling in any open space. It was a bone-chilling cold day but no one seemed to notice.

Sarah turned and looked behind her at the inspiring sight of the United States Capitol crowned by the bronze Statue of Freedom. She appreciated the symbolism of this female figure with its flowing draperies, the attached brooch inscribed "U.S.", and her right hand resting on the hilt of a sheathed sword. A laurel wreath of victory and the Shield of the United States is clasped in her left hand. She wears a helmet encircled by stars and its crest is adorned with an eagle's head, feathers and talons.

How significant, Sarah thought again, that the Statue of Freedom stands on a globe encircled with the words *E. Pluribus Unum*, "from many, one," the national motto at the time of her placement atop the dome in 1863.

Sarah mused, that motto could well serve our country today. We are so much stronger when we are united as we must be in time of war, she thought. We have to learn how to be united in peacetime too, so that we can address our people's needs.

As the Marine band struck up its stirring music, Sarah looked to the center of the National Mall and the obelisk of the Washington Monument, rising in tribute to the man called *The Father of Our Country.*

Our country is so young, she thought, we have been tested since the birth of this "experiment in democracy." But we are still vulnerable and there are many in the world who would do us harm.

In the distance, at the far end of the National Mall, stood the magnificent Lincoln Memorial. Sarah had walked to the memorial last night to look again at his face, hoping to absorb some of the strength, compassion and courage that Lincoln had needed during his presidency.

Midway down the Mall, Sarah could see women in white dresses, waving purple and gold banners, "Equal Rights for Women." The time is right, Sarah thought.

On Sarah's left, the round dome of the Jefferson Memorial brought memories of the brilliant leader who had drafted the Declaration of Independence and influenced the content of the U.S. Constitution. The Declaration's stirring words, "We hold these truths to be self-evident…" had set the Colonies on a new path.

The opening words of the U.S. Constitution had always challenged Sarah. It must continue to be, "We, the People," Sarah thought. We, *all of us,* every race, religion and gender, must eliminate the splinters and divisions, red states and blue states. It must be, We, *all the people* of the United States of America.

Her heartbeat began to accelerate a little as she felt the immensity of her approaching responsibilities. As she looked down the mall and acknowledged the memorials to so many wars and their heroes, Sarah's hands closed in commitment. We must honor the sacrifices of so many, she thought. We must serve as a beacon of hope and freedom for the world.

This must be my mission, Sarah affirmed silently, to remove the separation, bitterness and suspicions and bring unity and strength to our country.

She looked across the sea of faces in the audience. The faces of her parents, siblings, and their families and friends were clearly visible, perhaps, Sarah thought, because they had the biggest and proudest smiles. As did Uncle Dan and Aunt Lynn. Nearby were Tammy, Jordan, and Yolanda, her faithful teammates who had stood by her throughout her journey. She glanced toward James, Kevin and Heather who each gave her a thumbs up and a wink. Her daughters, Samantha, Summer and Malia, were grinning proudly at her.

Sarah stretched out her fingers, first touching the silver ring with its basketball glinting in the light, and next to it, the gold ring that said, "state champion." She turned her hand over, and on its palm was the word printed earlier by her mother: *Porivo!*

She smiled to quietly to herself. Practice is over, Sarah thought. If it is to be, it's up to me, and I'm ready.

I am a daughter of the game.

As if by cue, a flock of geese approached. As they flew overhead, their calls of encouragement rang in Sarah's ears.

Now is the time. It felt as though she had been preparing her entire life for this moment.

Sarah stood and walked to the podium. She faced the supreme court justice, placed her hand on her great-grandmother's bible, raised her right hand, and in a clear, strong voice, began, "I, Sarah…, do solemnly swear that I will faithfully execute the Office of President…."

"Hail to the Chief" rolled across the National Mall, and rippled across the United States of America.

MY HEROES

History of Women in Sports Timeline, 776 B.C. to 1960

The following events were selected to illustrate the efforts and accomplishments of women, defying safety, social mores and public opinion. See *Reference for total listing plus events into the current century.

776 B.C.   The first Olympics are held in ancient Greece. Women are excluded, so they compete every four years in their own Games of Hera, their Greek goddess.

1552   Mary, Queen of Scots (1542-87), an avid golfer, coins the term "caddy" by calling her assistants "cadets." It is during her reign that the famous golf course at St. Andrews is built.

1784   Elizabeth Thible of Lyons, France, is the first woman to soar in a hot air balloon.

⊰ 1805 ⊱   Madeleine Sophie Armant Blanchard sooed in the first of sixty-seven gas-powered balloon flights. She made her living as a balloonist, was appointed Official Aeronaut of the Empire by Napoleon, and toured Europe until she fell to her death in an aerial fireworks

⊰ 1811 ⊱   On January 9, the first known women's golf tournament is held among the town fishwives at Musselburgh Golf Club, Scotland.

⊰ 1850 ⊱   Amelia Jenks Bloomer begins publicizing a new style of women's dress that came to be known as "bloomers."

⊰ 1858 ⊱   Julia Archibald Holmes climbs Pikes Peak in Colorado (14,110 feet) wearing bloomers.

⊰ 1864 ⊱   Croquet is likely the first game played by both men and women in America and was played in the 1900 Olympics as a coed sport.

⊰ 1873 ⊱   Ten women compete in a mile-long swimming race in the Harlem River. Deliliah Goboess wins the prize, a silk dress valued at $175.

⊰ 1876 ⊱   Mary Marshall, 26, shocks spectators when she beats Peter VanNess in the best of three walking matches (called Pedestrians) in New York City.

⊰ 1876 ⊱   Nell Saunders defeated Rose Harland in the first United States women's boxing match, receiving a silver butter dish as a prize.

1881 Bell Cook of California and Emma Jewett of *Litchfield, Minnesota*, toured the country, competing in a series of 20-mile horse races. On Sept. 29, in Rochester, NY's Driving Park, the two compete, with Jewett winning for the first time when Cook was thrown from her horse with only half a mile to go. Jewett covered the 20 miles in 0:45.05. They each used up to nine changes of horses in a race.

1883 The first baseball "Ladies Day" is held on June 16 by the New York Giants, where both escorted and unescorted women are allowed into the park for free.

1884 Women's singles tennis competition is added to Wimbledon. Maud Watson wins in both 1884 and 1885.

1885 The Association of Collegiate Alumnae publishes a study which concludes that a study of women college graduates does not show any marked difference in general health, refuting the belief that college study impaired a woman's physical health and ability to bear children.

1887 Ellen Hansell is crowned the first Women's Singles tennis champion at the U.S. Open.

1888 The modern "safety" bicycle is invented with a light frame and two equal-sized wheels and a chain drive. Women take to the "wheel." More than a million American women will own and ride bicycles during the next decade.

1888 The Amateur Athletic Union (AAU) is formed to set standards in amateur sports.

◀ **1890s** ▶   The "Bloomer Girls" baseball era lasted from 1890s until 1934 with hundreds of teams playing.

◀ **1890** ▶   Nellie Bly (Elizabeth Cochran Seaman), as reporter for *New York World*, becomes the first woman to travel around the world alone and does it in 72 days.

◀ **1891** ▶   Beatrice Von Dressden, 14, of Buffalo, NY, makes her first parachute jump from a hot air balloon.

◀ **1892** ▶   The YMCA journal, *Physical Education*, devotes an issue to women, saying that women need physical strength and endurance and dismisses the popular idea that women are too weak to exercise.

◀ **1892** ▶   James Naismith invents the game of baske ball at the YMCA in Springfield, Massachusetts. Senda Berenson of Smith College adapts the rules for a three-court women's game.

◀ **1892** ▶   Hessie Donahue, who donned a loose blouse, bloomers and boxing gloves and sparred a few rounds as part of a vaudeville act, knocks out legendary heavyweight champion, John L. Sullivan, for over a minute after he accidentally landed a real blow on her during the act.

◀ **1893** ▶   Katharine Lee Bates climbs to the top of Pike's Peak and is inspired to compose a poem, "America the Beautiful."

◀ **1894** ▶   The first women's golf tournament is held on the 7-hole Morristown, NJ, course.

⊰ **1894** ⊱ Annie "Londonderry" Kopchovsky, 23, becomes first woman to bicycle around the world in 15 months, and she earned $5,000 along the way.

⊰ **1895** ⊱ Volleyball is invented in Holyoke, MA.

⊰ **1896** ⊱ The first women's intercollegiate basketball championship is played between Stanford and the University of California at Berkeley. Stanford wins 2-1 on April 4 before a crowd of 700 women. No men were allowed as spectators.

⊰ **1896** ⊱ At the first modern Olympics in Athens, a woman, Melpomene, barred from the official race, runs the same course as the men, finishing in 4 hours 30 minutes. Baron Pierre de Coubertin, founder of the modern Olympics, says, "It is indecent that the spectators should be exposed to the risk of seeing the body of a woman smashed before their very eyes. Besides, no matter how toughened a sportswoman may be, her organism is not cut out to sustain certain shocks."

⊰ **1898** ⊱ Lizzie Arlington becomes first woman to sign a professional baseball contract, appearing in her first professional game pitching for the Philadelphia Reserves.

⊰ **1899** ⊱ Three women create a stir when they compete in a "century run" endurance contest in bicycling. Irene Bush of Brooklyn rides 400 miles in 48 hours; Jane Yatman of Brooklyn rides 500 miles in 58 hours and Jane Lindsay rides 600 miles in 72 hours.

◄ **1900** ► The first women to compete in the modern Olympic games in Paris play tennis, golf and coed croquet.

◄ **1901** ► Annie Taylor, 43, becomes the first person to go over Niagara Falls in a custom-built barrel and live. She couldn't swim. Her comment on being retrieved, "Nobody ever ought to do that again." One newspaper account said, "It seems to us that she's getting a great deal of credit that should go to the barrel."

◄ **1908** ► Edith Berg becomes first woman to go up in an airplane. She was a passenger in the Wright Brother's *Flyer* in a demonstration in France.

◄ **1908** ► In England, Muriel Matters, a suffragist and balloonist, flies over the British Houses of Parliament, dropping hundreds of flyers urging "votes for women."

◄ **1910** ► Baroness Raymonde de Laroche passes her qualifying tests to become the first woman in the world to be issued a pilot's license.

◄ **1910** ► Australia's Annette Kellerman is arrested for swimming in Boston Harbor in an "indecent" one-piece swimsuit that exposes her legs.

◄ **1912** ► Harriet Quimby is the first woman to pilot an airplane across the English Channel. For most of the flight she was in fog, dependent on her compass.

◄ **1912** ► Swimming and diving debuts at the Stockholm Olympic Games, with 57 women from 11 nations competing in those sports, plus tennis.

❧ **1914** ☙ Georgia "Tiny' Broadwick demonstrated air-jumping techniques to the US Army in San Diego, CA, pulled her release manually, becoming the first person to make an intentional free-fall parachute jump from an airplane.

❧ **1914** ☙ The American Olympic Committee formally opposes women's athletic competition in the Olympics. The only exception is the floor exercise, where women are allowed to wear only long skirts.

❧ **1916** ☙ Sisters Adeline and Augusta Van Buren become the first women to ride motorcycles across the country from Brooklyn to San Francisco. They are also the first women to conquer Pikes Peak on motorcycles.

❧ **1917** ☙ Lucy Diggs Slowe wins singles title at the first American Tennis Association (ATA) national tournament, becoming the first female African-American national champion in any sport.

❧ **1918** ☙ Eleanor Sears (great-great-granddaughter of Thomas Jefferson) takes up squash, after excelling at polo, baseball, golf, field hockey, auto racing, swimming, tennis, yachting and speedboat racing. She accumulated 240 trophies during her career and demonstrated women could play men's games.

❧ **1920** ☙ Female swimmers become the first American women to achieve full Olympic status. Three events were held: the 100 meter and 300 meter freestyles and the 4 by 100 meter freestyle relay. Ethelda Bleibtrey won all three.

◁ **1921** ▷ Bessie Coleman becomes the first black licensed pilot in the world.

◁ **1922** ▷ La Federation Sportive Feminine International (FSFI) holds first Women's Olympics in Paris with teams from United States and four other countries competing in eleven events before 20,000 spectators.

◁ **1924** ▷ National Federation of Amateur Athletics - Women's Division (NAAF-WD) organizes and recommends that all competitive sports for girls and women be dropped, including participation in the Olympics. Most high school and college level teams were gone within the decade.

◁ **1924** ▷ In the first winter Olympic games, figure skating is the only event for women.

◁ **1924** ▷ The Amateur Athletic Union (AAU) holds first national basketball tournament for women with six teams.

◁ **1924** ▷ Aileen Riggin becomes first athlete to win Olympic medals in both swimming and diving. She becomes one of America's first female sportswriters.

◁ **1924** ▷ Helen Wills wins gold in both singles and doubles tennis in Paris Olympics.

◁ **1926** ▷ New York City native, Gertrude Ederle, 19, becomes first woman to swim the English Channel in 14 hours, 31 minutes, two hours faster than any previous men's times. She had won 3 medals in the 1924 Olympics, including one gold.

1926 The Women's World Games held in Gothenberg, Sweden. The Federation La Sportive Feminine Internationale (FSFI) had agreed to change the name of their event in exchange for the inclusion of ten women's track and field events in the 1928 Summer Olympics. The International Olympic Committee reneged and only included five of the ten they had agreed to.

1928 The Summer Olympic Games add gymnastics and five track and field events for women. Rules stipulate that women's shorts must come within 4 inches of the knee.

1929 The National Air Race, first major race for women, began in California and ended in Cleveland, OH. Competitors weren't allowed to use any navigational aids except paper road maps. The race was won by Louise Thaden.

1929 Women pilots organize The Ninety-Nines and select Amelia Earhart as their first president.

1930 Amy Johnson, Englishwoman, sets speed record flying from London to India in 13 days, while becoming the first woman to fly from London to Australia solo.

1931 Roberta C. Ranck wins first U.S. All-Around Gymnastics Championship.

1931 Lili de Alvarez wear shorts instead of a long dress at Wimbledon, shocking spectators.

◁ **1931** ▷   Baseball Commissioner, Judge Kennesaw Mountain Landis bans women from professional baseball (ban lasts until 1992) after 17-year-old pitcher Virne Beatrice "Jackie" Mitchell strikes out Babe Ruth and Lou Gehrig in an exhibition game for the *Chattanooga Lookouts.* Landis voids Mitchell's contract, saying baseball is "too strenuous" for women.

◁ **1932** ▷   Babe Didrikson scores enough points at the AAU national meet to win the track and field *team* championship single-handedly.

◁ **1932** ▷   Jacqueline Cochran gets her pilot's license. At her death in 1980, Cochran held more speed, altitude, and distance records than any pilot, male or female, in the world.

◁ **1932** ▷   Amelia Earhart, 34, becomes the first woman, and the first person after Lindbergh, to fly solo across the Atlantic in a red *Lockheed Vega* in 15 hours and 39 minutes.

◁ **1932** ▷   New York's First Lady, Eleanor Roosevelt, took a run down the bobsled run at Lake Placid when husband, Governor Franklin Roosevelt, presided over the opening of the Olympic Games.

◁ **1932** ▷   The US Women's Lacrosse Association is formed, holding first tournament the next year.

◁ **1932** ▷   Babe Didrikson becomes first woman to win medals in three events at Los Angeles Olympic Games. Women were limited to entering a maximum of three events.

◊ **1936** ◊ Formation of the All-American Red Heads Basketball team who used men's rules and played men's teams, winning nearly 90% of their games.

◊ **1936** ◊ Gymnastics for women added to the Olympics in Berlin

◊ **1936** ◊ Women win three of five places, including first, in the prestigious transcontinental air race for the Bendix Trophy. Women were allowed to enter for the first time in 1935 when Jackie Cochran entered the previous male-only race.

◊ **1944** ◊ The All-American Girls Professional Baseball League is formed.

◊ **L945** ◊ The *Minneapolis Millerettes* move to Ft. Wayne and change their name to the *Fort Wayne Daisies*. The *Daisies* win three division titles before the league folds in 1954.

◊ **1950** ◊ Babe Didrikson Zaharias is named "Woman Athlete of the Half Century" by the Associated Press.

◊ **1951** ◊ Althea Gibson becomes the first black player to compete at Wimbledon. She wins Wimbledon and is named Associated Press (AP) Female Athlete of the Year in Tennis in 1957.

◊ **1953** ◊ Women's basketball added to World Championships, U.S. wins gold medal.

◁ **1953** ▷   Jacqueline Cochran is first woman to fly faster than sound.

___

◁ **1959** ▷   Patty Berg hits hole-in-one in U.S. Women's Open, first woman to do so in USGA tournament. She was AP Female Athlete of the Year in Golf in 1955.

___

◁ **1960** ▷   Wilma Rudolph wins three gold medals in Rome Olympics.

___

◁ **1960** ▷   National Institutes begin to train future coaches and athletes. *The new era of girls and women's sports has begun.*

*Note: the historical events selected above are only a portion of the history that can be found at:

http://www.northnet.org/stlawrenceaauw/timeline.htm and other Internet sites.

Explore!

Q & A with the Authors

Q. Dorothy, I understand that you are the author of Two Rings: A Legacy of Hope. How long did it take for you to write it?

A. First, keep in mind that it took Marian about twenty years to gather the information for our first book, *Daughters of the Game - The First Era of Minnesota Girls High School Basketball, 1891-1942*. With that history to draw from and a lifetime of stories and experiences, it took five months at the computer for me to write the final manuscript.

Q. So you surprised Marian with the very first draft of the book?

A. (laughs) I decided not to tell Marian that I had started writing, in case it didn't seem to 'jell.' But it did. I invited her to lunch and asked her if she still would like to publish a book of historical fiction based on *Daughters of the Game*. She said,

'Oh, yes.' I handed her a notebook, and said, 'Here is the first draft of the book.' And you should have seen her face. It made my secret project very worthwhile.

Q. **Marian, clearly, Dorothy considers you and your research to have been instrumental in researching the history of the first era of girls' sports. What is your background in education?**

A. I grew up in Waterville, Minnesota, graduating in 1952 from Mankato State University with my B.S. degree. I earned my Masters' degree at the University of Minnesota in 1973. My first teaching position was at Stillwater High School from 1952 until 1957. I organized the premier synchronized swim club called the Aqua Teens and we competed in AAU competition. In 1957, I moved to Hamline University, St. Paul, and taught and coached synchronized swimming there from 1957-1964. In 1969, I was hired as a women's physical education instructor at the new Lakewood Community College. Times were changing and by 1970, I was organizing the women's athletic department. I became the athletic director for women's sports at Lakewood Community College from 1968-1987. It was during those years that I organized the women's sports program and coached volleyball, basketball, softball and tennis. In response to severe opposition to the women's program, I began to research women's sports history.

Q. **Dorothy, what is your background?**

A. I graduated from high school in Hawkeye, Iowa, and from Luther College in Decorah, Iowa. I taught from 1957-1959 in Ellendale, Minnesota and moved to Eden Prairie, Minnesota, where I stayed until 1970. During the turbulent 1960s, I began to advocate for expanding girls' sports into an interscholastic program. My involvement with committees at the state and national level resulted in an invitation from the Minnesota State High School League to join their executive staff. My responsibility, of course, would be to assist schools as they developed their new girls' sports programs. It was the door that we had all worked so hard to open, so I said 'yes' and stayed from 1970 until 2002.

Q. How did you two meet?

A. Marian: I was teaching at the college level and Dorothy was an administrator at the League office. We shared an interest in women's sports history and would talk whenever we crossed paths.

Q. What caused you to join forces for the Daughters of the Game book?

A. Marian: One day I was looking through boxes archived in the Minnesota State Department of Education and came across the letter from Harold Jack to the schools in 1938, telling them they should be dropping the girls basketball and swimming teams and replacing them with a Girls Athletic Association. That letter unlocked the door. I called Dorothy to share the information and we both knew that we needed to follow the trail until we understood what had happened and why.

Dorothy would provide me with television interviews during the girls state basketball tournament and women who had played in the 1920s were watching and they called to tell me their stories. And the information kept growing until there were tubs full of information.

In 2002, after Dorothy had retired from the League, she asked if I would like some help writing a book to preserve this history. I said YES!

Q. Your first book, Daughters of the Game, is nearly four hundred pages of history and photos. Was it difficult to get it published?

A. Dorothy: It was simple. We organized our own publishing company, McJohn Publishing. That way, we could develop the book that we wanted without anyone else influencing it. It simplified the process and we decided it would be worth our personal investment of time and money.

Q. Did the women pioneers of the early 1900s get to see their stories in print?

A. Marian: Sadly, some women died before they saw their stories in print, but most knew it was going to happen and that brought a smile. There were many women who did receive and enjoy their book. One woman said, 'Who would ever have thought that my story would be in a beautiful book like this!' That made it all worthwhile.

Q. Dorothy, with your own publishing company, did you and Marian have to do it all?

A. Yes, just like the 'little red hen.' The files of Marian's research filled several storage tubs and it all had to be typed into my laptop. The learning curve was nearly vertical (laughs).

After two hard years of hovering over a computer, sending out releases and getting permission from so many people and groups, the book was ready to go to press. Fortunately, my friend Claudia in Virginia could find answers to everything, from how to punctuate, to the history of the bicycle.

Q. Did you have a sales and marketing department?

A. Dorothy: Yes, you are looking at them. Marian and I were the promotion, marketing and accounting departments. The books and files are stored in our homes. We processed all of the orders and kept the books. We conducted over one hundred programs at historical societies, book clubs, community organizations. There are a couple Minnesota snowstorm stories we could tell too.

Q. What were some highlights of those years?

A. Dorothy: I enjoyed reading an article in the *Mpls Star Tribune* when our book came out in 2005 by Joel Rippel, a guy 'who gets it.' Soon after, the newspaper featured *Daughters of the Game* as one of eight books recommended for a holiday gift. Pretty neat stuff for novice authors.

A. Marian: Another highlight was when we received a national award from the American Association for State and Local History in Atlanta, Georgia. It was their Award of Merit for the preservation and interpretation of state and local history.

Q. You both seem to have a lot of interest in history. What prompts your interest?

A. Marian: I have always wanted to know why women were denied opportunities to do what they wanted in sports, in life, and in their careers.

Q. Dorothy, what about you?

A. There's a quote, 'Those who do not learn from history are doomed to repeat it.' We have to stop making the same tragic, senseless mistakes over and over again. One message in this book, *Two Rings: A Legacy of Hope*, is that women are ready to expand their involvement in the affairs of the world and all doors should be opened to them.

Q. Let's look at your new book, Two Rings: A Legacy of Hope. The characters are very sensitive to words directed at women, and stereotypes of what woman are permitted to do or how they should act. Why are you so sensitive to those subjects?

A. Dorothy: We are women who have personally experienced discrimination far too many times. In my stomach, I can still feel the sting of words. The first negative word I remember as a child was being called, or dismissed as a 'tom-boy.' I was, quite simply, a strong Iowa farm girl. I loved to do anything outside on tractors and in the fields, or playing Tarzan in the woods back of the farm with the neighbor kids. And believe me, no one called me 'Tarzette!' (laughs)

We know that words can be used to try to undermine another person's confidence and cause them to back away from something they are doing. Words are like little whips that definitely hurt. I didn't like observing another person getting some pleasure from causing pain to another.

Q. How did you respond?

A. When I was eleven, I threatened to beat up a neighbor boy who had been harassing me while we were threshing oats. We had a brief altercation. I have since decided that physical conflict is not the best way to resolve most issues. I prefer to use *words* and sound rationale to help people understand the options available and how to work together to achieve a positive solution.

Q. Did you experience conflict during your work as associate director at the Minnesota State High School League?

A. Yes, the purpose of the Minnesota State High School League is to provide schools with the 'vehicle' to set policies and resolve issues. They are usually significant, sometimes emotional issues with two options, and both parties feel strongly about their positions.

One situation is vivid in my mind. In the 1970s we were in a big controversy over setting the season for girls basketball. Some wanted it to be in the fall when the boys were outside and the gyms were open. Our position at the League was it should be in the 'traditional' winter season and boys and girls should share the facilities. Wow, that was a powder keg of an issue! As 'that woman' at the League, I was an easy target at meetings, on the telephone and in newspaper editorials.

One day, the weekly envelope of news clippings arrived on my desk. A male basketball coach had written a letter to newspapers around the state, alleging that the League's board of directors had capitulated to 'that woman' who was trying to 'ruin the boys sports program in Minnesota.' He defined 'woman' as a *'woe-man,'* i.e., 'woe' meaning 'causing misery and despair.' He said that Jezebel should be sent back to Iowa where she could 'ruin the boys program there.' It goes on, but you get the 'gist' of his frustration.

Q. **What did you do?**

A. (laughs) Well, *I* wanted to beat him up, but I used words instead, and kept talking and presenting the rationale for winter as the right season for both girls and boys basketball. And it was and is.

Q. **Dorothy, do you think that people are becoming more aware of words that should be eliminated from conversation involving women?**

A. Yes, we all have caring and fair people in our circles who only choose words that show respect to others. On the other end of the old bell-shaped curve are those who don't care and don't seem to mind showing their ignorance. The largest group of people in the middle usually try to speak respectfully but hang onto some old words. They would benefit from learning how to use appropriate language.

Recently, I heard a man greet a female colleague on a committee as 'little lady.' He may have felt it was an acceptable greeting, but to my ears it was *not* appropriate. Does 'little lady' show professional respect to a peer? Well, in my opinion, only

if the *paired* greeting to a male colleague is 'little gentleman.'
If you can't 'pair' the words, it doesn't work. Men and Ladies
- no. Ladies and Gentlemen - yes. Male and Female; Man and
Woman - yes. It's pretty basic and simple.

And, (smiling as voice raises in volume) there is a perfectly
good word to describe a female: WOMAN!

Q. What's your solution to the respectful language issue?

A. Marian: First, start at home with the family to discuss
appropriate words. Then the schools should step up and
encourage teachers to discuss it in their classes, insisting on
use of appropriate words throughout the school day. Follow
that with the workplace which is another huge arena open to
bullying and harassment.

**Q. Well, this has been an interesting subject. Are you ready
to move on or do you have more to add?**

A. Dorothy: Admittedly, I do get emotionally involved when the
words carry a message that is not respectful. It's an important
subject and needs our attention. In this book, *Two Rings - A
Legacy of Hope*, Sarah's concerns about the use of words and
labels may stimulate some discussion among our readers. Who
knows where those ripples might go?

Q. How did Sarah become your primary character?

A. Dorothy. The storyline is focused on a young woman search-
ing for her family roots in sports. During her research, Sarah
has many new experiences which open doors to even more

questions, and a growing frustration about how women have been treated in the past. She begins to feel a commitment to help bring about change.

Q. **Sarah finds information in diaries. How did you come up with the idea of using diaries to tell the story, Dorothy?**

A. *Desperation.* What could be the link between Sarah's world and previous generations? The answer was a diary. Many young women kept diaries during those years. So, a diary could tell the story of Sarah's ancestors when they were young women. The link was created.

Q. **How did the title, Two Rings: A Legacy of Hope, develop?**

A. A real woman, Ruth Dahlke, in *Daughters of the Game*, did lose her treasured ring in a local lake. So, in *Two Rings: A Legacy of Hope*, a missing ring sets the stage. And eventually a second ring emerges. Each carries its own message.

Q. **Your book is filled with so many stories. Are some from personal experience?**

A. Marian: (laughs) Yes, both Dorothy and I were raised in the Midwest, and we have many stories to tell and share. Stories bring 'life' to history and sometimes they provide a 'flashback' to a similar experience in the reader's life.

Q. **Were either or both of you athletes on your high school teams?**

A. Marian: I was in high school in Minnesota during the 1940s when there were no interscholastic teams for girls. I was one of the many young women with thwarted dreams, but I managed to be an athlete anyway. My brothers and I played touch football and softball. In the winter, we skied. When warm weather arrived, we swam and fished in the nearby Cannon River. I became a lifeguard and swimming instructor at a young age. I loved ice skating and later became a figure skater. But nothing replaced the lost dream of being able to play on a real interscholastic team in any sport.

A. Dorothy: In our rural schoolyard, I played a lot of Red Rover, and Prisoner's Base. And I was pilot of our World War II 'B-17 climbing tree' during recess where we flew our missions from its branches. In high school I played softball but no basketball, which I now regret, because I would love to tell you what a 'star' I was. (laughs). But it opened another door because I opted to be the student manager of the girls basketball team. Perhaps cutting oranges and picking up towels was good training for my future career. (laughs)

As a team, we traveled to Des Moines to see the Iowa High School Girls Basketball Tournament, an experience I will never forget. Schools in our region of the state won several state championships and there were individual stars who remain my heroes. Girls' sports in Iowa was and continues to be 'a big deal.'

Q. **What was the hardest part of the book to write?**

A. Dorothy: Easily it was Chapter 8, 'My Mother Played. Why Couldn't I?' That's the chapter that explains why girls and women's sports were dropped and sports for girls weren't available in Minnesota and elsewhere for several decades. The dream sequence was a way to tell the story by imagining how the NAAF-WD meeting would have sounded. And I enjoyed Sarah becoming a *mouse in the corner.* It made me laugh, and I try to laugh every day.

It would be easy to 'blame and shame' the National Amateur Athletic Federation-Women's Division whose actions caused such a national reaction, resulting in teams for girls and women being dropped across the country. We did benefit from their recommendation that physical education become a strong part of a school's curriculum. Today's concerns about obesity in children should motivate parents and schools to *bring back* the strong physical education programs that we once had.

Q. **Were you involved in breaking down the barriers and bringing girls and women's sports into the schools?**

A. Marian: Yes, Dorothy and I both were very active, I at the college level and she at the high school level. We were young physical education teachers who began to break away from the beliefs that sports for girls and women should be without any desire to win, no coaches, and awards. Our young women weren't satisfied with intramural level activities.

A. Dorothy: In the 1960s, we began to advocate for competitive sports for girls and women. We invited other schools to bring their students and we'd play our team against theirs. We kept score; we gave awards. We conducted gymnastics clinics and taught ourselves how to judge so we could hold meets. And it was a serious break with what was considered appropriate for young women at the time. It was risky for us professionally and in our own schools. But we believed in our cause and simply pulled ourselves up by our own boot straps.

It wasn't easy, but we did it anyway. State and federal laws put teeth into the movement. And the 'end of the story' is that girls and women's sports have become accepted and a part of the athletic programs in high schools, colleges and universities across the country.

Our brief description here doesn't do justice to the 'blood, sweat and tears' that were required of so many people to make it happen. Suffice it to say, our investment was for the right reasons. We changed 'the face of sports.' And we did make all the difference in the world for the 'Sarahs' out there.

Q. What is the primary emotion that you feel over those lost years between the 1920s and 1970s??

A. Marian: (shakes head) It's the sadness for all of the women who were born too early and were caught in those years without school-sponsored teams. They are still angry. Their chance to be on high school teams could never be recovered. While they can enjoy sports now, the loss of their high school years can never be undone.

Q. Dorothy, what can we learn from that time?

A. That we need to constantly be monitoring and resisting those who would try to slip below the radar and reduce opportunities for girls and women. And believe me, they are out there working away. So, pay attention and when you see something that makes your antennae vibrate, look into it, get involved, and stop it.

Q. **Marian, what makes you smile these days?**

A. Watching young women enjoy opportunities that, not so long ago, were denied to women. They see it as a normal part of their lives - as it should be.

Q. **Dorothy, you believe in preserving history. Why is it so important?**

A. Listen to this quote by Ann D. Braude, Ph.D.: *"Would each generation of women leaders have had to endure such a solitary struggle if they had known about those who came before them? One of women's greatest struggles has been that their history has not been preserved, and so each generation has had to rediscover over and over again the ideas and individuals that gave it strength"*

That means that we need to preserve our own stories first. Then share them, as we are doing with our books. Then, make it your mission to find another woman's life story that should be told and preserved, whether it be a mother, sister, friend, or a hero in your life. Write and share it through all the avenues available, i.e., ancestry programs, social networking, media, et al. Finally, support others who are on the road with you, such as the National Women's History Museum in Washington, D.C. *If we each do our part,* the pictures and the real stories of women's contributions throughout history will be available to all those 'Sarahs' out there and the generations to follow.

Q. Dorothy, is there a rainbow out there?

A. *Well, of course there is (smiles).* It does take rain to create the rainbow, so don't shy away from standing in the rain in order to enjoy the rainbow.

Q. Dorothy, how long did it take to write the Epilogue?

A. One morning, it just flowed onto the page. At first, I wasn't sure how Sarah's story would come to closure in this book until she began to absorb the importance of her legacy and express her desire to 'get into the game.' Then, all options were open. Of all the roads ahead, which will she choose to make a difference?

Perhaps selfishly, for our own dreams, we ask, *'where would we like to see her on a cold morning in January?'* There was only one place for our Sarah to stand. When that day happens, it will feel so right and we will always wonder, what took us so long.

Q. Will there be a sequel following Sarah's graduation from high school?

A. Yes, but we don't need to write it. It is *being written right now* by the many *'Sarahs'* out there in the real world. They will write their own stories. Each life will be a wonderful adventure, and one day, at the end of the rainbow, *one of them will become our President.*

Everyone smiles.

★ ★ ★ ★

BOOK CLUB AND STUDY QUESTIONS

1. If there had been no diaries, what other resources could have provided information for Sarah?

2. Were you aware of the introduction of basketball by Max Exner to the women of Carleton College? What impact did it have on women in Minnesota?

3. Do you have female ancestors who played basketball during the first era? If so, please describe.

4. How would you describe Patti's parenting techniques with Sarah? Were they effective?

5. What historical stories were unknown to you until you read this book?

6. The two events, *National Girls and Women in Sports Day* and the *Minneapolis Athena Awards* are actual events and open to the public each year. What did Sarah learn from them? What did you learn from them?

7. Were you aware of Amelia Earhart's connections to Minnesota? Does Amelia's life carry any message for you?

8. Did a particular chapter or story resonate with you? Why?

9. Do you have a suspect in the Chapter 5 "alarm caper" in the New Prague hotel? Who and why?

10. What was your reaction when you read the Epilogue? Did you anticipate Sarah's career path? If yes, what clues did you find in previous chapters?

11. Why do you think the author selected the title, *"Two Rings: A Legacy of Hope?"*

12. Which event in the *History of Women In Sports Timeline* was your favorite? Why?

13. If this book, "Two Rings," were made into a movie, who would you cast to play Sarah? Her mother?

14. Were you in school during the years of a Girls Athletic Association? If so, what memories do you have of those activities?

15. If you were in high school during or after the 1960s, what was your high school sports experience? Do you have a championship ring or a sports award? Please describe.

16. Who is a hero for you?

17. Do you believe that "society" could negatively impact opportunities for girls and women in sports again? If no, why not? If yes, how could it happen and what can we do to prevent it?

References and Notes

Abbreviations

AAHPERD - DGWS	American Association for Health, Physical Education, Recreation and Dance, Division for Girls and Women's Sports
AASLH	American Association for State and Local History
MSHSL, the League	Minnesota State High School League, state high school association
NAAF (WD)	National Amateur Athletic Federation - Women's Division
Daughters	Refers to the book, *Daughters of the Game - The First Era of Minnesota Girls High School Basketball, 1891-1942*

Primary Source

Marian Bemis Johnson and Dorothy E. McIntyre, *Daughters of the Game - The First Era of Minnesota Girls High School Basketball, 1891-1942* (St. Cloud, MN: McJohn Publishing, 2005)

Epigraph

References

1. Muriel Morrissey, *Courage is the Price* (Wichita, Kansas: McCormick Armstrong, 1963)

2. www.thefreedictionary.com/legacy.

3. www.webster-dictionary.org/hope

Preface

References

"Heroes," words and music by Ann Reed, ©1992 Turtlecub Publishing/BMI

"Look at Her Go," words and music by Ann Reed, ©1999 Turtlecub Publishing/BMI.

For more information about Ann Reed and her music, see www.annreed.com.

Chapter One: Sarah Gets an Assignment

References

Presidential Physical Fitness Award. www.presidentschallenge.org.

Notes

1. All references to Sarah's great-grandmother Ruby McConnell, are adapted from the stories of Ruth McCarron

Dahlke, Sherburn, *Daughters of the Game*, pp. 266-269.

2. The book's main characters are fictitious, including Sarah, her parents, and siblings. Patti, Sarah's mother, is a fictitious character, but the storyline wraps around the actual history of Patti Foley who did play on the Le Sueur teams in the 1970s. Sarah's principals, coach, friends and teammates are fictitious.

3. The names of the pioneer players and their stories are historically accurate and taken from the *Daughters of the Game* book. Some stories have been adapted to fit the storyline but can be found in *Daughters of the Game*.

Chapter Two: The Trunk and the Diary

References

1. http://www.thepeoplehistory.com.

2. http://www.thepeoplehistory.com.20s clothes

Notes

1. The 1924 Sherburn invitational tournament and its trophy are real; Ruth Dahlke's ring was real. It was lost in Fox Lake and is believed to rest there today.

2. The newspaper article, "Are Modern Girl Athletes Risking Their Looks?" is an authentic article and in the archives of McJohn Publishing, LLC.

Chapter Three: A New Game Comes to Town

References

1. "The Shot Heard Round the World," *Discovery YMCA*, *Spring/Summer 2001, 150th Anniversary Edition*, nos. 77 and 78 (2001): 26-29.

2. Carleton College 1892-93 yearbook, *ALGOL, Gymnasium Work, Spring Issue* (Northfield, MN).

Notes

1. The history of James Naismith, Max Exner and Carleton College is historically accurate. Carleton women were the first to learn how to play this new game of "basket ball" in the gymnasium of Gridley Hall.

2. On September 30, 2004, Eric Hillemann, archivist, Carleton College, Northfield, MN, provided research and photos that documented the introduction of basket ball at Carleton College by Max J. Exner.

3. The author of this book did interview the son of Max J. Exner, who lived in Ames, Iowa. He described his father as "the perfectionist's perfectionist."

4. Clara and her diary are fictitious, however, many young women of Carleton did learn to play the game of "basket ball" from Max Exner. Thus far, their stories have been lost in time, unless someday a real diary is discovered in another trunk and we can learn "the rest of the story." Could they be in your family's archives?

CHAPTER FOUR: BASKETBALL SWEEPS ACROSS MINNESOTA

References

1. Hult, Joan S. and Trekell, Marianna, eds., *A Century of Women's Basketball - From Frailty to Final Four* (Reston, VA: NAGWS and AAHPERD, 1991). Appendix, Women's Basketball Time Line, 427-430.

2. Hult, Joan S., "The Governance of Athletics for Girls and Women – Leadership by Women Physical Educators, 1899-1949" in *A Century*, 53-82.

3. Lawrence, Helen B. and Fox, Grace I., *Basketball for Girls and Women* (New York: McGraw, 1954), 191-228.

Notes

1. Clara's sister, Alice, and her letter are fictitious. Zumbrota's history of playing girls basketball can be referenced in Zumbrota High School, *Daughters of the Game*, 310. Zumbrota was playing basketball at least as early as 1904.

2. The Sherburn silver trophy is beautiful, very real and currently residing in the archives of *Daughters of the Game*.

Chapter Five: Where Did All the Snow Go?

References

Prosser, Richard S., *Rails to the North Star - One hundred years of railroad evolution in Minnesota* (Minneapolis: Dillon Press, 1966), 1-63.

Notes

1. Sarah's dream provided a way to describe an evening of girls high school basketball in the 1920s.

2. Marie's stories and the escapades in New Prague are real and can be found in her school's history, Belle Plaine High School, *Daughters of the Game*, 115-119.

Chapter Six: Why Did They Take That Game Away From Us?

References

1. Bellis, Mary, site curator, "The History of the Automobile, The First Mass Producers of Cars - The Assembly Line," *Automobile History - The History of Cars and Engines*, http://www.inventors.about.com/library/weekly/aacarsassemblya.html (accessed January 4, 2012).

2. Conrad, Dan, PhD., *Why Did They Take That Game Away From Us? The Story of Cokato High School Girls Basketball: 1903-1931*, published in cooperation with the Cokato Museum. Sources interviews: Lorraine (Kvam) Lee, Cokato, November 2005; Adalyn (Eckstrom) Wright, Cokato, December 2005, January 2006.

Notes

1. The descriptions of Howard Lake and its history are accurate. Vera Templin's stories of the snowstorm can be found in her history, Buffalo High School, *Daughters of the Game*, 129-132.

2. The interviews with Adalyn and Lorraine were conducted by Dan Conrad in 2005 and 2006.

CHAPTER SEVEN: UP NORTH

References

1. MSHSL, Official Handbooks of the Minnesota State High School League, 1924-1942, state tournament summaries. 2100 Freeway Boulevard, Brooklyn Center, MN 55430. www.mshsl.org

2. WeCoachU, a professional development/networking seminar sponsored by the Alliance of Women Coaches. www.gocoaches.org

Notes

1. Jeanne Knox is a real pilot, an officer and member of the Minnesota Ninety-Nines.

2. The Minnesota State High School League did conduct a MSHSL State Girls Swimming Tournament from 1924-1942. The history is accurately reflected in the names of the participating schools and the struggles to retain the

swimming teams before they were dropped. See *Daughters of the Game* for more information, p. 78.

3. Jean Frarey Walters of Virginia was a real swimmer in the 1942 MSHSL State Girls Swimming and Diving Meet and her father did fight to retain the girls swimming teams. The character of Tammy is fictitious.

4. Harold Jack was the Supervisor of Physical Education from the Minnesota State Department of Education and did send letters to schools recommending that they discontinue their girls basketball and swimming teams.

5. Nor'wester Lodge is real, as are Carl and Luana, and her blueberry pies.

6. Hibbing High School is a uniquely beautiful building. Everyone is encouraged to see it for themselves.

7. Gail Nucech is indeed a real person and a legendary coach.

8. Fraboni's Market is a real market and a key resource for authentic porketta.

9. Anne Govednik is Chisholm's legendary Olympic swimmer. Her story is historically accurate, including the role of the town whistle.

10. Lawrence Belluzzo is a noted historian of Chisholm and Anne Govednik.

11. For further information on the game of Sardines: www.wikihow.com/play-sardines

12. Dorothy E. McIntyre, the writer of this book, did experience the decision of the security guard at the Hibbing Airport as described.

Chapter Eight: My Mother Played, Why Couldn't I?

References

1. "Community Athletics for Girls and Women, A few questions posed from a study made in 1930, Platform of Women's Division, NAAF" (New York: NAAF-WD, April 1, 1931).

2. Alden, Florence D., Elizabeth Richards and L. Raymond Burnett, eds. *Official Basket Ball Guide for Women, 1918-1919,* (New York: American Sports Publishing Company, 1918)

3. Lee, Mabel, *Memories Beyond Bloomers – 1924-1954* (Washington, DC:AAHPER, 1978), 74-75

4. Minnesota Historical Society. Records and correspondence of Harold Jack, Supervisor of Health and Physical Education, Minnesota Department of Education, 1939, 1939. 51H14F-Dept. of Ed. P.E. Division of the Minnesota State Archives, located in the Archives/Manuscripts Division of the Minnesota Historical Society.

5. Norris, Anna, Dr. "The Beneficial Results and Dangers of Basket Ball," In *Official Basket Ball Guide for Women, 1918-1919,* edited by Florence D. Alden, Elizabeth Richards and L. Raymond Burnett, 71. New York: American Sports Publishing Company.

6. "Purpose of an Athletic Program," *Athletics for Girls – A Digest of Principles and Policies for Administrators and Teachers in Junior and Senior High Schools* (Washington, D.C., The Department of School Health and Physical Education of the National Education Association, 1933), 5-6.

7. *Standards in Sports for Girls and Women - Guiding Principles in the Organization and Administration of Sports Programs.* A Project of the National Section for Girls and Women's Sports of the American Association for Health, Physical Education and Recreation. A Department of the National Education Association. First Edition 1937. Copyright 1953, 5.

8. *Women's Division of the National Amateur Athletic Federation (NAAF-WD), Minutes of the Meeting: Resolutions adopted regarding Olympics, January 3-5, 1929,* New York City. From the files of Ola Bundy, former Assistant Executive Director, Illinois High School Association, Bloomington, Illinois.

Notes

1. Sarah's dream sequence is based on the platform of the NAAF-Women's Division. Dr. Anna Norris was author of the first draft of the platform. The quote by Mabel Lee is taken from her book, *Memories Beyond Bloomers*, 1978. Agnes Wayman's quote appears in *Daughters of the Game*, 75

2. Quotes from the letters from Harold Jack, Minnesota State Department of Education, to the schools are historically accurate and taken from his correspondence. Copies of the correspondence are in the archives of *Daughters of the Game*.

CHAPTER NINE: A PAUSE TO REFLECT

Notes

1. The description of the Le Sueur Girls Athletic Association (GAA) is fictitious but descriptive of the type of GAA recreational activities offered during those years.

2. The sisters of Sarah's mother, Patti, are fictitious in this chapter and developed to represent the opportunities and frustrations of many young women during that era.

3. Susan Alstrom, International Falls track star, is a real person and her experiences are historically accurate. She is a teacher at Buffalo Lake/Hector Schools and an accomplished coach.

4. The history of the girls basketball tournament is accurate.

Playoffs were held for the fall season schools and the winter season schools in 1974-75. The first statewide MSHSL State Girls Basketball Tournament was held in the winter of 1976.

5. The basketball editorials and articles are taken from the *Le Sueur News Herald*, following the 1975 tournament.

6. *A Prairie Home Companion;* http://prairiehome.publicradio.org

CHAPTER TEN: STANDING ON YOUR SHOULDERS

References

The website for the sponsorig committee for Minnesota's National Girls and Women in Sports Day, www.ngwsd-mn.com

Notes

1. NGWSports Day is conducted nationally and in Minnesota on the first Wednesday in February and the stories reflect the overall purpose of the event.

2. Music: www.annreed.com.

CHAPTER ELEVEN: FLYING THE BLUES SKIES OF IOWA

References

1. "Iowa Salutes the Iowa Girl - 72 Years of Iowa Girls State Basketball Tournaments." Video produced by Fletcher Communications Group, P.O. Box 21129, Des Moines, Iowa 50321. 1-800-728-4638

2. State Historical Society of Iowa, "Iowa Girls High School Athletic Union – Girls Basketball in Iowa," *The Palimpsest* XLIX, No. 4 (April 1968): 125.

3. Lovell, Mary S., *The Sound of Wings - The Life of Amelia Earhart* (New York: St. Martin's Griffin, 1989)

Notes

1. The author's description of the tournament is based on personal experience and information provided by the media resources of the Iowa Girls High School Athletic Union (IGHSAU).

2. The names of several of the outstanding Iowa players and their records are recorded in the media resources of the Iowa Girls High School Athletic Union. They are names known throughout "the great state of Iowa."

3. Sarah's Aunt Lynn is a fictitious character.

4. The history of Amelia Earhart during her years in Iowa and Minnesota is historically accurate.

Chapter Twelve: Returning to Her Roots

References

1. Foley, Jeanne, *Shooting Two - A Story of Basketball and Friendship*, Peppermint Books, 2010.

2. *Le Sueur News Herald*, Le Sueur, Minnesota; articles which appeared on and around February 26, 1975

Notes

1. Le Sueur does have all-school gatherings. The all-school reunion in this chapter is fictitious.

2. Patti, Sarah's mother, is a fictitious character but is based on real-life Patti Foley Good, who did play on the Le Sueur girls basketball team in the playoff year 1974-75. She provided stories from her experience, news clippings and tournament programs. Deb "Sox" Sunderman and Brenda Savage are also real people, played on teams with Patti Foley, and are really good basketball players.

3. Mildred is a fictitious teacher at Le Sueur.

4. The 1920s team names are real. Blossom's story is in *Daughters of the Game*, 199-200.

5. The Le Sueur team did lose in the finals of the winter season playoffs to Holy Angels by 2 points. Vicki Davis did officiate the game.

6. The letters and editorial are from the *Le Sueur News Herald*, preserved in the scrapbook of Patti Foley Good.

CHAPTER THIRTEEN: HEROES, WHAT CAN WE LEARN FROM YOU

References

1. Beck, Martha, *Steering by Starlight: Find Your Right Life, No Matter What* (New York,: Rodale Inc. 2008).

2. "Heroes," words and music by Ann Reed, ©1992 Turtlecub Publishing/BMI; "Look at Her Go," words and music by Ann Reed, ©1999 Turtlecub Publishing/BMI; www.annreed.com

3. Horne, Esther Burnett and McBeth, Sally J., *Essie's Story, The Life and Legacy of a Shoshone Teacher.* (Lincoln, NE: University of Nebraska Press, 1988); http://books.google.com/books/about/Essie_s_story.html

4. http://rootsweb.ancestry.com/~nwa/Sacajawea

5. http://www.naacp.org. Rosa Parks

Notes

1. Ed Lorence is a WWII U.S. marine and a hero.

2. The history of Sacajawea and Esther Burnett Horne is accurate, based on historical records and the personal contacts of this book's author with Esther. The author did visit Sacajawea's cemetery in the Wind River Reservation, Ft. Washakie, WY, and leave the Sacajawea gold coin near the left heel of her statue.

Chapter Fourteen: Pioneers Play Again

References

1. Hebard, Grace Raymond, *Sacajawea: Guide and Interpreter of Lewis and Clark* (Courier Dover Publications, MA, 2002).

2. http://www.daughtersofthegame.com

3. Website of All-American Red Heads by John Molina; http://www.allamericanredheads.com

5. *Spirit of '75, All-American Red Heads' 40th Anniversary, 1936-1976.* (Reunion publication) Moore's All-American Red Heads, owned and operated by Moore's Sports Enterprises, Caraway, Arkansas.

Notes

1. Aunt Betty is a real person and Marian Johnson's special sister, who lives near Grand Rapids, Minnesota. She makes aprons and has created a middy and bloomer uniform for Marian's book programs.

2. The All-American Redheads and individuals identified as members of women's professional teams are real people.

3. The pioneer women selected for the chapter, "Pioneers Play Again," represent the women who played from 1892-1942. They are real players and their information is accurate. See the book, *Daughters of the Game*, for their individual stories.

Chapter Fifteen: Myths, Stereotypes and Other Baloney

References

1. Anthony, Susan B., interviewed Nellie Bly, *New York World*, February 2, 1896, http:www.pedalinghistory.com/PHfaq.html (accessed January 4, 2012).

2. Carrol, Lewis, "Alice's Adventures in Wonderland," Avenel Books, New York, 94-96.

3. Mozer, David, "Chronology of the Growth of Bicycling," *Bicycle History & Human Powered Vehicle History*, International Bicycle Fund homepage, http://ibike.org/library/history-timeline. htm. (accessed January 4, 2012).

4. Victorian Station, Leisure Activities, "Bicycling," http://www.victorianstation.com/leisurebicycle.htm (accessed January 4, 2012).

5. http://www.forbes.com/forbeswoman/

6. http://www.forbes.com/2010/06/01/top-paying-jobs-college-graduates-entry-level-forbes-woman-leadership-careers.html.

7. Website for Alice Paul; http://www.alicepaul.org/alicepaul.htm

8. Website for National Women's History Museum; www.nwhm.org

9. First Lady Betty Ford quote; www.firstladies.org

Notes

1. Gen is a real and perfect dog and lives far away in Portland, Oregon.

2. The article, "Malice in Wonderland," portrays the boys as the 'new' sports program seeking admission and acceptance in the schools. It reveals how prejudice and discrimination appears from the other side of the mirror. It was admittedly written by Dorothy E. McIntyre.

Chapter Sixteen: It's My Happy Heart You Hear

Notes

1. "Happy Heart" was recorded by Andy Williams for the album, *In The Lounge with Andy Williams*. http://www.last.fm/music/Andy+Williams

2. The other favorite song of the Eden Prairie Happy Hearts was "On Our Way," the theme from *The Young Bloodhawke* movie. It was used as a marching-in song for their demonstrations.

3. The history and anecdotal stories of girls gymnastics is as accurate as collective memories can recall of events nearly fifty years ago.

4. Names of the meet personnel and gymnastics pioneers are real people. Pat Lamb and Ele Hansen were involved as described.

Chapter Seventeen: How Full is the Glass Today?

References

1. The website for the University of Minnesota's Tucker Center for Research on Girls and Women in Sport; www.tuckercenter.org.

2. Klobuchar, Jim. 1975. "He Enters A New Clubhouse," *Minneapolis Star*, February.

3. Smith, Robert T. 1982. *Minneapolis StarTribune*, March 21.

4. Klobuchar, Jim. 1994. "Girls tourney outshines dog-eat-dog basketball world," *Minneapolis Star Tribune*, March 22.

5. The website for Christine Brennan, *USA Today* sports journalist and author; http://www.Christinebrennan,com.

CHAPTER EIGHTEEN: COMING HOME

Notes

1, The history of the games between St. James and North-field is accurate. They did play a "Game of the Century" as described.

2. The character of Ray is representative of Ray Herman who was athletic director at Sherburn at the time of the school consolidation into Martin County West. He located the 1925 silver trophy. Erin Herman, his real-life daughter, is a coach/administrator in the Twin Cities.

3. Ruth Dahlke's silver ring was engraved inside the band, "R.Mc 1925."

4. Finding the missing ring is part of the fictional and happy ending to this historical novel. Ruth Dahlke's real silver ring remains at the bottom of Fox Lake. For the complete story, see the history of Sherburn High School, *Daughters of the Game*, 266-269.

CHAPTER NINETEEN: I BELIEVED MY MOTHER

References

Wilma Rudolph biography. www.notablebiographies.com.

Notes

Yolanda, the student, is the fictional relative of Wilma Rudolph. Wilma did have a sister named Yolanda.

CHAPTER TWENTY: STEERING THE SHIP OF CHANGE

References

1. http://www.goodreads.com/author/quotes/6117.Margaret_Mead

2. Bauck, Paula W. Bruss, *The History of Moorhead High School Girls' sports, 1957-1981.* Located in the archives of McJohn Publishing.

3. Bauck, Paula W. Bruss, *The Very Beginning of Girls' Interscholastic Sports in Minnesota under the MSHSL.* Located in the archives of McJohn Publishing.

4. McIntre, Dorothy E., 2005. "Reflections from the Front of the Bus," In *Stories by Minnesota Women in Sports - Leveling the Playing Field*, edited by Kathleeen C. Ridder, Jean A. Brookins and Barbara Stuhler, 152-167. St. Cloud, MM: North Star Press.

5. Edwin Markham. Poem "Outwitted" in The Shoes of Happiness and Other Poems, 1913; "He drew a circle..." excerpt: www.goodreads.com/quotes

Notes

1. Paula Bauck is a very real person who made significant contributions to the beginning of girls high school sports in Minnesota. She was a teacher/coach at Moorhead High School and active on the committees whose efforts resulted in the adoption of girls' sports in 1969 by the Minnesota State High School League. The history, names and dates are accurate. Paula has three sons. The young man is a fictitious grandson created to tell Paula's story.

2. The story of the emergence of girls and women's sports during the 1960s and 1970s is a history unto itself. An overview has been summarized here to provide a basic background for those who didn't live it. Your local school has its own pioneers of this era.

3. "What Little Girls are Made Of," comes from a 19th century nursery rhyme.

CHAPTER TWENTY~ONE: WHEN THAT HAPPENS, EVERYONE WINS

References and Notes - None

CHAPTER TWENTY~TWO: ONE STEP AT A TIME

References

1. Arnesen, Liv and Ann Bancroft with Cheryl Dahle, *No Horizon is So Far: Two Women and Their Historic Journey Across Antarctica* (Cambridge, MA: Persus Books Group, 2003)

2. http://yourexpedition.com/bae/ann-bancroft/

CHAPTER TWENTY~THREE: GET READY, WORLD! HERE I COME

References

http://about.poynter.org/abut-us/our-people/jacqui-banaszynski

Notes

1. Jacqui Banaszynski was a staff writer for the *St Paul Pioneer Press* when she wrote the article, "Girls basketball comes of age with grace, skill." While in St. Paul, she won the Pulitzer Prize in feature writing for her 1988 series on "AIDS in the Heartland."

2. The Minnesota State High School League sponsored the first statewide girls basketball tournament in 1976. The tournament annually crowns four champions: Class AAAA, AAA, AA, and A.

Chapter Twenty-Four: Athena, the Bringer of Victory

References

1. http://www.theoi.com/Olympics/Athena.html

2. Timeline of significant achievements; http://www.northnet. org/stlawrenceaauw/timeline.htm

3. Geisel, Theodore Seuss, *Oh, the Places You'll Go!* http.// www.goodreads.com/quotes/show/22842

Chapter Twenty-Five: All the Difference in the World

References and Notes

Eiseley, Loren, *The Star Thrower* (New York: Random House, 1978);

www.amazon.com/Star-Thrower-Loren-Eiseley/dp/0156849097.

Epilogue

Reference

1. Abraham Lincoln, quote by; http://showcase.netins.neet/ web/creative/lincoln/speeches/quotes.html

2. Statue of Freedom; http://en.wikipedia.Statue_of_Freedom

Q & A with Authors

References

Braude, Ann D., Ph.D., "Answering God's Call to Speak," *The Magazine for the Mary Baker Eddy Library for the Betterment of Humanity*; http://www.marybakereddylibrary.org

INDEX

Daughters of the Game
⧼ 1902-1976 ⧽

Brainerd Team, 1902 *(Courtesy of Crow Wing County Historical Society)*

Sherburn Team, 1925 *(Courtesy of Ruth Dahlke Family)*

Sherburn Invitational
Tournament, 1925
Championship Trophy
(Courtesy of Ray Herman)

Le Sueur Team, 1974-75 MSHSL Winter Season Tournament Finalists

(Courtesy of Patty Foley Good)

Saint Paul Central Team, 1976 MSHSL Class AA State Champions

(Courtesy of Lisa Lissimore)

About The Authors

★ ★ Dorothy E. McIntyre ★ ★

Dorothy E. McIntyre was born and raised on a farm near Hawkeye, Iowa. She graduated in 1953 from Hawkeye High School and received a Bachelor of Arts degree in 1957 from Luther College, Decorah, Iowa. McIntyre was awarded her Master of Education degree from the University of Minnesota in 1969.

Compliments of Ann Marsden Photography

McIntyre was a teacher at Ellendale-Geneva High School from 1957-1959 and at Eden Prairie High School from 1959-1970. In the 1960s, McIntyre began a lifelong advocacy for expanded sports programs for girls, and moved into leadership positions at the state and national levels. She started the girls gymnastics program at Eden Prairie High School.

In 1970, McIntyre was employed as an associate director at the Minnesota State High School League where she was active for the next 32 years promoting equity for girls and women's sports. The Minneapolis Star Tribune named McIntyre as one of Minnesota's 100 most influential sports figures in the 20th century.

★ ★ MARIAN BEMIS JOHNSON ★ ★

Marian Bemis Johnson graduated from Waterville High School in 1948 during the period when no sports programs existed for high school girls or college women. She received her Bachelor of Science degree from Mankato State University in 1952 and her Master of Education degree from the University of Minnesota in 1973.

Johnson was a physical education teacher at Stillwater High School from 1952 until 1957. She started the competitive synchronized swimming team in 1953. As a member of the faculty of Hamline University, St. Paul, from 1957-1964, she also coached synchronized swimming from 1968-1987. During this time Johnson was a pioneer in developing intercollegiate competitive programs for women. She was Women's Athletic Director at Lakewood Community College and coached volleyball, basketball, softball and tennis.

Johnson questioned why she couldn't play sports in the 1950s and her mother could in the 1920s, driving her research into the history of girls and women's sports.

ALSO BY DOROTHY E. MCINTYRE AND MARIAN BEMIS JOHNSON

Daughters of the Game

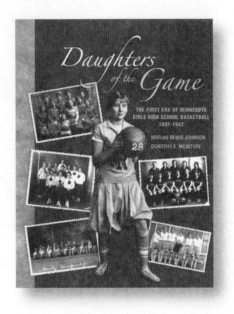

The First Era of
Minnesota Girls High School Basketball
1891-1942

www.daughtersofthegame.com